i

Capturing Dove

Louise Furley

CAPTURING DOVE

Louise Furley
Copyright 2021
All Rights Reserved

ISBN: 978-1-7378341-2-0
ISBN: 978-1-7378341-1-3

Cover art by *Pixel Mischief Design*

ALSO BY LOUISE FURLEY

Mafia Romance

Distilled Duplicity
His Winnings
Adara
Jozadak

Satan's Brood series

Devil's Prince
Devil's Seed

Dutch Military Special Forces series

Jungle Treasure
Jancarlo

Other titles

Jezábel and the Assassin

Solitar

Halo Valley

Isle of Orainn

List of the characters in Capturing Dove:

<u>Women</u>:

Dove, the female protagonist

<u>Female Passengers</u>:

Essie Cook
Kitty Moit
Chelsee Genise
Avril Izar
Robin Jacob

<u>Men</u>:

Tezer Corseque, the male protagonist

His team:

Garth Jefferson
Leo Panza
Reggie Lutalo
Nikolas Gazzola

<u>Extra Mercenaries</u>:

Zev 'Ziggy' Zigrid
Vigo Vedie
Reynaldo Silva
Clancy Bonds

Male Passengers:

Brock Disik
Ronald McCain
Paola Baretti
Tommy Tucker

Very very Bad Guys:

Yvetsky Braemont
Damon Philippè

Capturing Dove

Chapter One

"The bus is here," one of the men announced.

An ancient bus creaked and rocked down the dirt road. The bus that used to be white was now mostly burnt orange, stained with dirt and grime, and pitted with rust that had eaten away half of the lower section.

When it reached the old deserted station it came to a slow, hinge-squeaking stop. Shocks shot years ago, the rickety bus jostled for seconds after it stopped expelling grey clouds of noxious diesel smoke.

With no air conditioning, complaints and curses drifted from the open windows.

The doors opened and one by one the passengers clamored out into the roiling dust that huffed around the shaking bus.

Men and women alike, coughing and hacking, held their hands over brows to squint in the high sun's brightness, taking in the place the bus had deposited them.

Seeing a dilapidated building consisting mostly of crumbling bricks and splintered wood, an old railway station that hadn't been in service for over a quarter of a century, and nothing else for miles but wilderness, the complaints started anew, louder.

1

One passenger, handsome in a GQ model kind of way, smoothed his straight glossy hair straight off his forehead with his palms and scowled looking around in disgust.

His nose wrinkling, he sneered, "What the hell is this? This is no fucking Diamondbella Resort of the Région d'Obock the tickets described."

The rest of the passengers joined in grumbling.

The complaining stopped abruptly as numerous men dressed in camouflage stepped out from around the decaying building.

Every suspicious eye wide and confused turned to naked fear when they saw the men were armed, and the weapons were aimed at the passengers.

His brows drawn down in anger, the model looking man who had first groused took a cocky step forward and blared, "My name is Brock Disik. Now what the hell is going on here? I demand to have answers! The hell on wheels bus was bad enough, but we were told-"

One of the armed men wearing army green camouflage shirt and khakis, strode in heavy boots to the yapping man.

Raising his shotgun he set the end of the barrel to Brock's forehead. His voice icy and low, he ordered tersely, "Shut- up."

Brock froze, his mouth slammed shut.

The armed man, lean, muscular, sleek black hair and goatee, glared with dark surly eyes at Brock then turned his head slightly and nodded to a man appearing even tougher than him

The tough male dressed in camouflage pants and a tan T that outlined major muscle power stepped forward.

A sharp nod and the black-haired man said, "Chief, I think they are ready to listen."

The chief stood with his hands behind his back perusing the passengers under hooded eyes, making him look dangerous and aloof at the same time. He inclined his head to the black-haired man, "Thank you, Vigo," then he addressed the crowd.

His low masculine voice, commanding yet quiet, drew the audience's attention. Friendly and cheerful would be the very opposite of the demeanor this man exhibited. Harsh and hard would be a more apt yet understated description.

Face like carved granite, with a deeply domineering tone, he announced, "I am the chief, Tezer Corseque." A distinct chill savaged his words and was mirrored in his dark eyes.

"I am in charge of this…expedition." Tremendous biceps bulged and flexed under the shirt with his movements. His shredded chest molded into a straight V to hips as lean and taut as a jaguar's.

An elderly lady from the bus snapped, "Expedition? We did not come all this insufferable way for a stinking tour. We were told we had won three weeks holiday at the Diamondbella resort, a luxurious Shangri-La."

Her veined knobby hands set on bony hips. "This," she snorted while sarcastically gesturing with her head at the rugged terrain bordered on the west by thick jungle. A snarl curling her wrinkled lip, she continued, "Is not a Shangri-La."

The only building in sight was the decrepit station.

Corseque's curt mouth ticked up at a corner. "You are correct, madam."

Dismissing her, he turned to a man who strode up to stand beside him. Corseque announced to the group of passengers, "This is Captain Garth Jefferson, he is going to explain what is going to happen."

Dressed in army green khakis and an olive T-shirt that also displayed his thick yet without an ounce of fat physique and burly arms, Jefferson stepped forward.

A hint of mischievousness lurked in the blue eyes flitting back and forth over the group. He proclaimed, "All of you, every one, have been tricked into coming out here."

He waited while the collective startled gasps and denials spurted amid the bewildered people.

"You all know a Mr. Yvetsky Braemont," his mouth turned up at the string of sharp, guilty, inhales of recognition.

Nodding with a smirky smile, he went on, "Yes, you are familiar with Mr. Braemont. Then you know that in whatever various respect, each of you owes Mr. Braemont money that you have stolen from him or skated on repaying him." He paused then spoke over the stunned silence.

"Whether it was loans, theft in his clothing stores, theft of his jewelry," he shifted his eyes to a platinum blonde with a voluptuous body encased in a red, two-piece skintight pantsuit and enough makeup it could be seen from another galaxy.

The blonde frowned at him. Then, taking in the height and muscular breadth of Garth with the nice smile, blue eyes and short, dark wavy hair, her lids lowered over heavily lined cats' eyes in sultry solicitation. Her big full lips curved up in practiced allure.

Keeping his gaze traveling the crowd, Garth settled on a heavy man and an older, dark-skinned man standing beside him.

His eyes pointed on the two men, Garth Jefferson continued, "Some of you stole his stocks, others sold his ideas to other companies."

When both men flushed, Garth inclined his head to the old lady. "Some of you skipped out on rent you owed him."

At her sudden blanching, he looked around. Most of the people had paled or turned red and averted making eye contact with him, or Chief Corseque.

"So," Garth smiled, "that brings us to why you were enticed here."

The crowd of captive passengers licked guilty dry lips and shuffled nervously. A pin could be heard dropped in the dirt while they waited for his response.

Smiling, Jefferson advised them, "Mr. Braemont wants his money back. He has hired us," he swiveled and nodded to the armed men with him, "to bring you to him. He wants to see each of you individually, in person.

"Every one of you actually have underground warrants active for you instigated and held by Mr. Braemont. Some minor, some not so much, so we are fully within our rights to take you to him. We are not abducting you, technically, but somewhat like bounty hunters, we will ensure you face Mr. Braemont." *And his wrath.*

"So," the heavy man in his 20's stammered, "wha-what, uh where, I mean, surely Mr. Braemont isn't coming here?" He motioned his pudgy hands indicating the endless wild forest fringed by steep mountains.

Jefferson chuckled. "No, he is not. We are bringing you to him. Unfortunately there will be others looking for you as well. Other…hunters, and then there might be relatives searching for you, or the police, so we will be unable to take to the roads.

"We will need to keep under the cover of the forests, which means we will be travelling along the crest of the jungle, as we make our way up the Chaque Mountains."

He let the gasps circle then said, "Additionally, Mr. Braemont's place is actually quite inaccessible except by helicopter. There are lodges interlaced along the way for safaris that we will be staying at.

"Mr. Braemont wanted you all to have plenty of time while on the trek there to think about what you've done, and how you will pay him back." Jefferson paused.

Some of the people grumbled under their breath but most were too scared and shocked at his words to comment.

Hands curving over his strong hips, he continued, "It will be a difficult hike sometimes, he wanted you to suffer a bit. But, he's allowed the overnights in the lodges as the area is too treacherous to travel at night due to wild animals, and other dangers," he shrugged, "such as illegal loggers, trappers, drug smugglers, the list goes on."

Ignoring the protests and questions now shouted out in rising panic, he blithely went on, "We have several jeeps," he indicated three vehicles some of the legionnaires were sitting in.

The group tore their confused and angry eyes from him to take in the vehicles.

"They are not for you to ride in," he said with a smirk. "They will drive along perimeter roads to bring us supplies as we travel and clear recon as well as ferry your luggage."

At their outraged expressions and objections, a side of his mouth pulled up in a grin. "Be thankful you don't have to drag your own gear with you."

From the very back of the crowd, a figure separated and inched towards the skirt of the forest dense with trees a hundred yards away, then it ran flat out straight at them.

Chief Tezer Corseque, Garth Jefferson, and other men watched the woman run.

A hat covered her hair, but the men were all staring at her booty. Her clothes were loose but the round shapely butt jounced in a sensuous romp against the pants in her flight.

Muttering, "Wow," one of the soldiers grinned like a wolf. "Fucking hot ass."

Another commented with a snicker, "She runs like a girl." The others chuckled. Several started to move announcing, "I'll go get her."

"No," Corseque stated quietly. The deep timber of his voice rumbling low, he ordered, "See to the others. I'll get her."

Ignoring the complaints of his compatriots, Corseque darted across the grass taking a different path than the girl who had now disappeared into the leafy thicket.

Although a big muscular man, Corseque raced as silently as a jaguar on attack, bounding gracefully over dirt and rocks and grass into the woods.

They had been in the area for two days waiting for the passengers to arrive so there was plenty of time to explore the land searching for dangerous animals or lurking criminals.

In seconds he looped around the brush and stacks of trees and jumped out in front of the fleeing girl.

Startled, she almost ran into him. Letting out a squeal, she jumped to the side and took one step to dodge him but he grabbed her and hauled her up in the air.

Kicking and flailing her arms, she cried, "Let me go! Let me go!" She struggled wildly but her fists didn't even dent his thick chest. He held her as easily as he would a child.

Thrashing like a panicked trapped animal, she twisted violently trying to throw herself from his grasp. In the panicked scuffle she was oblivious that the buttons on her blouse had popped open.

Corseque set her on her feet with her back to him and grabbed her wrists pulling them behind her.

As she fought him, he bent her elbows and held her wrists in one huge hand, then wrapped his other around her body to hold her still with her slender back pressed against his broad chest.

Bending his head, his dusky voice cold, he said in her ear, "Calm the fuck down, woman, or I will break your fucking neck."

Panting, she huffed hysterically, "Do it, just do it, kill me- I only beg that you do it quickly-" her voice squeaked through her constricted throat. Her gasps for breath shallow and fast, she cried, "Please..." her chest heaved against his arm with her exertions and fright.

"What the fuck, woman? What is so horrible that you would rather choose to die out here in the jungle?" Scowling darkly at her, he grasped her chin and turned her head to force her to look up at him.

He stilled his reaction at the lustrous, golden green eyes luminous with unshed tears turned up in terror at him.

"Please, kill me or let me go," she cried, twisting in his clutch.

Gripping her chin tighter, his menacing eyes pierced lethal threat into hers.

8

Seeing the pitiless callousness in his gaze, already dizzy and weak, her eyes rolled back in her head and her knees crumpled as she blacked out.

Chapter Two

"*Shit-*" Still holding the woman, Corseque lowered her to the ground, her neck arched over his arm, her hair draped on the grass. Laying her on her back, he moved down beside her and threw a leg over her to hold her secure.

Hovering beside and over the young woman, he braced on one elbow, immobilizing one of her arms under his body, he pinned the other to the ground by her head.

The hat she'd been wearing had fallen off. Curls of hair so light yellow, they were almost the color of the silk that lines fresh corn, spread around her on the grass.

A few locks twirled in feather light ringlets on his tanned arm, lying weightless over the dark hair that covered his muscled skin.

Pulling his attention from the flaxen tresses, he commanded, "Woman, wake up, knock this shit off."

Her lids stayed closed. He studied her heart-shaped face in repose, complexion so wan and sheer it was almost translucent. She had small pouty lips that looked soft as sin to kiss.

Long lashes curled up on her high rounded cheekbones that were probably normally rounder when she had more weight on her.

He scanned her body. She looked like she'd been eating barely enough to stay alive. Probably why she fainted. Her limbs were slim to the point of thin, yet still she had insane curves.

His gaze moved to her chest. Her blouse was wide open exposing lush, creamy breasts mounding over a pink silk bra. His eyes scrolled down to her tiny cinched waist. He'd earlier caught a glimpse of her small but rounded ass, he felt the urge to see more of it-

Her lashes fluttered, then her lids cracked open. Seeing him looming over her, disoriented confusion clouded her eyes then she remembered, he had captured her.

Realizing he had her completely pinned down, she writhed under him stifling her screams, trying to buck him off her.

"All right now, calm the fuck down," his growl gravelly and harsh, their faces were inches apart.

As hitching gasps scraped out of her petrified lungs, he felt her frantic breaths, cool misty puffs on his mouth.

Pushing at him and twisting her body, she cried, "Get off of me you big brute, let me up!"

Looking down at the beauty staked under him, lying on her back, her arms pinned, writhing and struggling to get free, in full masculine arrogance he said, "You aren't going anywhere, sweetheart, until I let you."

Thrashing and squirming she kept fighting him. Not looking at him, she cried, "Get off of me!" With panting gasps she demanded, "Let- me- *up*," the words feathered out in a tight quiet scream.

11

Her chest brushed up against his with her frantic thrashing. He lowered his chest faintly mashing her bosom, pressing his rock solid pecs against her soft breasts.

He said coolly, "As soon as you calm down. I can lie like this all day until you are so exhausted with your feeble struggles and pass out, again. I won't promise what I will or won't do to you while you're unconscious."

Seeing the fright skitter across her pale face he told her, "When you stop fighting me, I will let you up."

She jerked at the wrist he held by her head but it was like he was holding her down with cement. Her other arm was trapped under his body, his strong and heavy leg easily held the rest of her immobile.

She tried one last wrench, grunting, "*Uh*," with the effort. Realizing it was futile, she finally submitted, her chest still pumping with shallow panting breaths.

He waited.

She didn't move.

He rolled off her and stood up.

She struggled to sit up, her palms braced on the ground behind her. Not looking at him she was unaware of his gaze on her open shirt, watching her breasts hitch and heave over the silk bra. He bent over, grasped her arms and pulled her to her feet.

Staring at the ground, the woman snatched her arms from his grip and steadied herself, then drew her fingers through the fair locks that reached to the small of her back.

"All right, we are going back to the station." He turned towards the path then halted when she said flatly, "No."

Forking his thick fingers through dark hair that was shorter on the sides than on the top, he dropped his rugged hands on narrow hips and glowered at her. "What?"

Very calmly, she said, "I am staying right here. You have no jurisdiction over me, you can't make me go with you. I am not one of them."

"Okay, woman, I don't have time for this shit. You come along peacefully with me or I will-" she suddenly darted away, dashing down the path further into the woods.

"Goddamned bitch-" Shaking his head, he jogged after her.

Not more than a dozen feet and he reached out and lassoed her waist with his arm bringing her to such a hard stop her limbs flew up in the air.

"Have it your way," he growled, bending over, "show everyone that fine ass of yours," and he threw her over his shoulder. Ignoring her protests he started back to the station.

She tried to kick but he had a tight arm over her thighs and a large hand on her butt. Her punches on his back garnered no reaction from him.

When they reached the clearing near the station he stopped. "All right, honey, you promise me you won't run and I will let you walk on your own. If you renege on the promise, I will bind your hands behind your back, and your ankles, and since everything out of your mouth will be a lie I will fucking gag you, and you will stay over my shoulder every fucking day until we reach our destination."

When she didn't move or make a sound, he swung her down and set her on her feet.

Gripping her jaw, he lifted it so their eyes connected. He said, "Well? Yes or no. Swear or not." His eyes dropped to the tiny plush lips pushed out in an unaware pout, which was in contrast to the defiant angry glare lancing at him.

"Okay," he sighed. "Fine." Catching her hands, while facing her, he pulled them behind her back holding them in one hand while he pulled a rope off his belt.

The glaring green eyes strained into fright and panic, she twisted from him but he held her taut and started wrapping the rope around her thin wrists.

Crying, "Okay, okay," biting back a sob, she jerked at her hands.

"Okay what? Be specific." He kept winding the rope around her wrists. Their eyes collided. Hers furious and frightened, his steely and enigmatic, bereft of even a hint of kindness or pity.

She stared up at the man who had the head and body of a poster for the perfect Marine. Many inches over 6 feet, he had high sharp cheekbones that angled into a square jaw that tapered to a strong chin.

A dark shadow covered his jaw even though he had shaved earlier. His dark hair was longer on top with the sides slightly shaved. His mouth was full, but hard carved, the slightly larger upper lip, chiseled but still the softest thing on him, gave him a hard sensuous look.

Under the tight tan T-shirt, powerful shoulders like cordons of stone ledged over a chest made of steel. With every move he made the tats on his huge biceps flexed. His strapping torso narrowed down to hips so sinewy yet lean even with a belt on his camouflage pants hung slightly.

Trying to keep her chest from touching his, she sighed heavily then murmured in a small tight voice, "I- I promise I won't run, today."

Hands still behind her back, her eyes rolled back up to his but he was looking down, at her open blouse that was now slipping back off her shoulders exposing her breasts mounded over the pink bra. Her chest rose and fell sharply in her anxiety.

"Oh! You pig!" She twisted hard in his grasp, but he didn't budge. Her voice high, she demanded loudly, "Stop it, stop looking at me!"

Holding her wrists behind her with one hand, Corseque moved the other to clutch her upper arm when she started struggling again, his thumb pressed against the side of her breast.

He didn't move, she was holding her breath. Then she struggled again. With every jerk of her writhing body the brushes of his thumb against her plump flesh made harder contact.

Her gaze fell to his pants and her cheeks flamed. Even in the camouflage pants she could see he had a blazing hard-on.

Angry at his manhandling her, she threw herself from his grip to get loose, her breasts jostled, and he was still staring at them under hooded aloof eyes. His inscrutable, dark menacing gaze drifted back up to her face.

The anger in her green orbs was pushed out by heightened fear. "Let go of me," she said with a jerk, her voice dipped down, drawn, tired.

One of his large hands still around behind her holding her wrists, the other clamped on her upper arm forced their bodies close, almost touching.

His breath sailed tendrils of light hair off her face, her chest still pumped with her panic and struggles. His eyes lowered to her open shirt that continued slipping down her arms.

The corner of his lip nicked up, his voice coarse and deep, he asked, "Well? What will it be, over my shoulder or you walk on your own? I don't intend on struggling with you anymore."

Her inhale deep, the sigh out heavy and beleaguered, she replied in resignation, "All right."

He stared hard at her for a moment, she glared back. He said tersely, "I'll untie you. Remember, you swore you wouldn't run."

"Today."

A ghost of a turned up lip, he parroted her, "Today."

His eyes drifted back down to her breasts. "Like I said, you run, you will be bound head to toe and I will carry you over my shoulder. Don't doubt I can do it. I've carried a lot heavier and bigger things than you for days, weeks, up and down jagged mountains, over broiling deserts, through thick swamps."

The dark eyes narrowed to pinpoints, he growled, "I do not make empty threats, and you will regret it if I have to chase you again. Do you understand?" He waited.

She stayed mute.

He sighed and started to retie the rope he had loosened.

Her voice shaky urgent, she said quickly, "Wait- wait, I said I promise. Stop. Please."

Now both of his arms were around her and her breasts were wedged hard against his chest mounding up like soft hills. His eyes dropped to them again before rising to her anxious face.

The dark orbs as sharp and hard as flint, he said, "Next time, I won't give you the time to fuck around, you will answer me right away. Got it?" His glare an iced threat.

Her eyes wide and unnerved, her entire body was shaking, she didn't respond.

"Oh for fucks sake-"

She nodded.

With a big sigh, he barked harshly, "Say it out loud."

She had a very slight accent it seemed she was trying to hide; he was trying to figure it out. His gaze followed her tongue as she licked her lips, wetting the soft pink pillows.

"Yes," she replied with a soft hush, "I understand you."

Glaring at her, he held her for a few heartbeats. They were both silent, breathing heavy. His gaze fell again to her breasts pushed up against him.

He released her. Nodding at her blouse, he said coldly, "Fix yourself."

He watched her fumble nervously until each button was done up. "All right, let's go."

Wrapping his long fingers around her upper arm, Corseque led her back through the last of the woods to the station.

Chapter Three

When they reached the station, Garth Jefferson was still instructing the group.

"Each and every one of you will obey Chief Corseque's every command or suffer the repercussions. When I say that, don't worry, we won't leave you here, that would irritate Mr. Braemont that he couldn't see you and get his money back. Because," he glanced around at the crowd, "trust me, we leave you here you will not make it out alive."

Moving past the cries of disbelief, he said, "But a person can still travel with broken fingers, arms, wrists, jaws, black eyes, torn ears, you get the point," he smiled slightly at the wave of gasps before fearful silence prevailed.

"Now," Garth nodded to another man holding a tablet and said, "Captain Leo Panza is going to read off your names. As he says your name you will step over here." He pointed to the side of the station.

When Leo moved up with his tablet, Garth tromped over to where Tezer Corseque was with the woman who had fled.

His brow arched when he heard Tezer say to her, "Remember, move and you'll be trussed like Sunday's turkey dinner." Then Tezer left her and moved away with Garth.

Peering across the grass at the woman who looked livid, Garth said with admiration, "Shit, Tez, Helen of Troy and her 1,000 launched ships has nothing on that babe. This one could beckon 100,000 sails. I can't say I've ever seen a more...beautiful, like, ethereal woman. She's like, hell, indescribable, bro."

His hands on his hips Tezer glanced over his shoulder at her and shrugged. "Yeah." He turned back to watch the roll call of the passengers.

Like many of the legionnaires, Leo Panza wore camouflage over his big, taut body. His nose was pure Italian but not overly large, and he had grey eyes from his Irish mother, and short dark hair from his father. He called off a name, "Brock Disik."

The man who looked like a model, smoothed his slicked back brown hair. With a strong yet lean physique, neat scrub on his handsome jaw, and conceited blue eyes, he stepped forward and answered, "Yes. I am Disik." He tugged at his crisp shirt tucked into neatly starched brown khakis.

Leo glanced at the picture beside the name and then at Brock. He clicked a check by his name then gestured with his head, uttered a short, "Over there," and looked down at the next name.

With a roll of his eyes, Brock stuck his vain chin in the air and swaggered over to where Leo had indicated.

Next, Leo called out, "Tommy Tucker."

A heavy man of around 26 shot a nervous glance around at the others before saying, "Uh, here."

Leo checked him off the roster and nodded to where Brock stood.

Leo would be calling out nine names in all.

The blowsy platinum blond simpered towards Leo as he called her name. She shook tits that were as huge as her ass, and clearly she loved and adored every voluptuous inch of her bountiful body.

"Uh, Katherine, ah, Miot," Leo said. Then frowned at her. "You don't need to come up here, go stand by the others."

Watching the roster called, Tezer and Garth both had eyes on the woman Tezer had brought out of the woods.

Golden green eyes dominating her pale face darted back and forth like she was preparing to run. There were only two female names left to call, but there were three still standing there.

Speaking quietly, Tezer said, "Go stand by her. Close."

"Yeah." Garth nodded and sauntered across the grass.

Seeing him coming towards her, the young woman's skin blanched further.

Tezer could see her body shaking from where he stood.

Garth went to her and stood behind her.

Feeling him right behind her, her shoulders turned rigid and she wrapped her arms around her body.

In the meantime, Katherine Miot was still approaching Leo, her painted on cats' eyes slanted at him like she wanted to lick his face.

Frowning, Leo said, "Miss Miot, we are not playing games here, go get in place."

"Oh, honey," she purred, "you can call me Kitty, all my friends do." She moved closer with her hand out, long nails almost to his arm.

There was no humor lurking in his eyes like Garth's, Leo's grey eyes were hard slate. "Miss Miot, go stand with the others, I won't say it again." His gaze bore into her hazel eyes, the threat crystal clear.

Beside him, a man as huge as Leo but with wavy dark red hair and a long square chin raised his shotgun at her, his dark blue eyes stared blankly at her. When he cocked the gun, everyone froze at the spine-chillingly loud sound.

Kitty's eyes widened, then narrowed to slits, but her smile stayed slick. She said saucily, "Fine, boys." Her gaze swung from redheaded Reggie Lutalo back to Leo's cold grey orbs, and smirked. "Don't get your dicks in a knot."

Tossing the helmet of hair-sprayed blonde hair over her shoulders, she turned, and swinging her big ass as hard as possible she sashayed over to go stand with the others.

Two women remained.

Garth lightly set a big hand on the young woman's slender shoulder. She trembled under his touch. His gaze slew to Tezer. But under hooded lids the chief's expression was indiscernible.

The other remaining woman appeared to be around 28. The perpetually angry Cleopatra-appearing woman had dark eyes that slanted naturally without liner. Her features were as sharp as broken glass with shapely yet thin lips. Her body comprised of pointy tits and narrow hips. She was decorated with a lot of tattoos and piercings, the one in her nose glinted in the bright sunlight.

When Leo said the name, "Avril Izar," the woman under Garth's hand twitched.

As the black-haired woman strode with self-importance over to join the group, the woman Garth held started to shift from him. He moved his hand from her shoulder to hold her arm.

21

Leo announced, "That's everyone."

The passengers and the mercenaries all looked at the young woman with the light blond curls.

Leo glanced at Tezer.

The chief gave an imperceptible nod.

"All right, everyone," Leo said in a loud voice, "we will be getting ready to head out. There are, uh, sort of latrines," he looked a bit sheepish knowing that they were much less than that, "for you to use before we leave. Come with me."

Several of the armed men in camouflage joined him as they prepared to herd the people.

Tezer Corseque strode over to where Garth and the mystery woman were.

Crossing his arms over his bulky chest, he looked down at the woman in Garth's hold. She stared back at him. He asked her, "Who are you?"

Her plush lips firmed, she said nothing.

Tezer glanced over her head at Garth, then back to her. "Your name is not on the list. Who are you?"

One of her shoulders pulled up in a slight shrug. "I told you I was not with them. Now, I will be on my way," she took a step but Garth's strong fingers were wound around her arm, she couldn't move.

She turned a haughty chin up at him and said again, "I will be going now. Let go of me."

Both men were quiet for a moment. For all her haughtiness, she was trembling like a leaf in a stiff breeze.

Tezer asked, "Why are you out here, then, why were you with them?"

Her smile stiff, tone politely cool, she replied, "I happened to get on the bus at the last stop hours ago. I wasn't aware it wasn't a- a public vehicle. The bus driver did not ask for a ticket or any money."

Tezer's brow arched at Garth, he muttered, "I will want to talk with Rey about that." Back to her, "Again, I ask you, what are you doing out here, in the jungle, alone? Where were you going?"

She tried to keep her head up, but her eyes lowered nervously. She was standing between two powerful, armed men, mercenaries apparently, alone out in the, as he said, jungle, and she was totally at their will.

Visibly gulping, she swallowed hard, blinked harder, cleared her throat and spoke around the knot in it, "I do not have to tell you anything. Now, if you please," she turned her head to glare at Garth's hand, "release me and let me be on my way."

The two men stood mutely studying her.

Huge biceps distending under the tight shirt, Tezer dropped his hands to his hips. "All right, I'm not going round and round again like we did in the forest. I will say this only once. Regardless of what you were doing out here, I am not leaving you here. You will be coming with us."

He watched her dark blonde brows fly up, pretty lips part.

"You will have one chance to tell me who you are and why you are out here. You don't, and my friend, here," he motioned with his head to Garth, "will take you back out to the woods and cut off one finger after another until you answer my questions."

Tears of fright blurred the golden green eyes. She closed her mouth and firmed her lips struggling to stop the trembling but couldn't. She lowered her head and stared at the ground without saying a word.

Tezer glanced over her head to Garth. Garth nodded. Tezer tried one last time to get her to talk, "Miss, answer my questions. Who are you and what are you doing out here?"

She kept her head down.

Releasing a heavy sigh, the chief looked at Garth then said to her, "Okay. Let me warn you, you pass out from the pain and he will revive you and continue. Take her, Captain."

Holding her arm, Garth pulled her like she was a puppet towards the woods.

Tezer crossed his arms again, his legs rigidly akimbo, and watched them leave. He moved to a raised area so he could see them, but they couldn't see him through the broad leaves.

Garth only took her a few yards into the brush.

He stopped at a tree stump that went higher than the girl's waist. He moved his hand to her wrist and forced her hand on the stump and took out a huge knife from a sheath at his hip.

He watched her eyes pop at the knife. The tears flowed out, she put a hand up to stop them but they poured over her shaking fingers plopping onto the stump her hand was on.

Garth stood over her staring down at her blonde head. He couldn't believe he was in the fucking forest with a young woman, really a girl, she looked to be in her late teens, that would put a playboy playmate to shame, and he was threatening to cut off her fingers.

"All right, Miss, you have one chance to answer the questions. You understand?" He stared down at her head, she said nothing, just sobbed silently.

"What is your name, and why are you out here?"

No response, she just cried.

With a grunted sigh, he pulled her hand up, twisting her body to look in her face.

Big green-gold eyes awash with tears that trolled down her face looked back at him in sheer terror, her hand shook in his grasp.

"Listen," Garth said, "you can't be out here for anything that could possibly be worse than losing your fingers." He waited.

Her eyes lowered and she turned her head from him, the blonde curls swirled covering half her face.

Muttering, "Ah fuck," he turned her and set her hand back on the stump. "Okay," he raised the huge knife in his hand so she could see it and aimed it at the index finger of her left hand.

Her arm was stiff as a board, body quaking, tears rolling. Keening sobs hiccupped out of her mouth, still she said nothing, just crunched her eyes closed and held her breath.

"Say your prayers," Garth mumbled and brought the knife to her finger- then a sharp whistle pealed through the trees. It was Tezer's signal.

"Oh," Garth said nonchalantly stuffing the knife back in its sheath at his hip, "we're being called back." Big confused green eyes rolled up to him. "We have to go." He tugged her hand. "Gonna have to finish this later."

At first she didn't move, it seemed her legs were too frozen to move.

Holding her upper arm, Garth pulled her with him. They pushed through the brush until they reached the others.

Garth walked her over to where Leo was lining the people up. He handed her off to Reggie. "Watch her," he growled and went to speak with Tezer.

Garth took one look at the young woman before he turned. Her head was in her hands, shoulders shaking with sobs. She'd turned to face the woods so no one could see her cry.

He strode over to Tezer who was on a satellite phone. When he reached him, Tezer looked at him with a brow raised in question. He frowned when Garth shook his head.

Tezer said into the phone, "No, she isn't talking."

Listening, he then said, "Yeah, she's young. We don't know who she is or what she's doing out here in the fucking wilderness alone. Has nothing with her, no bag, no purse, no cell, pockets are empty."

He nodded with the phone to his ear. "It doesn't matter anyway, if we leave her here she'd be dead before nightfall."

He nodded again. "Okay, copy, out," and clicked off the phone. "Here, Nik," he said handing it to a dark-haired man standing beside him then turned his attention to Garth.

"If I hadn't previously heard her speak, bro, with that hot little accent," his hands on his hips, Garth ducked his head and shook it with a wry half-smile.

"I would think she was deaf and fucking dumb. Hell, Tez, I had the fucking knife over her finger, asked her what her name was, she kept her head down and sobbed, but freaking would not answer. I couldn't fucking believe it."

Tezer curled his long thick fingers over his sinewy hips and looked through narrowed eyes over to where the girl stood.

"Yeah," he agreed. "I got the same shit out of her when I questioned her. There is something that she is more afraid of than being with us, or being left out here in the wild alone, or losing her damned fingers. She even told me to go ahead and kill her just make it quick."

He dragged a sleeve across his eyes then looked back at her.

Leo was getting everyone lined up; she was in the middle of the line with her arms wrapped around her body and her head down.

Most of the other people were chatting without a care in the world like they did this every day.

"Anyway," he continued, gruff annoyance dropped his voice lower, "one of the others already called Braemont and described her. He called me. He wants her. He said bring her and work on her on the way to learn her identity so he can do research on her. Thinks she could be a confederate, a spy possibly for other hunters hoping to take our prisoners from us and earn the cake themselves."

Garth twisted his neck back and forth to release the tension that had built from threatening the girl with his knife. "We can't leave her here regardless of what he said. This place would eat her alive. How's she supposed to contact her people with no phone?"

"Dunno. Don't care 'cause she ain't going to. I'll kill her if she attempts anything."

Giving his friend an odd glance, scratching his head, Garth said, "You recognize her slight accent?"

Tezer shook his head. "No, I can't place it. Don't think she's from Russia."

"So, she's not one of Braemont's fugitives and she's not a local." Garth glanced around at the dense forests surrounding them with the mountain backdrop. "Not that there would be any residents way the hell out here in this wilderness. It's a bizarre mystery why she's here with no possessions, no weapons, totally alone."

"Yeah, suspicious as all hell."

Garth's brow quirked with a wry grin. "Totally bonkers that those idiots thought there was some kind of Shangri La Resort out here in the wilderness of near Southern Siberia, Russia. Who even knew there was an actual jungle in this frozen tundra?"

Wiping his arm across his forehead, Tezer said, "All right, tell Leo to get them moving. I want you up front with me, Leo quarter way back. Zeg, Rey and that crazy freak Clancy spread throughout them. Have Nik and Vigo take up the rear. Ready?"

Garth smiled. "As I'll ever be. Weirdest mission we've ever done. Let's go."

Chapter Four

$\mathcal{T}$ezer and Garth hiked side by side along the grassy path. The group stayed near the woods but trod on an old path of smashed grass making it easier moving but were still under the canopy of the tall trees.

Behind them, nonstop grumbling and grousing rolled up and down the line. Periodically either Tezer or Garth would fall back down the line to ensure all was well.

Some people clammed up as they went by, some complained louder.

Tezer was halfway down the line when the old lady, Essie Cook, snarled at him. "You bastard," she spat taking him by surprise but it never showed on his stony face.

"What kind of lowlife thug are you to drag innocent people, especially defenseless women through this godforsaken jungle? Who raised you? A she-wolf?"

Tezer never slowed or responded.

When Garth made his trip she repeated her words.

Garth's mouth nicked up in a wry smile, he responded, "There's not an innocent person amongst you, and I'm thinking you have never been defenseless in your life." He chuckled at her scowl and kept moving.

When either Garth or Tezer passed the nameless young woman, she kept her head down.

They took a break after two hours of trudging through the mossy land.

"Gah-" Brock Disik dropped down onto the ground with a groan and leaned against a tree. He raked his fingers through his straight hair smoothing it back into place. Beads of perspiration lingered around his hairline. Several other captives plopped down with him.

A chubby girl with curly red hair squirmed until she was right next to him.

She smiled up at Brock, cheeks like freckled balloons. "Gosh, you seem to be having no problem hiking in this horrible wasteland." She pushed back a wad of curly hair damp with sweat off her face.

His eyes on the nameless woman sitting apart from everyone, he mumbled, "Yeah, well, whatever."

"So," she squirmed closer, pulling her dark blue blouse over her chubby tummy. Crossing her jean-clad pudgy legs she asked, "What's your name, handsome?"

At first he acted like he didn't hear her, then he glanced at her and gave her his megawatt model's smile. "I'm Brock, Brock Disik."

Round red cheeks peppered with freckles swelled with her grin. She ducked her head shyly and announced, "My name is Robin Jacob."

He tilted his head back to lie against the tree and yawned. With a bored tone, he responded, "Yeah, pleased to meet you. What was your crime?"

Robin squirmed closer and stared at him. His eyes were closed. Making a face that he couldn't see, she matter-of-factly told him, "Oh, I was a maid at his New York condo, and," her pudgy shoulders moved up then down, she leaned over closer to look at him.

"I pinched some clothes…and, uh, a bit of jewelry. No big deal." She dragged fingers like small sausages through the gnarly red hair to get the knots out. "What about you?"

He didn't answer her.

She poked him in the shoulder with a fat finger. "Hey, Brock, what did you do to get here?" She watched the frown mar his classical good looks. His nose was perfectly straight, the neat scrub made him look less pretty and more manly, his eyes stayed shut.

His mouth compressed and turned down at her poke, then they converted back to the nicely shaped but masculine lips with a slight upward curve.

One side of his broad shoulders raised in an indolent shrug, he answered, "Eh, nothing that freaking heavy. Just a couple years back when I was modeling I did a little wrong," his perfect teeth showed with his boasting smile.

When his eyes cracked open a slit to look at her, she twitched back so he wouldn't realize how close she was to him.

"I was a model you know." His lids shut.

"Yeah," Robin sighed, "you are so gorgeous."

The smile grew wider. "I know." His mouth opened wide in a rude, loud yawn. Not bothering to stifle or cover it, he said, "Anyway, there was this party for a bunch of us models, photographers and stuff at Braemont's condo in LA, and I kind of made off with a few sculptures, and a painting or two. I never thought he knew it was me.

"I tried to make it look like it was this bitch model, Glenna Millstream. Bitch thought she she was such hot shit. Anyway," he shrugged again, "whatever. I sold them all and the dough is spent so the old man won't get a nickel out of me."

Through another yawn, he mumbled, "Now," he squirmed to lie back further against the tree, "bug off so I can catch some shut-eye. Fuckin' slave drivers, I'm not used to such strenuous hiking."

Robin crossed her legs and leaned back against the tree next to him but shifted sideways so she could stare at him.

Robin was one of those girls that people always said if she wasn't so heavy she'd be pretty, and she believed it. Hell, she told herself, she was only pleasantly plump; guys these days liked a little meat on a girl's bones.

Off to the side, Tezer and his team, Garth, Leo, Nikolas Gazzola and Reggie Lutalo gathered in a loose circle to discuss how things were progressing.

Several feet away, the extra mercenaries Mr. Braemont had insisted on hiring to back them up, clustered together.

They consisted of Zev Zigrid, aka Ziggy, a blond mountain with a thick German accent.

Vigo Vedie, slick black hair and goatee, he was sleek and lean.

Reynaldo Silva, aka Rey. Self-acclaimed lady's man, his big brown eyes flicked nonstop over all of the women.

Lastly was Clancy Bonds. A light-skinned Black man with braids crossing from his scalp to collar tied at the end in short little bunches at the back of his neck. He had a thick beard and crazy eyes, talked about nothing but his past as an ex-boxing champ.

The group they were taking across the land mostly sat in clumps across the grassy clearing.

The women huddled together perched on fallen trees.

The male passengers and Robin, gathered around Brock. Eventually all the women except the nameless girl and the old lady, went to join Brock's group.

The old lady sat down in the middle of the clearing and bitched at no one in particular.

The mystery girl sat off by herself.

Tezer and Garth's hawk eyes rarely left her.

The blowsy platinum blonde with the huge knockers strolled over to Tezer's team. As she approached, her attention latched onto Tezer, the other men hid grins and deliberately wandered off.

Tezer lit a cigarette and leaned a shoulder against a tree. One hand in his pocket, the other holding the cigarette curved inside his palm, with a squint through a cloud of smoke he watched the bombshell approach.

Her voice deep and huskily sultry, she purred, "Hey, hotstick, I thought we could get to know one another. I'm Kitty, like in Kitty Kat." She ran a long nail down his brawny forearm. "Or," she giggled, "Some men like to call me *Pussy* Kat."

He said nothing, merely gazed at her through the haze of smoke from under hooded eyes that hid his thoughts.

Kitty moved closer, intentionally shaking her breasts to draw his attention.

His eyes dipped down briefly, her shirt was unbuttoned almost to her midriff exposing a lot of skin.

"So, uh," she inched closer until one breast was pressed against the arm with his hand in his pocket. "What are the, uh, sleeping arrangements going to be like?"

Her fake lashes flapped down, then up. She tucked in her oval chin to look up at him coyly through the long, thick lashes. "I'm more than happy to share a bed with a big strong hunk like you."

Tezer took a drag, inhaled deeply, blew the smoke off to the side and glanced down at her breasts. She wriggled them against his arm with a flirty giggle.

Finishing his cigarette, Tezer dropped it on the ground and crushed it with his boot. Without a word to Kitty, he pushed from the tree and traipsed to where his team huddled, sending him surreptitious grins.

Complaining at his boorishness, "Hey," a scowl pulled Kitty's penciled brows down, big lips twisted annoyed. "That is so rude." She glared at Tezer as he strode from her.

Then, a tiny smile curled one side of her wide mouth, she called out, "Playing hard to get? We'll see Mr. Chief, I love a challenge."

She chuckled to herself. "You'll have me in your bed by time the moon sets tonight!" Knowing no man could resist her, Kitty smiled and wandered over to join the others.

One of the jeeps suddenly appeared through low undergrowth.

Tying back his long fuzzy hair into a ponytail, Nik Gazzola helped Reggie and the hulking Ziggy take bags out of the truck then they went around handing out sandwiches and canteens to the group.

When the women asked where the bathroom was, they were appalled at the answer.

Rey Silva handed out biodegradable toilet paper with a sexy grin. "Right over there, ladies," he gestured to a clump of trees and bushes. "You might want to stay in at least pairs, the animals will be less apt to bite a lone bare butt," he teased, winking a brown eye. The long ponytail flopped on his back with his chuckle.

When the big blond mountain of a man, Ziggy, handed the mystery woman a sandwich, she shook her head.

"Thank you," she said politely, "but I am not with the group. There won't be enough for everyone."

Behind Ziggy, annoyed, Tezer barked, "There is more than enough for everyone." He moved to stand beside Ziggy. Both men stared down at the blonde beauty.

She looked up at them, shadows under her large eyes showed her weariness. "It's all right," she smiled at Ziggy, "I'm not really hungry, thank you."

"Uh, but Miss," Ziggy stammered, his German accent thickening, still holding out the sandwich in a huge, football sized paw.

Tezer took it from him along with a canteen and motioned with his head for the yellow haired giant to keep going to the rest of the people, then he crouched down in front of the girl.

It took all her might to not cower from him, but her rigid body and tight pulled in lips made it clear she was afraid of him. As she should be.

His thick torso blocking everyone's view of her, Tezer braced himself with a big hand planted on the ground. "All right. I am not going to argue about every fucking thing with you. We have a long way to go, you have obviously not had a square meal in a while. And when you drop dead from hunger, I will still drag your ass with us.

"We have more than enough food. So, eat the fucking sandwich and don't make me have to take my time and energy to have to keep telling you shit a grown woman should know and accept. Put the canteen around your neck." He thrust the sandwich in her hands and stalked off.

He didn't look back to see if she ate, he didn't want to return to her as angry as he would be if he saw the sandwich untouched.

He didn't look in her direction again until he returned to his men, then he glanced over.

Not a member of Tezer's own team, one of the hired mercenaries, Vigo Vedie had plunked down next to her on the grass.

Tezer's brows drew down low over the ridge of his forehead.

Normally, Vigo with his sleek black hair, glittering black eyes, svelte body of lean muscle was an exceptionally quiet man. But now, he sat with his legs crossed, smoothing his goatee with his fingers while chatting at the girl.

She nodded occasionally but never opened her mouth.

After a lengthy break, Leo trod back and forth telling everyone to get up and get going.

Groans and moans whined over the grass and rocks as people climbed reluctantly to their feet.

The old lady, Essie, refused to move. Leo traipsed over to her. "Mrs. Cook, you need to get up."

Her bony arms crossed, pointy elbows stuck out, her lip curled, grey curly hair fell over her brows. She pushed the round glasses back up her straight nose and said, "Get lost, little *I*talian boy, I am not moving."

"Okay," Leo said with a shrug, "we'll see you later."

He started to turn then swiveled back. "Hey, did you bring your camera so you can take photos of those hungry Mongolian grey wolves and golden tigers when they come out at twilight? It would be a good idea also," he paused as her mouth dropped.

Biting back his grin, he advised, "You should probably look for a nice rock to lay your head on, night comes quickly out here, you know? And, clearly there are no street lights in the jungle. Zero illumination. Nope, when the sun is down it is black as in you can't see an inch in front of you."

Her eyes widened behind the round glasses.

"And, remember, voracious animals can see much better in the dark than humans." Leo turned and strode from her. He could see by Garth's grin that Essie had scrambled up and was hurrying behind him.

Tezer stood to the side watching the people line up.

Most went right back to the place they had been before, some shuffled around as they made friends.

Three of the women stayed bunched together. Buxom Kitty, Avril with her diamond shaped face, witch's hair and angry puss, and Chelsee, a pretty girl with an Italian mother and Black father was around 25. She had thick caramel hair that waved past her shoulders and light brown eyes. Her hips were narrow and she propped up her small breasts in a push-up bra.

Chelsee Christine Genise hadn't taken her eyes off mercenary Rey Silva and his dark bedroom orbs.

When he glanced at her, she boldly stared back with a slight curve to her mouth overly plumped up with lip-fillers.

Tezer stayed in place watching as the group trod past him heading east.

Some of the people peeked at him as they went by, most were too scared to make eye-contact with the tough looking, unsmiling man with eyes so shadowy they were inscrutable.

The only one he really looked at was the nameless woman. His jaw worked as she moved slowly past him with her eyes on the ground in front of her.

When they had all gone by, he stayed in the rear with Nik and Vigo.

The group was entering thicker foliage but still on a grassy path, the path curved like a snake skimming through the grass in and around thick crowds of trees that had dropped half their leaves, and dotted with tall heavy bushes.

The people were talking quietly, most were concentrating on keeping one foot in front of the other as they were tired.

Then, Tezer's ears pricked up, he thought he heard a scream.

"Stay here," he said to Nik and Vigo and jogged up the line. He could only see a few feet of the line of people at a time the path was so curvy and densely shrubby.

He passed by where the nameless girl had been, and…he looked around, she was gone.

"Where's the girl?" he asked the people there. At their blank looks, he said with impatience, "The little blonde."

Everyone shrugged, shook their heads.

"Fuck-" he spat and jogged back to where they had just passed by, and paused, looking around.

Garth and Leo came down from the front.

"What is it?" Garth asked.

"The girl, she's gone." Tezer kept scanning the area. "Check, see if everyone else is here."

Leo dashed along the line. He returned in only a minute. "One of the passengers, guy, swarthy around 38, Paolo Baretti, is missing."

Without a word, seeing piles of autumn leaves crushed near the path, Tezer took off through the brush following the trail of smashed and scattered leaves.

Garth and Leo blinked then went right after him.

Tezer followed the disturbed ground and traced scuffled footprints in the dirt. He burst through the thick brush and saw the man Baretti dragging the girl through the forest.

She was fighting like hell. Baretti slapped her hard enough to stun her and she stumbled and fell. He stuck his hand in her long blonde curls and pulled her up by a fistful.

When she cried out he slapped her again and muttering curses, bent to throw her over his shoulder.

Tezer sprinted to the pair. Jabbing his hand around the back of Baretti's collar, he clutched it and jerked him back then slammed his fist into his jaw.

Hurtling back from the powerhouse punch, the man released the girl. She crumpled to the ground.

Tezer pounced on Baretti, punching him again and again. Baretti struck back, winged Tezer's cheek; Tezer twirled and slammed his iron-toed boot into his head.

Baretti dropped to his knees and Tezer fell on him pummeling until Leo and Garth raced over and grabbed his arms pulling him back.

Heaving and panting, Tezer shook the sweat off his face, wiped his eyes with bloody knuckles.

"Bro," Garth said, "we need to get him to Braemont alive, you can't kill him."

Tezer shook them off and scrubbed his arm across his face. "Yeah, we'll see."

He stomped over and glared down at the bloody mess of Baretti. "You fucking touch her, or any of the women again, you're dead. I don't give a fuck about Braemont." He turned abruptly, ordered, "Get him back to the line."

Garth and Leo picked Baretti up and dragged him back through the woods.

Tezer strode over to the girl who was on the ground. Her legs curled to the side, she leaned over with her palms flat on the grass, her eyes closed. She lightly shook her head as if to clear it.

Tezer crouched down. "Woman," he said harshly, stuck his thick rough fingers under her chin and raised her head.

The side of her face was red where the bastard had slapped her.

Tezer touched it lightly, then looked hard at her. "Your eyes are unfocused, are you nauseous or dizzy?"

She licked her lips and pulled her head from his hold. "I was…dizzy, I'm," she took a breath, "all right."

He moved to his knees, spread them and sat back on his heels. He waited, watching her trying to clear her head. Baretti was a burly man and he'd hit her hard. Thankfully it was with his palm and not his beefy fist, so delicate she could have been seriously injured or dead.

A few minutes passed then Tezer said, "Look at me."

She kept her head down.

"Look at me," he snapped and gripped her chin, lifted it and studied her eyes. They looked steadier than they had a few moments ago.

"I- I'm fine. Please let go of me," her voice very hushed, she kept her eyes lowered. "Just go on, leave me here."

Tezer stared at the mark on her face, he'd caught a glimpse of her eyes bright with unshed tears of pain.

He stood up then bent over, wrapped his hands around her upper arms and pulled her to her feet. He held her briefly while she gained her balance.

He waited another minute then led her out of the woods back to the path. Dried leaves crunching under foot, they dodged low spiky branches and went to the front of the line where Garth was.

Nudging her into the line, hard rugged face dark with anger, Tezer admonished her, "You stay up here. Don't make me have to go through that shit again. We've lost time. I will kill the next bastard that tries that shit, and I need to make sure everyone arrives alive," he turned from her and started walking back to check the line.

Her mouth dropped open, her dismayed eyes fired at him. She spouted resentfully, "That was not my fault! It is not my doing that you can't control your men, your hired animals-"

He swung around so fast she jumped back thinking he was going to hit her.

Bending over, he got right in her face. "He was a goddamned passenger, not one of my soldiers. You just stay where the fuck I tell you and keep the hell away from the men. All of them."

"Including you? I would be more than happy to keep clear of you. Way clear, like, I'll just leave now," she turned from him.

He snatched her arm and pulled her from the line to the side of the path.

Fuming, he ground out, "You just do what the fuck I tell you. No more. No less. Like I said before, you try to run and you'll be bound ankle and wrist. I'm not fooling around here, I have a job to do and you are not going to screw with it."

Sticking his roughly hewn, hard jawed face inches from hers he snarled, "Any other fucking comments little girl?"

That fired her ire up. She sneered, "How dare you boss me around, keep me prisoner! I am not part of this expedition, I am leav-"

41

He twined his fingers around her throat and pushed her backwards until her back was up against the rough bark of a tree. His face black and fierce, eyes frigid flint, he was over a foot taller than her and a 100 pounds heavier, all muscle, he leaned over and into her.

"This is the last time we're having this conversation. I am in charge here. Everyone does what I tell them. They don't, they end up critically injured, or dead."

He could feel her body trembling under his hand. Her eyes large and frightened popped wide like green-gold water lilies at him. Pieces of yellow curls stuck to the craggy bark of the tree.

She put her hands on his chest trying to shove him from her. He didn't budge.

His hand so big it covered her neck and collarbone held her staked to the tree. He grated through his teeth, "You are not leaving. You are staying with this group until I dump you with my employer. You aren't out here a minute and some fucker tries to abduct you and rape you, and you were helpless to stop him. Apparently you are too stupid or too stubborn to comprehend the lethality of this wilderness.

"Which is a moot point. You will stay with the group and do as I say. That is final. Don't fucking make me discuss this again because if we do, it will be with you bound and gagged and over my shoulder. Are we clear on this?"

She blinked at him and glanced up at his broad thick shoulders. His hand was still wrapped around her slender throat holding her against the tree.

Her chin trembled slightly over his hand. She brought her hands up to grip his forearms. They were too big and burly for her to wrap her fingers around in her futile attempt to pull them away from her.

He looked down at her small dainty hands trying to tug at his muscled arms then up to her angry but now frightened eyes. Squeezing his hand lightly around her throat, he growled, "Answer me."

It seemed a struggle for her to pull her plush lips apart and whisper, "I understand."

Still, he stared at her, scrutinized her every feature. He suddenly asked, "What is your name?"

She blinked startled at his abrupt question but didn't answer him.

Tezer sifted a few fingers over the red mark from Baretti, then released his hand from her neck. He had plenty of time to get it out of her before they reached the mansion.

He patted the underside of her chin and said roughly, "Not another fucking word about you leaving the group, my leaving you here. Not one." He grabbed her arm and brought her back to where the people were waiting.

They hiked on and on until the sun started down the other side of the sky. The men knew better than to keep the people out at dusk or later, hiking in a line they'd look like raw shish kabobs to hungry carnivores.

Leading the group, Tezer easily found the first lodge they were to stay in for the night. There was a padlock on the door, he twirled the combination, opened the door and then stepped aside.

Garth and Leo strode in first with their shotguns raised.

When they come out a few minutes later, Tezer said, "All right, everyone, inside."

The people wearily moved past him into the lodge.

As she passed Tezer, Kitty rubbed her body against his. He made no response and she kept moving with a slight pat to his cheek.

As Kitty's heartily curved body brushed his and her hand stroked his face, he looked up, the nameless woman was staring at him.

Her big green, tired eyes speared her contempt through the dimming sunlight at him. When she saw him looking at her, she dropped her gaze.

As soon as everyone was inside, Tezer waited for the last of the mercenaries, Clancy and Vigo to approach. When they stopped near him, he said, "All right, you two have first watch. You know what to do."

They both nodded silently and took off into the waning sunlight to patrol the perimeter.

Chapter Five

The rudimentary lodge consisted of eight rooms. Inside were two bathrooms, a kitchen and four dorm-like bedrooms, and a large living room.

One room was allotted to the six females, one to Tezer and his team of Garth, Leo, Reggie and Nikolas, one to the hired on mercenaries, Ziggy, Vigo, Rey and Clancy, and one to the four male passengers.

Everyone would be sleeping on cots. The women were to use one bathroom, and the men the other. The bathrooms had several stalls and showers.

Even as tired as they were, as soon as the passengers saw their accommodations, the grumbling and complaining started back up.

The legionnaires turned deaf ears as they stowed their gear and took turns showering.

Blond goliath Ziggy Zigrid, and Reggie Lutalo took over the kitchen and prepared a dinner of meatloaf and mashed potatoes with green beans.

When dinner was ready, the group gathered in the living room where folding tables were set up for them to eat on. Chairs were placed around the tables and people wandered about choosing who they wanted to sit with.

The three women, Kitty, Avril, and Chelsee sat down quickly and chattered while waiting for the food.

Elderly Essie Cook sat with two of the male passengers.

The second oldest of the group at 55, Ronald McCain constantly adjusted his glasses, a nervous habit, with either his fingers or just squinted them up with his nose. His hair had thinned exposing a dark brown dome, he went to the gym five days a week to keep in shape.

The other man at the table was the stout Tommy Tucker. At 26, he had straight straw colored hair, and round eyes placed close together. They were sunk in his doughy face and darted nonstop around the room.

Model Brock chose to sit with one of the hired on mercs, the local Casanova- Rey Silva. Red-headed Robin quickly sat down at their table.

Tezer sat huddled with his men. He kept his cool gaze on Paolo Baretti, the man who had attacked the girl.

Baretti sat slumped on the floor with his back leaning against a wall. His face was a mess, blackened eyes, bruises, swelling, he was lucky Garth and Leo had been there to pull Tezer off him or he would be one with the earth now.

The chief shifted his gaze to the doorway of the kitchen. The girl was in there. For some reason she chose to help Ziggy and Reggie cook. Tezer had instructed the red-haired Reggie to not take his dark blue eyes off her, even for a second.

Speaking of her, the young woman came out of the kitchen carrying filled plates. She took the plates to each table and set them down then went back into the kitchen for more.

After she set plates down at the table where Brock was, the model snaked his hand out and patted her on the butt as she kept moving, calling out, "Hey Goldilocks, come and try my bed, mine's the best of all the bears." He snickered at her scowl.

She stopped, glared at him like she was about to slap him, but he grinned at her with a dare, like the soldiers, he kept his big body strong too.

Staying out of his reach, her slight accent deepened as she threatened the vain man smirking at her. "You touch me again and I will stick a fork in your eye." Shooting him a fierce glower she hurried into the kitchen.

He called after her with a jeering laugh, "Yeah babe, you and what army? Come back beautiful, give this handsome bear a little Goldilocks kiss!"

Enjoying Rey's encouraging snickers, Brock grinned at the girl until she disappeared into the kitchen.

Then he sniggered to his new friend, Rey, "Babe is too steaming gorgeous she can't even make looking pissed bad. Such a bodacious ass, I'm thinking about which part of her anatomy I'm going for next."

Beside him Robin's round face turned bubblegum pink.

His shoulders hunched and head lowered, Tezer peered up at Garth.

Smiling, Garth got up and went over to Brock. Brock didn't look up, he had a fork in one hand and the other was on the table.

Garth slammed his fist on Brock's hand smashing it on the table.

Brock let out a howl, "What the fuck, man?" He dropped the fork and cradled his injured hand.

Still smiling, Garth said cheerfully, "Keep your hands off the women unless you are invited to touch them." He winked a mocking blue eye at Brock and trod back to his table shooting Tezer a grin as he took his seat.

Done cooking, Ziggy and Reggie came out to sit and eat.

Ziggy joined Rey and the now scowling Brock.

Reggie went to Tezer's table and brought the girl with him per Tezer's earlier instructions. After indicating for her to sit, taking his own seat, Reggie scraped long freckled fingers through his thick dark red hair before grabbing up a knife and fork and digging in.

The men talked about guns and sports, the girl didn't say a word and mostly pushed her food around her plate. She seemed relieved when dinner was done and she returned to the kitchen with Ziggy and Reggie to help with the dishes.

Garth stood up, moved a few steps from his table and addressed the occupants. "Okay folks, get a good night's sleep, take a shower if you want, we leave at dawn. You will hear three whistles, that means get up immediately, get dressed and come out here. Anyone lags in bed will have ice water dumped on them, whoever comes out last will be doing KP tomorrow."

His hands on his hips, he said, "Everyone is to go right now and hit the sack. You know where your assigned rooms are." He ambled back to sit at his table with his friends.

The main team, Tezer, Garth, Leo and Nik sat back and watched the occupants meander around the room.

The chubby redhead hung all over Brock gushing sympathy for Garth hitting him for absolutely no good reason.

Her cinnamon skin glistening, Chelsee in her pushup bra trailed over to Rey Silva, her flapping lashes made it clear she was interested in him. He didn't need to be told, he took her hand and led her down the hall towards the women's quarters.

Twining a lock of black hair around a finger, Avril watched Clancy the ex-boxer head her way. She had a perpetual angry look, as hard as her diamond shaped face, but it didn't put crazy Clancy off.

He set a hand on her boyish hips and stared blatantly down at her tits that stuck out of her T-shirt in points. Her sharp face still sullen, Avril reached up and stroked her fingers through Clancy's thick kinky beard.

The rest of the group mingled their way out of the room and down the halls where their sleeping quarters were.

Nik Gazzola got up and stretched. His job was to sit guard outside the women's room and make sure there were no uninvited nocturnal visits from any of the men. His long fuzzy hair tied back in a ponytail went past his shoulders, the green-blue eyes were a vibrant contrast to his olive skin.

When he got to the hall, Kitty was waiting for him. He didn't know why he was surprised, the full-figured girl had hit on Tezer and Garth already.

Still hanging in the dining area, observing the immediate pairing up of people, hanging in a clutch with the other men remaining at the table, Leo blinked, said surprised, "Shit looks like we're going to be a travelling bordello."

Garth chuckled. Tezer didn't crack a smile.

The dishes cleaned and put up, Reggie ambled out of the kitchen with the mystery girl in tow, he brought her to Tezer.

She refused to look at him. When Tezer stood up, she subtly took a step back.

He didn't say anything, just splayed his big hand on her slender back and started walking. She was forced to go with him or she'd fall over on her face.

Embarrassed pink crept into her round cheeks. When they got to the beginning of the hallway, he stopped and turned her to face him.

"I'm walking you to your room because I don't want a repeat of earlier today. Obviously you can't take care of yourself."

He kept going ignoring her angry gasp. "And," he hesitated, she had glanced at him for that second and now stared away from him. He lifted his hand and gripped her chin raising it to face him.

"It's a nasty habit to not look at a person when they are speaking to you. Especially me. I won't fucking stand for it."

When she refused to look at him, he squeezed her jaw until tears of pain sprung and she finally raised her eyes to his.

His growl commanding, he told her, "You look at me when I'm talking to you."

Thinking he was done, she pulled from him to walk on but he caught her chin again His fingers dug into her fair skin with ire. His temper deep in his grinding voice, "I am not done."

He waited until she tipped her golden green gaze back up to him. "There will be a guard posted outside the women's room, mainly to keep men from going in. The other women, except for you, are too smart to try to leave and go out into the dangerous night on their own."

Ignoring her gold brows slanting down and pursed lips at his insults he kept talking, "However, he will also be there to keep any stupid females from exiting the building. And, be aware, there are guards outside patrolling the area and will be all night. Do not even think about leaving, or you will be tied to a bed for the duration."

They glared at each other until she lowered her eyes. He released her. Setting his hand on her back again, he silently ushered her to the women's quarters.

Taking an annoyed deep breath, he muttered, "There should be extra toothbrushes and stuff in there." He didn't expect a response and he didn't get one. The thick square ends of his fingers pressed into the soft curve of her back.

When they reached the room assigned to the females, the door was open. Nik was standing to the side of it waiting until all of the women were inside.

Essie Cook was bitching a blue streak at Nik who was totally ignoring her, his gaze was directed down the hall slightly past the room where Avril and the Black boxer Clancy were making out like horny dogs.

Tezer looked at Nik who rolled his blue-green eyes. Hair loose from the ponytail sprung around Nik's head like a fuzzy halo. Without a word to her, Tezer gave the mystery girl a slight push to send her into the room.

She didn't acknowledge him as she went in.

The old lady followed in after her still bitching and cursing.

Before he could leave, having given up on Nik who ignored her passes and had briefly disappeared into the room to ensure the window was secured, Kitty slinked back out and put her hand on Tezer's chest.

"Oh my God, Chief, you are a hunk, so strong," she groaned, stroking her hand up to his shoulder then headed down to his belt.

He caught her wrist just as it went down further past his belt. Standing behind her back, Nik had returned and was grinning like a jackass.

Tezer dropped her wrist and without saying anything strode off down the hall.

Behind him, he heard her say to Nik, "Well, he's not interested, tonight anyway, I'll try you again. What do you say, handsome? I love a man with long hair, and yours is so curly." Her voice dropped into a husky drawl, "Nikolas Gazzola, you have such pretty eyes for a man, they're bluish-green like little lakes."

Tezer knew as a good friend and part of his team he'd worked with for years, Nik would brush her off too and do his job guarding the door.

In the morning, everyone was tired but it didn't decrease the grumbling. They had breakfast and were out the door and on the trail. They hiked for a couple of hours before taking a break.

After the break and back on the trail, Nik found Tezer. "Listen, Tez, that old lady is freaking crying like a baby. Wailing on and on she won't shut up. She's driving everybody at the end of the line crazy. Clancy and Ziggy and even some of the passengers are threatening to kill her. You have to do something."

"Yeah? Like what? What do you expect me to do?" The chief kept walking.

Tugging the band out of his hair, Nik combed his fingers through the dark tightly curled locks and then wrapped the band back around his ponytail. He continued traipsing alongside Tezer. "Why don't you have someone talk to her, calm her down. Seriously, Tez, I'm not kidding, tempers are flaring back there. Old bat's gonna get hurt."

"Have who talk to her? Everyone hates her, she bitches nonstop and has a worse mouth than any of the men. She's nothing but a nasty shrill." Tezer sent periodic glances over his shoulder to ensure the nameless girl was right behind him.

She'd put her hat on and tried to tuck all the blond ringlets up in it but several tendrils swirled around her face.

"Tez, you don't want to show up to Braemont's with one less than ordered."

Sighing hard, "All right," Tezer said to Nik. "Go back to your position, I'll do something."

When Nik sank back to the rear of the line, Tezer slowed his step so he was walking even with the mystery girl.

She did not even glance at him, her small nose stuck up in the air.

Tezer tried to match his long strides with her shorter ones to stay beside her. Gruff with his usual cold tone, he said to her, "Tell me what your name is."

That her head twitched to look away opposite of him let him know she heard him although she said nothing.

"I'll get it out of you one way or another, save yourself pain and humiliation and tell me now." He observed her fair skin pale further, even the pink in her cheeks fled. Still, she remained mute.

Garth called back over his shoulder, "We'll break in five."

Tezer nodded, stuck his hands in his pockets and said to the girl, "I need you to do something."

Stiffly, her head quirked warily at him but she didn't look directly at him or speak.

He wanted to stab his fist in her hair and snatch a hunk of it and jerk her around to look at him, but he stifled the urge. "We're taking a break in a minute. The old lady, Cook, has been kicking up a crying jag. It's driving everyone nuts."

Her eyes on the trail, she murmured, "So?"

"She is driving everyone crazy with her wailing to the point that people are threatening her life."

The girl glanced at him in surprise, then turned quickly away. "That's ridiculous."

"I wish it was. But it's true. I can't control everyone all at the same time. My men need to have their weapons on them, so I can't guarantee they won't shoot her."

An elegant snort came out of her plush lips. Now she deigned to look at him with a wry curve to her feminine mouth. "Oh come on, they are your men, you are the chief, the one in control, as you are always telling me, so, control them."

Bristling, his lips crimped holding his temper in, he looked at her marching next to him.

Although petite and thin, she was doing better than most of the other women and some of the men too. The sun shone on the loose buttery tendrils lighting them like they were flax to be woven into a gossamer quilt.

"There are four men who are my regular team. They are tough as nails and honorable to a fault. The other four men are mercenaries hired on by my employer. They, unfortunately are wild cards. Then there's the male passengers, as you saw with the asshole that attacked you.

"I can't be sure any of them won't lose it and take out the old broad. And," he took a deep breath, looked down the line with his exasperated exhale, "even the females are claiming they're going to wring her scrawny neck if she doesn't shut up."

"Why are you telling me this?" She kept her eyes straight ahead.

Biting back his pique at her not even glancing at him, Tezer forced himself to stay cool. "Because you are going to go talk to her when we break, calm her down."

"Me? Why me? I want nothing to do with any of you. Ask one of the other girls." Now she shot him a scant glance and frowned at the big man with his dictatorial, uncompromising, Marine's face of sharp sculpted cheekbones, and strong jaw that always seemed to have a shade of stubble even shortly after he shaved. The dark eyes as usual were iced stones.

He answered her, "The rest of them are useless. They hang like in a clique and make fun of others. The one with the big tits keeps adding more makeup even while we're hiking in a jungle for fuck's sake."

Ignoring her frown at his language, he went on, "The slut with the long brown hair, Chelsee, is too busy hanging all over the men as is the one with the black spiky hair. Even the pudgy redhead is mean to the old lady and sticks like glue to that guy who thinks he's a movie star. So," he shrugged, "that leaves you."

Her nose in the air, she sniffed, "You are terribly judgmental and have a vulgar mouth." Now she shot him a glance.

He stared blandly at her.

Impatiently, she pushed at the wisps of hair the breeze tickled her face with. "I do not want to talk to anyone. I want to pretend I am not even here and hope everyone else does too. So, leave me alone."

They were nearing an open space with large rocks and boulders the people could sit on for their break.

Tezer shrugged. "Okay. Whatever. Don't help her, make sure you step aside from the blood splatter." He strode away quickly before she could retort.

"Why you- you horrible-" she broke off. With his long legs he was already out of earshot. The awful man was lighting a cigarette as he joined his friends.

"It figures," she groused, "he's a smoker. Typical for a self-involved egotistical male." Out of the corner of her eye she saw Essie Cook, tears streaming down her gnarly face, boo-hooing loud, ear gouging like nails on a blackboard wails, wander over to stand near a ravine. *A little too close*, the girl thought to herself.

Huh. So what, what did she care? She was not a part of these criminals, and murderers for hire.

She glanced around looking for somewhere comfortable to sit where no one else was. Seeing a nice big rock she headed towards it. She'd almost reached it when she could hear the old lady wailing and saw half the group giving her the evil eye.

Two of the men had their hands on the pistols at their hips and were directing fuming glares at her.

Blaring her woes, Essie crept closer and closer to the edge of the ravine. Several people looked like they were thinking about giving her a push off the cliff.

Huffing her annoyance, the girl quickly strode over to the older woman.

The nearer she got, the louder the wails, and the closer to the edge Essie moved.

"Mrs. Cook," the girl said softly, coming to stand in front of her.

Essie wasn't looking over the ravine, she had her side to it. She didn't acknowledge the girl, just kept crying.

The girl set a gentle hand on a bony arm and said, "Mrs. Cook, please, come over and sit down, you need to take a break, get some rest," she babbled on about nothing while slowly, gently maneuvering the woman away from the edge of the ravine and to a big boulder she could comfortably sit on.

Settling Essie down on the boulder, the girl sat beside her.

But the old lady kept crying. The younger woman rolled a compassionate arm around her bony shoulders and gently patted her arm while whispering soft shh's near her ear.

"Now, now, Mrs. Cook, tell me what has you so upset. You can talk to me, I won't blab your business." She kept patting her lightly.

Her cries grew quieter, but Essie kept sobbing.

The girl murmured, "It's okay, we're all scared. It's okay to be frightened."

Essie took her glasses off and set them on her lap then wiped at her eyes with her shirt sleeves. Taking a few deep shuddering breaths, she said, "How did you know that I was crying because I'm scared?" She partially turned to face the young woman.

The girl shrugged, said kindly, "Because, like I said, we're all scared. Even the men. We don't know what's ahead, or what can happen to us out here in the wild."

Essie nodded, sniffed, wiped her weary eyes. "Yes, you're right. I'm scared out of my wits." Wrinkles wound around her withered lips and circled the bleary eyes.

The girl hugged her softly. "I know. And you are probably so very tired, I know I am. All this hiking and hiking, gosh, if I'd known I'd have brought my darn bicycle."

"Ha!" the old lady burst out a laugh. She lifted her shirt hem to dab at her eyes. "I'm with you, at least we could be sitting while moving. Of course my balance isn't what it used to be."

The girl smiled. "At least we aren't alone out here facing whatever, you know?" She dropped her arm and folded her hands together in her lap.

The older woman slipped her glasses back on and peered watery blue eyes through the round lenses at the girl. "At least we know why we're here. Why are you here? A young woman all alone in this godforsaken treacherous land?"

The girl's eyes lowered, the smile fell. "Oh, I really don't mean to be rude or- or unfriendly, but, I just can't tell anyone."

"Oh." Essie patted her knee. "That's okay honey, we're all entitled to our secrets. What's your name? I haven't heard anyone say it."

Bending over slightly, the girl blinked, still staring at the ground. Then she sat up straight and pushed the long blonde hair off her shoulders letting the curls flow down her back.

She smiled kindly at Essie. "Please don't be offended, Mrs. Cook." Drawing in a calming breath and letting it out slowly she said, "I...just can't tell anyone...who I am. My name. I," her lids lowered over pained gold green eyes, "if anyone knew my name I would be in...danger."

Her smile weak, sad, she said, "So you understand that I'm not being rude, or dramatic, I just can't..." Tears bubbled up, her throat tightened. Blinking rapidly to hold back the tears she looked away.

"Oh, honey, don't be upset. You don't have to tell anyone." Essie patted the girl's knee. "But we can't call you 'hey you' or 'what's her name' or the foolish Goldilocks that idiot Brock calls you." Both women laughed at that.

"So let's give you a temporary name. What do you think?"

The girl put her palms behind her and leaned back. Arching her neck, she let her head drape back and stared up at the sky, swallowing her tears. Sitting back up straight she grinned at Essie Cook. "I think that's a great idea. But how do I choose something?"

"Hmm," a finger to her chin, Essie looked around the area. "I think something, not a real name, something sweet, like a flower or an animal…" a bird flew from a branch in a tree nearby, its wings fluttered against the drying leaves making them rustle.

Watching it fly away, Essie said, "I've got it, what about Dove?"

The women stared after the bird until it was a dot in the sky.

The girl sighed, smiled at Essie. "Sure, I think that's a nice name. You can call me Dove, Mrs. Cook."

Essie grinned at her. "That's great. Since we are now official friends, you may call me Essie. All right?"

The girl, now named Dove, nodded happily, the two new friends hugged.

Essie said, "I feel a lot better now, Dove." She grinned, wrinkles deepened around her mouth, crinkles cut like bike spokes around her eyes. "Thank you for helping me." They hugged again.

Across the clearing, Garth nudged Tezer in the side. "Well, would you look at that." Tezer, Garth and Leo watched the women hugging.

Leo muttered, "Huh. That old battleax, I would have thought she'd eat that girl for dinner."

"Yeah, me too." Garth nodded with a smile, mischievous blue eyes sparkling with humor. "But it looks like they're best buds now. Go figure. Huh Tez?" He jabbed his friend in the side again.

"What do you think, Tez, now we don't have to find a place to bury the old lady's body, and the ice princess' heart isn't ice after all, it's soft and sweet like melted sugar."

Tezer grunted. "Whatever, as long as the old bitch stopped crying. Let's head out."

Chapter Five

They were all exhausted, they'd been hiking for most of the day and tempers were becoming frayed.

Garth and Leo had to break up a fight between crazy Clancy with his wild chocolate eyes and the giant Ziggy.

True to his nickname, Clancy was whooping and yodeling while dancing foolishly around the muscle-bound blond, mocking his accent.

He grabbed his crotch jeering to Ziggy to come take him. "*Dah*, come on big boy," he taunted, "I hear you Germans like men with dark meat. Come and get me!"

Ziggy had enough and the two men tussled for a few minutes before laughing like a rabid hyena, crazy Clancy ran off.

Then later, Brock and Vigo went at it. The two men were rolling around on the ground throwing punches.

"Hey, come on, knock it off," Garth ordered while grabbing Brock's arms and jerking him to his feet while Leo got a hold of Vigo. Brock was big and strapping, Vigo's sleek body was long lean muscles.

"He talks shit, man," Vigo growled, jerking his head at Brock. Sweat dripped down to his black goatee. His dark eyes narrowed at Brock. "He says he's fucking the girl, Goldilocks, and that's bullshit."

With smooth suave strokes of his fingers, Brock combed his gleaming brown hair back and grinned smugly at him. "You don't know, you're just jealous she chose me over your skinny ass."

"Oh yeah? I'll show you skinny you fucker-" Vigo made to leap at Brock but Leo held him back.

"Knock it off," Garth ordered. His normal good humor was stowed behind a tough mien, the usual mischievous blue eyes threatened his own beat down if they didn't stop. He slapped his hand on Brock's chest and gave him a shove back.

Leo did the same with Vigo, while asking, "What girl?"

Vigo scowled at him then at Brock. "The blonde honey, Goldilocks. You know, the little one with the face of an angel and the body made of pure sin, the one they're calling Dove. That prick says he fucked her, it's a lie."

Brock smirked at him and taunted, "Jealous asshole."

Garth's face darkened, he glared at Brock. "I know for a fact you haven't been near that girl, you loud-mouthed fuck. She's not been alone for a second." He hauled off and punched Brock in the jaw. Brock stumbled backwards then fell on his ass.

His normally cheerful expression turned hard as cold steel, Garth bent over him with his fists raised and warned, "I hear you talk shit about her again Vigo won't be the only one fucking you up. I'll be next in line behind the chief if he hears about this shit."

Brock stayed down. Garth was over 6'5" of pure solid muscle. He had that tough Marine look about him same as Tezer and Leo.

Leo asked Vigo, "What's this about calling her Dove? Where'd that come from?"

Fixing his shirt and wiping his knuckles on his pants Vigo shrugged. "She wouldn't tell anyone her name so I hear the old lady decided to call her Dove."

"Huh." Garth looked at Brock, jerked his chin at the handsome man. "Get up, get in line, and keep your trap shut. Got it?"

Muttering to himself, Brock climbed to his feet and brushed off his khakis. The four men trotted back to the line and immersed themselves in it and kept moving.

Garth strode up to where Tezer was. "Hey," he said to the chief.

"You knock their stupid heads together?" Tezer asked him keeping walking.

Garth grinned. "Yeah. Jerks. Acting like 8th graders. Hey, they said the old lady gave the girl a name. Calls her Dove."

His step slowed, Tezer glanced at his friend, brows raised. "Yeah?"

Nodding, Garth tucked his hands in his pockets. "Have to call her something."

Hard line of brows lanced down between Tezer's irritated eyes. "Braemont has called me twice a fucking day asking me if I got it out of her yet. He said knock her around, she'll talk. I tell him she won't talk, she's tight lipped, he tells me to use something to open them."

"Oh yeah? Like what?"

Twisting his torso, Tezer checked the line behind him and saw she wasn't in sight.

As he stepped out of the line, turning around to go look for her, he replied, "He said pry her mouth open with my dick, and push the words out of her with it. He's calling later. Wants to be on the phone with me while I do it. Sick perv."

He took off striding down alongside the line of people. The trail had curved like a snake, around trees, shrubbery, uphill, down, half the people were not in sight.

As he passed a thicket of trees he saw the bright sunny hair a few dozen yards away.

The other girls were circled around her.

"Ah shit-" he moved more quickly.

Like juvenile schoolgirls, the women were shoving her back and forth between them cackling like scathing hens. When she tried to veer away from them, Kitty grabbed her arm and yanked her back into the middle then shoved her at Chelsee.

Screaming with laughter, Chelsee pushed her at Avril. Avril caught her arm and held her while redheaded Robin threw out a freckled hand and gave her a little slap, then they all laughed.

Avril pushed her back to a mocking Kitty who sneered, "Fly away little Dove, what's the matter, someone clip your wings?"

Robin looked up and saw Tezer coming, she blurted, "Girls!" getting their attention.

They stopped pushing the girl around and acted like they were just rambling along the trail. Kitty sauntered up to meet Tezer.

She wrapped her arms around one of his arms and hugged it against her breasts. "Chief," with a pout she tilted her head and gazed up at him, her broad lips curved in a blatant sexual invitation. "When are we getting together? How about tonight? We can find a private-"

He yanked his arm from her grasp and moved past her heading towards the mystery girl.

Kitty whined after him, "Oh come on, Chief, we were just mocking her stupid accent and messing a little with her. She needs to get toughened up, she's too soft. Right baby Dove?" she sneered spitefully at the young woman.

Beside her, Avril whispered, "Never mind. We'll get back at her later. Come on, I see a building, it must be our lodge for tonight." She hit Kitty's arm, and the three women hurried up the trail with Robin bouncing after them.

Rubbing her arms, the girl walked on as if nothing had happened, but Tezer could see her face as pale as a mist over a winter pond, and her neck bumped from swallowing convulsively.

She pretended Tezer wasn't heading straight for her. She kept walking until he planted himself directly a couple of feet in front of her blocking the path. She had to stop or run into him. Keeping her eyes averted, she wrapped her arms around her body and stood silently.

"What the hell was that all about?" he asked tersely. He could see her fighting back tears of frustration. His gaze dropped to her arms in the short-sleeved shirt.

One of the girls had reluctantly loaned her a pair of jeans, blouse and clean underwear so she could wash her clothes and have something else to wear while they dried. It must have been Chelsee, although taller and heavier she was the closest to the girl's size.

His eyes dropped to her blouse, he could see her tits molding way out of the too small bra, *yeah, Chelsee's*. It was a good thing she would be needing a sturdy jacket in the next days, those full tits would attract too much male attention.

She mumbled without looking at him, "It was nothing."

He stared at her, at least she'd learned to answer him when he asked her a question. His gaze went to her arms, bruises were already showing from the girls roughly pushing her around. How juvenile of grown women. And this young woman clearly hadn't the strength, height, weight or skills to fight off four bigger females.

She started to move around him, he wound his fingers lightly around her arm avoiding the bruises. She was so slim his hand almost went around it twice.

The tone of his voice cold, he said tersely, "My employer is calling tonight. He is tired of your games. He wants to know what your name is. Tell me now and avoid a load of shit that I will have to do to you if you don't."

She had turned her face away from him, the soft curls covered half of it.

The days were sunny and balmy, but late in autumn a slight chill was sinking in. Now that the sun was heading towards the west a breeze had picked up. It eddied through the tops of the trees rattling the few clinging leaves while birds squawked and swooped around looking for places to roost.

They were standing on a dirt path that wound around the forest so they were mostly out in the open with tawny hills bordering them that sloped up to rocky mountains in the far north.

The breeze lifted the bottoms of her curly locks shifting them gently around her body as she remained silent.

"All right. Don't say I didn't warn you. You aren't going to like Braemont's methods for my getting the information out of you." Gritting his teeth, he spread his big hand on her slender back and nudged her to move up the path.

Nik appeared from the brush zipping his pants. He looked up in surprise at Tezer with Dove. His eyes shifting around the trail, he asked, "Where is everyone?" His fuzzy black hair normally in a ponytail fluffed around his shoulders.

Tezer stabbed an inscrutable look at his teammate and replied with cold anger, "Where the fuck were you?"

Nik's eyes flit nervously back and forth at the trail, Dove, back to Tezer. "Uh, I had to take a leak, man." Seeing dark red staining Tezer's neck, falling in step with them, he asked, "Something wrong? Something happen?"

Her lips bunched, Dove gave him a small smile of sympathy.

His hand still on her back guiding her up the slight incline, Tezer growled, "We will talk later."

Nik wisely kept his response to himself and followed the couple up the path.

An hour later, in the lodge for the night, the table in the big drawing room was big enough to seat all the people at the same time.

As usual, the girl, Dove, avoided everyone by staying in the kitchen to help Ziggy and Reggie cook dinner.

Conversation flowed sporadically up and down the table. The people were getting to know each other and were conversing more comfortably.

Tezer sat at one end with Garth, Leo, and Nik. When the food was prepared, Ziggy, Reggie and the girl carried in platters filled family-style and set them on the table.

Under his normally hooded eyes, Tezer watched as the girl leaned in and out to set food on the table. Most of the men were watching her. Several looked like they wanted to take a bite out of her.

The one who had snatched her, Paolo Baretti, sat slumped over his plate. He watched her too, but was sneaky about it. He thought no one could see his earthy eyes following her under partially closed lids and hidden by thick lashes.

Unconcealed avarice glinted under the cover of those lids, along with hostility. Feeling Tezer's glare on him, he averted his gaze to the window.

When they got done serving, Reggie brought the girl to Tezer who had left a space next to him for her, then Reggie sat down.

She stood awkwardly, not wanting to be that close to the chief. Her eyes flicked up the table looking for a space to sit but she was only met with lustful gazes from the men and enmity from the women, except for Essie Cook who waved a wrinkly hand at her.

She started to walk towards Essie when Tezer pushed the chair out next to him with his foot.

"Sit," he grunted stuffing a piece of bread in his mouth, he didn't look at her. She hesitated, he growled under his breath, "I will sit you down, so do it yourself or enjoy more humiliation."

Still paused, she looked over at Essie who had pulled her lips in masking her expression.

Tezer set his bread down and put his hands against the table as if to shove his chair back and get up. She sat down. He put his hand to the back of her chair and helped her push closer to the table.

They both ate silently while Tezer's team chatted around them. When dinner was over, Tezer wiped his mouth with a napkin and tossed it on his plate.

The girl quickly got up and went to pick up her plate to go help the men wash up in the kitchen. Tezer reached over and grasped her wrist.

He tipped his head back and observed her through lowered lids. Deep voice cold like the bottom of the ocean, he said gruffly, "No. Not tonight. You're coming with me." He could feel her wrist stiffen with the rest of her body.

"Uh," she tugged at her hand. "I, uh, need to help in the kitchen, everything is always left to the two men that-"

Still holding her wrist, he shoved his chair back with a loud scrape on the wood planked floor and stood up.

Gravelly low with impatience, he said shortly, "It's their job. They want help they'll make the passengers do it."

Without another word, he started walking. Since his grip was like an iron vice she had no choice but to go with him.

There were more rooms in this bigger lodge. The women were still all ensconced in one room for their safety, but most of the men were only double to a room. Tezer had a room to himself, he brought her there.

He opened the door and drew her in.

Once they were inside he released her wrist and locked the door. He heard her audible gulp as she stepped away from him, her eyes wildly scanning the room for an escape.

Chapter Six

His dark gaze unfathomable, Tezer stared at her while saying quietly, "This is your last chance. Tell me who you are. You don't, and I have my orders how to proceed to get you to talk. I'm to fuck it out of you."

Her big golden green orbs wide with fright, she gulped again silently and took another step from him. Her attention flit to the window.

"You won't even get it open before I get to you, honey, and forget the bathroom, the door will go down easily, trust me. Now," he trod to her in half the steps she'd taken to move away from him. He threw his arm out and grabbed her wrist again.

"Last chance, tell me who you are." He pulled her close so she had to tilt her head back to look up at him. Her body quaked so hard he could feel it in the current of the room.

Remaining mute, she stared boldly at him for as long as she could watching his face harden. The planes in his sharp cheekbones grew sharper, his mouth firmed into a harsh line. The evening stubble on his clenched square jaw made him appear all that more ruggedly sinister.

She kept her gaze off the big bicep that pumped in the arm that held her.

He didn't say anything while he pulled her to a desk against a wall. There was a length of rope coiled on it like it was there waiting for this moment. He picked it up.

"No, please," she cried, her eyes goggled huge at the rope, breath came out in a panicked rush.

Holding the rope, he inclined his head to her, Dark orbs ruthless, he said, "Tell me your name."

She lowered her head and mumbled, "They call me Dove."

Not what he wanted to hear. Seeing the blonde put up a wall shutting him down, he turned her around and caught up both her wrists, pulled them behind her back and tied them together.

Her chest hitched with the sob she swallowed. He gripped her arm and brought her to the bed and pushed her to sit on it. She barely made a ripple in the king-sized bed when she sat down.

Tezer glanced at the window, traipsed over and closed the curtains then returned to her, the corner of his mouth tugged in at her cringe from him.

He bent over, slipped his hands under her knees and back and lifted her to sit back against the headboard, then he climbed on the bed, the mattress sinking under his weight, and moved to straddle her legs.

Her back against the headboard with her hands tied behind her, she couldn't move at all with him on her legs.

A big solid mass of muscle looming in front of Dove, close enough she could smell his aftershave still there from this morning, mingled with his natural masculine scent and a hint of smoke from a cigarette. The denim of his jeans rubbed against hers.

Her voice a strained plea, hushed but bewildered, she asked, "Why can't you just let me go? Why are you doing this to me?" She quivered at the sight of the big man, even in a khaki shirt his chest bulged and his biceps flexed.

Tezer's dark eyes bored into hers. Full mouth grim, he dragged one hand through his thick hair. She looked about to explode with sheer terror. He had never bound a woman or a child before, only dangerous men.

It was the second time he'd tied her, the first was just a threat to get her to comply. Her wrists were so small, he felt like a monstrous beast handling her like that, and now, what he was about to do to her.

Nonetheless, he said, "It's simple. All we're asking is your name. My employer wants to know it, and why you are out here, a woman alone in this harsh treacherous land. You talk, and we're done here and you can go to bed." He waited.

She glared up at him. "Why is it all right if a man was out here alone? What's the big deal that I am?"

He looked at her like she was a simpleton. "Because, sweetheart, a man has at least a fighting chance to survive out here, you have none. To find a young female by herself in these parts, in this wild jungle, there's something not right.

"At the very least you should be armed, but you don't even have a hairbrush for fuck's sake. Now, tell me why you are here and we're done for the night. I'll untie you and forgo what I have to do to you next to get this information out of you."

She looked down and closed her lips tightly.

His sigh ground from his solid chest. "All right, it's your choice."

Her eyes followed his moves as he reached out and clumsily unbuttoned the top button of her blouse with his big fingers.

Trying to twist away from his hands, she cried, "Stop! What are you doing?"

He undid the next button. "Any time you want to talk, honey," he shrugged, "just start and I'll stop," and undid the next button.

"Please, don't, I- I can't tell you, please don't do this!" Sobs bubbled up her chest and into her throat, tears started to fall.

Undoing the last button, he said, "You can't tell me, and I can't stop," he spread the lapels of the blouse open. "We have to know if you are here for illegal acts or what. The more tight-lipped you stay, the more suspicious we are."

He lifted the long curly hair and set it to fall to the sides behind her back. She was wearing a black lacey bra that was too small to hold her breasts, they spilled over the diaphanous cups.

His skin darkened, pupils flared. He stared at her chest for so long she started squirming trying to get away from him.

The dark eyes rose to her terrified greens, her lips trembled so hard her teeth were knocking. Without a trace of kindness, he insisted quietly, "Tell me."

She looked at him and bit her small, full lips to keep them from trembling. When she didn't answer him, his attention lowered from her chest to her pants. He unbuckled her belt, undid her jeans and pulled the zipper down.

Her rasping sobs filling the room, his intent gaze moved to the matching lace panties behind the open zipper.

Someone knocked at the door.

Tezer moved and slid off the bed and went to the door. He opened it.

Reynaldo Silva was there with a satellite phone in his hand. He peered around Tezer and saw the girl on the bed, obviously distraught, restrained with her shirt wide open, pants undone. It looked like the chief was in the process of raping her.

Tezer moved to block his view.

"Hey, Chief, bro, boss wants to talk to you." He handed him the phone, licked his lips and craned his neck to see the girl behind him. "Listen, Chief, you gonna pass her around when you're done? I'd like first shot at-"

Tezer took the phone and shut the door in his face.

He snapped, "Corseque," into the sat phone then tucked it between his shoulder and ear to listen and walked to the bed, stood beside it and looked at the girl.

Pillows bunched up behind her, she was trying to get up, roll to the side to get away. He sat on the edge of the bed, laid the phone down on the mattress, wrapped his hands around her waist and dragged her back to lean against the pillows.

She clamped her legs together as if that could keep him from undressing her further.

Tezer put the phone back between his ear and shoulder. Shifting up the bed so he was close to Dove, facing her, he moved his arm across her to set his hand on the other side of her hip on the bed preventing her from rolling away.

"No," his eyes like impervious black discs contemplated her, he said into the phone, "don't know who she is yet."

Nodding at what was being said to him, his gaze scrolled from her terrified eyes and over the lush breasts, down her flat belly then lingered on the black lace exposed in her open jeans.

She struggled to move away from him. He lifted his arm and set his huge hand in the upper middle of her chest. His palm was over the swells of her breasts.

Her heart pounded at his hand. She made a sharp move to sit up and skirt across the bed, his hand was still on her chest, he moved both hands to her waist to pull her down to lie down on her back.

Tezer nodded with the phone at his ear. "All right, let me see if I can put words in her mouth." Setting the phone on the bed, he grasped the bottom of her face, and turned it towards him then lowered his mouth to cover hers.

She tried to pull her head back from his sudden kiss but she was flat on her back, there was nowhere to go. He moved his lips over hers trying to get her to open her mouth, she wouldn't.

Sitting up, he pulled a gun from the back of his pants and put it to the side of her mouth and said, "Open it, or I will shoot. You may not die, but you will lose some teeth."

Her lashes flew up in shock. Face rigid as a statue, her gaze skewed up at him but she kept her now very trembling mouth closed.

He pressed the gun against her skin and commanded, "Open."

Tears sliding out of the corners of her eyes, she parted her lips. Tezer set the gun down on the bed.

Wrapping one hand around her upper arm, he cupped the side of her face with the other and seized her mouth with his.

As he had suspected, as his lips touched hers a frisson of electricity resounded through his body. He'd known kissing her would shoot the top of his head off, but he had no choice. Even as she fought him, his lips demanded her submission.

Just like he was as a man, his kiss was as hard and harsh, on the edge of violent.

She tried to turn her head from his, but he spread his fingers on the side of her head holding her like a thick web, and drew her into a fiery, flint-striking-steel firestarter that burned a hole in his groin and spread like a red-hot cyclone through his body. He felt electric shocks stinging through his bones, down to his toes.

He swirled his tongue over the outside of her mouth, nipped her upper then lower lip, sunk his tongue between her soft lips to penetrate the inside, to taste her tender flesh, then sought and found her reluctant tongue.

Tezer felt every sensation amplified; his dick throbbed, skin heated, mouth prickled and his brain sizzled. Like Death Valley in the dead of summer his body was scorching hot.

This was so not what he wanted. A big damned mistake.

Her soft lips quivered against his full, rough-hewn mouth, her body shuddered in his hands with her fear. The more ardently he kissed her, the tighter his fingers wrapped around her arm squeezing harder.

Pressing more fiercely on her to cement their meshing, Tezer sucked her lips, licked them, then slid his tongue over her teeth before penetrating her mouth again to find her tongue and suck it.

His all-consuming kiss deepened, his mouth moving with rough sensuality over hers, still she trembled. She let him do what he wanted but she didn't respond.

The more the kiss intensified, the more Tezer's body heat hit her in waves- now her lips moved faintly, against her will, with his.

His heart raced, a vein at his temple throbbed. Tezer practically shoved his tongue down her throat. But, she stopped responding to his assault, she fought him, trying to turn her head from his. The salt of her tears tingled on his tongue.

Breaking from Dove with heavy breaths, his chest pumping, Tezer leaned back and stared at her, his hand still cupping her face. He brushed his thumb over the satin skin of her cheek, her eyes so frightened they screamed.

Tezer could see his reflection in her tear-blurred gold-green spheres. He saw his pupils were blown, totally dilated. Except for the white-hot flames streaking though them, his eyes looked like black quartz, and just as hard and cold and impenetrable as the rest of him.

Releasing her face, he dropped his hand to her belly, then lower where her jeans opened. His strong fingers spread over her pelvis right to the edge of the lace panties.

Her flesh quivered under his touch. With a sharp exhale she cried, "Stop, please, let me go." Her face expressing her acute distress, she looked imploringly at Tezer, appealing to him for her release.

His fingertips stroked under the lacy border of the silk over her abdomen; her hips twitched at his escalating carnal contact. He peered at her under lowered lids; she was now staring in wide-eyed terror at his hand.

Fingers strolling over her skin soft as a baby's moved down, close to, almost touching her private parts. His fingers felt like they had seductive magnets on them, compelling them to move lower. They burned to feel her woman's plump slit, slide a thick finger up into her warm soft sheath-

Sitting back on his heels, Tezer drew his hand off her body and set his palm on the mattress. His voice deeply husky, rasped, "Tell me who you are."

Golden green eyes twittering with her fear fell to his crotch where his erection was clearly outlined. A hard long, thick ridge raised in his jeans. Blinking rapidly, Dove turned her head, her chest heaving, she sniffed back the tears, but still did not say a word to him.

The white hot flame in his dark eyes lowered to her bosom. Drawn like a bear to honey, without thinking Tezer leaned towards her and put his mouth on the swell of her breast and sucked the plump flesh.

His mouth on her bared skin, dark hair brushing the sensitive skin of her neck and under her chin, Dove shuddered and begged, "Please, stop, please," she squirmed but he still held her arm keeping her secured.

He licked and nipped her flesh like she was cotton candy, then suckled the top of the soft swell. It brushed his cheek when it rose before falling with her frantic breaths.

Tezer sat back and looked down at the red mark he left on her breast then up to her, his lips as damp as the flesh he just sucked.

The pale skin of her beautiful face was pinched and streaked with tears. His gaze dropped as if it pained him to look at her.

Then he raised his eyes again, still cold, hard, dark under a fringe of long lashes, he repeated, "Tell me who you are."

She stared at him like she couldn't comprehend what kind of monster he was.

He had just performed an intimate act on her, joined their lips like lovers, kissed the hell out of her, put his mouth on her breast. Yet, except for his bulging manhood straining at his pants, he was just as implacable as ever. She turned away without a word.

Tezer waited only a second then picked up the phone. Into it he said, "So far your way is not working." A small shake of his head, his eyes rose to hers. "No. Not doing that. I'll get it out of her before we get there."

His gaze still on her, he clicked the phone off and stuffed it in his pocket. Her head was turned from him, she was still struggling to hold back the rain of tears, her chest hitched with broken breaths.

Suddenly he snatched up the gun, gripped her chin to face him and put it to the corner of her mouth and snarled, "Tell me who the fuck you are or I'll shoot."

Their eyes crashed, connecting. Hard, dry sobs wracked her chest, her mouth stayed closed.

"Fuck-" Tezer barked and rolled off the bed. He set the gun on top of the dresser then returned to the bed and sat down beside her.

Moving both big hands around her arms he pulled her up to sit.

Her breath held as he faced her. He reached both hands around her and plucked at the ropes on her wrists. While he untied them, her face pressed on his neck, her breasts rubbed against his chest, his erection was about to burst out of his jeans.

Tezer had to fight the insane urge to keep her clasped hard against his body, in his arms. When he got the rope undone he tossed it.

Her arms hurt, ached from being restrained, she tried to rub them but couldn't move they were so stiff and sore.

Tezer watched her struggle, his gaze fell to her breasts cradled in the black lace, her shirt had slipped off her shoulders and bunched at her elbows.

He lifted his big hands to her slender shoulders and rubbed them. Her head lowered and tilted, the long curls draped over her face hiding it.

Silently, he moved his hands to her arms and gently massaged them, then he stroked down to her forearms while carefully pulling them forward until she was no longer stiff or in pain.

Dove kept her head down, not looking at him. When he released her, she rubbed her arms, holding her breath for his next assault.

But he stood up. Her eyes flashed to him to see what horror he planned next. His gaze slid down her body, pausing at her bosom. His pupils expanded again, gleaming black at the mark he'd given her.

Scowling at him, Dove covered her breasts with her arms, her eyes dropped and widened at his erection which was still as long and hard and straining at his jeans. To her, it was as if his penis was separate from him, it wanted her, he did not.

Without expression, he watched her looking at his crotch. Realizing this she quickly looked away, pulling her lips in to stop their quivering.

He palmed his hardened cock to rearrange it and started towards the door. Before he reached it, she said, "You are the worst excuse for a human being I've ever met."

Hesitating, he swiveled slowly back to face her. A small crooked half-grin creased his face. "Yeah. I probably am."

Watching her shrink back from him, he said, "I did no wheres near to you what my employer insisted I do to get you to talk. Since I couldn't get your name out of you, now you will have to suffer his ideas to pry it out of you…when you meet him." He turned to the door.

She spoke again. "Huh. How's it feel to be a disgusting scum of the earth pimp? Selling a woman to an ogre. Apparently he is worse than you, but I can't imagine it."

His entire body went rigid, he didn't turn around. His hand on the doorknob, he said over his shoulder, "Fix your clothes and come to the dining room. Don't make me have to come back here for you. I promise, you won't like it."

Yanking the door open, he stomped out slamming it behind him.

Chapter Seven

Dove sat in a muddled pool of shock.

Huh. Dove, she was already getting used to the name. Not really a name, just a species of bird. But that was okay, she didn't want to be anything. Not a woman, not a person, nothing.

Her awareness was keen on the door expecting it to fly back open and the bullying brute to come stomping in, rip the rest of her clothes off her and beat and rape her.

With a sick shudder, she rolled off the bed quickly getting to her feet. Waiting for her legs to stop wobbling, she buttoned her blouse and fixed her jeans.

She strode over to the window, pushed the curtain aside to peer out.

The sun had set, they'd had a late lunch, the people would be gathering for a late dinner. *He* expected her to trot out like a programmed marionette and sit down with him and the others like he hadn't just embarrassed and humiliated her beyond existence.

She couldn't believe she'd run from the frying pan and got captured by the fire. Dove scrubbed her hands over her eyes then down her face. Her luck the past year or so has been as if she was cursed. Everything that happened next was worse than the last.

Leaning towards the glass, she shook her head with a rueful smile, no, nothing could ever be as wretched as what she'd escaped from.

Even the brute forcing her to kiss him moments ago, his tongue all over the outside and the inside of her mouth, on her breasts, licking and sucking her flesh. Unbidden, a flash of heat flared between her legs.

Ugh, he may be a lowlife mercenary scum, the heat flooded her extremities, but he could kiss. Harsh, hard, aggressive, against her will he had pulled her with him in his body boggling kisses.

Looking out the window, she saw Vigo and Ziggy go past on patrol. Hmm. No escape there. Propping her elbows on the sill, she bent and rested her chin on her hands and wondered why he had kissed her.

It was hardly any kind of severe punishment or abuse to make her talk. No, kissing was something done between lovers, not something made of hate or anger, or in the chief's case, indifference. Perhaps he thought he could break her down through humiliation and pure submission.

The way he looks at her, completely blank, except when he's scowling or displeased. But even though there are those flickers of emotion, mostly he has no affect at all.

Just as unemotional as a hired killer should be. A sociopath with no conscience and no mercy. Her fingers drifted to her lips, but he sure as hell could kiss. Even with no experience, she could still tell the man could kiss.

Shaking the lingering feeling of his masculine tough lips on hers, she remembered the feeling of him undoing her clothes and impassively gawking at her like she was an inanimate object. A doll, a mannequin.

Except, *oh, there was that flush of heat between her legs again*, there was no mistaking that erection that could pound iron pegs into the rocky ground. She wrapped her arms around herself.

It was huge and thick, and hard, and she was terrified he was going to rape her. He was too big, she was too small, he'd damage her, hurt her if he tried to impale her with that monstrous thing.

She shook her head again to dispel the picture, and the feeling of being pressed against his powerful chest. Embraced in those big arms, breathing in that virile scent. She needed to get going. She didn't want to be still here when he came back to get her.

He might carry through with his threats, rape, shoot her- wait- her eyes flew to the dresser. The gun. She didn't notice him take the gun with him.

She dashed over to the dresser, her stomach fluttering like crazy. It was there. Oh my gosh. She reached for it, carefully, she knew next to zero about guns. Picking it up with both hands, it was heavy, and cold, cold metal in her warm palms.

But it was her freedom. Her heart surged, she could now get away from here. If anyone tried to stop her from leaving she would shoot them right between the eyes. Her mouth twitched in a slight grin, well, maybe just threaten them with it.

Straightening her mouth into a determined brave line, Dove cautiously moved to the door and turned the knob.

It was unlocked.

Huh. He was so arrogant that she couldn't escape he thought she would just trot down the hall and to the dining room per his orders.

A snort scrounged out. Well, isn't Mr. Tyrant going to be surprised when she doesn't show and he comes looking for her and the dove has flown the coop!

Slowly opening the door, she poked her head out and looked up one side then the other of the hall. Empty. Thank God. Everyone must be at dinner. She'd better hurry before the *master* came for her.

Practically tip-toeing down the wood floor, her hair swinging back and forth and behind her, Dove headed for the nearest exit.

Her heart hammering like hummingbird wings against her ribcage, she put a shaky hand on the door handle and pulled it open, then out the door on rubbery legs she went.

Taking a deep breath, she couldn't believe she'd made it! Almost home free. She just needed to avoid the patrols. She would just stay inside the alcove and wait for them to pass then she'd run for it.

A few minutes and Ziggy went by to the north, a few seconds later Vigo went to the south. Carrying the weapon in both hands she started to run for the forest-

"Oh!"

Tezer stepped right out of the shadows and right in front of her, just like he had the day he captured her.

"Going somewhere, little Dove?" he mocked. His large thick fingers curled around his narrow hips, staring down at her, the corner of his manly carved mouth tilted up.

Backing up, she raised the heavy gun and aimed it at him. Damn, it was so heavy, and she was so scared, she couldn't keep it from wavering. "D- don't move. Just stay where you are or I'll shoot. I am leaving, and you are not stopping me."

Brows arched still mocking, he grinned. "Oh yeah? Where do you think you're going? I told you, you wouldn't last an hour alone out there." His eyes dropped to the weapon aimed all over his torso in her shaking hands. The tilt of the side of his mouth nicked higher.

Her arms were quickly tiring. "I don't care. Where I came from, and with you and where you are taking me will be much worse than taking a chance out there on my own. Besides," a lock of hair was floating around her face.

She wanted to brush it back but she couldn't let go of the gun, she shoved her shoulder at it. "I have a weapon now. It will keep me safe."

He crossed one arm over the other in front of his chest and smirked down at her. "Oh yeah? Is it going to fill in also as a flashlight, a blanket, fire to keep you warm at night, fire to cook what you aren't going to be able to shoot to eat, because any fool can see you know nothing about guns."

"Huh. All I need to know is how to pull the trigger."

"Hmm." His lips turned up. "You ever hear of a safety?"

She frowned. Then shook her head. "No, you can't trick me with that. You didn't turn anything on or off when you were shoving the metal barrel at my mouth." Her anger at him doing that to her flushed up her neck and made her face shiny red.

He actually laughed. "Okay, all right. You got me. There's no safety on that gun. So you'd better be careful before you hurt yourself with it."

Her brows drew down hard, furious at his chauvinist treatment of her all the time. "I'm not the one that's going to get hurt. Now, get out of my way, I'm leaving. You try to stop me I swear I will shoot you."

His mouth still turned up in a sarcastic smile, he said, "Okay. Go ahead, because I'm going to show you how easy it is to take that gun away from you. I've been playing with you or I'd have done it already." Like a damned huge ox he took a step towards her with his hand out.

"No!" She yelled in a panic, "Stop! Don't come any closer!" The gun was wavering all over, tears of fear and frustration floated in her eyes making everything blurry.

He took another step, smug look on his harsh face, huge calloused hand snaking out like he knew she wouldn't pull the trigger.

"Please," she cried, "don't make me shoot you. Please, Chief, just step aside and let me go. Please."

Shaking his head he said, "Sorry, I can't do that. Now, give me the gun," he moved almost a foot from her with his hand close to the weapon.

"No! I will shoot you- stop!"

He reached for the gun, she turned her head and closed her eyes and fired.

Expecting an ear-shattering boom, Dove heard nothing but, click, click, click as she repeatedly pulled the trigger.

When he snatched the gun out of her trembling hands her eyes flew open. The heavy weapon fit neatly into his big hand where she couldn't even hold it with two of hers.

Stuffing the weapon in the back of his jeans, he said, "I had already taken the bullets out before I put the gun to your face. I didn't want it to go off accidentally. I left it there on purpose to see what kind of balls you have. See if I could trust you not to run."

His gaze swept her head to foot and back, mouth ticked up. "You got 'em, balls, baby, but not big enough little girl. And," he sighed making tsk tsk sounds. "I obviously cannot trust you not to be stupid and try to leave."

Dark eyes narrowed as his mouth slashed hard. "See what happens if you don't know what the fuck you're doing with a weapon? It can be taken from you and used on you. Women can be so stupid."

She froze, oh no, what torture will he inflict on her now?

His lip curled smugly. "I knew you couldn't do it. You are too sweet. I've seen you in action, you couldn't hurt a fly, Goldilocks." With two fingers he flicked a long flaxen curl off her shoulder, a mocking smirk rumpling the severe planes of his face.

"That's why I sent you to talk to the old lady, you're the only one here with a heart." He chuckled shortly. "You've never even said a harsh word to anyone." The smug curl turned into a bitter twist, he murmured, "Except to me."

Dove was so infuriated she could scream. "You are an unconscionable junkyard dog with a heart of stone, you treat me abominably. You sexist pig, you have no right to hold me prisoner, no right to- to-" the red in her cheeks deepened.

Sputtering, she yelled, "You have no right to touch me, undress me, force your horrible mouth on mine. I should have- shot you!" Then she remembered it would have been to no avail, the gun wasn't loaded.

He threw his hand out and gripped her chin hard, the smile was gone. Tone disparaging, he said coldly, "I don't give a damn what you think of me. I have a job to do."

He shook her jaw ordering her, "Don't fucking ever do that again, hold a gun on me or any other man. Another man might not be so forgiving and make you eat it."

His fingers tightened bringing her face closer to his. "And for God's sake, you never close your goddamned eyes and turn your head when you're shooting at someone. What the hell kind of maneuver was that? Even if the gun was loaded you couldn't have hit me, or the side of a barn, and it made it child's play to take it from you."

Eyes piercing her with anger, shaking her jaw he growled darkly, "You hear what I'm saying, woman? Don't touch my guns, don't aim a gun at me or anyone else unless you know what the fuck you're doing. Same goes for knives, you're the one that will get hurt."

He gave her another shake to make sure she got it. Then said, "Now, we're going in to eat while I think about your punishment for daring to take my fucking gun and then aim it at me and threaten me with it, and," he pinched her chin, "again trying to run. Maybe a good hard spanking on that tight little bare ass of yours- huh?"

Seeing her fear, his mouth shut, teeth grit, the vein at his temple pounded.

Dove fought to keep the tears at bay, she'd be damned if she let this horrible man make her cry again and get enjoyment out of watching it.

Her heart sank. Not only had she failed miserably, he was now even angrier at her and threatening punishment. Her hands itched to cover her behind, but she would never give him the satisfaction of knowing he frightened her.

Of course when he twined those long fingers around her arm to lead her back inside he had to be able to feel her body shaking. The adrenalin, the excitement of escape, then the fear and disappointment of failure raced and pummeled through her body, sucking the air out of her lungs.

Dove pushed up her slumping shoulders. Her lips pressed tightly together, but if he thought she was done trying to escape, he was in for a rude awakening.

The asshole.

Chapter Eight

The next day, in the lead, Tezer was silent beside Garth as they trudged with the people continuing their journey up and down soft hills and winding their way through the least dense area of the forest.

Before he saw her, Tezer heard a coarse elderly voice beside his elbow.

"You," Essie Cook slapped his arm and snarled at him.

Without moving his head or slowing his pace, Tezer bit the inside of his mouth to keep from either laughing at the old bag or knocking her down. He could hear Garth's snicker next to him.

"Problem, Mrs. Cook?" Tezer sighed with sarcasm glancing down at the elderly woman as she tried to keep up with him.

"Yes, dammit," the snarl nasty, "I don't know what you did to that poor girl you son of a bitch, but it must have been bad. She cried all night. Tried not to, but I could hear her swallowing the sobs and sniffing back the tears. She wouldn't tell anybody what you did, but I have my ideas." Her infuriated blue eyes behind round lenses strode with disgust down his body then glared up at him.

Frowning, his lips tight, Tezer growled his reply, "It's none of your business, old woman. Get back to your place in line."

The veined hand slapped his big arm again. "She doesn't deserve to be brutalized by the likes of you, Mr. Chief. She's sweet and kind. She's obviously running from someone that is trying to hurt her, and you-" her entire wrinkled pale face screwed up in a grimace.

"You do everything you can to hurt her too. You are a disgrace to the human race. Nothing but a big arrogant bully that preys on defenseless women." Her bony chin snapped up and she turned and stalked back down the line to where she had been.

Tezer glanced over his shoulder, his brows drew down. Dove was not where he told her to stay, right behind him.

She was several people down, the older man, McCain was yammering in her ear. She smiled politely, friendly at him. She has never smiled at Tezer.

Pulling his lips in a grim hard line, he told himself he didn't care. He had a job to do and that was all that mattered. Let the old bag think the worst of him.

Undoubtedly Rey Silva had blabbed to everyone he had been in the process of raping the little blonde when he brought him the phone.

One shoulder shrugged. He doesn't owe anyone any explanations. A dark flush rose up the back of his neck heating his skin. He rubbed it.

The picture of Dove with her hands bound behind her, blouse and pants open, slid unbidden into his brain. It was just as bad as if he'd raped her. He had tied her, half undressed her, touched her against her will, forced her to submit to his rough kisses, held a gun to her face for cripes sake.

What a man. Tough guy. Pushing a little girl around to get something as simple as a name out of her. The picture of her helpless, so fucking sexy, the way she tasted, those soft tits pressing into his hard chest, her mouth. Hell, she had even responded at one point to his kiss, shit- his dick was hardening.

"Old lady reamed you a new one, huh?" Garth teased. He didn't know what Tezer had done to the woman either, but he knew Tezer would not rape a helpless unwilling woman.

He glanced at his friend's flushed angry face.

But Tezer had done something that had upset Dove drastically, and brought ruddy color up to his neck and the tips of his ears. The vein at his temple beat like a clock.

"Whatever." Tezer motioned with his head. "We're almost there, I can see it lighter up ahead, the trees are thinning."

When the group emerged from the forest they found themselves alongside a rushing river. A couple of people headed straight to it to wash their hands and faces.

"No, keep away," Tezer called out. "The river is treacherous. It's a torrent, like a flash flood, it's fast and gets very deep a few yards down. Wait until we get inside to wash."

Assuming they would all listen to him, he strode towards a slope that led up to the lodge they were staying in tonight. He stopped to have a few words with Garth and Leo while they waited for the rest of the group to catch up.

Brock Disik, preening like peacock, came out of the woods smoothing his hair back. Even tromping through the wilderness his stubble was neatly trimmed close to his handsome face.

Right behind him, Paolo, sullen, still sporting a black eye from Tezer's beating trod out next.

Ziggy was talking to the older man, Ronald McCain who stumbled out huffing and puffing.

Vigo, Rey, crazy Clancy were taking turns giving fat, wheezing Tommy Tucker a push up the slight incline.

Lastly, the women came dawdling with an impatient, annoyed, frustrated Nik behind them. Their catty gossip and foolishness were driving him up a wall.

Half his long curly hair had escaped its bind and floated around his disgusted tanned face.

The women were pulling on jackets. They had steadily moved uphill towards the mountains and the air had chilled, the temperature dropped.

Dove and Essie stood by the water. Spotting them, Ziggy traipsed over to join them. Too far to hear their conversation, Tezer's eyes tapered to slits as he watched them while listening to Leo describe the next leg of the trek.

Huge like a WWE wrestler, the more Ziggy talked, the closer to Dove he got. His big paw was on her shoulder, then her arm, he picked up a length of her hair, let it curl around his hand before draping it down her back.

"Hey!" Tezer yelled to them. "I said get the fuck away from the water!" He jerked his head motioning them away. "Get them away, Ziggy. *Now*." Assuming they would do as he ordered, Tezer turned back to his friends as they started to head for the lodge.

Someone screamed-

The men swung around. Kitty and Chelsee were waving and jumping and screaming, Avril pointed at the water-

Essie had gotten too close to the edge and had slipped into the rushing river. It snapped her up and was already hurtling her downstream.

Dove ran right into the water and tried to wade after the old lady.

Tezer made a mad dash to the river with Garth and Leo at his heels.

Shouting, "Dove! Get the fuck out of the water!" Tezer raced to the river.

Essie had caught onto a sharp rock that jutted out in the middle of the water, she was shrieking in terror. Dove continued making her way to her.

The water slapped and pulled at the women trying to suck them both along. Dove's arms were up and out, parallel as she tried to keep her balance. The water was swirling around her waist, the yellow hair like a flapping flag, she was stumbling and flailing.

"Dove, get the fuck out of the water!" Tezer kept shouting running almost to the bank.

But the petite woman was still trying to get to her friend.

Essie's grey curls were barely visible over the white rapid foam spraying and crashing over her, only her tiny wrinkled hands were visible still clutching the rock. But the thrust of the wild water was grabbing, pushing and pulling at her, she wouldn't be able to hang on much longer.

The water smacked Dove in the back knocking her over. Stumbling, she fell on her hands and knees. When she tried to stand back up the savage water beat her down and shoved her, bouncing and dragging her tumbling over the rough river bed.

Throwing his gun and phone to the ground Tezer ran straight into the river trying to keep Dove in his sight. The water was crashing over her head and dragging her. She struggled to her feet, the waster smashed into her like a fluid wall.

"Goddammit Dove!" Tezer yelled. "Get the hell out of the water!"

A wave hit her like a punch knocking her off her feet and shoving her face first into the torrent.

He reached her in seconds. Bending over, Tezer grabbed her shirt and jeans and wrenched her up out of the rapids.

Gasping and spitting, choking, Dove croaked, "Let me go! I have to get her- she'll die!" Spasms of coughing wracked her.

"Goddamn bitch," Tezer cursed, holding her up against his chest. The rough water buffeting around his waist he turned and literally threw Dove in the air at Garth, who easily caught her. "Get her the fuck out of here, Garth, up to the lodge-"

"No!" Dove screamed, fighting to get out of Garth's hold. "I have to help her-"

Tezer pivoted back around to find Essie.

Only one tiny hand was visible gripping the rock.

Tezer dove into the raging river and swam towards her.

Before he got to her, the river ripped her from the rock and hurtled with her in its deadly grasp-

Tezer swam harder, faster, she went under. With every other stroke he looked up to locate her.

On the shore, the group was gathered watching with hearts racing, it didn't look good for the old lady.

"Put me down!" Dove screamed at Garth.

With a lop-sided grin, and a twinkle in his blue eyes, Garth set her on her feet, but wrapped his arms around her so she couldn't go running back into the deathtrap.

Breaths held, they all watched Tezer's dark head bobbing as he swam like a shark, and groaned seeing Essie disappear and not pop back up.

Tezer saw her go under. Keeping an eye just ahead of where he saw her disappear, he increased his stroke and in a couple yards dove down, underwater he saw the grey hair and the blue pants she wore rolling over and over in the battening current.

In seconds he got to her, reached in, grabbed the back of her shirt and hauled her up. Using the lifesaving rescue hold, he moved her on her back and wrapped an arm across her chest and swam back to shore.

Leo, Nik and Reggie were there to help Tezer out of the water.

Carrying Essie who hung lifeless in his arms, Tezer slogged a few drenched steps before dropping to his knees on the grass and laying her down. He looked up at Dove through the water that still slewed down his face and hung on his lashes.

Garth held onto one of her arms. Her clothes were sodden, she looked like she was in a wet T-shirt contest. The too small bra with her breasts overflowing was like a second skin, her freezing nipples were pebbles. Long wet hair streamed down her back and she was shivering.

With an elderly woman's life hanging on the hinge, the other men lining up to watch the drama were all ogling Dove's soaked body, her nipples, and lower where her jeans clung to her woman's V. So much for humanely worrying about the old lady.

Tezer shouted at Dove, "Get into the goddamned lodge." Kneeling over Essie, he turned his attention to her and set his ear on her chest to listen for breath, then put two fingers to her neck to feel for a pulse.

Glancing to the side he saw no one had moved. "Get her the fuck out of here and into dry clothes- now!" he barked at Garth.

"No- I have to help, I have to see if she's okay- she'll be sacred of you-" Dove cried, fighting Garth's hold.

"Goddammit, Garth-" Tezer gripped Essie's chin and tilted it up. He was pinching her nose and pressing his mouth over hers when Garth literally dragged Dove up the incline to the lodge.

She fought him and yelled the whole way. At the top, she dug her heels in and spun around. Garth finally tossed her over his shoulder and carried her inside.

Down by the bank, after only a few chest compressions delivered by Tezer's beefy hands, Essie was coughing and spitting up water.

Tezer lifted her to sit and holding her against his chest, he draped her so her arms and head hung over his shoulder to his back. He patted her back gently while she coughed and sputtered, gasping for deeper breaths.

When she was breathing steadily, Leo and Reggie helped Tezer climb to his feet with the elderly woman in his arms.

They walked up the hill to the lodge, the rest of the group chattering like excited magpies around them.

Inside, Vigo and Clancy had gotten a good fire going. Dove was standing near it shivering, beside her Garth was arguing with her.

Moving across the room, Tezer said to Kitty and Avril, "You two come with me." The look on his face and the deep timber of his angry voice made them not hesitate to follow him.

He marched over first to Dove and Garth.

She had her arms wrapped around her saturated body, but she was shivering like a tuning fork. Ziggy and Paolo were standing in front of her, blatantly staring at her frozen nipples poking out of the wet shirt.

Still carrying, Essie, his voice low and harsh, Tezer stuck his face near Dove's and ground out, "You get your fucking ass into a room and take off those wet clothes."

Hair dripping around her body, speaking through chattering teeth, Dove rattled, "I- I- don't have anything to put on. These clothes are- are borrowed, the other jeans and shirt I have are wet from washing them this mor- morning."

Beads of water clung like raindrops to her long curly lashes. She swiped at them but more came from her wet hair. She sputtered through the chattering teeth, "They- the girls said they would- wouldn't loan me anything else." Her fearful gaze on Essie in his arms softened as she realized the woman was breathing.

"For the love of-" His eyes like black slits, Tezer said to Garth, "Get her something of mine to wear."

He stuck his face in Dove's and snarled below his breath, "If you don't go right now and change, I will have Garth strip you and do it for you. We clear?"

Ignoring Garth's agreeable grin, he turned his back on them and strode off down the hall where the women's quarters were.

When he moved into the room, Kitty and Avril stood awkwardly with annoyed expressions on their heavily made up faces.

Tezer could not understand it. They were deep in the forest, heavy hiking every day, not only why did they bother with the makeup, but when the hell did they have time to do it? Garth had everyone up and moving before dawn. Whatever. Tezer was a guy, he would never get it. Nor did he really give a shit.

He moved to a bed and said over his shoulder, "Get an extra blanket and put it on the bed."

Kitty and Avril stood gawking condescending at him like they didn't take orders from any-

"Now!" he barked.

They jumped and ran to get the blanket. When they returned and spread it on the bed, Essie's bones and teeth were clattering with her chill, Tezer gently set her on the bed.

Muttering, "All right," he leveled his glower to the two girls. "Help her get undressed and then dressed in dry clothes. Wrap her in a blanket, dry her hair with a towel. I'll have one of the men get in here and get a fire going in the fireplace and someone to bring her hot tea."

His lids drew down with a terse look at the women who weren't moving. "I will not say this twice. Do it right now or I will toss you both outside on your asses and you can spend the night out there."

He bent over Essie and smoothed the wet grey curls off her forehead. Her blue eyes looking up at him were watery and wavy, the terror she'd just survived still shrieked from them.

In the softest voice any of them ever heard from the big, tough as nails man, Tezer said, "You are safe now, Mrs. Cook. You will be cared for. Just relax and let the girls help you."

With fear and confusion, she murmured weakly, "I- I lost my glasses." She blinked big globby tears.

"Ah. I'm sorry about that. I will see to getting a fire going to warm you." He gently brushed back a wet grey curl, patted her arm lightly then left the room.

Down the hall and to the great room, he saw Reggie and Nik putting a grate over the fireplace.

"I need you to get one going in the girls' room."

The two men nodded and took off to do as he bid.

To Rey, Tezer said, "Get a cup of hot tea for the old lady. Fill it with sugar and milk, she'll need the boost." Then he strode off out of the room and down the hall.

After quickly changing into dry clothes, he entered one of the bedrooms.

Garth was talking to Dove who was staring out the window. She wore one of Tezer's flannel shirts and a pair of his boxer shorts. The shirt went to her knees and the boxers so big, looked like a skirt on her.

Her hair was a sodden mess down her back. She was still shivering.

Tezer looked at Garth. With a big grin and a wink, Garth left the room.

Grabbing up a towel, Tezer went to Dove and dropped it on her head.

"Hey-" she protested.

Ignoring her yelp, he rubbed the towel roughly over her head. She gasped and made to get away from him.

Keeping her still with his hands on her head he barked, "Stand fucking still. I told you, if you don't do as I say, I will do it for you. If you haven't the sense to dry your hair," his exhale harsh and irritated, "I'll fucking do it, and you will have to endure any discomfort." He rubbed the towel without gentleness all around her head.

Under the towel she mumbled, "You have a filthy mouth."

With a small chuckle, he replied, "I don't spend a lot of frivolous time with women, I forget some of you have delicate sensibilities."

Before she could comment, he pulled her over to the fireplace Ziggy and Leo were building a fire in and rubbed harder.

Drawing the towel down the length of her hair, Tezer took note of Ziggy staring at her, all of her, like he wanted to lick her like she was lollipop. Tezer sent him a hard look and jutted his chin.

The big blond German took the hint and he and Leo left the room.

Tezer sat on the bed and pulled Dove to stand between his legs with her back to him. Taking his comb out of his pocket, he tossed the towel on a chair and starting at the bottom of her long locks. He surprised both Dove and himself by gently combing her hair.

Dragging the comb through the thick locks, he scolded, "Worse than no sense to dry your hair before you get sick, you didn't have the brains to get out of that fuck- uh, river. What the hell were you thinking? The rapids hauled off with Cook, you think as small and delicate as you are you had a better damned chance than her?" He yanked on her hair.

"Ow! Hey-" she rubbed her head where her scalp stung. "I couldn't let her die. You think I could have just stood there and watched her get washed away?"

Sticking the comb in his pocket, he turned her around to face him and gripped her upper arms. "I yelled at you to get out. Didn't you see me coming? Didn't you hear me shouting at you to get out of the river?"

The pink plush lips firmed, she aimed a derisive glare at the rugged hard-edged man. "And exactly what did that mean other than you like to bellow and shout out orders?"

A muscle quirked on the side of his mouth. He squeezed her arms and glared back at her.

"The point to following my orders immediately is to save lives. Yours, Cook's. Everyone on this mission. I was coming to get the old lady, I didn't need to expend my energy dragging you out of the water too." His mouth quirked again at her scowl.

The gold blending with the green in her eyes like Christmas tinsel, she blinked at him. Unaware her lips bunched in a sexy pout, she dropped her gaze from the chief to the floor.

Quiet for a minute, Tezer stared at the top of her head. He heard her sniff and knew she was fighting to not cry in front of him. He curled one big finger under her chin and gently raised it to see he was correct. The greens were swimming with unshed tears of golden lava.

She tried to pull her head from his clasp, but he lifted her chin higher to make her look him in the eye.

"Dove," his mouth tugged up at the name the old lady had given her. "Did you think I would let Mrs. Cook die?" His head lowered towards hers, their faces bare inches apart.

His long lashes swept down his sharp cheeks then back up. For once the cold ruthlessness in his eyes had warmed, turning them into smoldering coals.

Brushing at an escaped tear as it slipped over her round cheek that was turning pinker, he asked quietly, "Did you think I would have let you get swept away, Dove? Did you think I would not come for you?"

Her mouth was dry, cheeks darkened. She looked at his smoldering eyes like they were hot black pools that were drawing her in, pulling her under.

"I- I," her throat bobbed with the swallow, she licked her lips. Another tear rolled out. "I would think since I wasn't part of your…mission, that you would not risk your life…for me," the tear slid to the corner of her mouth.

"Ah, little bird, you need to rethink." He bent his neck further and put his lips on the tear, gently licked it, then brushed his lips very lightly over hers.

His lids slid down to cover the now glowing coals of his dark eyes and regarded her confused look. The gilding in her orbs melted like liquid gold, blurring the normally sharp crystalline of her irises.

Footsteps coming down the hall pulled the pair apart.

"Hey," Leo started as he poked his Italian nose in the doorway. Grey eyes took in Dove's flushed cheeks and dropped to the bulging front of Tezer's jeans.

Seeing his friend's annoyed glare, Leo grinned and said, "Dinner is ready. Didn't know if you guys knew it."

Chapter Nine

Essie Cook was too weak from her ordeal to walk the next day.

Tezer went to the women's room to see her.

The door was open, he knocked lightly as several of the ladies were inside doing various things; painting their toes, fixing their makeup and styling their hair. Today there was time for grooming.

At his entrance, with a small squeal, Kitty tossed her brush on the dresser and ran over to him. Wearing her red jumpsuit, she almost knocked him over throwing her big voluptuous body at him.

"Oh you gorgeous man, did you come to see me?" Mashing her big breasts against his chest covered in a dark blue thermal, she shoved her pelvis at his and rubbed salaciously back and forth over the front of his jeans. Her long arms twined around his neck as she contrived to plant her wide full lips on his.

Growling an annoyed, "Dammit Kitty," Tezer grabbed her hands and pulled them from behind his neck. He moved her away with a scowl. "I came to check on our patient."

He turned a gentle eye to Mrs. Cook who was bundled up in the bed. Going right to her before Kitty could grab him again, he sat on the edge of the bed and smiled down at the elderly woman.

"Hey," he said quietly and waited until her tired eyes cracked open.

Her fear and anger of him was gone. He had saved her life, had given her mouth-to-mouth. She couldn't fear a man who did that no matter how fierce he looked and acted.

Words wobbly, she whispered through her sore throat, "Chief, I," she blinked hard, moistened her lips. "I didn't get a chance to thank you for risking your-"

Cutting her off, he said, "Ah, I'm just here to see how you're doing." He set his hand on her forehead and frowned. "Are you feeling bad, Mrs. Cook?" Her skin was overly warm.

The crepey eyes fluttered and closed.

Tezer stood up and headed for the door. Before he got to it Kitty threw herself into his arms again knocking the air out of him with a woof- Then she slapped her lips over his before he could speak.

At that moment, Dove, who had been helping clean up in the kitchen came in with Nik who was keeping an eye on her.

A gasp caught in Dove's throat, her hand went to her mouth taking in the pair in their clinch.

"Listen," Tezer said to Dove while grabbing at Kitty's arms, but Dove strode past him and hurried into the bathroom they were lucky enough to have in their room, and closed the door. The lock made a loud click.

Angry, Tezer threw Kitty's hands down and cursed at her. "Goddammit woman, I've told you to keep your hands off me." His boots clomped hard on the floor as he strode with furious steps down the hall.

When he was gone, Kitty swiveled around and grinned wickedly at her friends. Her long fingers curled on ample hips, she lifted one to tuck up under her curly platinum hair frizzing at her shoulders, it was requiring more hairspray.

"Good move," Avril complimented her with a sneaky grin.

"Yeah." Applying pink lipstick to her lips that would clash badly with her red hair, Robin added with a nasty snarky tone, "That ought to put a stop to anything that might be brewing between the chief and that blonde bitch."

Still fluffing her hair, Kitty sniffed with her nose in the air, "I don't need to worry, a big man like him is not gonna have any interest in that tiny dainty thing. All brawny man like him, is gonna want all robust woman." She turned to smile broadly at her reflection in the mirror and said, "Like me."

Due to Mrs. Cook's declining health, the group ended up staying an extra few days at the lodge.

Dove stayed with Essie 24/7 feeding her soup and hot tea. Then she switched to cold tea and iced compresses as the elderly woman grew alarmingly feverish.

Not liking the way her skin was burning up more every day, Tezer had contacted one of the jeeps to come and get Mrs. Cook.

He called in a helicopter but they had to wait for it to get there. It was stationed now a few miles away at a good clearing waiting to ferry her to the hospital.

Tezer stood back while Dove said goodbye to her friend. "You take care and get well, Essie, I have your address, I'll write you."

She leaned over, hugged Essie then kissed her soft wrinkled cheek. "You are my only friend here, I will miss you so much." She gave her another kiss then turned and ran to the lodge before she broke down in front of the sick woman making her feel worse.

Hearing their conversation, clearing his throat, Tezer stepped forward to speak to Essie. Patting her shoulder, he said gruffly, "You get well now, you hear?"

Bundled under several blankets, the lips creased with lines drew up weakly. "Always giving orders, young man." She smiled with affection at the big brutal man. "Thank you for saving my life. But Mr. Braemont-"

Tezer held up a hand. "Ah, don't worry about him. Your debt has been paid, he will leave you alone."

Her mouth dropped. "But-"

"It's no big deal, it wasn't that much owed. You were poor and skipped out on your rent, so what. Forget about it. Now, safe journey home, Essie Cook, we will check up on your health status."

Tears slipped over the fevered cheeks. "Thank you, Chief, you are a- a hero. Oh, I forgot," she reached back and pulled a chain off her neck. She handed it to him. "I meant to give this to Dove. Please see that she gets it? I hope it will protect her like it has me."

She set it in his palm. "And, Chief," she looked him in the eye, "take care of her. She's in dire trouble and can't get out. Don't throw her to yet another ravaging wolf."

Nodding, he looked down at the necklace, a cross with a leafy vine strung around it. "I'll get it to her." He closed her door and slapped the side of the jeep telling the driver to head out.

He saw her small thin palm wave at him through the window as the jeep rolled down the gravel drive to the woods.

A few hours after they started out the next day, contrary to the weather report they continued to scan, a heavy rainstorm struck.

The group had to seek shelter in a cave until it was almost dark before it let up.

Leading the group back out a few hours later, Garth found a space that was relatively dry as it was on the curve of a hill and had been the first area to get the rain.

The cave was likely, judging by the scat and small bones littered around, home to someone, they decided it best not to be there when it came back.

Grumbles and complaints abounded after dinner was cooked over a fire.

Tezer gave the order for everyone to spread out the blankets they were given and use their canteens for pillows.

The satellite phone to his ear, he stood at the side of the open area and instructed Garth, "I want the women together and the men spread out in a circle around them."

He nodded to Rey Silva and Clancy, who had surprisingly kept his crazy in so far. Maybe it was because the four women, Kitty, Avril, Chelsee and Robin were making their way through the hired-on mercs and the male passengers.

The only men who refused to accept their generous offers for sex were Tezer and his team, Garth, Leo, Reggie and Nik. They had no desire to stick their wicks in inkwells every other man there has been dipping in.

After finding yet another discarded condom yesterday in the grass outside the lodge, he'd lost his temper and cursed them all until he was blue in the face. He'd threatened if he came across another shred of litter, especially of the rubber kind, heads would roll.

"Indiscriminating pigs," Garth had grumbled, glowering at the highly promiscuous crowd. "At least clean up after yourselves you gross assholes. Don't want some ignorant bird or animal choking on castoff latex."

Avril had even taken a turn with the older man Ronald, but right now, wacky Clancy had his hands up Avril's shirt fondling her. She was giggling and half-heartedly telling him to stop.

Rudely, Tezer said with crude curtness to Clancy, "Bonds, get your hands off her tits and go with Rey for first watch."

Clancy's black face wreathed with annoyance. Now his eyes displayed the bugged-out weirdness Tezer was used to, Clancy started to scowl at Tezer. But seeing the look on the chief's face, he snapped his lips closed.

The hair that had escaped the tight braids in rows over his scalp furled in a brown corona around his head. He slathered his tongue all over Avril's diamond hard face before swatting her on the butt.

Then he took a healthy handful of her ass, squeezed hard and left her to join Rey on patrol.

Rolling his eyes, Tezer turned his attention back to the phone.

Besides Essie's ill health, the storm had also backed them up and put them slightly off course. He was under orders to tell Braemont every glitch they encountered along the way.

Shaking his head, he moved away from the group as they settled on the hard ground, some going for a last minute bathroom run, or rather bush run.

Into the phone, holding his patience and gruff tone in check, Tezer gruffed, "No, she still hasn't told me. No," he shook his head again, "she hasn't told anyone. If she had, it would have been the old lady but she didn't."

Essie Cook's harsh words at him a few days ago about how badly he'd treated Dove that she had cried all night, sifted through his mind as he listened to Braemont bellyache.

He replied to Braemont's bitching, "We got her prints, scanned 'em and sent them in, she's not in the system, and there were no wants on her anywhere."

To himself he thought, that means she was likely running from a person, probably a man, rather than the law. His hands curled into tight fists, he pressed the phone hard against his ear in his anger.

"Listen here, boy," Braemont's voice barked out of the receiver, "you are too much of a fucking pussy to get a tiny bit of information out of from what I hear, a petite young woman." His sigh arrogant and loud, he sneered, "Don't worry. I don't have your wussiness, I have ways of getting information out of even the most tight-lipped person."

Tezer could practically hear him rubbing his palms together and see his evil gluttonous smile through the phone.

"Yeah," Braemont continued, Tezer pitched the end of the phone up so he could barely hear the man's crass chortles, "actually, I'm glad you failed. I'm looking forward to this little hottie and forcing the information out of what I hear are perfect rosebud lips. I can already see those crystal teardrops falling from those big golden green eyes they've described to me."

A pause, Tezer figured the man was adjusting his cock as it hardened.

Then, Braemont went on, his voice a little deeper, tighter, "And that bitchin' body, she's got all the men there panting after her tail. I've got plans all right. Yeah, don't bother asking her any more. I'll handle it-"

Tezer clicked the phone off. Let the bastard wonder whether the connection got lost or he hung up on him, he didn't give a fuck.

Tossing the phone to Nik as he passed him, Tezer had to take a short run to burn off his fury. Afterwards, he endured a freezing bath in a pond and dressed in clean clothes he'd left there before heading out on a trail.

When he returned, everyone was lying down on the hard ground. He thought they were all asleep. But he was mistaken.

The women were bunched in the middle, the men scattered around them. Several fires were kept going to keep the animals at bay, and Vigo and Ziggy had relieved Clancy and Rey of patrol duty.

In fact, Tezer looked away quickly, Clancy was under blankets with Avril and it was clear by the way his ass was bumping up and down and the audible grunts, the pair was going at it.

Off to the side, Robin had pulled her blanket as close to Brock as she could get, her hands were under his blanket. It appeared they were on him, stroking his dick but Brock was locking lips with Chelsee.

Glancing around, Tezer saw blowsy Kitty cuddled with Rey under her blanket.

Tezer turned away in disgust. Bunch of no self-respecting rabbits. A leafy rustle of bushes stopped him as he was taking a step further out of the tree-line. Brows drew down in an iron line over his eyes tapered in suspicion.

Ziggy had moved stealthily out of the brush and was now standing over one of the women.

Tezer already knew who it was. The only female in the crowd not rutting with someone, Dove.

His own steps silent, Tezer made his way stepping around bodies to come up behind Ziggy.

The blond giant was crouched down beside Dove, her body suddenly jerked, her scream muffled. Ziggy's hand was over her mouth and he was trying to get her over his shoulder with his other hand.

With the snarl of an enraged gorilla, Tezer hissed, "*Put her down, motherfucker.*"

Ziggy froze.

Dove was kicking her feet but she couldn't speak with the giant hand covering half her face.

Tezer's deep voice, guttural with pure lethality, he spat out a curse, "I'll fucking kill you where you stand if you don't do it *now*."

Ziggy laid Dove back down on her blanket, pulled his hand from her mouth, and stood up.

Both hands up in surrender, Ziggy said quickly through his German accent thick with fear, "Hey, Chief, no harm no foul, bro. I uh, wasn't going to do anything with, uh, to her. Just wanted to have some alone time to, uh, talk-" before he got another word out, Tezer's fist swung pounding into his face.

Dove had to roll out of the way as Ziggy toppled crashing to the ground.

Hearing the commotion, heads popped up.

Leo and Garth were instantly at Tezer's side.

Bending over, the chief scooped up Dove's blankets and canteen, curled his fingers around her arm and pulled her to her feet.

"What the hell, Tez?" Garth was pulling a flannel shirt over his T.

Hard voice grating with suppressed rage and threat, Tezer grunted, "It's nothing. Get that fucking garbage out of my sight before I end him." His hand around her arm, Tezer walked Dove over to where he'd placed his blankets.

Releasing her, he spread her blanket down, dropped her canteen at the head and pointed with a rigid arm and ordered harshly, "Lie down."

"But, I don't understand, what did I do?" Her voice still throaty with sleep and heavy eyes confused, Dove looked up at the fiercely angry man glaring down at her.

"Just lie down," he demanded brusquely.

Still not moving, last thing she wanted was to be sleeping beside the raging Hulk. "Why are you mad? What is going on? He said he wanted to talk to me, but then he started picking me up."

His head dropped back, Tezer stared up at the night sky. The dark clouds had moved on letting the mild cool light of the silver moon and stars to shine.

Taking a deep breath and exhaling slow, hands on his hips, he looked down at her. Seeing the naiveté in her large eyes, he said calmly, "Dove, you did nothing wrong. I am concerned for your safety. You will sleep beside me. That's all."

He glanced over her shoulder, Garth and Leo were dragging an unconscious Ziggy off into the bushes for a talk.

His gaze back on her he caught her brief quail at having to lie beside him. With an annoyed snort, he said crossly, "Don't worry, I will keep my hands to myself."

Then a twinkle in his eye, he twittered, "Can I assume the same about you? Am I safe from your lustful roaming fingers?" Even as he said it a tingle ran up his legs to his groin. Her aghast expression eased his anger and made him chuckle.

"I- I would never, I mean, I-" she stammered taking a step back from him.

"Okay, calm down, honey, I'm just teasing you. Come on," he said more gently, "lie down, I need some rest." He didn't make any moves towards her to show her he had no designs on jumping her bones.

It took her several beats of staring at his angular face to see if she found him trustworthy before she sighed, and sank down on her blanket. Really, she had no choice, he would make her do whatever he wanted.

When she settled, Tezer dropped down beside her to lie on his back. His hands resting under his head with his elbows out he whispered, "I was just kidding about you keeping your hands to yourself. Feel free to touch me," his voice deepened, "anywhere."

At the sound of her sharp inhale and rolling to her side to face away from him, and her snapping her blanket over her body, he assumed she had no intentions of doing so.

Sighing, he closed his eyes and listened to the forest settling down for the night. At least for the non-nocturnal beasts.

He couldn't have been asleep for a few hours when Tezer, feeling something strange, his eyes levered open. *Oh fuck-* he was wrapped around Dove. Her back was pressed against his chest, his knees tucked under hers.

Worse, he was holding her tight against him, his hand was up under her shirt, the crescent of his palm just touching the under swell of her breast and his thumb was right between her breasts.

He sucked in a short breath and held it. He needed to get himself extricated immediately. While thinking how to do it without waking her, he was acutely aware of her soft curvy body curled against him, her chest rising and lowering softly, he could feel her heartbeat.

He knew why he'd woken. He didn't sleep with women. He fucked them, and preferred to sleep alone and not have to wake up and see the tousled sleepy face of the woman and her smudged makeup the next day.

But Dove hadn't maneuvered herself into his arms, he was the guilty party. If he didn't move soon his throbbing erection pressing against that sweet little ass of hers would surely wake her. That drama he didn't need. Especially after he'd told her he wouldn't touch her.

He was a lot of shit asshole to her, but he didn't want her to think he would not keep his word.

Yet, he laid there not moving for another minute feeling her so tender, so trusting, so soft in his embrace.

Ahh, holding his breath again, he carefully, gently, removed his hand from the silky skin of her ribs dragging his palm down the flat of her belly before slowly sliding it off her side.

He had to take another breath, he should have just moved his hand instead of choosing to detour and feel that pure skin of hers.

His other arm was under her neck. That took longer to move without waking her.

Finally, he rolled on his back and stared up at the sky.

Chapter Ten

By the time they reached the next lodge everyone was dragging their feet. It had been a long journey, and not over yet.

Going inside the musty building, Kitty hauled her canteen off her neck and leaned against a wall. Seeing Tezer, the last one in, she said, "Hey, Fearless Leader, show us where we're to bed down tonight."

Shrugging out of the backpack he carried, Tezer watched Dove and Vigo head to a big couch and plop down next to each other. His face impassive, he trod over to Kitty and said, "Let's go, I'll show you."

She perked right up. Hurrying to catch up with him, she slipped her hand through his arm before he was halfway across the room.

Out of the corner of his eye he could see Dove staring at them. Her expression totally unreadable. She turned and smiled at something Vigo said.

Irritated without knowing why, Tezer strode through the room and down the hall allowing Kitty to cling to him simpering God-knows-what, the entire way.

When he reached the room, he pulled her arm from his and gestured inside. "There. The jeep already dropped your shit off." He spun and left before she could stick her talons into him again.

Dinner was fairly quiet, everyone was too tired to talk much. As soon as they were done, people scattered to their assigned rooms. As usual, Dove went into the kitchen to help clean up.

Tezer and his team were having a brief meeting in a small study.

Looking at Reggie, Tezer's eyes scrunched for a second, then his brows shot like boomerangs up his forehead. He asked Reggie, "Why are you here? Aren't you supposed to be cleaning up with Ziggy?"

Reggie looked at him. "Huh?" Shaking his head, he replied, "Na, I think maybe Rey is there with him."

Garth said, "A few more days and we should be-" he broke off when Tezer strode out of the room without a word. Garth looked at Leo, Nik and Reggie, they all shrugged, who knew what bug was up the chief's ass.

It had hit Tezer like a hammer that Dove might be alone in the kitchen with Ziggy. The fucking beast who had tried to make off with her in the middle of last night.

Rushing down the hall he held a hand up halting Kitty as she slid off a chair and tripped over to him in high heels. *High heels*? Tezer thought, *in the jungle*?

"Chief, honey," pressing her arms together to increase the already enormous cleavage she had, Kitty cooed, "come and visit with me now that you're done with your boring old meeting. We can, hey-" he moved past her without a glance in her direction.

As he stormed into the kitchen, he glanced around, it wasn't that big of a room. Ziggy was at the sink, Rey carried dishes to set on the counter beside him. They were the only ones present.

"Rey, man, where's the girl?" Tezer asked from the doorway.

"Huh?" Rey crooked his head towards him. "Who?" Seeing Tezer's face set caustic, impatience furrowing his forehead, Rey's mouth tipped in a smirk. "Oh, Goldilocks."

"Fuck, Rey." Taking a step further into the kitchen, his mouth harsh with no patience for nonsense, Tezer glared at the man who thought he was God's gift to women.

"Okay, okay, geesh," Rey inched back. "I walked her to the women's room. She can't go out either of the two doors without passing all the rooms. The women's quarters are at the end of the hall, the only exit is this way. She's not going anywhere. Do you want me to go get-"

Out the door, Tezer jogged down the hall to the women's room. Without knocking, he threw the door open-

The room was empty.

Everyone was in the great room chilling after dinner.

Scanning the room, he saw the rumpled cots, bathroom door open, clothes strewn about, and the curtains by the window fluttering. It had grown so cool outside there was frost on the ground, no way the girls would have left the window open.

Moving to the window, he looked out. The night sky was cloudy, pitch black. He looked down, there were footprints directly under the window in the crystalline frost and they led away from the building. "Motherfucker-" he spat and raced out of the room.

Grabbing a jacket on the way out the door, Tezer ignored people that called out to him. Slipping the jacket on as he jogged around the building to the window, the crisp air bit at the bare skin of his face and hands.

When he reached the window he looked down. Yeah, those were definitely footprints. Small, female ones. He tracked them as they crushed the frost heading towards the closest clump of leafless trees. Winter had come quickly upon them as they ascended the mountain.

The further he moved from the house the darker it became as he left the building's outside lights.

Keeping an ear perked, Tezer kept scanning the darkness listening, looking for color or movement. His heavy boots crunched the stiff grass as he tromped following the prints.

She must have just left the building because he saw a flash of her white blouse through the tall craggy legs of black trees. *Damned bitch- not even a fucking jacket-*

Sprinting after her, Tezer saw her slip, loose stones and dirt slid, the ground disintegrated under her feet.

Arms flailing, with a yelp she tried to grab at a skinny sapling as gravity pulled her over a chopped off overhang, down a rock-jagged gaping gorge.

The sapling bent under her weight, both hands wrapped around the skinny tree were sliding as hoarse screams pelted from her frantic throat!

Skidding to her, Tezer dropped down on one knee, his other foot stuck out in front of him as a brace. He grasped her wrist and grappled around the ground to hold onto something- anything.

He searched the dark quickly and grabbed ahold of a stump sticking out of the hard-packed earth. A burrowing grunt razed through his clenched teeth as he struggled to keep a grip on her flailing body.

Tezer could hear her sucking in raw terrified huffs, and her feet scrabbling against the side of the chopped dirt wall trying to climb up. "Hold on," he urged as he dragged her chest, belly, then thighs up onto the cold ground.

Lying on her front, Dove's panicked breaths rushed fast and frantic. Tezer flopped down beside her on his back, his chest concussed like a gasping fish out of water.

His head hurt with his harrowing fury, he rolled over, grasped her shoulders hauling her to sit and roughly shook her.

"Goddammit, Dove, what the fuck is the matter with you? Don't you listen? You don't have the brains God gave a gnat for fuck's sake!" He was so mad, so...so scared, he wanted to beat her.

But her head was down, the long curls a thick curtain over her frightened face as she realized how close a call she had, hit her. Her shoulders convulsed with hysterical crying at her near demise.

If she'd fallen over the steep cliff, her body would have banged and crashed down the harsh mountainside before coming to a deadly crush upon the rocks at the bottom that she could not have survived.

"Ah shit-" he pulled her into his arms, her face buried in his shoulder.

She cried her terror into his shoulder as he cradled her head, his arm holding her safe against his stalwart body. It took many long moments before she could draw in a long traumatic breath.

When her sobs subsided, Tezer stood up, pulling her up with him. Her body shook so hard her wobbly legs threatened to toss her back down to the ground. Curving a muscled arm around her shoulders, he held her until her feet steadied and her heartbeat, and his, slowed to normal.

Shrugging out of his jacket, he draped it over her shoulders. Then he rolled his arm around her back and walked her across the crunchy frosted grass back to the lodge.

Inside, Rey handed him the sat phone with a nod that it was Braemont.

Raking a hand through his short hair, Tezer brought Dove to a couch in the living room. "Sit there," he ordered gruffly, "don't move one fucking muscle."

"I'll watch over her," Brock said cheerfully plopping down beside her.

Biting off what he was about to say, Tezer shot Dove a furious glare, and a warning to Brock who wasn't looking at him then strode to the other side of the room to answer the phone.

Leaning a shoulder against the doorway between the kitchen and the living room, catching his breath and letting his racing pulse settle, Tezer wiped his sleeve over his eyes and glanced around the room as he listened to Braemont's barking.

Avril, Ronald, Reggie and Tommy Tucker were playing cards. He presumed Tommy was losing judging by the beads of sweat rolling down his heavy face.

Chelsea and Vigo were playing a board game, and Paolo sat slumped in a chair appearing to have his eyes closed but his head was facing the couch Dove and Brock were on.

Robin bounced over and plunked down on the other side of Brock pushing into their conversation.

Tezer smothered his moan seeing Kitty come slinking in wearing tights and a cropped shirt that did little to hide her massive bosom. She headed straight for him.

She leaned her back against the other side of the doorframe, put her hands behind her back to clutch the frame and arched her spine to thrust her breasts up.

The brazen woman tilted her head back resting it against the door, so she could look down at Tezer with the sultriest smile she could craft. The tip of her tongue became visible as it wetly slathered her lips.

The phone to his ear, Tezer looked away from her. Peripherally he saw Dove still wrapped in his jacket, cast periodic, wary, nervous glances in his direction.

Lids tapered to slits, his gaze direct and level at her, the promise of punishment glittered in the dark depths. The damned pig-headed female was relentless in her escape attempts.

She had no clue what kind of perilous land was out there. He figured as soon as the fright of tonight faded, she would be at it again. She looked away when she saw him staring at her.

Hardly listening to Braemont's babble, Tezer could not fathom what Dove could be so petrified of that she would run off into the wilderness in the cold dark night, without a flashlight, a weapon, even a fucking jacket.

Throwing down her cards, Avril stood up with a stretch. Admitting defeat, Chelsee left her game. Tired of being ignored by Brock, Robin went over to stand with Avril and Chelsee.

Winking at Kitty, Avril said, "Come on, let's hit it, dawn comes too damned early," her sharp mouth widened in a big yawn. The four headed down the hall to the women's quarters. Dove awkwardly climbed to her feet to follow them.

Protesting, "Hey, hon, you don't have to go," Brock went to snag her wrist but she stepped out of his reach.

Her voice still shaking from her ordeal, Dove said quietly, "Um, I guess I'll see you tomorrow." Her smile crooked, self-conscious. Pinpricks of unease poking the back of her neck, she headed down the hall the girls had gone to.

Tezer grabbed her arm stopping her. "No, you're coming with me."

Boy he moved silently and fast for such a big man. Not looking at him, Dove said, "But, uh, the girls' room, I, uh, it's time for bed."

"Yes it is." He changed her direction and started walking back down the opposite hallway.

"But," she dug her heels in and tugged at her arm. It did her no good.

He brought her to the room he was staying in and pulled her inside, then shut, and locked the door. Turning to her he caught her cringe and step back from him.

Taking another step back, while gaping around looking for the nearest escape, she asked, "Why have you brought me here?" In her apprehension, her vague accent laced more thickly in her soft, nervous voice.

He trod across the room while taking his watch off and set it on a table on one side of the bed. Pulling out his wallet, several knives but leaving one on, he also removed a gun from behind his back and laid the weapons on the table.

His shirt out, he looked like the kind of man who spent a lot of time at the gym. The shirt snug around his broad solid shoulders hung loose at the inner curve of his lower back. Jeans clung hanging just a bit on his lean hips.

With calm nonchalance he nodded at the bathroom. "Go get cleaned up, I'll get you a shirt to sleep in."

Blonde brows jumped over eyes that flit back and forth like green ping-pongs. "What?" Her head turning towards the door she took another step back.

Watching her panic rising, he said coolly, "Yeah. You're staying with me."

"No, but," her fingers plucked nervously at a curl as she inched to the door.

He didn't move, expression made of granite. "Yeah. You're with me. No one will try to abduct you, or hurt you like those bitches pushing you and fuck knows what else they do to you when you're alone with them in the women's quarters."

Now he did move a foot towards her. "And you won't try any more escape attempts. I'm a very light sleeper, the door is locked and I will hear that old weathered window squeak open."

Lifting a duffle bag onto a chair, he rifled inside, pulled out a shirt and tossed it to her.

Surprised, she fumbled it then caught it up against her chest.

Tucking his hands into his pockets, he motioned with his head to the bathroom. "Now. Go clean up, put on the shirt, we'll be sharing this bed."

"Uh, no uh, I'm fine in the women's quarters. I'll just, I mean, my toothbrush, uh," her feet shuffled nearer to the door.

The room was small with the bed, a couple of chairs and tables, a raggedy rug covered most of the wood floor. So big and strong, Tezer seemed to fill the room with his heat and energy. Dove turned towards the door.

The coldness in his tone chilled the closed in space. "I said you are staying here. Use my stuff."

He almost smiled at her mouth twisting at the grossness. "I've had my tongue down your throat, sweetheart, you can use my toothbrush."

The stillness, rising heat in the air, and blooms of pink in her cheeks indicated they were both remembering his assault on her when Braemont had ordered Tezer to use forced sex as a weapon to get her to talk.

At her movements toward the door his mouth firmed. "You have one second to get your ass in there and do as I say or I will do it for you."

They played glowering stand-off for a few seconds before, with her head tilted away from him, she trod into the bathroom, shut the door, and locked it with a deliberately loud click.

Tezer let out his held breath.

Stripping down to a T-shirt and briefs, he tucked the gun and knives under his side of the mattress, except for the one knife he kept on his ankle.

The bathroom door opened slowly, she came out like a fair shadow preparing for the worst.

As she moved from the doorway, Tezer went by her, snapped, "Get in the bed," and disappeared into the bathroom leaving the door partially open.

Setting his jacket on a chair, Dove stood, knees knocking. Surely he brought her here to assault her. But, she looked down at the shirt she wore. It was the second time she'd worn his clothes.

The other girls were very stingy with their loaners. If he was planning on raping her, he wouldn't have given her his shirt. Would he? A sigh trickled out, her shoulders relaxed slightly.

Treading in bare feet to the bed, she pulled the covers back and anxiously slid in, faced away from the side he had set his belongings on and pulled the blanket up over her, covering half her face.

Her insides were still quaking from her near death fall. He had rescued her for the second time. That Braemont man must be paying him a fortune to bring her to him.

When the door opened, she didn't move, not even to draw a breath.

When he turned out the light and the mattress sank and rocked as he slid in next to her, she didn't blink. When he rolled towards her and braced up on one elbow, she still didn't breathe.

"Dove."

Every bone in her body turned to jelly.

Devoid of inflection, Tezer said quietly, "I am not going to touch you. If you try to run again, I will bind you like I told you in the beginning. Do not leave this room." He waited, she didn't move or respond.

Then her voice small, quiet, she said, "Thank you, Chief, for uh, saving me." She was quiet after that.

He laid his head down on the pillow and listened to her rapid shallow breathing until it slowed, deepened. He could palpably feel the rigidness in her body seep away as she fell asleep.

Tezer sighed. It was going to be tough for him to sleep in the same bed with her, with her in only panties and his shirt. He pushed at the throbbing hard length in his briefs, but she wasn't going to be able to slip out of the room and hurl herself unwittingly off a cliff again.

He must have finally drifted off when something jarred him awake. He wasn't alone in his bed. He jerked up, swung his head to the space next to him, then relaxed, it was Dove.

His eyes narrowed in the dark at her.

She was thrashing, crying, mumbling in her sleep. When her body writhed off the side of the bed and she started screaming, he instantly stretched across and caught her arm, preventing her from falling. He pulled her back safely onto the mattress.

But now she was screaming and fighting him, terror radiated violently out of her in hysterical waves.

Tezer wrapped his arms around her to hold her from hurting herself. She must be dreaming about her earlier brush with death.

Her back pressed against his chest, his mouth near her ear, he spoke quietly, "Dove, Dove, it's okay, you're dreaming." Hell, she wouldn't respond to Dove, that wasn't her real name.

Stroking her hair, he murmured, "Shh, wake up honey, you're safe, wake up, it's…ah, Tezer…wake up."

Her chest heaving against his arms, sobbing, she choked in terror, "Stop! Please-" Struggling to break loose from his hold, she begged, "Don't hurt me anymore!" A sob of excruciating pain burst from her as she screamed hoarsely, "*Please!*"

His arms tightened into steel ropes around Dove, she couldn't get away. Her head fell back, mouth open in a strangled cry, "Please, it- hurts-" gasp, "so- bad- *please*," she sobbed.

"Shh, honey, you're safe, baby, it's Tezer. You're dreaming, wake up." He kept talking quietly, calmly, softly whispering in her ear, gently rubbing her arms.

Gulping great gasps of deep breaths, her body felt different, she was coming around. It wasn't the fall she was dreaming about. Someone was violently hurting her.

"Dove- it's okay, I won't hurt you, I swear, open your eyes."

The room night dark, stiff in his hold, chest hitching, in rasping fear and confusion, she whispered, "Chief?"

She was awake, he loosened his hold. She lifted her hands and gripped them on his powerful forearms crossed over the front of her.

Looking down she saw she was wearing an unfamiliar shirt, she could feel the muscles in his chest hard on her back, the side of his face pressed against her hair.

His night whiskers catching the locks, wisps of hair fluttered with his every exhale. His deep voice a rumble, he murmured, "Shh, you're safe now."

Blinking into full consciousness, she saw she was on a bed, wrapped in Chief Tezer Corseque's arms. "Uh, why, uh..."

He felt her tighten up again. "It's okay, you were dreaming." When she pushed, he let her go.

She moved away, looked around. Then she remembered, he had forced her to stay with him.

Tezer shifted back to lean nonthreatening against the pillows stacked behind him. "Dove," he said quietly, "I was not harming you. You had a nightmare."

Eyes wide as blue plates, inhaling deep breaths for calm, she just blinked at him, prepared to flee if he made a move towards her.

Forehead knit in frowning thought, he pondered, "It was about why you're running, why you're alone out here in the middle of nowhere."

Studying his tough face in the dimness, she lowered her eyes, shook her head.

"Look at me." He waited. She glanced up briefly then lowered her eyes again. "Tell me." Folding his hands together he rested them benignly on his stomach and asked, "Are you running from the law?"

Wordless, she shook her head. Keeping her eyes down, curtains of blonde hair waved down the sides of her face and over her shoulders.

His dark brows rose as he thought. Then they drew down like angry swords as he surmised, "Then it has to be a man."

Her eyes popped up at him before she quickly looked away, licking her lips.

Tezer reached out and put his hand on her arm. "Dove, tell me. Tell me what's going on. If someone is after you, if they hurt you, I'll take care of it, him, whatever it is. I can make it go away. Even if it's the law, I can help you."

Pulling her knees up, she wrapped her arms around them and stared blankly across the room. A shaky sigh heaved out. "It's…nothing. I just had a bad dream. I'm all right now. I'm, uh, sorry I woke you." She shuffled down in the bed with her back to him and laid her head on the pillow.

He stared at her in the dark. He'd heard her scream, saw her face while she was in the throes of the nightmare, heard her words pleading to not be hurt anymore. She was not all right. He moved to lie down.

She was so scared, too scared to talk. And she didn't trust him to tell him so he could help. Like he could blame her.

The next time he woke, he was curled around her like when they'd slept outside. Except now his hand was under the shirt cupping her bare breast, his raging erection dug into her backside like it could bore through his briefs and her panties and get to her.

His hand involuntarily clenched over her firm globe, she wriggled with a sigh, her butt snuggled against his swollen shaft.

A thought flashed through him. He could be inside her in one move. Who could she tell? He'd make her like it.

With his strength it would be easy to overpower her, force her, pull those pretty thighs apart and shove in, even from behind like this-

Tezer drew his hands from her warm feminine body and rolled off the bed.

He got up and pulled his jeans on, buckled his belt, and then moved to a cushioned chair to sleep the rest of the night.

Chapter Eleven

The rain kept them from leaving the next day.

They had enough food to hold them for a few days, all of the lodges had generators and extra gas out in secured sheds.

Well after dinner, most of the men were sprawled around the living room watching a hockey game on satellite TV. Beer bottles in hand, some were shouting, some muttering, a lot of curses flew around the room. Occasionally a fist was shaken at the screen.

The women were in their room doing their nails, hair, gossiping, discussing their sexual exploits and comparing stories. Their laughter grew louder as they provided grades to the men they'd been with on the trip, charting length, skill, stamina and creativity.

Dove was sitting in a chair near the sofa Tezer and Garth were lounging on. Tezer had informed her since she'd tried to run again and almost fallen into the gorge, that she had forfeited any privacy. From now on she was to stay with him, at all times.

She had found some wool and knitting needles tucked away in a closet, and was working on the half completed sweater that was in the basket. She set the work down and stood up.

His eyes on the television, Tezer asked brusquely, "Where are you going?"

Slightly startled, she didn't think anyone even noticed she was there. With an annoyed sigh and rolled eyes, she said, "To the bathroom."

Not looking at her, he said, "I don't need attitude. Don't go anywhere else, come straight back."

Rolling her eyes again, she muttered, "Yes Master." Before she could take a step, his hand swung out, he snatched her arm and dragged her to bend over to look in his eyes.

"I said," he growled squeezing her arm, "I don't want attitude. You give me good reason to know where you are since you're determined to kill yourself out in the wild, and for some reason half the males here think you're fair game.

"Until you tell me what has its hold over you, and I'm sure you won't try to run again," he pulled her closer getting in her face, "you will do as I say. With no attitude. Got me?"

Mortified, hoping no one in the room noticed their exchange, with a contemptuous glare, she muttered, "Yes, sir."

He held her another minute to make his point then let her go.

Straightening up, she tucked her loosened blouse back into her jeans, her cheeks flushed at his dominating treatment of her in front of the others.

Rubbing her arm, she walked away muttering under her breath, "Master." Out of the corner of her eye she saw he heard her by the lifting of one side of his mouth.

With a mirthless grin, he said after her, "You're going to pay for that."

She kept going unsure if he was amused, or pissed.

Tezer kept one eye on the game and one eye on the hall to the bathroom, irritated because he had his mind on her and was missing plays on the game.

Beside him Garth roared, cheered at a goal, went to clink bottles with him then saw his blank look.

"Ah," Garth snickered, "funny to see a guy all fucked up over a babe he isn't even fucking."

Tezer ignored him, Dove was finally coming down the hall. But, Rey Silva swaggered out of a doorway and stopped her.

Tezer couldn't hear him, but Rey was talking to her. She shook her head with a polite smile and made to pass by him. Rey stuck out his arm, put a palm on the wall to block her from moving. He bent his head and said something quietly to her.

She shook her head again and tried to move past him but he kept his arm like a fence keeping her blocked. He stroked his other hand down her arm then picked up the end of one of her long curls and rubbed it between his fingers.

She snatched the hair out of his hand and shoved past him, but he pushed her against the wall and moved his arm close to her body to keep her from leaving.

A deep growl rumbled in Tezer's chest. "Go get her," he said to Garth, knowing if Tezer went they would be short a man for the rest of the trip.

With a big grin, Garth got up and ambled over to the couple.

His eyes slit in ire, Tezer watched Garth set his hand on Dove's shoulder, he saw her jump at the unexpected touch. Then saw her visibly relax with a warm smile when she saw who it was.

A vexing twinge pricked his stomach; she was never relaxed around him, never smiled at him. She liked Garth. Of course Garth wasn't a mean tough shit and a bastard to her like Tezer was.

He watched Garth tell the man to drop his arm, let her go, and get lost. Rey started to argue with him, but Garth dropped his arm around Dove's shoulders and guided her away and back to the living room.

Tezer felt his stomach twist, he'd never gotten disturbed over a woman before. She was worming her soft way under his tough skin. The damned female was holding dark secrets, she inexplicably keeps trying to run out into the vast treacherous wilderness where she would meet certain death.

His eyes twitched to Rey who still stood in the hall glaring at Dove and Garth. Tezer felt unfamiliar possessiveness. His ass burned every time another man was even near her. It made him sick. He had no interest in her. Surely it was just a unique effect of the mission.

He scrubbed his fingers down his face. He needed to put her back in place as just another female. He's been too soft on her. Well, that ended now.

As she started to sit in the chair she'd been in before, Tezer moved over on the couch. Without looking at her, he nodded to the space between him and the arm of the couch and snapped, "Sit here."

Garth patted her on the shoulder then moved down the far end of the sofa and plopped down on the old yet still thick cushion.

Brows furrowed at Tezer's order, Dove continued onto the chair.

Now Tezer turned his implacable stare to her and said coarsely, "I said sit the fuck down here."

Not wanting a scene, with a deliberate sigh, Dove sat down on the sofa as close to the arm and away from Tezer as she could get.

The room erupted in a cheer as the team made a goal. Tezer turned his attention back to the television.

After a few minutes, Dove murmured, "I'm tired, I'm going to go to-"

"No."

Staring at his stiff profile, she said calmly, "I'm tired. I am simply going to the girls' room to go to bed."

He suddenly put his hand around her neck under her jaw and pulled her over so she was off balance and had to set a hand on his thigh or she'd topple over into his lap. "I said no. You sit there and shut up."

Affronted at his words, she huffed, "How dare you talk to me like that. You are a big rude bully-"

Below his breath, he lashed at her, "You want to flap your lips, honey, we will go to my room right now and I will give your mouth something to do."

At the confused look on her face, he grabbed his crotch and the dawning hit her.

Her face reddened. Closing her mouth she crossed her arms and sat back against the side of the sofa, muttering, "Repulsive tyrant."

He grasped her hand, yanked it over and forced it palm down on his groin watching her face as she felt his erection swell.

Holding it there, his lids low over barely visible thundercloud eyes, his soldier's face like sheet metal so hard and sharp, he said quietly, "You got something to say to me?"

He'd show her how a pissed off mercenary would treat her, let her get a glimpse of what she could expect if she ran into one while escaping into the jungle.

She tugged at her hand, but he pressed it down harder. His cock thickened, hardened, lengthened under her hand.

"Let go of me," she whispered fiercely pulling at her hand.

"Oh, you still want to talk? Let's go to my room," he cupped his hand over hers making her squeeze his hardened manhood and glared straight into her furious eyes.

Her gaze dropped first, she shook her head.

Staring at her, he forced her hand to squeeze him again, then released her.

She shifted back to the end of the couch. Curling away from him, she kicked off her shoes, pulled her knees up and wrapped her arms around them.

His eyes were back on the game, but he wasn't seeing it. He was hoping she wouldn't cry. Without looking at her, he could tell she wasn't scared, well, maybe a little; no she was more angry at his boorish behavior. Too bad.

At the end of the first quarter, Dove's eyes drifted closed. Slowly, her body slumped, then slid over near his, until she sank down on the cushions and settled her head in his lap. Facing him, her knees bent, her hand shifted onto his thigh.

Tezer didn't move. His legs felt like they were burning. Still semi-hard from earlier, his groin swelled painfully, pinching inside his jeans. He looked down at the sleeping woman who had made herself cozily comfortable with her face on his thigh and her mouth so near his-

Around the room the men were yelling at the game but their roars didn't wake her. She just snuggled more against his crotch, her hand moved up his thigh.

An odd feeling swarmed in his belly, it rose to coil around his heart. Of its own volition, his hand moved to her shoulder, then he was stroking her hair.

Garth brought him another beer and wriggled his eyebrows at Dove asleep on his lap with her mouth and small hand practically on his groin, and Tezer stroking her hair that spread out like a yellow shawl over his legs.

Taking the beer, Tezer gave him a frown telling him to bugger off.

Laughing, Garth flopped back down on the couch and turned his attention back to the TV.

After a while, realizing he wasn't watching the game, Tezer slid his hands under Dove and held her against his chest as he stood up.

In his room, he laid her on the bed and pulled the blanket over her then he gently lay down on top of the blanket, fully dressed except for his boots.

Closing his eyes, he hoped she wouldn't have another nightmare. It was an agonizing thing to experience and he hated feeling powerless to help her.

Chapter Twelve

Again the rain kept them trapped for another day.

Tezer and his team were hanging out in the small study playing poker, some of the group were washing clothes.

Loud voices carried down the hall. Someone sounded upset. The men kept playing. Tezer and Nik shared a pack of smokes.

Leo waved at the cloud of smoke that wafted towards him. "Hey, bros, ya ever hear those things cause cancer?"

"Yeah," Nik tossed down a card, "quit whining like a baby, you in or out?"

"Chief!"

The men looked up, chubby Tommy Tucker panted in the doorway.

Blowing out a stream of smoke, Tezer muttered, "What?"

Tommy bent over put his hands on his pudgy knees as he tried to catch his breath. "It's," he gasped, "the older guy, Ronald," gasp, he wheezed gulping air.

"What about him?" Garth asked while dealing another hand.

Bent over, Tommy drew in big breaths, "He's out there, outside," gasp.

Leo's brows arched his disbelief. "In this storm?"

Nodding, still catching his breath, his belly wobbled as Tommy wheezed. "Yeah, he- he was looking out the window and a, a- deer was lying on its side on the ground. Ronald's one of those uh, PETA people, loves animals."

He sucked in a deep breath. "It looked like the deer was injured, so, he went out to help it, but," wheeze, gasp.

"But what?" Stubbing his cigarette out in an ashtray Tezer pushed his chair back.

"It's a- big dark storm. I was watching through the window. I think a, I don't know, maybe an animal, a bear or wolf, couldn't hardly see but a shadow jumped at him and knocked him over. Then the storm, I don't know, he stumbled to his feet and ran with the thing chasing him."

Standing straighter but still breathing heavily, Tommy cried with worry, "It's been like twenty minutes and he hasn't come back, and the deer is gone."

"Shit." Tezer jumped to his feet and strode out of the room. By the time he grabbed his jacket and hat, Garth, Leo, Nik and Reggie were going out the door with him.

The rest of the group gathered in a bunch in the living room, half with their faces pressed against the window with concern.

Thirty minutes later and no one had returned.

Dove left her spot at the window and headed to the kitchen to make a pot of tea and heat up some soup. When they all returned, hopefully with Ronald in tow, they were going to want something warm.

"Hey," Rey said sauntering into the kitchen, "you need some help?" He moved to where she was stirring a pot over the burner.

Her eyes glued to the back window, Dove shook her head. "No, I'm fine, thanks."

"Uh huh." Rey sidled over next to her.

There was a ruckus at the front door, and it burst open.

The five men blew in half-carrying, half-dragging Ronald McCain.

They dragged him to a chair and helped him sit. The men peeled off their wet jackets hanging them on hooks by the door to dry.

With wide eyes, Chelsee stepped over and asked, "Is he okay? What happened?"

Panting slightly, Leo told her, "He got knocked down and chased I think by a small panther. When he got to the woods he grabbed a tree limb and whacked the animal until it ran off, but he got disoriented and lost, tripped and fell into a pond."

"Yeah," Nik joined in. "Apparently swimming isn't his forte. Tezer tracked him and found him. Then jumped in and pulled him out." He glanced over at the shivering soaked Ronald. Garth and Reggie were helping him back up to go take off his wet clothes.

Tezer left to hit his room to change. When he returned he looked around with a frown. "Where's Dove?" he asked Chelsee.

"Oh," Chelsee fidgeted with her thick caramel hair, twisting it and twirling it around her fingers. Her eyes slanted to Kitty curled up in a chair.

Kitty tilted her head up in a signal, then smirked.

Smiling at Tezer, Chelsee informed him, "Goldilocks is in the kitchen. She and Rey wanted some…you know…alone time. He had his hands all up her," she cocked her head with a coy grin and squeezed her own tiny breasts, "you know."

Mouth firming into a grim clench, Tezer turned from her bee-lining for the kitchen not seeing Chelsee and Kitty share a smirk.

Clomping to the kitchen, a red haze clouded Tezer's vision, and it got worse when he moved into the kitchen and saw Dove and Rey standing very close together.

Rey had his mouth near her ear and was speaking quietly into it. She was stirring something in a saucepan.

"Dove." Tezer noticed her shoulders go rigid, neck stiffen. "Come here," he ordered with a cold bark.

With a sigh that told him his commanding her irritated her, she turned around. His gaze flickered from Rey's smug smile to- his brows sprung like they were yanked up by a string.

Dove was wearing a tiny cropped shirt that showed her midriff and was thin enough he could see the too small bra she wore, the top button on the shirt was missing.

His stunned gaze fell to the skin-tight pants she had painted on. Her feet were bare, hair tied back in a ponytail. Her face looked like a fresh sixteen, her body, pure adult, sinfully lush ambrosia.

Rey's eyeballs were all over her tits like hands fondling her.

"What the fuck have you got on?" Tezer snarled while jerking his head at Rey to get out.

An obnoxious snicker on his lips, Rey took a long look at Dove's chest before he strolled out.

Tezer snapped at Dove, "Turn that shit off and come with me."

A line cut between her brows. "What? It's soup and tea for you men, you're wet and cold, poor Ronald-"

Tone a feral threat, sounding like ground gravel, he snarled, "I said, turn it off and come here." His high spiked cheekbones darkened and cut sharper than chiseled rock, the full lips tightened into a pricked slash. He looked as ferocious as the storm outside beating at the lodge.

Dove knew glowering at him only made him madder but she did it anyway. *How dare he order her about like a dog.*

Turning her back to him, she rotated back to the soup and grasped the wooden spoon that was in it, and stirred. The long ponytail swished across her back as if mocking him.

She didn't hear him move, he was always as swift and silent as a jungle cat, but she could feel the heat burning from his strapping body. He was behind her, almost but not quite touching her. The hair on the back of her neck sprung up, her fingers tightened on the spoon.

She was proud of herself for not flinching when he reached down in front of her and turned the two burners off, but it was hard to swallow past the lump in her throat.

Winding his long fingers around her arm, Tezer didn't say another word to her as they left the kitchen.

When they moved through the living room, Tezer was more than aware that every male eye in the room was on her chest.

The midriff-baring shirt was tight, her breasts molded in it like soft round pillows and they jiggled being not secure in the too-small bra. The pants she had on were so tight he could see the outline of her tiny panties cupping her firm rounded ass.

Conversation stopped as everyone watched Tezer, his face an impenetrable mask, lead Dove out of the room and to the hall that led to the men's quarters.

In the hallway, she jerked at her arm knowing it was useless and snapped, "How dare you treat me like this, and in front of people! You are a sexist brute. You can't-"

Thrusting her into his room and slamming the door behind him, he held his big hard fist up. "This says I can do anything I want. The strongest leads, the strongest commands, the strongest survives to protect the weak."

"I am not weak! I-"

Cutting her off again, his gaze seething with ire dragged down her body like a rake. "You are indecent, you look like a whore."

Her mouth dropped, eyes widened. Nettled, slapping her hands on her hips, she retorted, "How dare you! I am washing my clothes, I have nothing but borrowed things to wear."

His big hands clenched on his lean hips, he snarled his fury while staring at her body. Heat rushed up his own limbs and torso like a scorching wind, his balls tightened painfully. "That's no excuse. You know you can wear my stuff. There is no excuse to be parading around like a slut."

He knew he sounded like a jealous boyfriend, but he told himself that wasn't it, it was his duty to protect all of the women from unwanted advances, and even dressed in a burlap sack she was walking, body-scalding sex.

Before she knew it she flung her hand out and slapped him. He didn't even blink. But seeing her grab her hand with a cry, a slight smirk rode up the side of his mouth.

"Ah, it seems you have never struck anyone before. Chalk that up with the gun experience."

Her scowl at the reminder made him grin with a nasty edge. He asked curiously, "Why didn't you hit me with your fist me instead of that little ineffective slap?"

Holding her hand to her chest, she said, "I don't know how to punch, I thought I could break my hand. You're such a brick wall."

"Oh, I see," his tone snidely sardonic. "I thought all whores knew how to punch."

Reacting to his deliberate goading, she swung at him. He caught her fist and pulled her close to him.

Looking down, seeing her anger slide into fear, Tezer said with silky intent, "Ah, did I mention every time you hit me, or try to, because there is no way you can hurt me," his arrogance knew no bounds, he continued with a masculine sneer, "you will forfeit something." He drew her in closer, watched her lashes flutter in growing trepidation.

"Forfeit what?" She futilely pulled at her hand. "I have nothing."

His face shadowed with scrub inches from hers, looking down at her, he taunted, "Yes you do. Go ahead, try it again. Try not to hurt yourself too much." He laughed and twisted out of range of her thrusting knee, and kissed her fist in a mock showing her who was in charge.

Furious, she spurted, "You are just a plain stone-cold hearted bastard."

His gaze scrolled down her figure then back up to glint tauntingly at her. "Oh yeah? I'll show you cold hearted. I told you that you would forfeit, this time it's your insolent mouth."

Suddenly snaring her arms, he pushed her back against the wall, cupped her face and kissed her wildly, incessantly, letting all the heat he'd suppressed boil out. His mouth besieged hers relentlessly until they were both panting and delirious.

Drawing away from her to take a deep breath, Tezer studied her reaction. The gold in her eyes seared over the green, dazed and bewildered, damp lips parted eliciting stunned, soft, rapid breaths. Her chest heaved and hitched with fast shallow breaths.

In a steeping low voice, he said thickly, "How's that for cold hearted?"

Blinking back the disoriented fog, her small pink tongue circled her lips. He grabbed her behind the neck under the ponytail, pulled her to him and kissed her fiercely again.

Her hands went up to brace against his chest, but he pulled her closer forcing her hands to slide off his chest, her fingers clutched wildly at his big arms.

Biceps so huge she couldn't get a grip, his intense kiss growing almost violent as he plunged his tongue into her mouth, sweeping the inside of her silk cove, tasting every inch of her.

Then he chased her tongue, sucking, tugging, tasting, his breathing deepened, quickened, he was holding her so tightly she could barely suck in air.

Her head spinning, Dove pushed at him until he fought through the cloud of throbbing desire that had overtaken him like a descending thick fog, and released her face.

The steam of lust slowly cleared from his white-hot eyes. His chest pumped so hard it beat against her breasts, a trickle of sweat slid down his temple.

Gripping her upper arms, between short, rapid inhalations he uttered, "You want to provoke me again, woman? Go ahead, try to strike me, next you forfeit that blouse." His gaze dropped down the front of the tight shirt and back up to her alarmed eyes.

Her face displaying her shock, Dove endeavored to push him back and couldn't. It was like trying to move a tank.

Hooded eyes probing her disconcertment, he murmured with a wolf's leer, "And then next it's that tiny black lace bra I can see through that shit blouse."

She protectively put her hands up in front of her chest.

He smirked. "So, keep trying, little bird, I don't mind. There's a lot more you can forfeit, trust me." He waited like a preying eagle over an exposed mouse, she said nothing, just stared at his tough Marine's chin.

He propped a hand on the wall next to her head and said with mild sarcasm, "So, we done here?"

Staring at his chin, she didn't move.

Tezer gripped her collar with both hands, his fingers on a button. "I asked you, are we done here or do you want to play some more, 'cause I'm game. Don't answer me and the shirt goes."

Her head jerked up but her eyes stayed on his chin. "Yes, I mean no," took a shuddering breath. "I, we're done."

Frustrated that she would not look him in the eyes, he said waspish, "You sure, 'cause I don't mind, I have the time. You dress like a whore, hook up with every fucking guy here, and I'll treat you like one."

Her grimace reached up to rebuke the darkness in his eyes. He clutched her chin with his thumb and finger and asked snidely, "You got something to say?"

She started to shake her head, then angrily hit him in the chest with both fists. "You have no right to do this to me, no right to keep me prisoner! No right to tell me what I can wear and who I can be with. You are nothing but a brute and a coward!" She broke from his clutch and started to run.

That she didn't deny she wanted other men detonated his fury. He shot out one hand snagging her forearm.

Slowly pulling her back to him, his face a mask of coarse frost, he said, "So, that's the way you want it?"

Her shoulder bunched up, she kept her forearm rigid, head tilted in defiance and cried her frequent refrain, "No, let go of me." She hit at his chest again but it was like hitting rock. He didn't even flinch.

"You can't tell me what to do. If I want to be with- with Rey, or, whoever, you can't make me-"

The rage building, deafening him, he put his hands on her shoulders and pressed her down until she was on her knees. Yanking the band off her ponytail he stuck his hand in the back of her loose hair, grabbed a handful, and at the same time unbuckled his belt.

Anger and fright battling inside her, Dove screamed, "Stop! You're a pig, an animal! Let go of me!"

He unzipped his pants and pressed his hand over his briefs, over his already hard cock. "I'll shut your smart mouth, Dove, see if you can talk with my dick in your mouth."

Holding her hair, he shoved her face against his manhood, over the briefs, forcing her mouth over the thick iron ridge. She put her hands on his thighs to resist.

Rubbing her face against his erection, he fiercely ground out, "Now tell me how much you want to be with the other men here."

Punching his thighs she screamed, "You're a pig! You can't make me do anything I don't want to!"

Pulling her up to her feet by her hair, he snarled in her face, "That's not enough to shut your mouth? Fine, I've had it with you."

Swinging her around so her back was against his chest, he shoved his hand down inside the front of her blouse so hard a button popped off. He kept moving his big hand down and over her lacey bra and grasped her breast. His other hand went to her belt and tugged at it.

"No! Stop, please, please, Tezer. I- I'm sorry," Dove cried, clutching his muscular forearms to stop him.

His mouth against her ear, he gripped her breast, yanked at her belt and whispered wickedly, "You really want me to stop, little Dove? I bet your sweet little pussy is wet; you liked our kisses as much as I did. I bet you are soaking wet for me, am I right?"

Her lips pressed tightly together, she wordlessly shook her head.

"I'm going to find out." He pulled her belt open, undid the top button on her pants.

"No please, Tezer, I'm sorry, please don't." Sobs choked out her tight throat.

He jerked his hand out of her blouse, swung her around to press her bosom against his chest and shoved his rough hands down inside the back of her pants under her panties to grip her bare ass.

"*Now* you apologize? After deliberately baiting me? Maybe it's too late for that. Maybe I'm tired of your smart mouth, your puny little attempts to hit me, taunting me with other men." He squeezed her ass so hard his fingers dug into her crack.

Both hands on her butt, he pulled her hard against his engorged erection, so hard his iron shaft pushed through his open pants and through her jeans and panties to fit ridged up the cleft of her womanhood.

Her hands flat against his shoulders she cried, "Stop! Don't you dare touch me, get your hands off of me!"

He held her so tightly her breasts were wedged hard against his chest keeping her completely inert.

"You provoke me, little bird," he growled in a guttural rasp. "Flaunt that fine body in my face, so fucking sweet on one hand," he squeezed her bottom, "so damned ballsy on the other. If you were a man you'd already be dead. I wish half my men had your balls."

Kneading her ass, a groan curled from him, his fingers slid into her crack.

She moved her hands down now in tight fists pressed against his chest trying to push him away.

"What?" he asked with a cruel smirk. "You done with that smart mouth? Done running that ballsy mouth? Wait, that's right, but of course, you don't have balls, do you?"

He suddenly covered her mouth with his, seizing control. Hard, dominant, forceful, he moved his hand down under the curve of her butt, his long fingers almost to the opening of her womanhood when he froze.

Turning her face from his, she whispered, "Tezer…" Her taut voice constricted, she squirmed against his hand, the warm pressure of it, his fingers on the crest of her core.

His voice dropped in husky incredulity, he rasped, "You are wet, Dove, you are fucking wet. For me."

"Please, Chief, don't," her voice broke. She stopped squirming, it only forced him to grip her harder to hold her still and bear his fingers closer to her tender sex.

He didn't move for a few seconds, as if fighting with himself. Then, he carefully drew his hands out of her pants. Forcing down deep cool breaths, reaching for calm, he fixed his own pants, then hers, straightened her blouse, she didn't move a muscle.

Stepping back from her, his head down, he mumbled, "Let's go."

Softly, eyes gleaming golden with suppressed tears, she pleaded, "Please, Chief, let me go. Your employer can't be mad if I escape. He's never seen me, he will forget he wants you to bring me to him. Just let me-"

Anger burst from his grim mouth, "All right. That's it. That's what you want, let's go." He wrapped his thick fingers around her arm and started walking her to the door snatching up a sweater.

"Chief-"

"It's fucking, *Tezer*," he snapped, his furious eyes raking her.

She looked up at him. His face as usual was a hard implacable mask. Releasing her, he handed her the sweater, his hot gaze streaming down the front of her aiming at her chest.

Her nipples were hard, poking out of the thin blouse, the button he'd inadvertently torn off exposed some of her ample cleavage.

"Put it on." He stomped over to a case, unlocked it, removed a shotgun and locked the case.

She pulled the sweater down over her head, tugged it down to past her thighs. He strung his long fingers around her arm and resumed walking her to the door.

"Chie- uh, Tezer…" Tremors suddenly shook her tense voice, "W- what are you doing?"

His mouth clamped shut hard. The corner of his jaw ticking, he continued walking her out the door, all the way down the hall to a back exit, pausing to grab up someone's shoes by the doorway and passed them to her.

He waited while in bewilderment she put them. Holding the door open, he motioned for her to go out. Leery, she nervously passed under his arm.

They stepped outside. It was just dusk, hanging between dwindling light and approaching shimmering twilight.

150

His hand on her back, he led her to a four-seater jeep that the men used for reconnaissance and bringing supplies. He opened the passenger door, said curtly, "Get in."

Balking, "Chief," her eyes skipped around the grounds for a place to run.

Gesturing with his head, he barked, "Get. In."

She looked down at the shotgun in his hand, swallowed hard, then nervously climbed in.

He closed her door then trod around to climb in behind the wheel. He started the jeep up and drove across the expanse of clearing in the waning light.

They were silent while he drove for a few moments under the dark sky, the jeep bumping and jostling, rocking and jarring over the rough terrain of rocks, holes and thick tall grass. The shotgun was on the floor between him and his door.

Her hard swallow audible, Dove worked to steady the shaking in her voice. "Are you...going to kill me?"

His eyes flicked her a glance that said nothing, the corner of his lip twisted.

Driving a bit further, he pulled the jeep over and parked in a lodge of trees. Shutting off the engine, he got out and went to get her.

He opened her door but she stared at him, not moving. He took her arm and pulled her out. The shotgun in one hand, he held onto her and strode through tall grass to the woods.

"Chief, please-"

"Be quiet. Don't say a word." He brought her to the shelter of a grove of dense trees then stopped. It was even darker inside the coterie of mostly leafless trees. He cocked the gun.

Dove was visibly shaking.

Tezer rolled his arm around her shoulder and led her to a thick, tall tree and placed her to stand next to and slightly behind it.

Beside her, he nodded his head slightly, whispered, "Look."

But she was staring bug-eyed at him waiting for him to shoot her. He wasn't looking at her, he was staring out to the field. She turned to see what he was looking at.

The night was approaching fast, it was hard to see with no lights at all and a bare blur of orange sinking down the horizon. But then Dove saw some movement.

In the distance, but near enough to see, her heart fibrillated like she'd stuck her finger in a light socket.

A lion.

They were watching a lion lurking in the tall grass. A real, live, man-eating, flesh ripping, lion. She slapped her hand over her mouth to stifle her gasp.

Terrified to look at it, but compelled to, she saw it had something bloody in its mouth and was dragging it to a thick brush. Keeping her hand over her mouth, her belly blew in and out with her petrified breaths.

Beside her, his hand on her shoulder, Tezer stood motionless, the cocked shotgun in his hand.

Suddenly, another lion leaped out of nowhere.

Behind her hand, Dove sucked in a sharp intake of air.

The one cat dropped the prey and instantly the two ferocious felines started fighting, snarling ripping, roaring, clawing.

Her hand fell numb, Dove's mouth dropped open in a scream, Tezer clapped his hand over it.

They watched, silent, wide-eyed as one lion killed the other then took the original kill, some kind of bloody gazelle, and ran off with it disappearing into the brush.

Her system in overload, Tezer's assault, perplexed over her own feelings and her body's reaction to him, now, in the dead of the forest, she'd watched two kings of the jungle duke it out with flesh tearing claws and rapier teeth, until one was dead.

Dove struggled to catch her breath, fought the heaves that bubbled up her throat to puke, she pressed her hands over her fluttering stomach.

His hand still on her shoulder, Tezer said quietly, "That gazelle is you if you go out in the wild alone." His hand moved to the back of her neck, his fingers twined around it tilting her face up to his.

Her eyes quivered laden with fearful tears, her legs shook, she could barely feel her body it was all rubbery. How had she ended up in this vicious jungle, a prisoner of ruthless mercenaries?

She thought she had run from danger, escaped it. But now… Her diaphragm panting in fright, she leaned forward into his chest, put her face against his slabs of steel and buried her weeping fright into his jacket, inhaling the smoky leather.

Tezer slid his arm around her, holding her tightly against him and laid his head on the top of hers.

When her trembling dissipated some, he whispered, "We need to go. It's not safe to stay here."

Back at the jeep he helped her climb in. Good thing, her legs were like sponges, barely holding her up. They didn't speak on the way back.

Buckled in her seat, Dove tucked her hands between her legs to still their trembling.

As he parked and shut off the engine, she put her shaking fingers on the door handle.

Tezer set a hand on her arm and told her, "Wait. Wait for me, Dove, to come and get you. There are animals here too, you just can't see them."

Her face shone ashen in the rising moonlight. She pulled her hand back into her lap. Tezer got out with the shotgun, he'd already carefully checked the perimeter as he drove in and parked.

Opening her door, he unbuckled her seatbelt as she seemed incapable of stilling her quivering hands enough to do it herself.

He helped her out, then wrapped his hand around her shoulder tucking her in tight against his side. "Stay close to me, you're smaller, an animal will go for you first." He walked her back into the lodge.

Inside, as he closed the door, he said, "Now, go into dinner, I'll be there after I put the gun up."

She shook her head slightly. "I- I'm not hungry."

He cupped her jaw lifting her head up and told her, "You will do as I say. You're already too thin. Go and eat. I will be there in a minute."

They stared eyeball to eyeball, she blinked and he let her go. She turned from him and went to the dining room.

Moments later, when Tezer entered the dining room he saw her just sitting still and ashen, staring down at her plate. Giving her some space, he moved on and took a place further down by Garth and Leo.

Later, watching Tezer watching Dove, Leo said, "Why don't you fuck her already. It'll straighten her the fuck out and you're wound so tight you're about explode."

Chapter Thirteen

 $\mathcal{T}$ he next day after several hours of tromping through the willowy grass, laces on her hiking boots untied and flopping over her feet, Kitty scuttled up to traipse beside Tezer.

"Honey," her voice a low coo, "how much longer? When are we going to get to wherever it is that you are taking us? Or," she slid one finger down his arm. Surprising, all the hiking and roughing it, her manicure was still perfect.

While others played cards or board games, Kitty worked on her body, hair, nails. She said with a slight tease, "Are we in a twilight zone where we just keep walking and walking, never arriving at a destination?"

Turning his head slightly, his gaze traveled over the huge breasts, doubtful they were real, that poured out of the half unbuttoned, tight, khaki blouse.

His eyes continued down further to the slight pouch of her jiggling belly, and below that to the camel toe clearly displayed in the pants that were made of a weird silver metallic, like tinfoil incasing her long legs.

"Just another few days and we'll be there." He wanted to look behind him to ensure Dove was close by, but he

155

kept facing forward. "We are going to a real place. You all are to be guests of Mr. Braemont until he is satisfied you paid him back in some way for what you stole from him."

The big lips curved up in a sly smile, she batted her long fake eyelashes at him. "Well, I say good luck with that." Motioning behind them with her head, she asked, "What about Goldilocks there, what happens to her when we get to Braemont's?"

His lips firmed, Adam's apple bobbed with his deep swallow. "You need to move on back in the line, Miss Miot. I have to concentrate on the topography."

A pungent laugh bubbled from her slick red lips. "Ah, I hit a sore spot. So, are you just dumping her there and moving on? Is she like a gift for Braemont? You going to tie a red bow in your gift's hair?"

The vein at his temple beat at the same pace as his jaw worked. Through grit teeth he said, "Get back in line. Now."

Another laugh spilled out, "So, you dump her in his kinky hands, and believe me, I know from whence I speak, that leaves room for me."

Her fingernails stabbing into his arm, she said with a sneer, "Chief, Tezer, she is too…" she glanced over her shoulder sliding a denigrating look at Dove then turned back to Tezer. "Young, dainty, delicate like an easily smashed flower."

She skimmed her hand up his arm, moving closer to him. "I on the other hand, enjoy a …" her eyes skated down his hard chest to the front of his denims, "robust man." She purred, "I like it rough, honey, I can see it in that steel glint in your eyes that you do too."

Rubbing his brawny arm, she purred, "Aggressive, forceful, ah, I bet you're dominant and forceful in every…thing."

His eyes forward, unblinking, acid scouring his voice, he ordered, "Get back in the line, Miss Miot, I won't tell you again." Jaw tight, brows hard, he looked as chilling and dangerous as he sounded.

She slid her finger back down his arm, whispered, "See, honey, like I said, you like dominance. We'll talk more later." Scoffing a choleric glare at Dove walking behind Garth who was right behind Tezer, she strutted back down the line to join her sniping friends.

The day of hiking ended early, the group was thrilled to come in sight of the brick lodge they were to stay in for the night.

After dinner, the people broke up into their regular cliques. Kitty, Avril and Chelsee disappeared into the back room where they were sleeping to gossip.

Robin followed Brock around like a pesky flea to the point that he just tuned her out, looked right through her while the men broke up into teams for card games.

Tezer looked up from his cards to see Rey usher Dove out from the kitchen. Rey's hand on Dove's shoulder drew Tezer's attention, puncturing the distance between them with a knifing glare.

She didn't see it because she was saying something to Rey, but the Casanova caught the warning and smiled, smugly squeezed her shoulder, and bent slightly to dip his nose into her hair.

Brows daggered down and hard over the ridge of his forehead, Tezer's eyes almost disappeared beneath caustic hooded lids.

Rey brought her to Tezer who sat back, leaning against the chair staring at them, his face was blank but his eyes blazed. His hand wrapped around a bourbon, neat, his fourth.

Dove said quietly to Tezer, "I would like to take a shower and go to bed. I'm…" she smiled slightly, "I just want to go to bed."

Tezer raised his barbarous gaze to Rey and jerked his head.

Hugging her to him, Rey offered with a lewd grin, "I'll walk her to the women's quarters."

Everyone knew Dove was sleeping each night with Tezer, but she didn't seem happy about it and refused to discuss with anyone rude enough to ask if they were having sex.

People either believed they weren't because there was such animosity between them. Some said he raped her every night which was why she was so sad and angry.

When they talked about it, Kitty's mew a jealous wail, exclaimed that she would love it if Tezer raped her. That brought sarcastic laughter.

Brock had told her, "You can't rape a willing participant."

Such black wrath flamed from the chief's eyes to Rey, Rey felt it like he'd been zapped 1000 volts with a Taser. "Yeah," he mumbled to Dove, "see ya tomorrow, hon."

His arm still draped around her, Tezer's brows drew down further at it. Gingerly sliding his arm off Dove, Rey grinned weakly and left to join one of the card games.

His expression inscrutable, Tezer said to Dove, "Go ahead." She nodded and turned to go, he caught her wrist, she turned back.

He said, "My room." He watched her glance around to see if anyone heard him. It didn't matter, they would all know when her cot in the women's room stayed empty, as it had been.

"Use my shower," he said shortly. He'd already secured the window so she couldn't get out it.

"I'll, uh, get my toothbrush and um, shirt, and go there." She turned from him again, waiting to hear him stop her, but he said nothing, just stared at her walking out of the room.

Playing another hand, and tossing back a few more straight bourbons, he was distracted from his game waiting for her to come back and pass through the room to go to the hall to his bedroom, to shower naked in his bathroom, then climb into his bed, wearing his shirt.

The men joked and chatted around him as he finally watched her walk by under his lowered lids.

He hoped showing her the lions that she would give up trying to flee the group. He shook his head, but she was damned stubborn. She was determined to flee and jeopardize her life.

She couldn't comprehend there was nowhere for her to go out there. He played a few more hands then tossed his cards in.

"You done?" Nik asked him dealing the cards.

"Yeah." Tezer tromped out of the room unaware that his friends were grinning at his back.

There was a bet going on whether Tezer and the mysterious girl were ever going to really hook up. As surly as he was they were sure he wasn't getting any.

Tezer opened the door to his room.

Dove was sitting on the bed near the headboard, in front of the window looking out. Her entire back was bare, her legs curled to the side, her hair waved over one shoulder.

She held a sheet loosely in front of her. The single lamp by the bed made her appear an ethereal Madonna in the faint golden light, sad, and achingly lonely staring out the window into the sightless night.

Not expecting him for at least another hour or so, she was startled at the door opening.

Keeping her back to him and not veiling the aversion in her tone, she said, "What do you want?"

Chapter Fourteen

Tezer moved into the room, closing and locking the door behind him. His hand on his belt he said, "Since you asked, I'll tell you what I want."

His eyes swept down the nude length of her back and her side, the side of her breast was exposed.

Taking a step closer, he said, "My first choice is, you drop that sheet, lie down on the bed and spread your legs, and I will take you first viciously hard, violent, fast, then after we catch our breath, we'll do it again but this time slow, languorous, until you're begging me to let you come. After that we can improvise."

His lips pulled in wryly at the surprise, and fear flashing on her face as she turned to face him holding the sheet trying to cover her front.

He moved a step closer. "My second choice," he tugged at his belt buckle, "is you drop the sheet, come here, get on your knees, take me in your mouth and look up at me through those long lashes with those sweet eyes as you suck me off."

At her shocked expression, he rubbed his erection that was already a long, thick club in his jeans.

161

Whimpering softly, "Chief, please," shocked at his bold crass blatant sex talk, Dove gripped the sheet tightly in her fists.

He grunted, "Tezer," and trod closer to her, his eyes glittering with lust and warning, formidable, and unstoppable. Unrelenting.

As he moved to the bed, she backed up against the headboard trying to get away from him.

"Tell me, Dove, which is your choice? I'm up for either of them. We can start with you lying on your back and I'll show you what I can do with my tongue, make you come a few screaming times. Then, you're small, I'll need to stretch your pussy, and impale you with my fingers until you're good and wet, and ready for me."

A flame kindled in his dark eyes stroking down her body confirming his intent. "How many times do you think I can make you come before I bury myself inside you? I can't wait to start counting."

He leaned over and set a hand on the bed, and then a knee pushed down the mattress, and he reached for her. Chocolate brown hair growing out flopped over one searing dark eye, evening scrub made his face shadowed like that of a brigand.

Through the full, sculpted lips, his voice a rough purr, he said, "I'm big, you're petite, my little bird. We'll need a lot of time, ah, preparation, to make you ready to be able to take me…every inch of me, baby."

"No, stop," Dove whispered, putting her hand on his chest as if she could stop him.

His eyes dropped to her small hand on his powerful chest, feeling the heat radiate from it spreading in hot spokes throughout his body. His gaze moved to her slender arm that he could break in a heartbeat with his huge fists.

The side of his mouth twitched, brows arched. "Really, Dove? You think you can stop me from taking what I want?" Desire changed the harsh grin, soothing the hardness. The lines around his mouth yielded as his eyes glimmered with heat.

Tezer edged towards her, forcing her elbow to bend with his weight, until his breath warmed her face. His lips parted slightly in anticipation, as if about to claim hers.

The mattress sank and rocked with his onward movement. Like the lion stalking the gazelle, his male heat reached her before his body did. The muscles in his chest and arms flexed and hardened with every move he made, becoming an indomitable flesh and bone wall in front of her.

His kisses had made her wet before, he would kiss her now until she was delirious, hot and wet and wanting him.

But, her palpable fear of him washed over Tezer in distraught waves.

Pausing, his deep voice for once without tyranny or cruelness, he said softly, "Dove, give me a chance, you don't need to fear me. I swear I won't hurt you, I will only bring you pleasure. You know we are meant to be. I've resisted the insufferable temptation to touch you, bring you to share this explosive passion.

"I feel you are attracted to me, I can feel it, see it, when you look at me. Maybe you're not as entranced by me as I am with you; I want you so badly I can't think straight. But, the more we are together, the stronger your feelings will build."

Dove's hand still pressed on his chest, her cheeks blossomed with pink. Her gaze traveled his hard face, up to the dark burning eyes, down to those sensual lips, but she said nothing, didn't move.

His lashes lowered as he beheld her agitated eyes then the vulnerable mouth he wanted to kiss. "Although you've tried to hide it, avoid me, avoid making eye contact so you can't see my desire…and I can't see yours…" he sifted a thick finger, his male fingertip square and broad, down her leg.

Deep voice lowering, he said, "It's there. Let down your walls, baby, let me in. Tell me what you're hiding from, I can eliminate it. Whatever it, or who it is that frightens you so, it will be out of your life, out of existence, just tell me. I swear I can take it out."

After he fucked her a few times he could draw her in, make her want to stay with him even after the fucking mission was over. She would find out then that he has no intentions of letting her go. Never had.

"Chief," strident but soft, as if she hadn't heard what he just said, she said, "you can have your choice of any of the women out there. Why would you want to have someone who does not want you?"

A scowl shifted over the desire tendering his lips, darkening his face, but he still moved closer to her. He said gruffly, "*Tezer*, dammit Dove, not Chief. I don't want any other fucking woman, I want you."

So close now he could smell her fresh female scent that stirred his groin, hardening it further, see the sheen of her fair hair in the faint light.

"I've treated you roughly because I've tried to keep my distance, keep from doing exactly this, what I've wanted to do since those goldy-green eyes ensnared me the day I took you."

Though unable to hold him back, her hand stayed on his chest. "No, I see, I get it," she said with self-disparagement. "You've had them all and you only want me as the last conquest of your little mission?"

His face stiffened with anger. Voice a deep growl, his words slow, barely audible, he sneered, "Are you calling me a man-whore, little bird?"

She continued to ineffectively push at his chest but he leaned into her, bringing his angry hard face so close he could see her pupils flash, feel her shallow breaths on his mouth.

"You think I just fuck any female that walks in front of me? That's your opinion of me, Dove, that I nail every woman within sight?" He shoved his hand into her hair and gripped it in his fist, forcing her head up to his and grabbed the front of the sheet as if about to rip it off her.

"That I don't have respect for my own body, or what I say to you about how badly I want you and only you is false? That I lie?"

Streaks of white heat, from anger and lust sparked in his eyes so brilliant and close to hers, Dove was sure he had seared her own orbs. So close she could see each individual black lash surrounding the fierce dark eyes, lashes too long for a man, especially an iron-tough one like him.

He smelled faintly of liquor and smoky cigarettes, imbued with his subtle yet dominant masculine scent. Other than his fist in her hair, without physically touching her it still felt as if his sinewy body enveloped her like that jaguar he reminded her of.

Stalking through the thick jungle about to pounce on her, take her down. He held her head almost immobile, tilted up and back, forcing her to gaze straight into his wrath.

"Chief," she glanced down at those chiseled sensual lips and back to his frightening glare. Biting back her fear, she said with bitter apathy, "You're a man. Men have no feelings but what is between their legs and where they can put it."

"*Tezer,* goddammit," he cursed, knowing she deliberately called him Chief to keep them impersonal. *Well, fuck that.* The lines in his stern face hardened, an irritated gleam skewered her through furrowed slits.

"We'll see how demeaning you are when I am plunging between your willowy white thighs, honey." He lowered his head, his lips seeking hers, to seize her mouth in a wrathful, lustful, hungry kiss as his hand gripped the sheet more tightly and he started to pull it away.

The words flooded out with her cry, "You are a brute, a crude horrible brute that's holding me prisoner!"

His dark whisper, she could feel on her skin, "Yeah, I am. Let me prove it to you right now, little Dove." His mouth almost upon hers, long lashes hiding his eyes.

She turned her head with a choked sob, "Please, I can't take being raped again!"

He froze. "What?" His sharply hewn face scrunched with confusion and anger. "What the hell are you talking about?"

Her head down, she didn't reply.

Pulling her head back up with her hair still wrapped around his fist, he roared, "Answer me! Did someone here touch you? Hurt you? I will fucking kill them!"

She turned her back to his fury, but he still held her hair. With her hair held up, the loose sheet draped down revealing a tattoo low on her shoulder, letters that marked her ivory skin.

His eyes popped, he felt his stomach drop like a sickening lead brick. Grasping her shoulders he turned her completely around revealing her entire back.

His shocked exhale blew tendrils of loose blonde hair over her shoulders. He held a hand up, his palm an inch from her back, wanting to touch her because he couldn't believe what he was seeing.

Her back was crisscrossed with fading marks he hadn't seen from across the room. Now he ran a gentle, light palm down her back over the almost healed slashes.

She winced as if they still hurt. His hand on her back, his other on her shoulder, he gently turned her to face him.

"What the hell? Who did this?" he demanded.

Her head still down, tears fell, she mutely shook her head.

He clutched both her shoulders about to shake her, then stopped. Squeezing them gently instead, stilling the roar that crashed through his skull, he forced himself to ask quietly, "Dove, tell me, who the fuck did this to you? I will tear them to pieces."

Eyes bursting at him with shame and terror, she cried, "My name is not Dove! It is why I am running and hiding. Now, please- leave me alone." She glared at him through flowing tears. "You're a hypocrite you were about to do the same thing to me."

His head shook slowly in his shock. He said with gentle sincerity, "No, Dove, never. I may push you to break down your walls, but I would never force you. I would never strike you. Never."

She dropped her head in her hands and wept.

Stunned, shocked, Tezer didn't know what to do. He gathered her against his chest, his hand cradling her head.

Stroking her hair, his lips against her fragrant locks, he murmured, "Tell me, Dove, tell me who did this to you. I will avenge you, I swear on my honor, I will remove him from this earth."

She pulled from him, her hands covering her eyes. "Please, I'm begging you, just leave me."

"The tattoo, he did it, didn't he? His initials? Like branding ownership?"

"God, please, Tezer, leave me alone."

He couldn't move. Aghast at someone whipping her, branding her, after he…brutalized her. Tezer just stared at the young woman that was in such despair.

His stomach churning, voice filled with anguish for her pain he said softly, "Dove, baby, let me help you."

She kept her back to him. "Please," she wept wearily, "leave me alone."

Sighing with the rage of his impotence to make her trust him, to punish the man that did this to her, he said quietly, "When we get to Braemont's I have to stay until he is satisfied he's gotten his quarter out of the people.

His voice almost quivered with anguish and rage over her pain, what she'd suffered. "Then I'll take you some place safe. I planned to anyway from the beginning, but I want you to be thinking about it now. Knowing I will take care of you."

"Tezer-"

"And the fucking monster that did that to you."

She kept her back to him, her shoulders shaking with her weeping. Voice catching, she murmured faintly, "Please, leave me alone."

His gut ached, but he did as she asked.

Standing outside the closed door of his bedroom, he leaned weakly against the wall, listening to her faint sobs, feeling like a knife twisted in his gut.

He finally accepted, knew all along that she meant so much more to him than the sex he craved with her, and more than just feeling protective of her. He needed to be inside holding her, comforting her, getting out of her who the hell did that to her. Making her feel safe.

Dragging a sleeve over his face, he forced himself to tread down the hall, one heavy step in front of the other. In a daze he headed for the study.

Garth and Leo were there on their laptops.

"Hey," Garth said not looking up, "the way you swaggered out of here with all that booze in you we figured this was the night. The night that you and Dove-"

Tezer plunked down in a chair. The appalled incredulity etched lines in his agonized face.

His eyes narrowed on his friend, Leo said, "What's wrong, Tez?"

That got Garth's attention.

The two men looked at Tezer. They'd never seen him so...upset.

Nothing ever broke that icy veneer of his.

Nothing.

Chapter Fifteen

He didn't want to, but Tezer waited until very late knowing she'd be asleep before he returned, and then rose the next day before she awakened.

In the morning, Dove acted as if nothing had happened, except she never quite looked him in the eyes.

He observed her throughout the early morning, washing clothes, helping prepare breakfast and clean up after. Tezer figured she always did it to avoid the rest of the group, and him.

She tried to stay clear of the women, they were mean and cutting to her, and the men wanted to touch her, fuck her. Him included.

His gaze fell on Kitty holding court in the living room. Although she'd slept with most of the men, except his close team, the other guys still clustered around her.

Undoubtedly due to the blouse she had more open than not, her thin tights like a second skin, outlined her every curve, including the ones between her legs. He looked away in disgust.

The woman had no shame, displaying every private part of her to all the men that should only be between a woman and her lover. He snorted a short laugh, yeah, except Kitty had a lot of lovers.

She'd brazenly, wantonly chased after him the second they started on their journey. His shutting her down, rejecting her was probably why the girls treated Dove so badly.

Not only was he forcing Dove to sleep in his room, his attention seldom left her whenever she was present. And when she wasn't, she was on his mind. Wondering who she was, why she was running, did she desire any of the men in the trek?

He'd felt her response to his kiss, and he could tell she looked at Tezer differently that the others. He laughed to himself, yeah, that was because he was so cold and cruel to them all, and a molesting bully to her.

He told the people this morning at breakfast that this would be their last day in the jungle.

Tezer was on his way to get his gear packed when he stuffed his hands in his pockets and pulled out the necklace Essie Cook had given him to give to Dove. Huh, sturdy little thing it survived several washings. He stuffed it back in his pocket.

After getting his gear packed up, he announced to the others that in an hour they would be leaving the lodge and should arrive at Braemont's estate in less than three hours.

Everyone fluttered away, excited and apprehensive, to pack up their stuff.

The room empty, Tezer wandered over and sat down in a chair to enjoy the quiet. His eyes flickered as Dove entered the room.

She hesitated when she saw there was only him present. Her gaze darted back the way she'd come.

"Don't leave, Dove. Come over here and sit down." He pointed to the sofa cater-corner to his chair.

Her head twitched to the doorway then back to him.

He sat at ease, his hands resting on the arms of the cushioned chair, legs relaxed, he even gave her a crooked smile.

Wariness of him made her steps slow, but she trod over to him. As she was about to sit, he reached into his pocket and she paused.

"Here," he said softly, "I have something for you." He pulled the chain out and dangled it so she could see what it was. "Mrs. Cook gave this to me to give to you the day she left." A bit sheepish he grinned. "I, uh, kinda forgot about it."

Her eyes rolled a flash of golden green. "Men," she snorted. "You guys have memories the size of peas." She held out her hand.

He pulled his hand back slightly, one brow in an arc over a twinkling dark eye. "Oh yeah? And this is from one of the female sect that goes all wacky hormonal every month."

At his grin at her pursed lips she suddenly snaked her hand out to grab the necklace from him.

Laughing at her efforts, he tucked it quickly in his palm, the mischievous grin a highly unusual expression to see on his rugged face. Then teasing her, he dangled it in front of her again.

A smile tugging at the corner of her petal lips, she said, "Well, I think-" then reached out to snatch the necklace-but with the clap of a triumphant laugh he closed his fist and pulled it back to his chest so fast she almost fell on top of him.

She had to throw her hand out on his thigh to break her fall, then the other hand fell on his other leg to keep her balance.

Both hands on his thighs and bent over, she was almost on her stomach in his lap.

He flipped the chain like a pendulum back and forth in front of her. "Ah, I like this position. You have my permission to stay in it if you desire."

Grinning at her consternation, his eyes dipped to the collar of her blouse that dropped exposed cleavage, then twinkled back up at her.

"Huh." With a grunt she pushed to her feet. "I'm done. I refuse to play childish games."

Before he could respond she started walking past the chair, just as she was next to him, she reached out to snatch the necklace but with a burst of laughter he held it out of her reach.

"Oh, you…" she growled at him. "That's it. I'm done, you are so juvenile." Her nose in the air she stomped past him and a few steps behind the chair.

Then with rapid tiptoes she rushed back, leaned over the back of his chair and flung her hand over his shoulder to grab the necklace.

Like lightening, he caught her arm and pulled her over his shoulder, clinching his other hand on her side he pulled her down to his lap with her squeal of surprise.

With a hoot, he blurted, "I've battled men with experienced sleuthing skills honey, you amateurs haven't got a chance."

"Hey!" she squawked, landing across his lap on her back with a flourish, arms and legs in the air. "That's cheating!"

"Oh yeah? All's fair in war and teasing. This is what happens to people who get caught," he tickled her until peals of screaming laughter gushed out of her mouth.

She twisted and rolled, giggling and squealing lying on her back across his legs, trying to catch his hands to make him stop.

Out of breath she finally yelled, "Okay! Okay! I give up!" still giggling at his fingers tickling her sides, scrunching her neck when he tickled it and behind her ears.

"Yeah?" he chuckled, continuing to wriggle his fingers around her body. "You surrender? Say Tezer wins!"

"I will not- eee-" His fingers were all over her sides and belly until gasping and laughing she cried, "Okay! I surrender, you win!"

He stopped torturing her and pulled her up to sit on his lap.

"Wait!" she warned trying to slip off his legs. "I'm too heavy. I'll squash you, *oo-*"

He stood up, one hand spread under her back the other under her legs, he raised her over his head laughing at her shriek. "I can certainly bench a measly 100 pounds of soft and squirmy."

"Put me down!" She giggled between shrieks.

He lowered her to cradle in his arms. Her face tilted up to his, his mouth inches away from her lips, he almost kissed her. Then he sat down with her on his lap.

Grinning broadly, he held out the necklace.

Smiling suspiciously, she looked down at it then up at him to see the rare gleeful playfulness in his dark eyes. Even the sharp planes in his face were less severe.

"Here, let me put it on you."

Eyeing him warily, she turned slightly and lifted her hair. "Can I trust you?"

"Huh-" his snort of pretend hurt feelings. Then he said solemnly, "Of course you can, little Dove. Always." Slipping the chain around her neck, he closed the clasp then lifted the metal to lie neatly on her breastbone.

She dropped her hair. They both looked down at it. Touching it lightly, Dove said a little wistfully, "It's beautiful. I hope she's okay. I told her I would keep in touch because she can't call me-" she broke off, lips drooping sadly.

"Hey," Tezer said, lifting her chin. "How about when we get to Braemont's you call her to see how she's doing? She should be out of the hospital and home by then. Leo called yesterday to check her progress. She's doing fine."

Her sad eyes flit up to him, the sadness turning to hope. "You think we can call her?"

He nodded, still holding her chin, his other hand slid down from behind her neck to gently clutch her upper arm. Their faces were bare inches apart.

His voice low and quiet, he said, "I promise, honey." Their eyes connected, she didn't look away. His drifted down to her plump lips, then back up to her eyes, the green had shimmered into sheer gold.

Tilting his head, his gaze dropped to her lips again and he covered them with his. Softly he kissed her, gently nudging her lips apart to push his tongue inside. And he was surprised, pleasantly, when she responded, tentatively stroking his tongue with hers.

His hand moved from her chin to cup the side of her face, the other to her back to bring her closer as the kiss deepened. When he felt her hands skim up his chest to wind around his neck, he slit his eyes to look at her, to make sure it was what she wanted too, that she wasn't feeling forced.

175

Her eyes were closed. Satisfied, closing his, he encased Dove further into his embrace, savoring the exotic taste of her, inhaling her exclusive woman's fresh scent.

The more he tasted, lapped, the more of her he wanted. Her soft curves pressing all over his slabs of muscles created sparks of fiery adrenalin that shot to his manhood, making it train engine hard and roaring to take her.

His brain swirling in erotic euphoria Tezer could think of nothing but being inside her. The kiss unleashed any restraint he had left. His fervor increased, burned, devouring her more intensely. He had to have this woman.

Splaying his hand tight on her back, he slipped his thumb in the corner of her mouth to touch her lips, her tongue, while he kissed her. A tiny moan oozed from Dove surprising them both.

Dizzy with a consuming flush that ricocheted through her body and into her head, deafening her, Dove melted into him. Her breasts wantonly pressed against solid rock pecs, arms like flexing iron held her breathtakingly close, solid hands caressed her back with rampant strokes.

His relentless mouth extracted everything from her, her walls, her fear, her secrets, leaving a racing wildfire between her legs that swelled her breasts, caught in her throat and scorched her brain.

Tezer drew back slightly to see her face.

Scant inches apart, they were mirror images of flushed skin, parted lips damp and swollen. Dazed eyes roamed each other's heavy lidded, passion filled orbs, rapid shallow inhales from panting chests.

He licked his lips, he had to have her. All of her. Now. Right now. Murmuring, "Ah, Dove," Tezer pulled her back and captured those ravening plush lips-

"Geez, get a room," Garth dripped sarcasm laconically from the doorway.

Tezer ignored him, but Dove pushed at his chest pulling her mouth from his.

"*Damn*," Tezer groaned with a rough exhale. Cuddling her against him even as she struggled to get up, he glanced over her head at his friend. "Don't you have something to do? Pack? Take a walk?"

Dove broke from his embrace and scrambled off his lap. A blushing smile at Garth, she mumbled, "I uh, have to, see if I left anything, uh, behind," and without a backward look at Tezer she hurried off to the women's room.

Which showed how frazzled she was. She had very little and what she did have was in his room.

"Hey, thanks a fucking lot, bro," Tezer snarled at his friend, stretching to sit up straight in his chair. He tugged his shirt down and pushed at his pants to give his bulging erection more room.

A big grin crimping his face, Garth chuckled, "Yeah, well, be glad it was me and not one of those other assholes. They already treat her bad enough." He strolled into the room.

Combing his fingers through his lengthening hair, scowling up at him, Tezer groused, "Nice timing. I'll never get her back all soft and hot like that again."

Leaning a hip against a table, Garth crossed his arms, still grinning at his friend's flushed, stringently angled face, mussed hair and obvious hard-on.

Recalling Dove's pink face and lips plumped and red from his kisses, he said, "You're not giving yourself enough credit bro. Believe me, she was all into you. But she is the kind that needs patience and softness, you are too tough with her. She is not one of those strong brassy liaisons you normally pick up that don't mind being cursed at and treated coldly and crudely like shit. Man, Tez, she's the long-term relationship kind."

Leaning forward still raking at his hair and tugging at his pants, Tezer growled, "I know." He looked up at Garth through a swath of dark hair that needed cutting. "You find anything on her?"

Shaking his head, Garth replied, "There's nothing to look for. I checked missing persons in this country, but she might be from anywhere. With her accent, we already figured she wasn't from here. But, without a name there is very little to run a search on."

Rubbing his eyes, Tezer sat back and said, "I know. But I've been thinking. I think she's running from…" His mouth twisted, eyes eclipsed sheathing his temper. "I think it's a man. A guy," he scraped in a breath, sighed it out. "I think a man hurt her. Abused her. She, uh," he glanced around to make sure they were alone, his skin paled, "she was, uh, whipped."

His eyes widened, Garth made a sound of disbelief.

Tezer lowered his voice, "I think she was held prisoner…and tortured. The bastard," he dragged his hand through his hair shoving the long front back out of his eyes. "I think after he, ah, assaulted her, he like branded her. Tattooed his initials or some shit on her."

Garth's mouth dropped. "Bloody-motherfucking-God, Tez, what the fuck?"

Nodding, Tezer set his hands on his thighs. "Yeah. She won't tell me. It explains why death at my hands or the jungle's doesn't scare her. It doesn't measure up to prolonged rape and torture."

He stood up. "We'll be heading out in an hour. I want you to take that time and do another run on her. Check the underground, dark web shit. Look for stuff like, oh, bounty hunter kinds of bulletins, the personal kind, offering rewards for discreet information. With her unique beauty and the...tattoo, it might be enough to pull something in."

Scrubbing his fingers down his face, his voice sour, Tezer said, "Chances are, the way she looks, the fucker will be looking for her, wanting her back."

Making notes on his phone, Garth nodded.

His hands on his hips, head lowered, Tezer glanced up at Garth. "And he's got to be raging mad that she got away from him, and, will take it out on her if he catches her."

Garth stared at him speechless, trying to digest what he'd just said. Then he choked out, "I bet there's a reward for her capture and return. That's why she wouldn't tell us her name. God, Tez..."

"We need to find him first."

Garth's mouth a sick curl, through clenched teeth he said, "We find him, Tez, we're taking him out."

Tezer nodded, that was a given. But first, he needed to figure out how to keep Dove out of Braemont's clutches.

He wouldn't have told Braemont at all about her but one of the other men had called him and told him about her the second that'd taken the group over when they got off the bus.

It was without question that Tezer would never have left her, a lone woman, there at the closed ancient station in the perilous forest, in the middle of nowhere.

Even if she was not a young, stunning female he'd instantly fallen head over teakettle for the second his eyes lit on her. He would leave no defenseless woman alone in the Russian wilderness, regardless of the secrets she was hiding or any agenda she'd planned. Now he realized her only agenda was staying alive and out of the grasp of the fiend that sought her.

When they reached Braemont's, at first he had thought he could secrete her at the huge estate until he completed his mission and then could get her out.

But, Braemont not only knew about her, but was dying to see her. And, if he had half the testosterone that Tezer had, he'd want her, and would undoubtedly plot to keep her.

Just like Tezer was.

Chapter Sixteen

Although they were coming to pay the piper, the group was glad to be in sight of Braemont's estate. They were all bone weary of traipsing through forests and jungles and fields and mountains.

The estate's external perimeter was surrounded and concealed by thick barely penetrable woods. Virtually impossible to get there by vehicle, even ATV's, access was by helicopter only.

Half a dozen copters were on the grounds in hangers. Once they passed through the dense flock of trees and scrub, they could see the estate standing out in the open surrounded by just enough clearing for the copters to land.

The main section of the stone and brick building was three stories, with four equal sized wings like solid limbs spreading out in all directions.

Numerous other structures, garages, stables, barns, etc. were scattered throughout inside the perimeter grounds.

The center door opened and a handful of servants sprinkled out down the steps and across the lawn heading for the group. Tezer had called ahead when they were nearing the house.

Nervous, excited twitters from the women were steep contrast to the low, stilted conversation of the male passengers.

Tezer's men ushered the people to merge with the servants so they could be brought inside and taken to where they would be staying.

The chief breathed a sigh of relief seeing the last passenger disappear into the mansion. He had his arm around Dove and they were flanked by Garth and Leo.

Under his arm he could feel the rigidity in her shoulders as unyielding as wrought iron. She wasn't shaking, yet.

Quietly he said to her, "We need to head on inside." Starting to walk, he stopped when her feet didn't move. He nodded to Garth and Leo to go on ahead, then he faced her.

Blocking her view of the mansion with his strapping broad shoulders, his fingers itched to touch her, he resisted.

Remembering Garth's words of not being so tough with her, he forced the tension out of his hard lips. Consciously making his mouth firm but gentle he said, "Dove, honey, we need to go inside."

"No, Tezer." All big eyes, like golden sea moons, she was the picture of dread. Shaking her head, she pushed the yellow hair off her shoulders. "If I go in there, someone will…tell, please, he'll…find me." Her hands clasped in front of her like prayer.

"Dove-"

"He…they will come and take me, please, don't make me." Tears lurked but she sniffed them back.

Feeling like an overpowering brute, he took one of her hands and threaded their fingers together. "I won't let that happen. You need, must, trust me, Dove."

Ernest strength emanated from his dark spheres fringed with long dark lashes, lingered over her lovely face.

She stared at him for a long time. Taking in the sincerity in his bold eyes and the power that fairly exuded from his entire body, his bangs so long they kept flopping over his eyes softening the harshness of his severe face, making him look endearingly boyish.

He lifted their hands and kissed the back of hers, his cleaving gaze promised her with his words, "Trust me, baby."

"Tezer, I can't." She tugged at her hand but he held it.

Working to keep his voice calm and gentle, he said, "I will not leave you out here. It would be certain death. Take your chances inside. With me."

He wanted her to make her own decision, but, if she made the wrong one she'd be over his shoulder and he did not want her to suffer that humiliation.

Her sigh drained through her entire body, turning everything to rubber. When he started walking still holding her hand, she went with him.

He brought her up the stone steps to the wide stone porch and inside the mansion.

The outside of the mansion was strong and formidable like Tezer.

Inside was like a rich and glamorous show.

Gilded paintings and gold-leaf designs covered the beige walls, fireplaces of onyx and gold warmed in the frigid weather. Dark orange and peach striped floor to ceiling drapes matched the thick rugs.

Antique white furniture looked chic but sturdy enough for a big man to lounge comfortably. Ornate chandeliers draped through every room.

A servant met Tezer and Dove, she bowed with a strict face as she said, "Please come with me. Mr. Braemont awaits you in the lounge."

Following the maid, Tezer set his hand on Dove's nape, she was stiff as a board, legs like fence posts.

Traveling through the grand foyer, open and bright with gleaming paneled floors, partially covered with Indian rugs, they passed an ivory staircase curving up the middle of the room with black, graceful wiry curlicue iron railings.

Continuing on, they passed under immense arches and down several wide corridors.

Dove already knew she'd never find her way back out.

The maid turned into a room and just at the threshold she stepped aside. She said coolly, "Sir." As soon as Tezer and Dove entered, she slipped silently away.

"Corseque," a man in a suit that boasted an expensive weave greeted Tezer with a drink in his hand. He was in conversation with Garth, Leo, Nik and Reggie who had been ushered to the room while Tezer was outside trying to convince Dove to enter the mansion.

The man ended his dialog with Tezer's men then unhurriedly approached the couple.

Yvetsky Braemont spared Tezer a brief nod and slight smile before turning his attention to Dove. His bearing, expression, exhibited polite disinterest.

Barely concealing a gasp, Dove was taken aback, as was everyone when first experiencing Braemont's phenomenal eyes.

His freaky yet stunning irises resembled the aurora borealis, the northern lights. Waving bands of blues and violets flowed and glowed like the natives described as dancing spirits of the dead.

When they zeroed in on Dove, the pupils ballooned, almost entirely encompassing his solar eyes.

As if feeling the metamorphosis, Braemont lowered his lids until only a strip of the enigmatic colors sifted out.

Tezer had met Braemont several times through other acquaintances, in restaurants, bars, parties, even some here at the estate, and he had seen the man brazenly seduce women with just a fleeting look of those spellbinding eyes. That and his wealth.

Tezer kept his hand on Dove's nape. He could feel her skin warm, whether it was due to anxiety or attraction to Braemont, he didn't know. He'd prefer it was neither, he'd prefer it was her enthralling reaction to his hand on her body.

It would be difficult to compete with the handsome, wealthy man with the unusual, yet alluring eyes. Braemont kept his streak of cruel sensuous predilections under wraps. If his true depravity showed on his face no woman would come within a hundred miles of him.

"You made it and with only one casualty." Braemont shook Tezer's hand.

At Tezer's raised brow, he replied, "The old lady, Essie Cook. However," his slick smile diffident, he said, "you made good on her debt, so I suppose that will be satisfactory. Of course you won't earn the pay for her."

His brow ticked up, but Tezer made no comment. He felt Dove's surprised look at him, she hadn't known he had paid Essie's debt. Hell, he was rapidly losing his tough guy image.

Dark auburn hair perfectly coiffed gleamed under the bright lights, the glossy locks combed straight back. Braemont parted his perfect lips in a semi-smile exposing brilliant white teeth, more so against the bronze tan of his skin.

Devastatingly handsome with a strong chin and bold yet not large nose, thick wavy hair, those extraordinary eyes, he had the build of a man who worked out strenuously.

Braemont was almost as tall as Tezer, his chest defined but not as muscular and cut as Tezer's. And although Braemont was trim, Tezer's hips were lean, sinewy, from running up mountains, climbing trees, swimming rapid rivers, and leaping over bogs of quicksand.

Braemont probably had 12 or 13 years on Tezer making him around 40.

"Corseque," his voice cultured with a slight accent, his eyes never leaving Dove, Braemont said, "you have not introduced me to your...*my*, guest."

Clearing his throat, Tezer said coolly, "Dove, this is my employer for this mission, Yvetsky Braemont."

Braemont's smile widened, he raised his lids so the unusual eyes gleamed at her and he held his hand out. "Please, um, Dove, you may call me Yves, you know," he purred like a hungry lion, "like the eve of twilight."

Dove didn't move, or smile. Her gaze dropped to his proffered hand then rose to his polite tanned face.

Tezer's fingers tightened, curling half on her shoulder and half on her neck.

Lowering his hand, the smile of a shark's, Braemont said to Tezer but looked at her, "I don't recall you mentioning that she is deaf, or cannot speak." His gaze boldly scrolled up and down her body, his pupils sparking like flare guns shooting into the night.

"Braemont-" Tezer started but Dove cut him off.

"I have nothing to say to you, sir. You ordered, paid, Mr. Corseque to bring me here against my will. You had no right." Piercing him with arrogance and anger, she said, "And I will be leaving immediately."

Silence.

Then, Braemont's short laugh roared out, he grinned at Tezer then said to Dove, "Oh, you do have a biting tongue, my dear."

Leaving the implication on his face what he'd like her to do with that tongue, he said, "Come, you cannot run right off when we've only just met. You must be weary, would like a rest, a bath, dinner."

He waved at the maid who had reappeared in the doorway. His gaze left Dove for only a second then returned. The full force of his blazing desire rawly visceral, like he wanted to climb right into her skin with her.

Her stomach lurched with his blatant creepy interest. "No, I said I will be leaving." Dove went to move to the door but Tezer's grip held her. Under her breath she seethed her endless refrain since she'd met him, "Let go of me."

Behind them, the rest of Tezer's team was led out by another servant. They all shot both Tezer and Dove commiserating looks.

Aware Braemont was watching their exchange with great interest, Tezer murmured, "We've discussed this. You will stay here until my mission is done then-"

Braemont cut Tezer off, "Come along, dear, don't be difficult. You are well aware that Mr. Corseque will prevent you from leaving the estate. So, do yourself a favor, relax, accept my hospitality. We will discuss your leaving after you have all rested and eaten. All right?"

His auburn brows arched with a friendly smile. Not waiting for her to respond, he continued on, "Now, Miss Mandrake will show you to your room where you can freshen up." He held his arm out indicating the maid with the strict face and tight brown bun twisted on top of her head who had reappeared.

Tezer moved Dove slightly behind him. "Ah, sorry to upset the donkey cart, Braemont, but Dove stays with me."

Braemont's body was bayonet sharp, rigid, dangerous. He finally moved his gaze from his relentless perusal of Dove and settled his solar eyes on Tezer. "Corseque-"

Tezer's response was chilled, neat and clipped, "It's not debatable." The two men held an unblinking, unwavering, visual exchange.

Braemont would have to garner his people to fight Tezer and his men if he wanted to separate him and Dove.

Braemont hired Tezer for this mission due to his reputation for fierce, inexorable combat and success of other missions. To try to fight him without more resources might not bode well. Braemont relented.

Hiding his irritation and ire for both Tezer's insolence as well as not having Dove ensconced alone where he could get to her, Braemont plastered his polite, friendly smile on his handsome face. "Of course. As you wish. Miss Mandrake will show you to *your* room."

Tezer didn't smile, or make any kind of response. Under his hand Dove was just as rigid as before. He dropped his hand to her waist, turning her to follow the maid.

"Corseque," Braemont drawled, waited for Tezer to look at him. When he did, Braemont said, "We will discuss, *this*," indicating Dove, "later."

Not responding to his employer, his expression stoic, Tezer guided Dove out of the room to follow the maid.

She led them back down wide halls of beige and dark orange carpeting and picture lined walls.

They came to a broad curved staircase that they climbed to the second floor. Heading to a wing of rooms to the right, the maid passed numerous doors before stopping at one.

She opened it and stepped aside for the couple to enter. It was luxurious as was everything in the mansion, but more on the masculine side with heavy furniture, dark carpets and brocaded, antique white drapes.

Miss Mandrake said, "Sir, can you find your way to your friends' rooms or shall I wait for you to take you there? They advised me that once you were settled they would desire to meet with you." Her pale face with jutting cheekbones and thin lips held no expression, as if she was a robot.

"I know where they are, thank you. You can leave." Tezer closed the door before she even stepped away.

Dove moved to the window. The window overlooked the back of the mansion's gardens and lawn covered with the early tawny winter grass.

Tezer trod over to stand beside her. Knowing she would not be communicating with him first, he touched her arm to turn her to face him.

"Dove, I will get you safely out of here. Just," he dragged his fingers through his hair. "Trust me. Don't fight me. Whatever I say, just…follow my lead. You want to argue, wait until we are in private."

"Why am I to stay with you and not have my own privacy?" She looked up at him with slight irritation.

He stuffed his hands in his jean's pockets and hunched his big shoulders. He looked at her then let his gaze fall to the floor before sighing heavily and looking back up at her.

"Ah, I'm afraid you won't be safe alone. Braemont wants you. Bad. I can't protect you when you're down some wing, at the end of some infinite long hall."

Brows low over her concerned eyes, mouth tight, she asked, "Why did you bring me here if you fear him...uh, doing something to me?"

Pulling his hands out of his pockets he crossed his arms. Under the jacket his biceps bulged. Shaking his head he rolled his eyes wryly and replied, "I am not going to have this fucking fight with you every fucking minute."

Her eyes popped at his cursing and harsh voice. His dark brows were angry sabers over flashing dark eyes.

She looked away, towards the window but he cupped her jaw and turned her to face him.

"For the last time, you would fucking die out there. I will not let you out that door alone. Between the treacherous wilderness and the fucker who hurt you, and is as you, and I fear, looking for you, you won't stand a chance. I have to stay and complete this mission, then," he let out an aggravated exhale, "as I promised you, I will take you some place safe until I can eliminate your threat."

Softly, she asked, "And, who will protect me from you?"

His dark eyes about blasted her with fury at her words. He released her and crossed his arms, dropping his furious gaze to the floor. What she said was true. It was already a losing battle to keep himself off her.

When he didn't respond she turned back to look out the window.

Her tone snarky, she commented, "Maybe you need to go get your money, you know, that you earned for bringing me, and the others here. You know, like a pimp."

The air leaving his lungs was like crushed rocks. His voice tight with severe aggravation, he said, "I was hired to bring those people here. It's not normally the type of work I, my team does. However, Braemont is a friend of a friend who asked me to do it due to the extreme perilous territory leading to here. And protecting them from the other dangerous hunters that were after them.

"Braemont is paying some steep cake for these people, therefore every mercenary and bounty hunter in the world was looking for them. Dove," his lips bunched, he swiped a hand over his jaw.

"They are felons, every one of them. Except maybe Essie Cook, but even she had robbed him. Those passengers would have been arrested or captured eventually by either the law, or, the unlawful."

A deep exhale burned his lungs, his chest inflated with a jagged breath as he worked to stay calm. "I did not, and am not accepting payment for you." He snatched up her arm but she jerked it from his grasp.

The anger coloring his face, furrowed his brow, brought his deep voice low. "You need to stop with the injured attitude, Dove. I don't want to hear that crap, that word pimp come out of your mouth again. Don't test me.

"If I was a pimp I would have fucked you the first night I took you. And every night since." A sneaky hint of a leer heated his eyes that rolled down her body. "And the days, too. And," he narrowed his eyes at her, "I would have left you alone in that room with Braemont."

Covering her gasp with her mouth, she quickly looked away from him.

Staring furiously at her profile, Tezer watched her throat bob as she swallowed nervously.

"I need to go meet with my team. Do not leave this room. There are men, people, all over this place. No one will be out for your good. They are all loyal to Braemont. Lock the door until I return. Don't answer it to anyone but me."

She didn't respond.

"Dove," the irritation was back in his voice. He slid his hand around the back of her neck and pulled her to face him.

The golden green was dark, tumultuous with her tension.

Tezer lowered his voice, shook the anger out of it so it was calm, quiet. "Please do as I ask." The plump lips stayed closed. Sighing again, he bent and set his lips lightly on hers.

He felt her stiffen in his hand, but she didn't pull away. He bent his head and kissed her without aggression but still hard, with aching want and hunger. When her lips parted under his onslaught, he gently thrust his tongue inside to mate, to meet hers.

Already his body heated, his pants tightened. He pulled back while he still could. Her lids covered her eyes, lips dewy and still slightly parted. He couldn't read her, and that drove him crazy.

"Uh, all right. I'll be back. Stay here." He bent and gave her a swift kiss then left quickly or he would be all over her.

Tezer easily found where Garth, Leo, Reggie and Nik were lodged. He'd been in the mansion a few times and had made it his job to study the outlay and know where every room, nook and cranny was.

He met briefly with them, shocking them with his idea regarding Dove. Then he left so everyone could shower and rest before dinner.

Chapter Seventeen

After a long shower, Dove dressed in Tezer's shirt and boxer shorts.

She was drying her hair when a knock on the door made her pause in mid-brush. Assuming it was a maid, forgetting Tezer's order to not open the door to anyone but him, she opened the door. And frowned.

Kitty was standing there, wearing a coat. She held the sides of the coat wide open revealing she was totally naked underneath it. She looked as surprised to see Dove as Dove was to see her.

But she quickly gathered her wits and closed the coat. Her tone nasty, she snipped, "The chief told me to meet him here. Why are you here?"

Dove was still in shock at seeing Kitty's zaftig body displayed like a Renoir nude painting. Her mouth hung open, no words tumbled out.

Rolling her lined hazel cats' eyes, snapping the coat shut, Kitty said with a haughty sneer, "Where is he? Is he here? They told me this was *his* room."

Her gaze sliding away from the big voluptuous woman with the platinum curls lined in black roots that bounced stiffly around her shoulders, Dove muttered, "Uh, Tezer is not here. He's meeting with his men."

Kitty's disparaging gaze rolled up and down Dove's petite frame. "So, what are you doing here?"

Shrugging one shoulder, Dove replied, "It's really none of your business. Shall I give Tezer a message for you?"

Pushing her way inside, Kitty's wide lips curved up in a tart smirk. "Actually, Goldilocks, I saw Tezer ten minutes ago when he told me to meet him here. He said if you were still here to tell you to get the hell out. Get your skinny ass down to the women's rooms. The maid has my room ready for you and a dress for you to wear to dinner."

Her sneering gaze swept Dove's figure as if it was nothing but a pile of mud. "Although, it's doubtful anything will make that body look good." She sauntered past Dove not bothering to button her coat.

"Um, Kitty, I don't think-"

"Yeah," the buxom blonde reeled back on her, "that's it, don't think. I know you're jealous of me. You think Tezer would want your scrawny little body when he can have this?" She opened her coat again flashing Dove her naked, Rubenesque full figure.

"Anyway," Kitty moved close to Dove making the smaller woman back up. "Tezer said he was tired of your shit, that now that we're here he's turning you over to Braemont."

Shaking her head, Dove objected, "No, he said-"

Moving closer, Kitty nudged Dove towards the open door. "Yes, little bitch. You ever heard of an odalisque?"

At Dove's blank look Kitty sniggered. "Of course not. You're too straight, too green to know of such pornographic things." Her smile ridiculing, she explained,

"Tezer has sold you to Mr. Braemont as sort of a- a- female slave. Like the kind in a harem."

She poked a finger in Dove's chest pushing her into the doorway. "A sexually desirable woman, an odalisque, to be kept captive, locked in luxury, only taken out when the master desires to be with her."

Her gaze streaked down Dove, railing back up with her signature sneer. "Braemont has animalistic insatiable tastes. With his immense wealth, he normally has groups of women hanging around. You know, like movie stars do. Scantily clad women in bikinis, draped over him, and scattered around like potted plants. I hear he's kept his calendar cleared…for…you."

"No, you're wrong, Tez-"

"Yes," she mimicked, cutting her off again. "Tezer said for you to get your tail to my room and stay there until dinner. Now, go!" Kitty grabbed Dove's arm and shoved her out of the room and shut the door in her face, and locked it.

Dove stood staring at the door, her mind spinning. She didn't know what to think. Tezer had seemed, sincere, intent on keeping her with him, claimed he wanted to take her somewhere safe.

She turned slowly, dragging her hair back in a tight clutch behind her head and then dropped it. Blonde curls sprung down her back.

A hollow pit grew in her stomach. She finally admitted to herself that it had felt so…good, so right, in his arms, kissing him. The big bad mercenary had been so gentle with her, teasing her.

Chagrined, Dove realized her feelings for him were growing. Surprisingly, she liked being with him, sleeping with him. She felt safe, wanted him to kiss her, make love to her, but, her cheeks flamed, she feared it too.

Brows dragged down in consternation and heartache, she had to acknowledge it, he'd duped her. How embarrassing, how humiliating. He had brought her to Braemont intending on leaving her with him after all.

She thought about the way Braemont had looked at her. If he'd had a fork she would have been gobbled up. Her legs moved unsteadily down the hall.

Maybe Tezer told her that he wanted to help her only as a ruse to keep her quiet. Compliant. Until he and his men left, and she was left alone with…

Her steps slow and awkward, she shuffled along the carpet wondering, how had all this- horror- happened to her? She had been a hardworking woman starting college, minding her own business, when-

A maid came out of a hallway.

"Um, Miss," Dove stammered, "can- can you please help me?"

"Certainly madam." The maid gave her a stiff polite smile and a short bow.

"Uh, I need to go to…um, the room of Kitty, um, that is Katherine Miot's room."

At the maid's confused look, Dove said, "Big blonde with uh, a full kind of figure."

Confirmation, and disgust spread over the maid's plain face, she nodded. "Of course. Come with me."

******

Tezer left his friends and went back to Braemont's study to tell him his plans. As he approached the door he heard someone in with his employer.

A male voice said, "So once you have completed your…transactions with your…guests, what are your plans for the woman? She is extraordinary, as they told us."

Footsteps shuffled around on the carpet, bottles clinked on glasses.

"Yes, she is. My men are here and getting into position outside to escort Mr. Corseque and his men out of here. When he's gone, I will keep her in the violet room. I'm even thinking she'd make gorgeous children, and a fine wife. It's time I settled down." Braemont's accent marked him as the speaker.

A light chuckle, the other man said, "Doesn't she have to be at least somewhat agreeable to this?"

"Huh," Braemont grunted, slurped his alcohol audibly. "You remember what area of this country we're in? Women's rights haven't made a big splash here yet. And remember, I own the city this land is in. Besides, no one knows who she is or even that she's here.

"There will be no one coming here looking for her. So, no, I don't need her acquiescence. It would be nice, ah, of course, but," audible ice chinking against glass, "that will come in time.

"My money, I can offer her every luxury. I'm fit, good looking, I have an arsenal of sexual skills in my carnal bag, and the toys to go with it." Coarse laughter from both males ensued.

Braemont went on with natural arrogance, "It won't take long to win her over. Not that her desires matter."

Male laughter blended until one man couldn't be delineated from the other.

The other man said, "So, I heard the chopper come in. I take it that's your Aunt Mary, Uncle Jim and the two cousins?"

"Aye, dinner will be in less than an hour."

The voices lessened to mere rumbles as Tezer moved away from the door.

He travelled the length of several corridors passing through wide open spaces covered with peach and gold-veined marble floors, blush walls and opulent furniture.

Glass cabinets displayed antique china plates and statuettes, while larger alabaster and marble statues of mostly nude women, goddesses, graced the inside as well as the gardens outside.

Taking the stairs two at a time, he trod down hall after hall until he reached his room. He knocked on the door and said, "It's me, Dove, open up."

The door swung open, his mouth dropped.

Kitty, wearing only a big grin and high heels, held her coat wide displaying her sybaritic nudity all the way down to the neat Mohawk strip over her private parts. "Chief," her purr oozed, "I've been waiting for you."

His eyes flit around the room. "Where the hell is Dove?"

She tripped up to him in her steep heels shaking her enormous breasts in his face. With a pout on her red glossy lips she told him, "She's gone, sugar, come here to mama, let me show you what I can do for you."

He stepped out of her reach with a mean grimace. Staring directly at her eyes, low and rough, he snarled, "Tell me right now where she is, Kitty, or, trust me, female or not, I will fuck you up." His fearsome glare drilled into her with his vowed threat.

Feeling his fury like a hot murderous wind, Kitty closed her coat and stuck her nose in the air. "She's in my room. I told the maid to bring her dress there. If you will excuse me," she sniffed insulted, said with a snotty scoff, "I have to get dressed for dinner. We're all to meet in thirty minutes."

She looked down her nose at him, it wrinkled. "You could use a bath yourself and a shave." Her head snapped up and she stormed out the open door.

Shaking his head at her brazen audacity, Tezer started out the door to go find Dove, then glanced at his watch. Shit. She was probably in the midst of getting dressed. He'd have to wait until dinner. Now he wouldn't have time to warn her of his plan.

After seeing Kitty and guessing what she probably told Dove to get her to leave his room, Dove would have lost any trust she may have finally gained for him.

Cursing again, he closed the door and went to gather clean clothes for after his shower.

He rubbed his lean jaw, yeah, he needed a shave too.

Chapter Eighteen

His fingers drumming impatiently on the table, Tezer glanced for the tenth time at his watch. Where the hell was she?

"Chill, bro, she couldn't have left the building, there are guards everywhere. She's not with that prick Braemont," Garth nodded to the head of the table where Yvetsky Braemont was holding court. "She'll be here."

His shoulders hunched, Tezer gripped a wineglass in his hand and glowered at the door.

The other occupants of the room held zero interest for him. The passengers gabbling like idiots, interspersed with the mercenaries and a flock of other guests, filled the long elegant table.

Braemont's aunt, uncle and one of his cousins were seated up near Braemont, the seat beside him was vacant.

The relatives gazed curiously around the table at the assortment of people.

Braemont had briefly filled them in why these people were guests at his estate. The civilians owed him money, the mercenaries were waiting for the mission to become complete then they would be paid the rest of their money and they would take off.

Kitty Miot flirted outrageously with Braemont. She leaned over, allowing her breasts to almost fall out of the severely low cut dress.

"Now Yves," she cooed, "you know I have no cold cash, all my money is tied up in stocks and such. But," her cat's eyes slit in a leer, "I could consider working off my debt." Her lurid gaze sliding up and down his nicely constructed form in the designer suit made it clear about how she planned on doing just that.

Twirling his wineglass in his hand, the deep red wine swirled around the crystal goblet, Braemont was sitting back relaxed, his heavy-lidded solar eyes narrowed at her.

A half-moon smile lifted one side of his mouth in satirical counter. His eyes, like Tezer's, flicked like the second hand on a watch at the wide double doors that were thrown open with servants traveling to and fro through.

"My dear, I have already experienced your… opus. I have other ways for you to truly work off your debt; to pay back for those pilfered jewels, gold and cash, and other things you made off with. Which," his gaze slid like an oil spill down her body, "don't look like the clothes would fit any more. Fondness for the carbs, hon?"

Her painted on brows flew up to the dark roots of her platinum hair. "Why, how dare you, I'll have you know-" Kitty stopped when she saw red staining Braemont's cheeks and his suddenly glowing eyes pasted at the double doors.

A maid had finally brought Dove.

She paused with painful uncertainty and shyness in the doorway. All eyes were on her.

Tezer had hoped the dress Braemont had for her was more modest than the transparent, micro short fuchsia dress Kitty was billowing out of. It was. Barely.

Like a bandage dress, Dove's outfit was shimmering sapphire. Clinging fiercely to her figure, soft bands wrapped around and around and down to flare at a short skirt. As short as the skirt was, it had a slit near her inner thigh.

Spaghetti straps came from the sides of the bodice by her slender arms to tie behind her neck, forcing her perfect plump breasts to mold over the low décolletage.

The flaxen locks were swept up to one side into a partial French braid then the fat curls waved loose down over her shoulder and back. The girl looked super-model ready to strut down the walk.

She stood mortified on mile-high sequined heels.

Tezer went to push his chair back but Braemont was closer. He was up and to Dove before Tezer would be able to get around the table. *Bastard planned that.*

Garth set a hand on his arm. "Wait, bro, it's not the time. Besides, there are no other empty chairs for her to sit next to you." Garth had brushed his short curly hair like mad but it still waved around his head.

His head lowered, Garth rolled his blue eyes around the table. Everyone was staring with blatant interest at Dove.

Hovering in the threshold like a glistening sexy fairy, so stunning she appeared otherworldly, Dove looked petrified and would have opened her fairy wings and flown away- if she had them.

If Kitty could have killed her, stabbing her with her livid resentful eyes, Dove would be lying bleeding on the floor.

Glowering through tapered lids, Tezer watched Braemont slide his arm around Dove's bare shoulders and lead her to the table. His splayed hand slid slowly down the curve of her back, then he helped her to sit in the chair he'd kept unoccupied beside his own seat.

His body rigid as solid rock, fury roiled off Tezer like a building on fire. But he forced himself to sit back and unclench his fists.

The servants were bringing everyone individual plates of seared prawns with melted butter, linguini layered in a lavender scented, delicate cream sauce and petite filets. Along with curried greens, warm rolls, the wine goblets never dipped below half full.

Tezer kept his eyes on his plate, occasionally glancing at Garth who kept a rambling monologue beside him hoping to keep the chief calm.

Tezer didn't dare look at Dove, he was so pissed that Braemont had dressed her like a sparkling bauble, flaunted her in that X-rated outfit that showed her every curve. The short skirt and high heels made her gorgeous legs look long and lissome.

Keeping his head down, Tezer's gaze skewed slightly taking a quick peek at her then he closed his eyes with a grunt. Her damned tits were on display, round and soft, he couldn't look around the table, he'd want to punch every fucking guy that was leering at her.

They were all staring at her, including Braemont's uncle, who was a minister.

Tezer's fingers twitched, he wanted to get a washcloth and wipe that caked makeup off her face, it covered her natural fresh glow and made her look like an exotic dancer.

And, like every other man there, he imagined laying her on his bed, shoving his hand up that slit skirt to capture her womanhood in his palm, while pulling down the bodice, palm a delicious tit and plant his voracious lips on her bare- *ah*, he was only causing himself discomfort.

With Garth's voice buzzing in Tezer's ear, he just ate, ignoring one of Braemont's cousins, Ashley or some shit, trying to flirt with him.

Fluffing her ginger curls, Ashley could swat flies batting those false eyelashes so hard like black whisk brooms.

Carrying on a one-sided conversation, Garth picked up a buttery prawn by the tail and rambled at Tezer, "Look at red Robin, that pudgy girl just never gives up on that asshole Brock."

At Tezer's disinterested grunt, Garth continued, "Even now, she has her hand under the table on his dick while he's preening and hitting all over Braemont's cousin Frannie. Don't know why, she's plain as a box, but with those big thick lips, he's probably thinking she gives good blowjobs."

Tezer grunted again, twitched Ashley's hand off his arm, and shoveled in a piece of filet then washed it down with a healthy swig of pungent burgundy.

After pinching off the tail, stuffing the shrimp whole in his mouth, Garth spoke while chewing, "I see that witchy Avril with her cone tits still has it going on with that crazy black as spades Clancy freak."

He picked up another prawn while still chattering, "Ah, but Clancy is putting the moves on the heifer, Ashley is it? The one next to you that is clearly offering herself, her body that is, to you on a silver platter."

Chomping the shrimp and guzzling a beer, Garth kept on, "The older guy, Ronald is still a scared rabbit, shifts his glasses like he has Tourette's, he's shaking like a palm frond in the wind, obviously freaked over what Braemont is going to do to him."

Garth's eyes shifted down the table. "The blond giant Ziggy and pervert Paolo that attacked your girl disappeared right after the first course. I think they're hitting the bar in the den."

Hoping to keep the chief calm with his nonsensical prattle, Garth droned on, "Any second whiny Chelsee with her flat butt and vanilla chest will follow them. I can see her constantly looking at the door. I think her and the Zig got it going on now that Reggie's done banging her."

Muttering beside him, "When the hell did you become the town gossip?" Peripherally, Tezer could see Dove looking at him, the hurt clear on her heart-shaped face. She obviously believed whatever swill that goddamned Kitty had fed her.

Without the rouge someone had painted on her, Dove's fair skin would have been pallid. If she felt she couldn't trust him, she'd start working on escape plans again, just throw herself from the sauce pan to the broiler, or whatever the hell the saying was.

He knew she wouldn't be able to read him, his face was a blank stone, his eyes cold and flat. He couldn't help it, he didn't need the rest of the assholes there to know what he was thinking, feeling.

Dove's big eyes floated around the room avoiding eye contact with everyone except Garth and Leo who smiled their friendliness and warmth at her. She lowered her long curled lashes like shields, hiding the fear that shone from her orbs like golden green torches.

Finally, flaming crème brulee all succulent caramel sweet and crunchy was served, some had coffee.

When the last fork was set down, Braemont stood up. "Let's all go into the salon for brandy." He held his bent arm out to Dove, "Allow me to escort you my dear."

She stared at his proffered arm, then pitched a glance at Tezer. His attention was on her. All she would see was his impassive gaze like discs of obsidian ice, his mouth the usual inscrutable grim line.

Again, everyone was watching her, she couldn't refuse Braemont's arm. Swallowing her sigh, Dove stood up and smoothed down the skirt that had ridden up her thighs when she sat. Her breasts bobbled with her movements.

When she looked up at Braemont, his extraordinary orbs were glued to her chest.

As she set her hand reluctantly on his arm, she glanced again at Tezer. Still inscrutable, his skin darkened, mouth a bare slash, eyes bolted on her hand touching Braemont.

The rest of the table rose, babbling like banshees, and filed out of the room trailing Braemont.

Braemont had Tezer seated at the far end of the table, away from him and furthest from the door, so the majority of the people were crowded between Tezer and Dove.

Braemont led the group to an airy room.

Three huge arches curved over windows that opened to the back terrace. The arches rose up to the vaulted ceiling with arced beams that crossed over to either side of the room.

Black iron encased chandeliers were the only cascades of color against the cream walls.

The people wandered in and sat on chairs with powder blue seats, and on several divans of cream with indigo pillows as dashes of color.

The seating and tables circled an oval rosewood and glass coffee table, everything was grouped on the stenciled orange and pale brown center rug. Glass and marble tables were placed between chairs.

Several maids in black pantsuit uniforms with gold bow ties and matching gloves slipped around the room serving after dinner drinks.

Braemont clustered his relatives and a few of his male guests around him and Dove providing a human fence around them.

Tezer's fingers twitched with the irresistible urge to tighten around Braemont's neck until the man's auburn head popped off like a cherry bomb. He abruptly left the room.

Stalking down the hall to the first exiting door he could find, he snatched it open and stormed out. If he stayed one more second, Braemont would be dead and his men would be shooting at Tezer and his own team, with Dove in the crosshairs.

Leaning against the cold stone building, he lit a cigarette. Watching the smoke unfurl and float up and away, Tezer strived to get his temper under control.

He unclenched his jaw to take a bigger drag, sucking the smoke down his lungs, his diaphragm tightened. Exhaling, he blew out his tension with it. He shouldn't be whining, he had known all along that when he brought Dove to Braemont the fucker would be all over her, claiming her as his.

Finishing the cigarette, he dropped it and toed it out with his boot. Feeling calmer, he stuffed his hands in his pockets and made his way back inside.

When he reentered the salon, he could tell the people were already getting tipsy. Between the wine at dinner and now more cocktails, shrill laughter and bawdy jokes rebounded around the cylindrical room.

Across the salon, still in a clutch of people, Braemont had his arm around Dove. His hand was easing down her back until it settled in the lower curve of her spine. Almost on her ass.

She didn't see Tezer come in, she was too busy discreetly trying to disentangle Braemont's paw from her butt.

Nudging Garth with his elbow, Tezer strode uncompromising through the crowd straight to Braemont.

When Braemont saw him coming, he gestured with his head to his men to block his approach.

But this time, Tezer wasn't allowing anything to get in his way.

Chapter Nineteen

$\mathcal{M}$uscling through Braemont's human fence, Tezer slid his hand around Dove's shoulders pulling her from Braemont's grasp.

Braemont had to let her go or there would have been a tug-of-war right there if he didn't.

Drawing a surprised Dove against his chest, Tezer brushed his lips over hers then said, "Sweetheart, I missed sitting with you at dinner. But," he smiled, a real smile, so rare his friends in a huddle nearby jabbed each other in the side and grinned. "Of course we will have the rest of our lives to have dinner together every night, right, baby?"

Around them, chatter ceased, everyone's rapt attention was on the scene playing out. Braemont looked about to wrest Dove from Tezer's hold and then have him beheaded, but the words Tezer said sunk in, and his angry look turned to puzzlement. He retorted, "What the hell are you talking about, Corseque?"

Tezer smiled down into Dove's starkly confounded eyes, and lowered his arm to twine their fingers.

Turning them to face the room, with a huge grin he proclaimed, "Ladies and gentlemen," he nodded to his team, "my friends, I am proud to announce that this beautiful woman has agreed to become my wife."

He set his hands on her shoulders and moved her to face him and said, "Yes, we are proclaiming our engagement."

When Dove's mouth dropped in shock, he captured her lips, straightaway thrust his tongue into her sweet cove, and instantly burned through an intensely exquisite kiss.

One of his hands slipped around to net her head with his long fingers, the other spread against her back. Half his hand splayed on her soft, bare skin of the low backed dress, their heads tilted to opposite sides to seal their mouths.

Dove's baffled hands perched on his shoulders as Tezer continued the enrapturing kiss, so heated, it looked to the group in the room any second the couple was going the way of nova stars bursting in a gamma explosion.

"Corseque," Braemont growled trying to get Tezer's attention. But Tezer was too busy consuming his new fiancée to hear anyone or see anything.

"Dammit, Corseque," he thundered, "stop this improper display at once and explain yourself!"

Tezer drew both hands up to cup Dove's face, his face was mere inches from hers. Neither moved while catching their breath, and Tezer worked to settle his body down, as always, he had an erection whenever near her.

A rose sheen lit Dove's cheeks, lids heavy over eyes that were a mesmerized mist of confusion, and passion.

Her lips parted, he put his finger gently over them and whispered, "Shh, later when we're alone."

When they broke apart, some of the people present cheered and converged on them to offer their congratulations. Others, like Kitty, stayed back.

Her painted face set like Mt. Rushmore, Kitty's wide mouth twisted, the cats' eyes so enraged they were almost closed.

Braemont made a poor job of hiding his livid expression. Struggling to suppress his fury, his neck worked with hard swallows, jaw clicked and flexed.

Barely under control, his anger punched around his words, "So, *Corseque*," he said Tezer's name with a hiss, "what a...uh, surprise. You didn't mention anything about this during any of our...conversations." One brow rose in suspicion then lowered with the other to send scathing poisonous arrows at Tezer.

His arm tight around Dove's shoulder ignoring her slight struggles to get free, Tezer smiled. "Yeah, well, she only just agreed to marry me, uh, today. Right, sweetheart?" He nuzzled her nose with his then kissed her lightly.

Her lips didn't move under his, he could see the shock and mistrust spiraling in those beautiful eyes. Silently he cursed Kitty for throwing a wrench into his plans to tell Dove ahead of time what he was going to do.

Braemont was so incensed his face was almost purple. The freaky solar eyes blazed with blues, greens and spears of violet. He knew Tezer lied but he couldn't call him on it.

His own plans of taking Dove as soon as the mansion was cleared of all the damned people, were blown out of the water like a cannonball fired into the mix.

Then, a conniving evil smile pushed his lips up. He said, "That is wonderful news, Corseque, Miss Dove," he nodded to Dove letting his covetous gaze trail down her body and up before looking at Tezer.

"I am pleased to tell you that you can marry right here on the estate. My uncle, James Braemont," he motioned to the dapper man in his sixties smiling broadly at the couple, "is a minister and a notary, and he can perform the ceremony." His eyes glittered pleased at the panicked look on Dove's face, then frowned at Tezer's soft smile.

"Um, but, uh, I- I can't," Dove stuttered. "My uh, family, I have to, uh," her mind spun, she couldn't think of anything to say.

"I think she's saying," Tezer hugged her, "that she'd like to marry at home where her family can be present."

"Nonsense," Braemont crowed. "She has no passport or identification to allow her to leave this country. She marries you and that issue can be resolved with the greasing of some corrupt official palms."

His hands clasped behind his back, he rocked back and forth on his wingtips grinning broadly like a pleased papa. He was positive Corseque was just trying to cockblock him and once he was faced with a real wedding, the mercenary would run for the hills, and Dove would be his.

Tezer had already contemplated the issue of her identification. He knew she had none, when he'd taken her she had nothing, not even a toothbrush with her. It was like she got up in the middle of the night and fled with only the shirt on her back.

She tried to push from his embrace, he held her tight, feeling the panic shivering through her body. He cursed Kitty again. If he'd been able to speak to her ahead of time, Dove wouldn't have to go through this turmoil.

He said to Braemont, "We will discuss your offer and get back to you. For now-"

"Not at all, Corseque, this will be my gift to you. You two will be married, right here, tomorrow." All mirth and pleasantry bled from the solar eyes leaving sheer threat pulsing through them.

He leaned over and whispered in Tezer's ear, "A crew arrived earlier, so now I have enough men here to prevent you from leaving with her. Since you blurted out this marriage shit in front of my relatives, I offer the wedding because I can't have bloodshed in front of my aunt and uncle."

Making a pretense of straightening Tezer's collar and patting him on the shoulder, he whispered, "So, you either clear your ass out of here, without her, or you two marry tomorrow. You try to leave with her not wedded, you and your men won't leave here alive, and I will get to keep my prize."

His lascivious gaze slid over, coiling like a snake around Dove. Calling Tezer's bluff, he was positive Tezer would run for the hills and leave her behind before binding himself to a woman. The chief's hard ways were legend. He had never been seen with the same woman twice.

Clearly horrified at the whole wedding thing, and feeling like Braemont's eyes were like roaches crawling all over her body, Dove trembled and subtly burrowed under Tezer's arm, tucking in against his chest.

Squeezing her shoulders gently, Tezer said, "But of course. We appreciate your kind offer, and will accept it. Thank you. For now, I'm afraid my fiancée is very tired, and overwhelmed by all this attention, so we are going to go to our room."

Braemont leaned in and murmured, "My uncle will need to have her real name for the license. You may give it to him and I will ensure no one else sees it, including myself. See, I can be magnanimous, even when you bleeding try to cheat me out of my coveted prize."

He slapped Tezer hard on the back. Looking at Dove, he saw the pinched lines around her mouth as she kept a lid on her trembling lips. Her skin was white as a sheet, the big eyes radiating frantic alarm.

Tezer stared unblinking at the other man, his mouth tightened into a hard line. "Send someone with the time for tomorrow, we will be ready." Without another word, his arm around Dove, he turned and walked across the room with her to the doorway.

On the way out, he only glanced at his team. Garth was covering a grin with his hand. Leo's grey eyes were thoughtful. Nik's fuzzy hair tied back, he nodded with a slight smile. Reggie winked a dark blue eye at Tezer and smiled warmly at Dove.

Tezer and Dove walked in silence up the stairs and down the long hall to their room. He opened the door, nudged her inside and closed the door, locking it behind them.

Tezer strolled across the room to the table beside the bed. Keeping his back to her, he took out his wallet and cell and set them on the table.

He'd kept a small gun tucked into the back of his pants, he pulled that out along with a knife in his boot and set them on the nightstand. He was giving her a moment to compose herself. Then he turned to face her.

She had moved to stand by the window. Staring out, she didn't blink, didn't move, didn't seem to be breathing.

Tezer trod slowly over to stand beside her. "Hey," he joked, "not thinking of jumping, are you?" Then his skin paled when she shrugged not denying it.

Finally she turned to face him. "I- don't understand, Tezer. What is going on?"

He wanted to sift his big hand around her head and hold her while he took her lips with his, hard and hungry, but she was already freaked and he needed to explain. He took her hand and brought her to a chair, then pulled another one in front of her.

"Sit down. Please." He didn't have to tell her twice, her legs were shaking, she could hardly stand anyway. When she sat down, he dropped onto the other chair.

When he leaned forward setting his forearms on his knees and twined his fingers, she sat back as far as she could, away from him, her back rigid against the chair.

Ah, she looked so confused and scared. "Dove, I had planned to tell you about all this before...dinner, but that fucking, sorry, woman, messed me up with her fuck- uh, sorry, antics."

"Tezer, I don't-"

"Baby, that bitch lied. You have to realize that. If I had wanted her I had the entire trip to do her. She makes my gut churn, I feel like upchucking every time she touches me. When she realized I wasn't in the room, she pretended that we had an assignation, pretended she wasn't aware you were there. She fucking knew. The whole scheme was to drive a wedge between us."

Dove brushed her knuckles over her eyes but said nothing.

"Dove," he said softly, "don't let the bitch win. This is about you and me and no one else."

Her chest heaved with a deep sigh. "But this- this wedding! We- you can't be serious?"

He reached for her hand but she pulled them both into her lap and clenched them together.

Sighing, he told her, "I had no other choice, honey. Braemont was not going to let me leave with you. He flew in reinforcements, too many for my men to combat. If I tried to take you out of here, he would have killed my men."

"And you," she breathed softly.

Nodding, Tezer replied, "Yes." He sat up, leaned back in his chair and crossed one ankle over his knee then stretched his arms out along the arms of the chair.

It took an effort to keep his eyes on her face and not scour that luscious body in the revealing dress. If he didn't, he'd have her flat on her back and be doing what he'd thought about at dinner, shoving his hands up that tiny skirt- *ah*, he shook his head.

"Anyway, I know his Uncle, James Braemont, he is a minister. I've heard that he is a strict man of integrity, however, he will do anything his nephew says over all else. Yves Braemont can snatch one of his daughters at any moment and put her in danger, or do an abundance of other dastardly things to him or his family. So pleading our case to him would be to no avail."

Dove sat still as stone, her fingers threaded tightly together on her lap. The fact that she was considering his words was clear in the furrowing of her forehead and the firming of her lips.

When she bent to unclasp a high heel, she was unaware of the jolt of fire that lanced into Tezer's groin as her breasts bounded over the bodice of the low cut dress, about tumbling out.

Still bending over, she undid the other shoe and slipped them both off and slid back into the chair.

Dark color flooding up Tezer's neck was the only thing revealing the lust that struck him like a comet, other than of course the boner that was straining at his pants.

Tezer raised his eyes before she could see him leering at her woman's flesh. If she realized the thoughts that cartwheeled around inside his head at the moment had nothing to do with the wedding plans, she'd freak.

He was picturing how many different ways he could take that sexy as hell dress off her before laying her naked body down-

"But, I still don't understand, explain this, uh...foolishness about getting..." she made a face, "married," said it like it was a dirty word. Lifting her arms she plucked pins out of her hair and slowly unraveled the French braid.

His mouth dry as the desert, Tezer was hypnotized watching her, so feminine taking her hair down like a woman getting ready for bed with her lover...*he wished*-with him.

Her raised arms caused her breasts to lift and push together. His eyes bulged; he thought he was going to have a heart attack trying to clamp down his flaming carnal urges, his mind fogged with blind lust.

Desire had torched through Tezer the moment that first day he'd seen her detach from the other passengers and try to flee into the woods. When he'd grabbed her up as she ran between the trees he thought his head, and dick, would explode on contact. And the intense feelings had only climbed until he was fair to bursting with the want, the need of her.

He could hardly keep a train of thought. In a second he would not be able to stop himself from leaping up and damned jumping her and fucking her, or come in his pants like an inexperienced teen.

Tezer wasn't used to holding back when he wanted something, especially sex. There were any number of willing wenches all over the world to satisfy him without his ever even having to utter a word.

But no, he has to have irresistible desire for this female, to the point no other women were even visible to him. And this senseless possessiveness, not to mention the stinging rage of jealousy he'd never experienced before in his life.

The even more shocking thing was that it wasn't just the extraordinary lust he felt for her, the girl had snuck in and stolen his heart. Hell, he wasn't even aware he had a heart. His friends had always told Tezer that he was a cold, ruthless son of a bitch.

After sex with a woman it would have been remarkable if Tezer even recalled her name, if he'd bothered to ask what it was in the first place. The kind of women he got off with didn't usually care who he was either. And that had worked for him. Dove was on a whole other planet in an entirely different stellar system.

He not only desired her, he genuinely liked her. He enjoyed talking to her, playing with her, spending time just being with her. When he wasn't with Dove, his thoughts continually bounced back to her.

Tezer could not contemplate a world, his world, that didn't have Dove in it. His eyes narrowed on her as she moved.

When she fluffed her hair, combing the locks back off her shoulders and crossed her legs, the skirt slipped up almost to her apex.

That she was totally unaware of it, or the effect she was having on him, always had on him, made it all that much more body-vibrating *hot*.

Chapter Twenty

Tezer abruptly stood up and turned his back to her, taking a few steps away.

A deep breath held, shuddered, then his exhale was long, roughly slow, he dragged his fingers through his hair that needed a trim. The back had grown enough to curl over his collar and the front flopped with great annoyance in his eyes.

With short thrusts of aggravation he jabbed the hair back. Taking another deep, slow breath he turned to her. Keeping his eyes on a spot over her shoulder, he explained why it was necessary that they marry.

"There is no other way. He will never let you leave, there will be no one to help you. I knew he would want you," he shook his head with a wry smile, "but I underestimated how much he'd go through to keep you. He wholly plans on slaughtering me and my men if I try to take you from the mansion.

"Even if I could remove you without my men dying, as he said, you have no passport or visa to get you out of this country. Or to get a job here, or, whatever. I could fly you out, illegally, but I'd need to get you off the estate first. His offer is the only way to get you out. He's just not expecting me to accept it. He thinks the thought of marriage will freak me out and I'll drop you like a hot potato and run for my life."

A brow rose over a distrusting eye, Dove told him, "It was your idea, Tezer, you said it, that it was your plan, not his."

"Ah," his head dropped, the hair flopped back in his face.

Lifting his head, he shoved the dark brown locks back. "Yes. It was my idea. Again, it was the only way to get you out of here. He wants to keep you. I knew if I announced our engagement in front of his straight-laced aunt and uncle, he would have had no way to refuse.

"His uncle may be pliable with Braemont's wishes, but his Aunt Mary is a buffalo, a severe fundamentalist. She would have pushed him to let us go, if we were married. If we weren't, she'd pay no attention to any of us and would care less what Braemont does with you."

Watching her expression carefully, Tezer sucked in a harsh breath. "I hate to go along with Braemont's orders, but I feel if we don't marry before his relatives leave he will prevent it and we'll be back where we started, with no way out for you."

Dove gathered up her hair pulling it around her front to fidget with the curls. "Then," she said calmly, "just leave me here. Take your men, and get to safety. I will eventually be able to...escape." Her gaze to him was rueful. "He can't be anywhere as diligent as you are in holding me."

Against his will, Tezer's eyes roved down her length. Her words about holding her turned to imagery in his head. He could almost feel her tangibly in his arms.

Shaking his head, he said, "No. If you stay here, you will never get away. I've heard from some of his men he has a room ready for you, one he plans on keeping you locked in. Permanently. He even planned on marrying you himself."

Dragging his hand through his hair again in frustration, he said, "And, uh," a scowl furled his brows, lips pulled down, "he also plans to impregnate you and not only get desired heirs, but use the babies to keep you from even considering escaping."

Shocked, Dove squawked, "But- but he can't force me to wed him!"

"Yes he can. You forget the specific area of the country you're in. As a woman, you basically have no rights. There would be no one here for you to talk to in order to help you get out. His Aunt Mary would be the only one, and Braemont will keep you from her. And, after tomorrow, she and James are gone."

He shook his head again. "No, the only way out of here is if you marry me. That's it." He gave her a moment to ruminate on that.

She turned to stare towards the window, he took the opportunity to soak her in. It was a mistake, his body flared all over again.

"But, Tezer, I don't understand, why would this man go to all this trouble to keep me? He doesn't even know me."

The corner of his lip lifted wryly. "You don't realize the effect you have on men, baby. They see you and they want you, at all costs. It's bizarre, but there it is." *Look at me, high jacked before I could get a steel wall around to protect myself from falling for you.*

"But-"

"I am not leaving you here. There is no other way. When we get you somewhere safe, if you want to, we will get an annulment or divorce."

Her brows tweaked in puzzlement. "If *I* want to? I don't under-"

"I'm done discussing this, Dove. We will marry tomorrow. After that, when the mission is over, that's when all those fools pay up what they owe Braemont, then we're out of here and we can move forward."

Her eyes narrowing with suspicion and uneasiness, she glanced at the bed and back to him. "What about-" she raised her head but dipped her gaze down. Then she glowered hard at him. "I am not sleeping with you. I mean, sex, I- we're…not… uh," her words fizzled out with her embarrassment.

Tezer lowered his lids to hide the lust that burned under them. If she saw how affected he was there was no way she'd agree to the plan. His eyes flit to the chair she sat in, he wanted to take her and bend her over it. Push up that tiny skirt, pull down her panties and nudge those pretty legs wide apart as he moved behind her-

With a thick tongue, he said quickly, "It's okay. There will be no sex. I won't demand my…husbandly rights."

A corner of his lip ticked up drolly. "This is only to get you out of here. I have no trick up my sleeve to fuck you. If I was going to do it, believe me, I would not need to marry you to take what I want."

At her swift sharp inhale, her hand covered her mouth, she shook her head. "That…you're talking about…forcing me," she whispered her fear of what would happen once she was legally his.

His eyes rolled heavenward, as if he was having an internal struggle. Already on the sharp slick edge of pushing her down and fucking her without her consent be damned, he sighed loudly.

"Yeah." He looked levelly at her. "You know I could just take you but I haven't. I'm telling you I won't." *Unless you provoke me*, "So, it's agreed. We will marry tomorrow."

If her face was any whiter she'd blend in with the evening's frost. Her eyes so big and traumatic like lighthouse beams in a fretful fog, she said quietly, "And…no sex, right?"

Shooting her a black scowl, he growled, "Goddammit Dove, you act like sex with me is equal to the worst fucking torture."

Seeing her frightened, wary expression, he sighed again. "No. I won't force myself on you, or expect you to…" annoyed at her look of relief, the sigh roughened, fell heavier, "give it."

Flicking his gaze over her, he said, "But, if you want it, sex, with me, please feel free to tell me or show me, whatever works for you. Know that it is understood that I won't at any time turn you down, even if I'm sound asleep or exhausted to death, or busy doing something," his lip curled up in a slight leering grin.

Mad that he was forcing her into a corner, Dove felt like needling him to take that smirk off his face.

Sitting casually back in her chair, she said with innocence, "So, what about if I…you know," she faintly smiled with rare coyness, "wanted to be with, you know, another man. Would-"

Exploding, he snarled fiercely, "Fuck, Dove-" and lunged at her feet.

She shrank back at the rage blanketing his face.

224

He knelt in front of her, put his hands on her knees, spread them, then pushed his hips between her legs, and watched the pink rise and wash over her creamy complexion.

One hand on her thigh, he threw the other up to grab her chin. "Get this straight, Dove, you will be my wife. There will be no other men for you. None. I find you with another man, I promise you now, I would never harm you, but he won't walk away on two legs. You want to fuck, you come to me. Only me. We clear?"

She fought to pull from his grasp but knew it was futile to try. He was too strong. Besides, she didn't blame him for his ire, she'd said it to piss him off, and it worked. Too well.

"Yes, Tezer. Gee you have a filthy mouth." Her hips wriggled trying to push from him, close her knees, but he was planted between her legs keeping them obscenely open, making her feel vulnerable.

The short skirt stretched tightly across her thighs, she knew he could see her panties, her cheeks blew up dark red.

Glaring needles at her, he held her face for a brief moment to make sure she saw he was not joking.

"What about you?" she asked nonchalantly.

Releasing her jaw, he muttered, "Huh? What about me?"

Ducking her head in embarrassment, Dove said thinly, "What about you and other women? You know, like…Kitty. Am I to…look the other way when you feel the need to…uh, you know, men have…needs." Her voice wobbled, after all, he was still between her legs forcing them to spread open.

Rolling his eyes with a growl, he declared angrily, "Good Lord, Dove, you fucking work my every nerve. I have no desire to be with any other women. Trust me. And let any shit that bitch Kitty said to you roll off your back, she has tried to drive a wedge between us since the beginning.

"If I wanted her I could have just gone to her room. I did not ask her to come to our room, and you fucking know that. I was practically screaming adamant that you didn't leave this room, you think I'd turn around in five seconds and tell her to tell you to get out so I could be with…that…blown up tart?

"You know damned well I could have had her every fucking day and night if I'd wanted to. But I didn't. I wouldn't touch that trash with a ten-foot-pole and gloves on. You are the only woman I've ever gotten involved with on a mission."

His angry labored breath coursed out. He said roughly, "I don't want to hear that bitch's name again. She is nothing to us."

Dove layered her gaze on him, her face a block he couldn't read. Then she said, "But other women, you-"

"Goddammit Dove!" he exploded. "*Stop it.*"

He moved his head closer to hers and stared hard into her eyes. "I do not want, I will not want to be with another woman. Believe me," he shook his head with a short laugh, "you are more than enough trouble for me. I don't need any more estrogen fucking with me."

Their eyes glowered at each other for a few harsh seconds.

Sucking in a frustrated breath, he said, "All right? Now, are we good on this whole marriage thing?"

Dove's lips puckered, then pursed. Her gaze scrolled from his harsh face down his steel armored chest, down to his hips keeping her legs spread open. His big hands squeezed her thighs in his irritation. Her cheeks flamed brighter when she saw his hard-on bulging against his pants.

Seeing her looking at his erection, slightly sheepish, Tezer shrugged. "Yeah, well, like you said, men have needs. But, honey," he cupped her chin again but gently, "what about you? Women have needs too. I know you feel something, Dove, I've literally felt the evidence of it."

He glanced down at his hand on her thigh and back up to see her blush deepen remembering when he had his hands down the back of her pants, his long fingers had curled up and felt her wetness, shocking them both.

Still kneeling between her legs, he let go of her chin and set both hands back on her thighs. The short skirt was stretched tight across her thighs exposing her panties. His gaze flickered down, he saw a tiny swath of ivory silk, and his erection turned to steel.

She seemed not to be able to move her eyes from his boner; she blinked, licked her lips but said nothing.

"Well?" his murmur seductive, velvety low. "What about your needs?" His hands so big they covered her legs. He slid them slowly up her thighs and watched the color in her face deepen further. Her mouth parted, she moved her eyes from his pants to watch his hands.

Swallowing hard, Dove murmured, "Uh, Tezer, please…"

He kept moving his hands up until they were under the tiny skirt and his thumbs pressed against her panties.

Feeling the heat of her sex through the silk on the pads of his thumbs, he whispered, "Don't you have needs too, Dove? Let me take care of them, I can make you feel so good…" He pushed the skirt up to fully expose the miniscule white silk panties and lightly brushed his thumb over her core.

The shiver struck her full body, washing up from between her legs to her shoulders. He watched her eyes roll back, her head listed, she licked her lips again.

Softly, a sensuous timber underneath, he whispered, "Just let me make you happy, let me make you come, baby. I swear, that's all. No sex, I won't push myself on you, I swear. *Unless you beg me to*- I only want to make you come."

Because if he got her to orgasm a few times, she would relax and he could take things further, maybe not today, but it would happen.

His hips between her legs forced them to stay spread open. Her hands were clutching the chair arms, her chest rising and falling drew his gaze to her beautiful tits.

The craving to pull the dress down to expose those amazing globes slammed into him, tearing through his heated body. He breathed deeply to still the overwhelming hunger to see her bare flesh.

He'd be a goner if he removed those panties and kept her legs spread showing her pink nether lips, and her breasts in their nude glory. Tezer could not believe the almost uncontrollable impulse he continued to have to just force himself on this girl.

Dragging ragged breaths up his tight throat, Tezer shook his head. She had such a hold on him she could never know how much.

Instead, connecting their eyes as if he could cast a spell on her, he brushed her core lightly with his thumb. Then did it again harder and watched her eyes roll back even as she struggled to overcome the feelings he was eliciting in her.

If, when, he was able sometime to get her to match his skyscraping powerful desire, they would be like lit dynamite together.

She didn't say anything or push him away.

He moved one hand to hold her where her thigh met her pelvis and slid the other one slowly into her panties. She gasped, shuddered, didn't say anything, her hips shifted on the chair.

He nudged her thighs wider by moving his body closer to her and holding her thighs apart. He stroked his hand inside her panties and down to caress her sex and almost choked. She was fucking wet. Her silk spilled onto his fingers.

Feeling his own body buckling, Tezer's breathing grew heavy, more rapid, his slacks were so tight he thought they'd split. He touched her sex, slipped a finger along her tender slit and watched her green eyes shiver and roll under fluttering lashes, her knees clenched at his legs.

He forced himself to move very slowly, gently, she was so skittish any rough or aggressive move would make her bolt. Aggression could come later when she was comfortable with him being inside her.

Dove knew she should stop him, but, goodness, she couldn't move, except to clutch the chair arms. Electric charges were firing in her core and gyrating, spreading throughout her body, she wanted more.

His fingers, gosh, she groaned, couldn't help it, she felt her mind cloud with pure rushing feeling. So intense, it built, stronger, he was bringing her up, to…she didn't know where...

Tezer stroked her feminine folds, then her silken slit. He smiled when a moan escaped her.

She clutched the chair so tightly her knuckles were white, and her hips squirmed against his fingers.

Ah, finally, she couldn't deny she was aroused, it gave him the green light to go further. When he touched her swollen bud, her hips tweaked, another moan scraped from her husky throat and the wet of her slicked over his fingers. Tezer thought he'd go ballistic.

Nudging her thighs as far apart as he could, he used his thumb to draw light circles over her clit; and resisted taking his cock out and fisting it when her hips revolved with his motions.

Under deep cover of his girlishly long lashes, he studied Dove.

Her eyes were closed, lids fluttering over them, face blushed pretty pink. Licking her lips, bosom billowing with thick breaths, her legs held forced open for his perusal, his touch.

When her purling moans hitched quickly and her bottom wriggled up the chair and her hips bucked to meet his fingers, a shudder rippled through Tezer.

He carefully slipped a thick fingertip just inside her wet opening- she suddenly sat forward shoving her lower half away from his hands, and slapping her hands on his shoulders pushing at them.

"Let me go. I want to get up."

Holding her taut with his hands, Tezer said, "Dove, come on, you're almost there, let me bring you over the top-"

"No. Let me up. You said you wouldn't force me."

At first he knelt like a stone, his hands on her thighs. His fingers slight inches from her sex, so close they itched and twitched to touch her. His tongue circled his lips crazy to lick her core, suck at her tender bits, taste her.

With obvious reluctance, he pulled his hands away, tugged her skirt down and stood up. At least she had gotten hot and heady, he had her primed now. She'd felt his hands on her pussy and liked it. It should be easier to get her to that point again. But not tonight.

She didn't get up, just sat, closed her legs and wrapped her arms around her body.

"Okay," he said with a laborious heavy sigh. "I'm going to grab some stuff and go bunk with Garth. You can stay here and not worry I'll...attack you."

He strode off quickly, his head spinning, clouded with desire, so turned on his legs were shaking. He had to get away from her or he'd break his word and throw her on the bed and fuck the very breath out of her, with or without her assent.

Slamming around, he grabbed some clothes and his toiletry case containing his toothbrush and shaving gear.

With his hand on the door, he paused. His head lowered, beads of sweat trickled down his temples.

Looking up at her through a lock of hair, he said, "No one will know I am not here, so no one should come. Don't leave the room. You can't get out of the building. There's a guard on every floor and outside and all around the perimeter."

He smiled drily. "There are men like me out there that want you. But they won't back off like I am. Stay here. I won't come back until tomorrow."

Dove sat unmoving on the chair. Sadness pervaded her eyes, and regret, and the depths still shadowed with fear. She didn't reply.

Her fear and sadness broke his heart. Some other bastard had hurt her so badly that intimacy terrified her. Tezer moved carefully back to her. "Dove," he stopped a few feet away as she cringed back in the chair from him.

Sighing his frustration, he said, "Tomorrow, tomorrow morning, I will come back. Then, you will have to tell me your name. Your real name. It has to go on the license. Maybe then you will tell me about…what happened, what made you run."

He studied her, searching for anything that revealed what she was thinking. Would she finally tell him? A few steps closer, ignoring her shrinking from him, he bent and tucked a couple of fingers under her chin and lifted it.

His eyes boring into hers, Tezer kissed her lightly, gently. Her lips pulsed against his, then firmed. He knew she responded against her will. That gave him hope.

That and the way her body had responded to his touch. He was pretty sure she was wet before his fingers had even touched her pussy, that was good. Something he could build on. He needed to eradicate the memories that evil fuck had imprinted on her so they could move on with their lives. Together.

He stood up straight, said, "Lock the door after me, don't open it to anyone except me, Garth or Leo."

Then he left without another word.

Chapter Twenty-One

Dove knew she wouldn't sleep and she was right. It was bad enough how he could bring her into delirious waves of rapture with just his kisses, *God could he kiss*.

All night she relived Tezer's hands on her thighs, pushing those strong palms up her legs until his fingers touched her, she shivered as if he was implanted right now on her body.

Her core burned remembering the feel of his fingers stroking her woman's sex. He had been right, her body was climbing the volcano, about to plunge over into the consuming blazing heat, the molten liquid melting her from the inside out.

But she stopped him. She had to. After what she's been through, she was never having sex again. Especially with a hard-hearted mercenary that only wanted her for sex, and not for her.

Tezer had once denied wanting her at all, but the fire that burned in his dark eyes when he looked at her was too white-hot to hide.

His kisses were too excruciatingly hungry, too aggressively intense for a man not interested in sex with her. Her body decided to go into another bone-bending shiver thinking about last night.

Kisses on the precipice of violent, it was like he tried to climb inside her, to feel every bit of her, drawing her with his powerful might to match him, respond with the same intense hunger. His hands so emphatic in their fervent handling of her woman's flesh, stroking her, yeah, he wanted her.

The wonder was why he held himself in check. He could rape her easy enough, get it over with, and as he said, there was nothing she could do about it. Why did he allow her to push him away, stop him?

Dove threw off the covers, not just her sex was heated, her skin literally sizzled all over. Sitting up, she lifted her long hair pushing it behind her back and wiped at her eyes.

She was supposed to be getting married today. The thought sent waves of panicked shudders down her spine, her stomach just flipped over and over.

Shuffling to the side of the bed she slid down to her feet. Glancing at the window she saw the sun had already risen. He would be there soon.

Another bought of shivers overtook her, some were quivers of fear of seeing him, others were scorching riffs of heat striking her female parts as if with a feverish paddle. It was almost as if she wished he *would* force her and take away her having to keep fighting him.

She hurried into the bathroom to shower.

When she was done, Dove had a towel over her head while she dried her long curls. Only wearing Tezer's t-shirt and her underwear, she padded to the dresser to grab her one pair of jeans and blouse one of the maids had so kindly washed and brought to her.

"Dove," his voice choked out in a rasped hush.

234

"Oh!" She dropped the towel in her surprise.

He was standing just inside the closed door. She'd forgotten he had a key.

Tezer didn't move, just gleaned every inch of her body from the nipples that poked through the thin shirt and the areoles dark circles around them, down to her hips. He wondered if she had panties on. Her legs and feet were bare.

As reliable as a sonar clock, his dick swelled. "Ah," surprised at the tremor in his voice, he was abnormally nervous. "I thought you'd be up and...dressed. I knocked but I guess you didn't hear me."

His eyes dipped as if they could lift the hem of the shirt and see under it. Her voice drifted into his lust-filled brain.

"Um, if you can give me a...minute, I'll get dressed." She hurried over to the dresser and yanked the drawer open.

He muttered, "Hell, don't bother on my account." His eyes followed her every move, from the way the T flipped with her movements showing flashes of pink lace. He wondered where those panties came from.

A scowl suddenly pulled his brows down. He snarled meanly, "Did Braemont give you those fucking panties? Because if he did, you are giving them back to him, no, I'm giving them back to him."

Rolling her eyes she looked at him in exasperation. "No. One of his cousins sent them with the maid last night..." she broke off, why would one of the cousins who she hadn't shared one word with, be so kind to send her underwear?

Her face colored, they probably were from Braemont. But, she snapped her head, she was not giving them back, she had so little to wear.

Reading her like a book, he had already come to the same conclusion. "Take them off. Right now, and give them to me," he commanded with his hand out like she was going to whip them right off and drop them in his palm. *He wished.*

Her face squashed in a mutinous frown, she snatched her clothes out of the drawer and marched to the bathroom.

At the door she turned to him and said defiantly, "I will not. And you will stop ordering me around. It is ridiculous for you to take what little I have and give it back because…well I don't know why it bothers you, but it makes no difference. I am *not* taking them off."

Her head snapped and she marched into the bathroom slamming and locking the door.

Tezer stood bemused staring at the door. She had to know it would take one kick and the door would be gone. Crossing his arms he considered her words.

She was right. She didn't have much to wear, and again, he was acting like a jealous boyfriend, which he certainly was not. But damn, it irked the fuck out of him that she was wearing something so intimate as panties given to her by another man.

A knock at the door broke his revelry. He opened it and let in a maid. She brought a tray with breakfast on it as he had requested, and set it on the table by the window then left with only a stiff polite, "Good morning, sir."

He was pouring coffee into the two cups on the tray when the bathroom door opened.

Dove came out warily, keeping her distance. She was well aware he could grab her and wrest her clothes off and take the offending panties. He had to admit the thought had crossed his mind.

He pulled out a chair. "Come and sit down. Stop staring at me like I'm a hungry tiger in a zoo." His mouth curved in a dry grin.

Gingerly, she slipped across the room in her bare feet and cautiously sat on the chair he'd indicated. She was wearing pink jeans and a white blouse with ruffled collar and pearl buttons.

"I ordered breakfast for us here in the room. I thought it would make you more comfortable than being in the dining room with all those freaks," *and that bastard Braemont, knowing she was wearing practically a thong of pink that he had touched, and knowing it would barely cover her twat -*

Her eyes tripped up to him, a small smile tugged at the corners of her lips. "That's not very nice, Tezer."

Shrugging, he lifted the metal cover off a plate and set the plate of eggs, bacon and toast in front of her. He did the same with his plate that contained triple the food of hers, removed the orange juices and butter, jam, and other condiments and utensils and set the tray aside.

"I'm only telling it like it is. Other than my team everyone else here is a freak." He sat down and took a sip of coffee.

He wore black jeans and a button down shirt with the long sleeves rolled up revealing those brawny arms. He caught Dove's quick glance at his arms then to his hands before she reached for her own coffee. He wondered, *was it in fear of his strength, or desire for what he could do to her with them?*

They ate, talking peacefully about the other occupants of the mansion. He told her some funny stories of his friends, mostly about Garth and Leo's crazy exploits.

When they finished, Tezer gathered up the plates. Dove got up and helped with the glasses and cups and they set them on the tray.

He took the tray and set it outside the door then returned and motioned for her to sit back down on the chair with a comfortable leather seat and back. When she did, he sat down opposite her again at the table, keeping space between them to keep her more at ease.

Leaning back in his chair, his legs spread like men sit, his heavy boots planted on the carpet, Tezer folded his hands in his lap.

"Okay, baby, it's time. I need to know your true name. As I said, only the minister and I will know it. I will redact your name on the copies I show to Braemont." His voice was cold as always, but a warm light softening his gaze shone at her.

"I hope, Dove," he said softly, "that you will also tell me about...what happened. Okay?"

Dove's eyes lowered to the table, then moved to one of his large hands setting on the tabletop. He had long, thick, manly square-tipped fingers, they were rough and calloused, scars crisscrossed all over them. Not surprising considering his choice of livelihood.

Her gaze shifted to his face. She could tell he was trying to sound kind, gentle, patient. It must be killing him. He was normally none of those things. No, the man was crude and rude, violent and tough, and icy cold. And patient? *Ha*, never.

Dove could see the smolder in his dark eyes as he beheld her. As much as he tried to quell, hide, his desire for her, it was impossible. She sighed.

"Dove?"

"Yes. I will tell you everything."

Chapter Twenty-Two

*H*er eyes flit to his strong face then to his solid broad shoulders, then lowered to her hands clutched in her lap.

Dove drew in a tense breath, held it while obviously contemplating whether or not she should tell him, then she let it out, resigned. She finally had to admit to herself she needed help.

Besides the lust he tried but failed to hide, his intense gaze on her was of caring and interest. He wasn't a man to pretend anything, she had to believe he was sincere, and honest, and meant what he said about helping her.

He could have hit her, abused her, raped her, passed her around to the other men, even left her in the wild. Tezer could have done all sorts of things to her in the time they traveled the jungle.

But, although she'd given him plenty of reason to, other than taking some liberties with her body and being chauvinistic and bossy, he had never hurt her. Quite the opposite, in fact, he had risked his own life on more than one occasion to save hers.

And, he had rescued Mrs. Cook. He might be getting compensation for the others, but he earned nothing for Mrs.

Cook, and had actually paid off her debt to Braemont out of his own pocket.

Even now, knowing how difficult this was for her, he sat with a calm, patient, nonjudgmental look on his face, and kept his aggressively strong body loose and as nonthreatening as he could.

After another deep inhale, she let it out slowly, then said, "My name is Savá Mariè Bretèche." She watched him, he didn't blink.

"Um, I don't know if you know anything about the French Southern and Antarctic Lands, the uh, *terres australes et antarctiques françaises*."

When he made no comment, she continued, "There are 300 plus islands owned by the French that form an archipelago."

A resolute exhale settled her rigid body. "Where I'm from, near the Kerguelen Islands, is one of the most isolated places on earth. It is raw and chilly with almost constant severe winds.

"There are no residents there, actually, but there are 100 or so fluctuating scientists, engineers and researchers. The islands have no airport so the only way to or from it is by boat."

She peered up at him. His eyes darkly penetrating, stared at her with acute concentration. She stopped talking, her gaze shifted to the window.

Quietly saying, "Dove," his head tilted, watching the ghosts of her past crawl mostly in disturbed mottled winces over her face.

She didn't respond, he gently said, "Savá Mariè." The unfamiliar name tippled from his lips as if he tasted it first.

She smiled at the foreign sound he gave it, her eyes turned up to him. He wasn't smiling, but he still wore the caring and patient expression.

Finally learning what her intriguing accent was that had bedeviled and bewitched him, he nodded for her to go on.

"Um, so, uh, my parents were scientists. They were very…not cold per se, but they were 150% wrapped up in their work. Well," her eyes lowered again then rose to stare bleakly towards the window. "I was attending college at a large and more heavily populated island when my…" her head tipped down, "parents, died."

"Oh, Do- **Savá**," Tezer said softly. "I'm so sorry."

Her eyes crunched closed hard before she opened them and looked directly at him. "Yeah. It was some freak thing where they were on a research boat studying the marine life surrounding many of the islands when a storm railed out of nowhere."

She blinked and turned her attention back to the window. "They, everyone on board died."

He moved to reach over and take her hand, then thought better of it and stayed still.

"Anyway," she said with a mild shrug, "I was discombobulated." She smiled slightly at the word. "To say the least. I buried them alone. I have no other relatives that I know of, then afterwards I headed back to college. I hadn't even finished my first term." Her lips bunched, she pressed her fingers against them.

"It was so hard, I'd led such an austere insulated life out on the island, I was…uncomfortable around a lot of people. There was very seldom anyone even close to my own age on the island. When I turned around 11, because some of the men on the island, uh…"

He watched her face darken with angry embarrassed heat. Softly, he said, "They were inappropriate with you?"

The long lashes swept down hiding her embarrassment. She nodded. "Yes. My parents kept me even more isolated in an effort to…protect me." Her lips twisted bitterly. "Heaven forbid they take me from that hellhole to a real home,"

Sucking down a ragged breath she changed the subject. "Anyway, many things like movie theaters, restaurants and shopping centers amazed me. I've still never experienced a mall but I have seen them on television."

A smile tilted the corner of his mouth up. "I can imagine." It also explained a lot of her reticence and confusion with sexuality and her own self.

Her short smile turned into a frown. "Yeah. Well, anyway, it didn't prepare me for a lot of things in life. One day I was on my way to class, still dazed, and had inadvertently wandered into a protest. I still don't even know what it was about."

Her face drained of color and a small tremble shook her hands. She clutched them more tightly to still them. "I was…uh, arrested."

His brows shot up in disbelief. He'd been in his fair share of jails around the world, but he could not imagine this delicate, elegant young woman tossed in the slammer with other degenerates. "Savá," he frowned.

She shook her head and smiled sadly at him. "Really, Tezer, I have come to prefer Dove. I feel it…cleanses who I was and I am a new person." She moved her twined fingers to rest on the table.

He nodded. "Go on, Dove." He smiled, he was used to the name Dove, it was who she was to him. A little soft bird seeking only to fly free.

"And, uh, I still do not want anyone to know…who I am."

"I understand." *For now.*

Her neck arched, she dropped her head back, looked at the ceiling as if garnering strength to go on. Taking a deep breath, she straightened her head and said, "So, I was brought in front of a judge. I had no parents, no money for a lawyer, I didn't know what I was supposed to do. I pled not guilty to stall for time to see if I could get some assistance."

A tiny snort bubbled and she said, "The judge himself came to visit me in jail. He said he wanted to help me." She regarded Tezer with her regular suspicion and distrust.

"I am not him, Dove," he said quietly.

She blinked at him trying to absorb what he said. Her pretty face hardened in a tight scowl. "Unfortunately, most of what I know about men is that they are not to be trusted and to…" her eyes accused him, "keep my distance for my own good."

His mouth pinched, he looked her hard in the eye. "I repeat, I am not most men, I am not that judge."

The yellow in her brows glinted in the light when they arched sarcastically. "Really? You basically kidnapped me. You have taken me and held me against my will. You have cursed and bullied me, you have touched me…intimately when I've begged you not to, and you are forcing me to marry you." She pulled and twisted her fingers as she grew more agitated.

There was nothing he could say to that. It was all true. He opened his mouth to say that he had to take her with them or she would have perished alone in the jungle, yet she still believes she could have overcome any obstacles whether they were predatory animals, human or otherwise.

She knew nothing of the steep ravines and flash floods, poisonous snakes and hidden sand bogs among a coterie of other deadly properties in the wilderness.

Tezer wanted to state that he had not harmed her and never would, but, he bit back a sigh, in her eyes he has hurt her. He stayed silent and waited for her to continue her story.

When she didn't, he prompted, "Go on, Dove."

Blinking back her infuriation with the male part of the human race, she coughed, clearing her throat. She said, "Yes. So, uh, the help he offered was that he would set me free, for a price."

Her face wrinkled in pained embarrassment, the pink drained to leave pale misery. "He knew I had no money, no family. His price was…uh, my body. I would agree to be his, you know, mistress, and he would see that the charges were dropped."

Tezer said nothing, but the darkness of his anger spread up his neck.

A few tiny coughs behind her graceful hand, she dropped it to clutch her other hand to continue mutilating her fingers.

Continuing with her story, she said, "Well, I refused. He got mad. He sentenced me, technically *sold* me, to a couple who ran a missionary here in Russia. Apparently he regularly supplied them with laborers. I was forced to work for them. I had no choice. In a foreign country, without identification or money, I was a prisoner. If I ran away, I would be captured and sent to prison."

They both sat silently. He stared at her, she looked out the window. He prompted her, "Then?"

Her attention drew back to him as if she'd forgotten he was there. Nodding, she went on, "I worked there and had to fight off Mr. Aiken daily. I even hacked off half my hair, wore clothes sizes too big to dissuade him, but," her sigh was sad, and angry.

Dove glanced up at Tezer, mortified having to tell him of her humiliating life. "After almost a year of it, his wife finally got tired of her husband's chasing after me. There were mostly females at the missionary. We built buildings or taught children. Mrs. Aiken," her gaze fell like a rock to the floor, "sold me. She sold me to-" she broke off as tears threatened to engulf her.

Tezer shifted his chair closer to her, but kept his hands in his lap. His voice soft, he said quietly, "You're not there anymore, baby."

Nodding, she dashed her hands at a few tears that fell. "I know."

"Tell me. Tell me what happened," he spoke softly, gently prodding.

Looking up at the ceiling while she tried to compose herself, Dove said, "She sold me to Damon Philippè." A sharp tremor rocked her body, her skin tinted green, she put her hand over her mouth as if to hold the horror in.

He wanted to hold her, protect her, comfort her, but Tezer knew while she told her story about these men who had hurt her, she wouldn't feel safe with any man's arms around her so he willed himself to stay still. He waited patiently, not pushing her.

It took a few minutes for her to calm herself before going on. She tucked her hands under her thighs.

Swinging her legs back and forth, her shoulders hunched, she said, "You, uh, already have figured out most of it. Yes," she ducked her head, "he chained me. He has an ancient but modernized castle, with," she choked a smile without mirth, "a real life dungeon underground. I was kept

246

in there much of the time. He…" her eyes went stark blank as she recalled her time with Damon.

"Uh," her breath shook, "he tortured me in- in different ways. He had… devices… apparatus. Apparently while he had me, he didn't bother any of the other women he normally used in…that way."

Her chest heaved while she tried to draw air through her lungs constricted with the horrendous memories. "Tezer," she broke off, her face red with mortification.

His face carved stone, eyes blazing, he said quietly, "Tell me." His gut clenched and revolted, but he wanted her to tell it so she could get it out, get the poison of what this man did to her out.

It was all he could do himself not to upchuck at what this beautiful tender girl had suffered. But, he'd known since the moment he'd seen the whip marks on her back that he would avenge her. The person, monster, that had done this to her would not live.

Dove lifted her shirt and wiped her eyes, cleared her throat before starting again. "He, uh, would slap me mostly, repeatedly, sometimes he'd punch me…then he'd laugh like an insane mental patient while he stripped me.

"He would force me on my knees, bent over on my stomach over a wooden stock with my hands, uh, stretched out in front of me," she gulped a hard swallow, coughed, "and he would chain me in place."

She raised her eyes to Tezer but couldn't read the dark hooded eyes. His mouth was a tight grim line.

Then, he already knew, but his voice a bare harsh whisper, "Rape?"

The words stayed bottled inside, she nodded. The tears fell. "In between whipping me he would…but thankfully he only raped me twice, he had been too ill in the beginning and I escaped right after the second…time," she drew an aggrieved shuddering breath, her face strained.

"But there were other things…please don't make me say…" her big eyes showed the pain was still too recent, she was wringing and twisting her fingers to death.

There was no way he could hear any more of what was done to this sweet, innocent young woman anyway. Tezer moved near to her and pulled her against his chest while she wept.

"God, baby, God," he couldn't believe what she had endured. He stroked her back while she cried, her sobs shuddering against his body, he felt them as if they were his own.

When her wracking sobs decreased and she took deep heavy breaths, he held her upper arms and pulled her back. He tenderly pushed aside the hair that stuck to her damp face.

"Okay," his own voice fell out shaky and taut, "now, that I know who he is-"

Her eyes widened in horror. Lips parting in frightened gasps, she cried, "No, no Tezer. Nothing can be done. He's wealthy and powerful and dangerous. Deadly. No. You promised you wouldn't tell anyone about me, you promised!"

Her voice edged to hysteria, she wailed, "He told me if I ever ran, he'd use the rack and bring in other men to hurt me and sod- sodomize me with- with *things*, big things, implements he-"

"Hush, hush, baby," he soothed her, stroking her hair. "I won't tell anyone now, I promise you." His team already knew she had undoubtedly gone through something like what she just described.

"No one is going to hurt you again. I will take care of this fucker- ah, monster. My team. Me and my team will wipe this vile creature, Damon the Demon, off the face of the earth and send him to hell where he belongs. I'll decide later how to handle that fucking judge and those slave-driving despicable missionaries."

Dove jumped to her feet exclaiming, "No! You can't go near Damon, he will murder you- and Garth, and Leo, Nik, Reggie! He will kill you all! Please don't-"

Tezer got to his feet and reached for her, wrapped his hands around her arms to hold her still.

His big body like a protective muscular cloak around her, Tezer said soothingly, "Calm down, nothing is happening right now. Except," he pulled her in close and looked down into tumultuous swirls of panicked golden green, "we are getting married."

She tugged from his grasp. "Tezer, please-"

"Hush now, honey." He reached for her again and palmed her face, thumbed away her tears. "Braemont expects us in an hour in the salon. I want to give you some space so you can regroup after having to tell me…your, uh, experiences without me looming over you."

Dove studied his expression expecting to see revulsion, or judgment, or condemnation for what she'd told him. But all that was there was his fury at what had been done to her.

Sadness for what she had suffered, and determination that he would do something about Damon Philippè. And since he knew her name now, he would be going after the judge, and the Aikens, too.

Tezer sat back down and pulled her onto his lap. Cradling her head, he drew it down to rest against his shoulder. They say silently for a while like that, with his arms around her.

His cell beeped. Sliding it half-way out of his pocket to glance at the text, he shoved it back in his pocket and told her, "The maid is bringing you a dress to wear. I'm going to go change. Garth will come for you."

He soothed his fingertips over her pale face. "Right now, all you concentrate on is our wedding. Save all the worry for tomorrow. Okay?"

"Tezer," her chest hiccupped with renewed panic telling her story brought, and now, Tezer wants to go face that very devil himself? "Please, you can't-"

He set her to stand then he got up. "Dove," his voice rough and firm but he said gently, "think only of our wedding, then a few days or so and I can get you out of here to a safe place. Your place. You'll make it all your own."

Her eyes volleyed from one of his eyes to the other. He was so stalwart, so calm, so strong and confident, maybe…

Tezer slid his large hand around to web the back of her neck and head.

Before she thought to ask where this 'safe place' was that he was talking about, she'd go berserk when he tells her it was his home, he planned on not filling her in on that until they were actually there.

His gaze warm on her, he said, "Trust me, honey. All will be well. I won't let anyone hurt you, ever again, never. But," he clutched her neck, "you have to do as I tell you. I can't protect you if you disregard my orders- uh, instructions."

Seeing the mutinous tug to her mouth, he said quickly, "Now, I'm going to go change. Do not open the door to anyone but the maid or one of my team. You, do- not- leave- this- room- without Garth. You got that? Do I need to put it in writing so you'll know I won't change my mind?"

Her lips curved with a shake of her head. "No, I don't have any desire to leave this room, Tezer. I'd rather you didn't leave-" she broke off with a frown. She realized she felt safe with him here, at the moment anyway. The thought of him leaving her alone made her edgy.

Biting back the smile that pushed the corners of his mouth up, Tezer was happy to hear she wanted him to stay, wanted his presence. Even if it was only for security, that would do for now.

He needed some time to himself too to calm the rage that scorched through his vengeful, tightly wound body after the horror she told him she had endured.

It was all he could do to keep himself from storming out of the mansion right now and seeking that motherfucker and making him suffer the same as what he had done to her before he took him off the planet.

They both turned at the knock at the door.

"Ah, that would be the maid. I will see you in an hour. Now," sucking down his fury, he pulled her head closer, tilting it up. "Do not fret about anything, all will be well."

His lips fell gently on hers in a light kiss, any more and he'd be kicking the maid out and tossing Dove on the bed.

He went to the door and let the maid in. As the woman entered, Tezer reminded Dove, "One hour, Dove. Do not leave here."

She nodded, too nervous to speak. In an hour she would be getting married to a virtual stranger. A killing warrior, a dangerous mercenary. Ever since her parents died, her life had spun violently on its axis and she was still spiraling out of control.

She looked at him. He was tough and courageous, his dark eyes heated when he regarded her. The valiant chief did not hide his desire or his caring for her. Dove realized he was a man of his word. He would do everything he could to help her and protect her. She murmured, "I won't leave."

One last look, and he was gone.

"Miss," the maid said to her, "Mr. Braemont asked us to see what we could loan you. One of the servants who is close to your size offered this dress." She held up the hanger.

An off the shoulder, cream and blush satin sheath draped from it. In her hand she held a pair of satin heels and a large tote bag. "I will help you dress and do your hair and makeup."

Dove stood numbly watching the maid hang the dress on the top of the door. She could not wrap her head around the fact that she would be marrying Chief Tezer Corseque in an hour. She didn't even know how old he was, where he was from, nothing about his family.

What was she thinking?

Chapter Twenty-Three

She was ready when Garth knocked at the door, his deep voice announcing his name.

The maid opened it for him then slipped out as he entered.

He wore a dark blue jacket over a white dress shirt and tie, and creased black pants. His short dark curly hair was as neat as she'd ever seen it, and the ever present twinkle in his mischievous blue eyes held a dash of kind pride as he smiled at her.

"You look amazing, Dove, breathtaking. I wish I'd gotten to you first that day the bus brought you all in."

Her cheeks tinted pink at his compliment, the sincerity of his words was clear in his bright eyes. But Tezer was his best friend, he would never hit on her after Tezer had staked his claim. And the chief had made his claim clear the second he told his men he was going after her.

And as much as he would deny it, Tezer had chosen this girl for his own the second he saw her fleeing into the forest. He had come out a gone man.

Garth chuckled, couldn't happen to a better guy. Once these two settled down and grasped that they had fallen for each other, everything would drop into place.

"Um, thanks, Garth. I'm…nervous." Her lashes fluttered with her nerves.

"That's good, you're supposed to be nervous on your wedding day. You ready to go?"

She stared blankly at him, debating what her options were.

Fussing with the silky hair that curled over one shoulder, she said, "Garth. I am marrying a man I don't really know, who is an admitted killer. He said we would get a divorce later when I was safe. But then, what happens to me? I'm so...confused."

"Hey," he said softly, "Tezer Corseque is one of the best men you'll ever come across."

He moved closer to her and agreed, "Sure, he's bossy and tough, but he's only dangerous to the wrong kind of people. He hasn't hurt you, Dove. In all this time, you must see he would never harm a woman, or a child."

He smiled down at her. "He has the strongest integrity of anyone I've ever known, and he will protect you to the ends of the earth, with his life if necessary." To himself he muttered, *as far as the divorce, not gonna happen.* Garth knew his friend well. He was never going to let this blonde doll go.

With a big reassuring grin, he held his arm out for her to take. "He's a good man, Dove, give him the chance to show you. Okay?"

Her eyes went from his friendly, trustworthy face to the arm he offered her. Biting her lip, she was not going to be a crybaby anymore, dammit. Letting a heavy exhale drag out, she slipped her hand under his arm and allowed him to usher her out of the room.

If she wasn't holding onto Garth, she knew she would have faltered. But he was strong, he held her upright on her wobbling legs all the way down the carpeted stairs, through the halls to the salon.

When they reached the double doors that opened into the salon, her mouth dropped.

Everyone that had been on the trek as well as all the occupants of the castle were present, including staff and security people. They were all dressed in the finest clothes they had.

The room hushed, all eyes were on her.

Garth took a small bouquet of pink peonies and white calla lilies from Braemont's Aunt Mary and handed them to Dove. She took them without looking. Her eyes were aimed at the head of the room.

Up front, Tezer stood with James Braemont, the minister who would be officiating.

Tezer's dark eyes cut through the room and fastened on Dove like she was the only person on the planet. The only time his gaze left her big eyes was to travel down to take in her dress.

It must have met with his approval because a corner of his mouth curved up and the gaze that moved back to her eyes was crazy heated.

Her dress clung to her elegant shoulders. A faint blush tulle swept over the low bodice, and the thin satin sheath skimmed down her curvy slender figure to pool in a short train behind her on the floor.

Only the tips of her satin toes peeked out from under the hem. Her bright hair was pulled up the side with the curls rolling over a breast and down her back.

She looked at Tezer.

It was odd to see the big, grim, rough and tough mercenary dressed impeccably in a black suit. The jacket stretched over his broad shoulders, the pants hung slightly on his sinewy hips. He wore black dress boots and a tie, the same blush color as her tulle, over a starched white shirt. How on earth had he managed that?

His hair was combed straight back, but an errant lock slipped down over one brow making him look devilishly rakish as hell. And so darned sexy.

Dove didn't want to find him so devastatingly sexy, she wanted to be able to resist his advances with no effort.

Yet, those smoldering eyes were already drawing a heated tightness between her legs; she could feel silky dampness filtering through her channel. The handle of the bouquet crunched in her anxious hands.

Soft music flowed from speakers in the ceiling indicating the proceedings were to begin. An iceberg of terror slipped down over Dove, freezing her feet to the floor. When Garth started to move, she was stiff as a porcelain figurine.

He bent his head to whisper in her ear, "You are strong and brave, Dove, I've seen it. Don't let fear of the unknown handicap you. One foot in front of the other, you can do it."

He gave her a few seconds to pull herself together, then started to walk slowly.

After another initial hesitation, lowering her eyes to the carpet in front of her, Dove forced her feet to move.

They took a few steps, she raised her eyes.

Tezer's were gleaming straight at her, his expression inscrutable.

Garth brought her across the room and to his best friend, who took a few steps towards them. His eyes twinkling, Garth grinned at Tezer, who looked as confident as ever, but unsmiling. As usual.

He nodded at Garth, but his eyes never left Dove.

Garth lifted Dove's frozen hand from his arm and placed it in Tezer's big warm paw. He gave her a kiss on her cheek before taking his place beside Tezer.

Tezer said nothing as he brought her to stand in front of the minister.

Leo approached them, and with a smile to Dove, he stood beside her as her witness.

Her lips parted in surprise, then she gave him a trembly smile of thanks.

He bowed respectfully to her and turned his attention to the Reverend James Braemont.

Dove peeked over at his brother, **Yvetsky Braemont.**

Everyone was sitting down, **Yves** sat in the first row of chairs. Kitty was practically slung over him. Her gown all gold glitter, and as usual, more of her breasts were out of it than in.

His hand high up Kitty's thigh over the slit that exposed her bare skin, Yves stared impassively, his unfathomable expression was directed at Dove.

Kitty darted one hateful glare at Dove, then turning to Tezer, her face softened briefly, before hardening into a resentful grimace. She wriggled so Yves' hand would move further up her skirt, his fingertips moved to just under it.

Willing Tezer to look at her, Kitty spread her legs enough to show she was commando, she wore nothing under the glittering dress, and it was his for the taking.

But Tezer only had eyes for the little blonde trembling in front of him.

The couple faced the minister while he read from the Bible, Songs of Solomon about love, and 1 Corinthians 13:4-7 that says "Love is patient; love is kind; love is not envious or boastful or arrogant, or rude. It does not insist on its own way; it is not irritable or resentful; it does not rejoice in wrongdoing, but rejoices in the truth. It bears all things, believes all things, hopes all things, endures all things." Then he led the congregation with their promises to support this couple in their new life together.

The minister nodded at Garth.

Garth held out his hand. In his palm were two white-gold wedding bands.

Dove gasped, she glanced up at Garth who shrugged, murmured with a crooked grin, "Fed-ex by chopper."

She stiffened. Her eyes on the rings she said under her breath to Tezer, "You said nothing about rings. Why do we have rings?"

Feeling his little bird about to take flight, Tezer whispered, "They are not handcuffs, Dove. They are part of the ceremony. Relax." The truth was, he wanted his claim on her clear as a bell.

He wanted every man to take one look at her and see his ring and know she's off-limits. But he couldn't tell her that, she'd freak. She thought this wedding was just a temporary fix to get her out of the estate.

His little bird would go psycho when she learned the truth; that she was going to be irrevocably tied to him. She deserved much better than him. Tezer tried to keep telling himself that he must free her once he had her safe. But, he knew, once he had her, fair to her or not, he was keeping her.

Reverend Braemont said more words then elicited their vows from Tezer first.

His voice quiet but firm, his eyes boring into Dove's as he slipped the ring on her shaking finger, he promised to lover, honor and take care of her until they died.

Then Dove's turn. She repeated his word, her voice was so hushed the people strained to hear her breathy whispers. She pushed at the ring but couldn't get it up his big finger, her hands were shaking so badly now.

Tezer just shoved it on and smiled down at her.

His heart twisted, she was so dreadfully uncertain.

The big green eyes swimming with gold tears, she looked like all she wanted to do was run. She stared down at the ring on her finger like he had tied a python around it.

"You may kiss your bride," Braemont announced in a cheerful directive.

Ignoring the swift panicked widened eyes, Tezer cupped her head with both hands and lowered his mouth to mount her feminine softness. Lip to lip, he licked around the inside of both her sweet lips before sinking his tongue inside laying claim to his beautiful, frightened, wife.

The rest of the world turned to vapor around them. Tezer was only aware of his and Dove's mouths joining, becoming one. His hands tightened around her face, his loins throbbed and hardened, he tilted his head to seal their mouths more tightly-

"Ahem," the minister cleared his throat. When Tezer ignored him, the minister set a hand on his shoulder, gingerly squeezed gently as the chief was known to swing first and ask questions later.

The room twittered. Tezer broke from his bride. Her cheeks flushed rosy, eyes heavy lidded and glimmering, yet apprehension hovered in their depths.

He brushed his thumbs over her cheeks and smiled. A soothing whisper minted her skin, "Relax baby, the hard part is done."

She gave him a quivering crooked smile.

He slid his arm around her shoulders and turned her to face the room.

James Braemont announced loudly, "May I present, Mr. and Mrs. Corseque."

At his words, Dove stiffened under Tezer's arm. Tezer gave her a quick hug and led her through the small crowd, nodding straight-faced at the well-wishes tossed at them.

Yves Braemont had also provided a reception. The man wasn't happy about the chief snatching Dove out from under him but he was a man who always saved face. Plus, he loved any excuse to throw a party.

The people danced, and ate and drank and made merry for hours.

However, after only an hour or so, Tezer was tired and annoyed at every man pushing to dance with his bride.

Seeing Braemont holding her breathlessly tight against his body, with his big slick hands all over her bare back while he looked down her décolletage, was the last straw.

Seizing her hand, he ushered his new wife as discreetly as possible from the big room decorated with pink and white ribbons and bows down a hall she'd never been in.

He led her to way in the back of the mansion. Then he opened a door and lifted her into his arms.

"Tezer! What are you-"

"Threshold baby, it's called carrying my bride over the threshold." He carried her in and kicked the door closed behind them.

Before setting her down, he held her in his arms and twirled her around, laughing at her squeals and giggles.

When he set her on her feet, she grabbed at his shoulders to steady herself and looked up at him.

One of the rare times she saw a real smile on his face, and the harsh planes were relaxed. The empty pits of his dark eyes held a soft warmth.

Letting go of his shoulders, she combed the loose ringlets of her hair with her fingers and asked, "Why did you do that?"

He shrugged a broad shoulder. "To calm you, ease those tense muscles. Your body has been as rigid as an ironing board all day. Like I said, the rough part is over."

She blinked at him then looked around. "Oh, Tezer, it's beautiful."

He had brought her to a glass enclosed atrium. Plants and colorful flowers bloomed everywhere. Heat or a fireplace was not necessary as the glass allowed the sun to soak its luxurious buttery warmth into the room.

Flowers stretched their ornamental blooms to bathe in the lovely light. Leafy green plants glistened, preening in the bright rays.

"Yeah, Come." He took her hand and brought her to a sofa covered in soft cream and helped her to sit.

In front of the sofa, on a table sat a crystal ice bucket containing a bottle of champagne with a cloth laid over it.

Tezer shrugged out of his suit coat, tossed it on a chair, then took the bottle out, unwound the wire and popped the cork.

The bubbly champagne effervesced over the top; he quickly picked up a crystal flute, filled it and handed it to her.

Surrounded by the lush garden of fragrant blossoms and rich greenery, her hands in her lap, Dove looked at the crystal glass with fizzing golden liquid and hesitated. "Uh, I don't really drink, I don't think-"

"Here," he grasped one of her arms, pulled it up and thrust the glass into her unsure hand. "Celebrate with me. It will help calm you. If you're old enough to be married, you're old enough to drink. Besides, it's not like you have to drive anywhere," he said with a dry half-grin.

Her brows arched, it was not like Tezer to joke. "Um, if you think it's okay," she took the glass.

He poured himself one, sat beside her and raised the glass to her and said, "To my beautiful bride."

Her worried expression brought a frown to his cool countenance. "What, what is it?" He tugged at the knot in his tie, loosening it, and opened the top button of his white shirt.

Clutching the flute with both hands, Dove said urgently, "I don't want you to go after Damon." She started to move off the sofa, her word came out more firmly, "You get me out of this mansion and I can hide. There is no need for anyone else to get hurt."

Tezer grabbed her wrist to hold her in place. Turning her slightly to face him, he said, "You are done running, Dove. I am your husband now, I will protect you and I will eliminate this threat from you."

Shaking her head, she moved again to get up. "No, I won't have it, Tezer. You don't know what you're up against. He…" her eyes flit up at him then away. "I've seen him kill." Her graceful shoulders shivered with the memories. The light left her eyes making them opaque green goblets.

She stared blankly at his hand on her wrist. Her voice soft she told him, "He is without compassion. He ruthlessly kills out of anger, punishment, and," she shrugged and her head dropped in inevitable hopelessness, "sometimes I witnessed him murder, just for the fun of it. No."

Setting the flute on the table she made a strong effort to get to her feet. "If you fight me on this, Tezer, I will march right back to the salon and tear up that certificate."

Putting his glass on the table, his mouth curved wryly, Tezer said with slight amusement, "Honey, it doesn't matter. You can burn the marriage certificate, but it won't invalidate it. It's a copy for us to keep. As soon as we all signed it, I had the original sent off to the clerk of courts in the main city." Already she was trying to back out of the marriage and it had barely been an hour.

Exhaling to release his suddenly taut muscles, Tezer forced the anger that boiled up inside his chest over Damon to chill out. Moving a hand behind her head cradling it, he grasped her arm to hold her, then bent and leisurely kissed her plush lips.

The kiss was not aggressive, or even steaming lustful, it was tender, long and dulcet. It was so long that when he finally ended it, he could see her head spinning, passion clogging the green-gold orbs. Blinking at him, she had forgotten what they were talking about.

He reached over and picked up her glass, tucked it back into her hand and reached for his own.

"We were toasting to us, baby, remember?" He held his glass out and clinked it with hers and smiled at her dazed expression. "To us, Dove. Drink up."

"Um," her dazed eyes contracted befuddled and wary on the glass in her hand.

His voice smooth black velvet, he told her, "Don't think, honey, drink."

When she still didn't move, Tezer cupped her hand and literally brought the glass to her lips and tipped it. She had to drink or it would pour down the front of her.

Tezer spoke about inconsequential things while continuing to urge her to drink up.

Every time she went to set her glass down he raised his in another toast. When her glass shrank to half-full, he would fill it so she was completely unaware of how much she was consuming. But he watched her carefully. He wanted her relaxed, and amenable, not passed out or sick.

Taking a careful sip, Dove eyed the bottle in his hand with suspicion. Her head was feeling bubbly with the bubbly. She felt slightly giddy. "Chief, tell me-"

Exasperated, Tezer growled, "Come on, Dove, I'm your husband. Cut that shit out."

She peeped at his scowling hard face; the hurt of her trying to keep a wall between them was clear in his frank eyes. "I'm sorry. Tezer, tell me about your family."

The hurt in his eyes turned to blank inscrutable discs as his lids lowered over them. "Ah, that would take a lot of time. I'd rather talk about them later, when we have some time really to ourselves. All right?"

What could she say? He had walls too. "I, uh, guess; if you're uncomfortable, but-"

"So," he said quickly while refilling her glass, "what did you think about Braemont's cousin, that girl, Ashley?"

Her words were slightly slurred, "The one with the orangey hair?"

Smiling, he took a sip of his champagne, nodded. "Yeah. She was all up over Clancy at the reception, and the witch was staring black daggers at her. I was expecting a girl fight any second."

She giggled, drank some and scolded him, "You are so not nice, Tezer. Just because she has black hair and a pointy face, Avril is not a witch."

Thoughtfully with a slurry grin, she muttered, "She's not a witch, but she sure is mean," more giggles bubbled out of her. She skewed a sly look at him, "The girls say you men like girl fights. I bet you were hoping for a knock down-drag out, bodice-ripping brawl! Right?"

He bent to set his glass on the table, then took hers and set it beside it. Moving his hand to brace against the sofa cushion, he cupped her face and leaned over, not stopping until he could reach her lips with his tongue if he wanted to.

He murmured against her mouth, "The only thing I care about, Wife, or whose bodice I want to rip, is yours." His mouth enveloped hers.

Chapter Twenty-Four

Lulling her into the kiss, Tezer moved his mouth so soft against hers their lips barely touched. He didn't pull her closer or harden or deepen the kiss, he just kept lightly as a hint touching their mouths together.

He smothered his smile when after a few minutes of cloud-soft wispy kisses, her hands strode up his chest, her fingers coiled tentatively over his shoulders.

He held her very lightly like she was cotton candy and kept his kisses feather strokes, even when she started digging her fingers into his shoulders and trying to kiss him back harder.

Soon, she grew frustrated with his gentle kissing. Her hands still on his shoulders, she frowned. Eyes wobbling slightly unfocused, she asked, "What's wrong, Tezer? Am I doing something wrong?" Her little pink lips pushed out in an intoxicated pout. "Now that we're married, you don't want me anymore?"

Keeping his smile suppressed, he responded, "Hmm, well, I know you don't want to have…relations with me. I am respecting your wishes. I don't want to get myself all excited and carried away with more…say…ardent kisses, and push myself on you. I have very little resistance when it comes to you, Dove. So it's better we keep it…mild. Right?"

His inner smile deepened at the frown of perplexity furrowing her brow and making her pretty lips pout more.

"But," her lower lip stuck out, her glazed eyes went from his dark orbs to his mouth, she licked her lips.

Tezer's erection already strained at his pants.

Watching her struggle with wanting him to kiss her more zealously, and suddenly not sure if he was still as hot for her as he was. Not sure what she should do or say, and following that pink tongue swirling around those luscious lips, all she had to do was look down and she'd see clear, thick hard evidence of his desire for her.

But he smiled innocuously, and said, "I don't want to upset you baby, so I'm keeping my hands to myself."

The lip pushed out further. Her words carried the slight slur and accent thickening, "But, um, kissing is okay, I think. What do you think?" She was growing confused. She wanted to continue but she didn't know what to do about it.

"Well," he put on a pretend frown and brushed her pouty lips with a fingertip, and smiled when she absently kissed it.

She didn't protest when he moved it to just past her lips to inside her mouth. "I don't want to, you know, pressure you, overpower you. Maybe," he trailed off watching her stare at his mouth.

Her tongue stirred, touching his fingertip. As soon as she did, he drew his finger from her mouth watching her unhappy expression. Her licking his finger made him think of other places she could put her tongue.

"Maybe what?" She brought her legs up and knelt on the couch facing him, bringing her body closer to his.

"Well, maybe if *you* kiss *me*, you know, then I'll know when to back off." Tezer had to purse his lips not to smile at the way her every thought traipsed across her face. Damn she was so young, so naïve, such an open-book. Fucking adorable.

Through the slightly drunken fog, she thought hard about what he said. "Um, okay. I think that would be…all right."

He didn't move.

Her perplexed frown deepened. "Aren't you going to, uh, kiss me?"

Now he let a tiny smile slip through turning up one side of his mouth. "No baby. We just decided you needed to come to me and show me what is all right with you."

"Oh. Okay." She wriggled closer on her knees and put her hands back on his shoulders then carefully put her mouth to his and kissed him gently. She leaned back. "Is that okay?"

The smile deepened, she would kill him when she sobered up and comprehended he'd manipulated her. He said nonchalantly, almost diffidently, "I guess. You need to do what you think is right."

She contemplated his mouth for a few seconds, then put her lips on his, tilted her head and kissed him harder.

When he showed little reaction, she gingerly licked his lips like he had done to her, then slid her tongue into his mouth and explored his masculinity, how different he was from her, how his musky maleness tasted. His mouth was harder than hers, but still soft, his lips were firm but soft.

Tezer feared his pants would split with his enflamed erection, his dick felt like a geyser about to blow. But he let Dove lead with her innocent experimental kisses.

Though he was more comfortable dominating in sex, she was doing a damned fine job, and her greenness was a turn-on itself. All her tentative little thrusts and parries titillated his mouth, he could feel it in his stomach and his manhood.

He put his hands on her bare shoulders delighting in the slender softness of them, then he skimmed his palms over the smooth skin of her back, her nape, and up her neck, stroking her entire elegant carriage.

She moved even closer to him, her hands slid from his shoulders to press on his chest. Pulling back slightly, she purred, "You are so strong, Tezer, I've never seen such muscles before."

Her fingers slid down his tie, then feeling brave, she tugged it out of its loose knot, used it as a rope to pull his head to hers. Her smile was wickedly wanton, and he freaking loved it.

"Feel free to explore them as much as you want, honey, any of them." This playing was fun, nice, hot. He'd never played with a woman before, they usually just got right to it, wham, bam.

Humming, "Mmmm," Dove pulled him with his tie until their lips met. His mouth barely pulsed when she kissed him, letting her lead. She slid the tie from his neck and tossed it on his jacket and put her palms on his chest.

Tezer could feel every nuance of her small hands spreading over his chest, cupping flinty muscles, feeling their hard, flexing play under her hands. Every caress went straight to his dick.

He stroked his hands down her bare arms below the off the shoulder dress and felt her squirm on the sofa until her knees were almost touching his leg. He faced her with one leg curved on the couch and the other planted on the floor.

So close, lids heavy with passion over her tipsy eyes drifted all over his face, from his hard chin and chiseled cheeks, to his eyes like liquescent onyx, to his lips, the top one sensuously slightly fuller than the bottom.

Her mouth as if drawn like a fish after bait fell fervent to his, so surprisingly unbridled Tezer felt his shaft bulge and jerk inside the black slacks.

His hands moved instinctively towards his belt to release his cock, but he managed to stop himself. He had to let her make the moves.

He slid his hands back up her arms, across her shoulders to her neck. His fingers glided over the soft skin of her neck, his thumbs stroking her jaw, he caressed her lightly but ensured she felt his every stroke.

Dove's face was glowing a dark pink. Dazed eyes glassy, she moved her head from his and put her fingers on the buttons of his shirt.

Her eyes shifted to his then to a button. "Can I," she looked up shyly at him again toying with the button, the liquor emboldened her, "unbutton your shirt and see…those…uh, muscles?"

A few loose tendrils of hair fell over one eye made her so sultry sexy it was a struggle for him to fight the urge to push her on her back and lift her dress- Only the flare of his pupils relayed his body's reaction to her words.

"Sure," he said casually, "feel free to do whatever you want." *Because turnabout is fair play-*

The tip of her tongue poked out the side of her mouth as she unbuttoned two buttons. "Oh, Tezer, I'd forgotten the few times I've seen you, um, without a shirt, you have…lots of dark hair." Her eyes sloped up to his. "Can I touch it?"

Realizing this may go where he hoped, Tezer growled, "Baby, I think we should go to our room where we have privacy. Someone might come in here. What do you think?" He still wanted it to be her decision.

Her head swung back and forth as she looked behind them and to the door. "Oh, I didn't think-" she blushed. "Maybe we, shouldn't," her gaze flit back to the partial exposure of his broad chest, the dark masculine hair behind the starched white, and she scrambled off the sofa.

"Okay." She tottered a few feet backwards when the alcohol hit her with the sudden movements.

"Hey," Tezer stood up and caught her arm. "Steady there, honey." Nonchalantly, he said, "Should we bring the champagne? There's still half a bottle."

"I guess." She turned blurry eyes to the bottle and shrugged with a smile. "Sure."

He didn't wait another second for her to change her mind.

Chapter Twenty-Five

$\mathcal{T}$ezer picked up his jacket and tie tossing them over his shoulder, set the flutes in the bucket, grabbed up the bucket, clamped his hand on her wrist and hurried her out of the atrium.

Tezer strode so quickly down the back hall to the back staircase to avoid running into other people that Dove gasped breathy giggles.

"Tezer! I can't keep up with you!"

"Uh huh," he mumbled absently, the only thing on his mind was getting her to their room and continuing where they left off before she sobered and grew doubtful and rigid again.

When he reached the room, he opened the door, handed her the ice bucket and swept her up into his arms.

"What are you doing?" She shrieked with laughter.

Striding through the door, he hit it with his boot to close it behind them and said, "Threshold baby, remember? That's what husbands do with their new brides."

Laughing she trilled, "But not every one of them, silly!"

He set her on her feet and took the bucket from her and set it on a table. He immediately poured her half a glass and

272

handed it to her. "Have a sip, you must be thirsty," he said cheerfully.

His cagey plan was to keep her slightly buzzed so she was pliable and wouldn't think. She'd been brutally raped as a virgin, and he needed to keep her tranquil, and aroused, so the horrific memories wouldn't flood out their own lovemaking.

"Oh, okay," she giggled taking the glass and a big sip.

Throwing his jacket and tie on a chair, Tezer maneuvered her away from the dreaded bed and to the divan in the room and nudged her to sit, then sat down next to her.

"That was such a pretty place, Tezer." Dove smiled thinking about the atrium.

"Yeah, it was. Drink up." He urged the glass to her lips. When she took a few more sips he took the glass from her and set it on the table.

Playing shy, he said, "You were, uh, about to, you know," he nodded down at his chest.

Her expression was befuddled. So green she needed coaxing. He picked up her hand and slid it inside his shirt under the few open buttons. "You have my permission to touch any part of me you want, nothing is off limits. You do not need to ask."

"Oh!" She giggled. "I remember." She flexed her fingers over the bit of hair she could feel. "You're, I mean, it, your hair, is soft. Or, actually roughly soft."

Tezer set his hands on her thighs, said innocently, "Go ahead, honey, unbutton the rest."

"Hmm." She stared at the shirt, nodded. "Okay," and fumbled the rest of the buttons open. A sexy smile rode over her face, pulling her delicious lips up.

"Tezer," she oozed, her voice husky, so sultry, Tezer almost gave up and ripped both their clothes off. But he restrained himself. She would run if he jumped at her.

It was frustrating as hell as a grown man to drag this out, but, it was also the hottest thing he'd ever experienced. Taking all this time with her was a million times better than having a quick fuck with someone like Kitty. Yuk, why did he even think of that bitch.

"Dove," murmuring softly, he labored to calm the scorching blood racing through his body setting off sparks and heat. He said casually, "That dress is beautiful, baby, especially on you, but," he eyed it slyly, "it looks a little uncomfortable. Do you have anything on under it that, maybe you could…"

He could have suggested she change into something else but didn't want to chance losing momentum. Besides, whatever she had on under that dress had to be a lot less than what she'd put on if she changed her clothes.

Dove looked down at the front of her dress a bit muddled, trying to remember when she'd gotten dressed. Her face brightened. "Yes, I have like a- a bustier kind of thing, like a lace corset teddy. It's really pretty, one of the maids loaned it to me."

"Uh huh." He nodded casually as if she said she was wearing army boots. "Maybe you'd feel more comfortable in the- what'd you say, teddy? I mean, you'd still be fully clothed, just more comfortable, right?"

She considered his words, her mouth pursed in thought. Then she shrugged. "I guess. But," she blushed again.

"But what?" His fingers were already moving towards her.

A shy giggle, her shoulder tipped up. "The maid had to help me into this gown. I don't think I can get it off without her help. I guess we need to call her to come and-"

"No problem." Tezer stood right up, grasped her hands and pulled her to her feet. "Turn around." Not waiting for her to comply, he put his hands on her shoulders and spun her.

"Uh, Tezer, I'm not sure…"

"You'll be fine, honey, if a maid can do it up, I can undo it." There were satin buttons down the back of the gown, he was already reaching for the first one.

"Oh, I didn't mean that, I meant," she trailed off, the liquor was affecting her thoughts.

"Oh," she sighed, giggled. "I don't remember what I was- oh!" While she was ruminating, Tezer had unbuttoned the gown to her waist; she felt the air brush against her back.

His hands on her waist, he turned her back around to face him. His eyes fell to the bodice of the dress. Without the constraints of the buttons, the front dipped exposing more of her cleavage.

Seeing his eyes charge with excited heat, his pupils enlarged at her bosom, Dove nervously looked over at the champagne. "I feel uh, maybe I should have some more champagne." She turned towards the table but Tezer's hands tightened on her tiny waist stilling her.

"I don't think you should have anymore right now, we shouldn't push it. You want to be relaxed, but able to feel what we're doing, and remember it. Now, where were we?"

He caged her mouth with his before she could object or think and instantly took her over. She melted into his mouth like hot syrup. He kissed her, drinking from her sweet fountain, drowning in her essence.

His lips slid from her mouth to behind her ear. Tezer remembered how sensitive she was when he had tickled her there. His licks and nibbles on her tactile skin sent a soft moan flurrying in her chest, her neck arched.

He licked around her ear. Her body twittered in his hands along with another fragmented moan, she tilted her head to give him greater access. He kissed from her ear, over her cheek and along her jaw to her neck.

Tezer was enthralled with the way she shivered and sighed a purr.

His mouth on her neck, he bit lightly then sucked until he marked her. Juvenile, yes, but he liked seeing it there, and another hot sexy sound rumbling deep in her chest told him she liked it too. Or at least the feeling of his mouth sucking her tender flesh.

Moving his mouth back to cover hers, nudging her lips apart, his tongue stole inside to find hers and skirmish with it. He lifted his hands to the top of her gown.

Keeping her occupied with the manipulations of his mouth and tongue, he slipped the gown down her front and down her arms.

But he had to look. He pulled from her, dropped his gaze and almost cried at the strapless, lacey corset that cupped her beautiful breasts like a man's hands.

His eyes about fell out of his head. His lips bunched, the only man's hands that would be cupping Dove's breasts would be his.

With his big hands he caught the satin dress and brought it down to her waist then lifted her arms out of the bits of sleeves.

Feeling the cool sinuous dress sliding down her body, Dove's neck arched and her face tipped up. The long curls pinned up on the side of her head slipped around her back and dangled in ringlets.

Then, her modesty prevailed. She straightened and put her hands on his chest. "Tezer, wait, I-"

His mouth back on her neck, he sucked then licked down to her collarbone. With little kisses he said against her skin, "It's okay, honey, you're fully dressed under the gown. Let me just," he kissed down to the swell of a breast, "help you off with it."

Keeping his mouth on the flesh of her ample globe, Tezer pushed the gown past her hips.

"Oh, Tezer, I feel, so..." her head lolled, breasts rose to his tongue and teeth biting and licking the richness of each mammary.

He tore his mouth from her breast to pull the rest of the dress down. "Good God, Dove," he moaned. Pushing the dress to the floor he gaped at the teddy.

It was pink and white lace that went from her bosom to snug between her legs, and, there were garters, *oh God*, and white fucking stockings, he was going to die.

He'd never seen anything so mind scrambling hot in his life. He crouched and lifted one high-heeled foot then the other to move the dress away, leaving it in a satin pile on the carpet.

He studied the corset. He wanted like hell to leave the stockings and garters on while, if- they made love, but to be able to get to her, he had to take the teddy off, and the garters and stockings were all part of it. Sadly the stilettoes had to go too so he could get the stockings off.

Last thing he wanted was to pause things, but he had to make sure she was all right with everything. He stood up and put his hands on her shoulders.

She tipped her head lazily up at him and smiled. Like a punch in the gut that smile did to him. "Ah, baby, I'm going to take off your shoes and stockings so you can…be comfortable. Is that all right?"

Her smile dreamy, sexy, her lashes lowered slowly then raised up to reveal the glimmering gold-green eyes.

"Sssure," she slurred and wriggled with her arms pressed against her breasts. The full flesh jiggled and mounded even more over the top of the teddy.

Tezer would love to dive into her cleavage, jump in with his whole body and slither all over her bare skin, licking and mouthing every silken inch of her. Slide his throbbing cock up and down between her fluffy breasts, he shook himself.

"Okay. Put your hands on my shoulders to balance."

She did as he said. He crouched down and slipped off one heel then the other, frowning sadly at them.

He pictured her legs wrapped around his hips with her wearing only the garter, stockings, and the heels digging into his back. But, alas, they had to go. Maybe next time he could entice her to wear just them while they-

When she swayed on her feet, he took that as an opportunity. Clasping her hand, he drew her to the bed.

"Let's get comfortable, baby, you were going to undo my shirt, and," he sighed, "I feel that you have quite fallen down on the job." He nodded to his shirt with arched brows like she was slacking.

With a giggle, she said, "I forgot." She reached for his shirt but he put his hands around her waist and lifted her up and set her on the bed. Then gently pushed her back inclining against pillows.

Laughing, Dove lounged back and watched as he straddled her hips. "What are you doing, Tezer?"

"I'm moving to where you can reach me, sweetheart. It's all about your comfort. Okay, go ahead, finish your job," indicating his shirt.

Grinning, Dove reached up and undid the rest of the buttons. Then she tugged the hem out of his trousers with both hands and slid the lapels of his shirt back to expose his purely masculine chest.

With an approving sigh, she put her palms on the dark hair that matted over the slabs of muscles. She tentatively brushed her hands up, letting the hair sift through her fingers.

"Soft and rough at the same time," she murmured, then rubbed harder to feel the muscles that lay bunched under the hair. Her fingers clutched at sinew and raked at hollows, her hands stroked up his chest to his big shoulders where she kept murmuring how hard and strong he was. When she dragged her fingers back down and grazed his nipples he twitched and groaned.

When her wandering hands moved under the shirt to feel his huge biceps, he trailed a finger over the swell of one breast then the other that mounded over the lacy bra. He slid the finger down between them.

Her spine wormed, her head fell back, and she rolled slightly with a hushed moan and shiver at his touch.

He slipped his fingers under the top of the corset-bra and pulled it down to completely bare her breasts. He could feel his eyes heating and glowing at her beauty. Perfectly round, soft globes, he covered them with his hard hands.

"Tezer," her whimper husky in her throat, her hands fell limply to the mattress. Her body lifted and rolled, arching against the pillows pushing her breasts into his hands.

Tezer still straddled her, hungrily gripping her woman's flesh.

"God in heaven," he groaned, "every single part of you is so fucking beautiful, beyond angelic." He clutched her supple breasts with his long fingers, squeezing their fullness.

"I'm fucking insane for you, Dove, my wife." Cupping her full flesh, he looked from her plump lips to her strawberry nipples, his hands and mouth coveted both.

Tearing his burning gaze from her bosom to her eyes, he told her, "The second you flashed those terrified, *angry*, golden green peepers at me, I was so gone. The whole journey, I had no idea how to handle the feelings you evoked in me. I know I was…a cruel brute."

She murmured, "You were so mean to me that first day, cursing me and pushing me around. Made Garth threaten to cut off my fingers…" her mouth puckered at the terrifying memory.

"Ah, honey, you know neither of us would have ever hurt you. It was a method," his head drooped slightly, "that I regret, and Garth really hated it. We are soldiers, I'm not used to…interrogating…females, especially ones I am so mercilessly attracted to."

The corner of his lip ticked up. "That's why I made Garth do it, I didn't want to appear that much of a sadistic beast to you." He kneaded her breasts almost too hard as his erection trapped in his pants, sought her female core.

"I'm sorry I hurt you, Dove, was cold and cruel. I just felt I needed to keep my distance, and I didn't know how to do that. I never get involved with any women on a mission. Never. So," his eyes lowered to her chest and blazed.

"I was crude to you, trying to make you not important to me, but," he bent and kissed the valley between her swollen flesh, his evening whiskers brushing the tender skin, "it was a losing battle."

Dove watched Tezer fondling her breasts with more and more aggression, harder. Her head fell back with an erotic sigh, his hands were so strong, so purposeful, so sexy. The way he looked at her, like he was a rocket ship, a projectile aiming to penetrate her Venus.

He took her lips, sucked the plush plums, whispered against them, "Tasty mouth," he leaned from her. "Ah, Dove," his palm tenderly swept her face.

"I'd never before experienced such an irrepressible urge that day I chased and caught you. I craved beyond belief, to push you down, pull those sweet thighs apart and fuck you until we both-"

At his aggressive words, she nervously pushed to sit up. "Tezer, I need to- to- go." Her hands propped behind her, she was oblivious that her ribcage curved, lifting her bare breasts to his face.

He couldn't resist, moaning, "Sweetheart," and grasped her ripe fruit with his thick calloused fingers, bent and swathed his tongue over a nipple. Her groan, a shocked cry vibrated with her body suddenly gyrating on the soft mattress.

Pinching the nipple between his finger and thumb, he turned to the other and put his lips on it, nipped it, bit it again, harder until she gasped with pleasured pain.

He licked it and sucked it, taking her entire areole into his mouth until she was whimpering, her body undulating under him. His man's organ was like a steel rod pressing at his pants, wanting inside her with his every heaving breath.

Caressing the ample swells of her breasts, Tezer's skin puckered at her moans. He lifted her slightly to her side, and rolled halfway down beside her.

Gripping one breast, he skimmed his other palm to stroke the inner curve of her back, and down to cup her bottom. He kneaded her ass over the lace with his big hand but he hungered for her bare skin.

Slipping his hand up the bottom of the teddy, his fingers slid along her inner crease, stroking, squeezing each rounded cheek. He lowered his head to hers and fused their mouths.

Both breathing harsh and shallow, his kisses suddenly quickened, escalating feverishly with growing roughness and voracity, his fingers aching for her flesh, he shifted his mouth to suck the mounds of her breasts.

Cradling a firm globe in his tough grasp, he bent to capture her nipple, pulling it into his mouth, searing it with the heat of his tongue.

He needed her desperately. His hunger turned him savagely violent, in a frenzy he jerked the top of the corset down to pull it off but couldn't get it over her hips, he wrenched fiercely at the bottom trying to rip the teddy off her.

His rapacious tearing at her lingerie panicked Dove. Her hands went to his chest while she twisted her body from his grasp. Shrugging herself to the edge of the bed and pushing at him, she cried, "Tezer, please, stop, you're scaring me!"

Blood coursed through his veins and rushed in his ears, his brain effervesced like the champagne, he couldn't hear her over his lusting rampage.

He grasped her wriggling butt with both hands to bring her back to him, pulled her tight against his raging hard-on and savagely devoured her mouth emitting feral guttural growls down her throat.

Impatient and incensed with desire, his brain shouted for him to rip off the swath of cloth that covered her privates and he could thrust into her- But, he felt her rigidity in his arms, her lips trembled against his rampant mouth. Slowly he became aware of her small fists pushing at him, her hands on his chest trying to futilely move away.

It was an effort to lift his lids heavy with rushing passion to look at her. When he saw her frightened face, he paused in his vehement onslaught.

His eyes dropped to her naked breasts wedged against the mat of hair on his chest, the fever fueled in him all over again, but he forced himself to loosen his grip and look at her face.

He moved his hands to hold her upper arms. "Baby, Dove, what is it?" But he knew, he'd lost his control and was too forceful too quickly and brought back the memory of that fucker's assault on her.

Her bottom lip quivered, she brought her hands up to cover her breasts. "Please, Tezer," she lifted her eyes to see the thatch of dark hair hang over one of his eyes that gleamed white-hot desire.

Biting back his disappointed sigh, Tezer sat up and pulled her up to sit.

Her hair had come loose and draped over the front of her body partially veiling her nudity.

"I…I'm sorry, Dove, I didn't mean to scare you, push you. I just," he shoved the hair back off his head. "You turn me on so fucking much I just went crazy and, out of control. I want you, baby, I want you bad. I… want us to…make love."

God, he felt like a wild animal. Never has a woman ever unleashed him like this before, totally vaporizing his self-control, making him attack her, forgetting she was still so innocent and fragile.

She pushed her long curls back with both hands and wriggled to make him release her arms.

"Dove, I'll take it slow, wait-"

Shaking her head she pushed at him again but he couldn't make his fingers unlatch from clutching her.

"Honey, kiss me, it's our wedding night," that was a mistake, he knew it as soon as he said it.

She raised flushed, angry eyes to his that he knew smoldered with his intense need for her. "You said, you promised, you would not want sex with me if we married." She jerked her body to get him to let go of her.

Another mistake, his gaze fell to her sumptuous breasts jiggling from her movements. His shaft flared, and she grew angrier, anxious, seeing his pupils heat up again. "Let me go." Her voice was firm but the quiver was there.

Refusing to let her get away, Tezer coaxed, "Dove, let me be your husband, baby, be my wife, let me make love to you. Let's consummate our marriage and move forward. I want a life with you-"

"Let go of me." Her head lowered, she was not going to make eye contact with him.

Defeated, he forced himself to release her.

She immediately scooted off the bed and frantically looked for something to cover her partial nudity. Spying his jacket, she scurried over and slipped it on then went to the dresser and grabbed up shorts and a T.

It killed him. Seeing her just about naked in his suit jacket was so fucking hot.

Raking his fingers through his hair, his voice was ragged with frustration and desire. "Dove, I didn't say I would not want sex with you, obviously that is not true. I said I wouldn't force you to have sex with me, but that doesn't mean we can't…if we want to."

He peered up through that lock that flopped back down over his dark eye. A lopsided grin turned up a part of his mouth, he said, "I want to." He watched her shuffling towards the bathroom.

Louder, he said, "And I know you wanted to. At least for a while there." He raised his voice, "You can't deny it," but he was talking to the bathroom door.

Grabbing the pillows and shoving them against the headboard, slamming his back on them, Tezer exhaled harshly and palmed his erection to move it to a more comfortable position.

A cold shower wasn't going to take care of this one. He eyed the bathroom door, how long would she be? The shower came on. Damn he'd give anything to be in there with her.

He unbuttoned his pants, unzipped them and took out his swollen erection. If he didn't take care of his hard-on she was not going to be safe from him. Fisting it, he pictured Dove laying under him, her naked tits bouncing, body writhing to his touch, eyes like willow glass, and he pumped vigorously until he got release.

Not the one he wanted, but at least he wouldn't be jumping her, assaulting her when she exited the bathroom. Because that's what his iron hard shaft wanted, and if it had ears, they would be closed to the word no.

When they were both…calmer, they were having a talk about this marriage of theirs. Yeah, he'd promised her he wouldn't make her, force her to have sex, and yeah, the truth was he had led her to believe he wasn't going to want or expect it from her.

He had to say that then or she wouldn't have gone through with it. But, right from the start he had planned on their union lasting, and lovemaking was sure as hell going to be a part of it.

Sighing, he reached for a towel on the table. That bastard had damaged her. It didn't destroy or ruin her, but she was broken. She could be fixed, he just needed to move more slowly, give her moments here and there to get used to them as a couple.

New plan. He would surreptitiously teach her to crave his touch. He smiled to himself.

Earlier, he'd gotten her hot, and had sneakily coerced her into being the aggressor.

It had worked, for a while. Until he'd turned into a deranged, out of control ravager.

Lesson learned. Tomorrow he would work his plan. Seducing his beautiful young wife. Yeah.

Chapter Twenty-Six

Tezer was pissed when the sun streamed into the room pushing up his hung-over lids.

He had left the room yesterday before Dove had come out of the bathroom. He didn't trust himself with her at the moment, and he knew she needed some space. He'd gone and found the guys in a billiard room drinking and shooting pool.

When he returned very late, and very drunk, to their room, Dove was sound asleep. She was under the covers, curled up, he noticed with a wry twinge, facing away from his side of the bed.

After a shower, he had changed into sweatpants and a T and lay down on top of the blankets. The more barriers between them the better.

Except now, as the sun had long past risen indicating afternoon, the bed was empty, as was the rest of the room.

She wasn't there. Instant anger snapped. She knew he didn't want her wandering around outside the room without him. Damn hardheaded naïve woman.

He quickly got dressed, slipped his wallet and cell in his pocket, his gun in the harness at the back of his pants, and stuffed several knives around the rest of his body.

When he went to the dresser to comb his hair, he saw her ring. Her wedding band.

He didn't know which emotion struck him more fiercely, fury that she took it off, or dread that it meant the marriage was already at an end. Shit. He'd pushed her too far too fast last night.

But if she thought their marriage was done, she had another thing coming. He swooped the ring up and slipped it into his pocket and left the room.

Taking the stairs two at a time, Tezer headed first to the living room, the great room where most of the people normally gathered. One quick glance and he saw she wasn't there.

He checked the kitchen and dining room next. Striking out, he was headed for the library when Yves Braemont came out of a corridor and stopped him.

"Corseque, just the person I was looking for. Didn't you get my calls?"

A grimace on his face, Tezer shook his head with a scowl. "No. I don't have time for calls, I need to find Dove. My wife." Damn, if anyone had told him six months ago he'd love saying those two words; he would have offed their head with a sardonic lancing.

"Didn't you just spend the night with her? I'm surprised you even let her out of bed. I wouldn't have. Get a fucking collar and leash for her for fuck's sake. Right now, I need you."

Tezer tried to walk around him but Braemont moved in front of him. "Braemont, get out of my way, you won't like it if I have to move you." Finding Dove was the only thing on his mind right now.

"No. Listen to me, you asshole. One of the girls is gone. The pudgy redhead. She got upset over Brock telling her to get lost and she fled outside."

Now he had a portion of his attention, Tezer growled, "So? She's fat, she's not going far."

Braemont rolled his eyes. "You are so crude, you dick. The second a person leaves the direct grounds and steps into the forest they are lost. And you know that. She won't last the night. You are the best tracker, you need to go find her." The solar eyes focused on his hired mercenary.

"You have other men-"

"None as good as you, and you are still under my payroll in regards to those people. It's your job to go retrieve her. I want my money back that she stole. Now," he huffed, "go fucking get her."

His fingers nimbly tucked at the few sprigs of silver feathering amongst the auburn hair at his temples while watching Tezer's scowl deepen.

"Fuck. Fine," Tezer sneered. "But I'm not going anywhere until I see Dove."

His annoyed sigh expressed through his nose, Braemont plunked his hands on his hips. "Fine. Your *wife*," that irked Braemont beyond belief, that Corseque had snatched the unique beauty right out from under his nose, "is in the game room."

At Tezer's arched brows in question he explained, "You know, down the east wing."

Before Braemont said his last word Tezer was already stalking down the hallway to the east wing.

Braemont yelled after him, "You see her for one second then you get your ass out there and get that round Robin!"

Tezer masked his scowl when he entered the room. Spying Dove through the group of people he went straight for her.

Brock stepped in front of him. "Hey, Chief," he held a cocktail glass, it was early afternoon. Waving the glass, he said, "Just wanted to thank you, Boss, for getting us all safely through that godforsaken jungle. I had my doubts a few times, like when that old bag fell into the drink-"

"Yeah, excuse me." Tezer started to push past him but Brock blocked him.

"No, really," his words slurred slightly, "and the way you snapped up that little honeypot. Hot damn, we all wanted to nail a piece of that-"

Before he slammed his fist in his face and ruined Brock's model looks, Tezer muscled past him and strode across the room.

The huge space was filled with arcade games, slot machines, two ping pong tables and a variety of other games. Dings and bells and whistles rang around area, laughter and squeals joined in the noise.

Dove was playing a game that had a shotgun shooting big game. Surrounding her were Rey Silva, Vigo, and crazy Clancy. Giant Ziggy stood so close behind her every time she bent to shoot at something her butt just about brushed the front of him.

She was oblivious to it, but the blond German wasn't. His face was red, gaze zeroed in on her ass.

Tezer's eyes narrowed at slick Vigo's hand on Dove's shoulder while he gave her advice.

Kitty, Avril and Chelsee lounged around the room watching Reggie, Nik, Garth and Leo play ping pong. The girls all held drinks that looked alcoholic to Tezer. *Geesh, it wasn't even five o'clock yet.*

He stalked through the rest of the room. By the time he reached her, Tezer's face was dark with wrath.

She had her back to the door so she didn't see him coming.

Barking, "Dove," he snatched up her arm and swung her around to face him. Again, another mistake, but he couldn't stop himself. "We need to talk." Ignoring the aghast look on her face; he literally dragged her out of the room, past the snickering crowd.

Outside the door he released her arm.

Her face was red with indignation. "How dare you-"

His arms crossed over his buff chest, he cut her off, "Where is your ring?" He nodded down at her vacant finger.

"My," she looked down and shrugged. "I, uh, don't know. I mean, I'm sure it's in the room. What-"

"You agreed to wear my ring. I expect to see it on your finger. At all times. It falls into the drain and disappears, I'll get you another one."

Eyes wide and bewildered she protested, "I don't see why it's a big deal if I'm not wearing-"

He grabbed her wrist and jerked her hand up. He had the ring in his hand and he shoved it on her finger. "Do not take it off again."

Her brows drew down so low and hard it looked like an angry yellow V between her narrowed eyes. "Tezer, you do not own me, and I will not have you pushing me around and telling me what to do."

He was just as angry. Leaning over to get in her face he said crossly, "You agreed that we had to make this marriage look real so everyone would believe it. You agreed it was the only way to get you out of here. I am only holding you to your agreement."

His nose rose slightly in the air, the haughty look on his macho harsh face almost made Dove laugh. But she bit her lip.

Letting the angry air out of her lungs, she said, "Fine. You're right. For some insane reason I agreed to your ridiculous plan and I will follow it. Until we're out of here." She knew she struck a nerve when his scowl darkened, then shifted at her sudden acquiescence.

"Uh, okay then." He leaned back out of her space, uncrossed his arms and stuffed his hands in his pockets. Watching her finger-comb her long heavy locks, he asked, "What are you doing down here?"

She blinked at him then glanced back at the game room. Her tone of redundancy clear, she said, "I'm playing games."

Rolling his eyes, he countered, "I know. What I mean is, what are you doing out of our room? You know I don't want you to be out without me-"

"Come on, Tezer. You are being too controlling. The other girls," she nodded at the room, "are out and about and no one is dragging them off to a dark corner assaulting them and locking them in their bedroom. I am fine. No one is bothering me."

He resisted grabbing her and shaking her to get her to listen to him. "Dove, raping a whore is an oxymoron. No one has to force a girl that already easily spreads her legs for every male in the vicinity. Each one of those bitches has fucked every man here except my team. Now they're going through Braemont's men like hot knives through butter. They are whores, you are not."

"Tezer! That's so- so- rude, so crass." Frowning, she sarcastically advised him, "There's been a sexual revolution you know. Women are no longer looked down on for celebrating their sexual freedom."

Now he did wrap his big hands around her slender arms squeezing them in anger. "We are not talking about every woman. We are talking about you. You are my wife."

He shook her lightly when she opened her mouth to remind him it was a temporary situation. "I've already told you, you are having sex with no one but me. Don't make me remind you of that conversation we had about this and you agreed to it."

She responded snootily, "Even a whore has a right to say no."

Sighing with annoyance, she vainly tried to shrug his hands off. "Tezer, I didn't say I wanted to run around town having sex with men, I was just pointing out that I am just fine. No one is going to hassle me. It's not like I'm going to hang around in dark corners."

"Dammit, Dove, trust me, you are not safe here." He wanted to drag her back to their room but it would only make her more antagonistic at his tyranny.

Forcing his fingers to unwind from around her arms, he tucked his hands back in his pockets or he'd make good on his inclination to throw her over his shoulder and march back upstairs.

Then he remembered damn Braemont. He told her, "Listen, the girl, Robin, apparently she took off, left the mansion and has fled into the woods."

"Oh no!" Dove's brows flew up in distress for the redhead. "Why? She's terrified of the forest, the jungle. She hated the entire trek here."

"Ah," he rolled one shoulder. "That ass, the movie star, Brock, was a bitch to her and I guess she just ran off blindly in her hurt. The problem is, is that if we don't find her before nightfall, she could, well, you've heard all my blustering at you every time you wanted to leave the troop."

"Will you go look for her?" Dove set a worried hand on his chest.

He didn't look at it. It burned through his shirt and strengthened his desire to toss her over his shoulder and take her to their room and continue where they left off last night.

Tezer pictured her in that fucking teddy thing. Pink lace pulled down to her tiny waist, exposing those plump bare tits, the garters, stockings, stilettoes, his hand up the bottom of the corset, the way her back arched while she writhed with little moans on the bed, *God.*

Sweat pooled at his temples, his palms were damp, his erection swelled in his jeans. She was his wife and he couldn't touch her, fuck her.

Hell, he pulled a hand out of his pocket and wiped his sleeve over his forehead. The sooner he left, the sooner he would get back and the sooner they could-

"Hey, Dovey, baby," Rey poked his head out the door and aimed his bedroom eyes at Tezer's wife. "It's your turn again, you coming back?"

She smiled at the bastard.

Tezer forked a pissed hand through his hair.

"Yes, I'll be there in a minute." She turned back to catch Tezer's black scowl.

"Dove-"

"Tezer, are you going to go find Robin?" she asked again hopefully.

His enigmatic eyes flashed a dark warning to Rey telling him, 'hands off.' He growled, "Yeah. I'm going now." He glared at Rey until the other man gave him a mocking grin and returned to the game room.

Tezer said to Dove, "Listen, while I'm gone, I want you to go back to our-"

Shaking her head, the blonde hair swished across her back. "No. I am an adult. I can take care of myself, and I will not be held prisoner, by you, or anyone else. Now, please, hurry and find that poor girl, she will be terrified."

"Fuck, Dove, listen," he reached for her but she leaned away from his hand.

"No."

The air whooshed roughly from his lungs. Yeah, he could forcefully remove her but he knew what that would get him. "I'm going. But when we come back, you and I are having a talk."

Seeing her brows draw down, he gently tucked a lock of saffron behind her ear. Then he slid his hand behind her head, tipped it up and softly kissed her. He breathed easier feeling her respond. Her avid lips pulsed against his and parted, letting his tongue infiltrate her comely mouth.

The tension lessened in his chest when he felt her soft curves melt against him. Tezer sank both hands into her fine-spun hair and lifted the bulk to settle behind her back. Then he cradled her face and pulled her closer, and kissed her with vital ruggedness until he heard someone clearing their throat.

He clamped the curses behind his lips as he pulled from her. Someday he would have her to himself, with no one else around to freaking interrupt them, and they'd have all the time in the world to enjoy each other.

Over Dove's head he saw Garth grinning at him with Leo, Nik and Reggie behind him.

Garth only grinned more broadly at Tezer's annoyed glower. He said, "Bro, Braemont called us. We need to get a hoof on out there and find that girl before she does herself in."

"Yeah," scowling at his friends Tezer gentled his expression when he looked down at Dove, he still cupped her face. Brushing his thumbs over the hollows of her cheeks, he bent and gave her a quick kiss. "I really want to lock you in our room upstairs, but," he sighed hard at her face stiffening with pique at his suggestion, "I have to let you do what you want."

He leaned over and whispered in her ear, "I'll work on my compulsions to protect you, keep you secure," he bussed the tip of her nose, "and push you around. In the meantime, please, be careful. Do not trust anyone. Do not go to anyone's room or anywhere alone. Hear me?"

Smiling, she stood on her toes and kissed him. "Okay, Mr. Bossy. You be careful, you're the one going back out into that danger zone."

"Come on, Tez, light's burning," Leo muttered.

"Yeah, yeah." He quickly kissed Dove and turned on his heel striding swiftly down the carpeted corridor with his men right with him.

Chapter Twenty-Seven

Tezer easily found Robin's tracks. He and his men followed the mushed grass to the woods.

Leo said, "She's already been gone hours so she has quite a head start."

Garth nodded, agreeing, "Yeah, but we're bigger and faster, it shouldn't take us but maybe an hour to find her."

Keeping his eyes on the footprints that stayed steady on a dirt path, Tezer glanced at the sky.

Grey clouds were gathering to the west. If it rained before they found her, her tracks would be obliterated and after that, chances of finding her would be very slim.

He squinted up at the clouds and crossed his fingers; they seemed to be heading towards the south, away from the area.

Tezer led the group. The men stayed in single file behind him without speaking unless it was necessary to point out a hole in the ground or animal tracks.

They kept a keen ear open in case the girl called out, or screamed while turning into some creature's dinner. Periodically one of the men would shout out her name then they would stay quiet hoping to hear the girl respond.

After close to an hour of hiking, they hadn't caught up with her. Trepidation was settling in as her tracks were further and further apart as they started to cross over more rocky and less dirt or grass.

Now, it had been some time when they'd last seen a footprint.

"Fuck," Tezer cursed coming to a stop.

"What?" Garth came up to stand beside him. The others quickly joined them.

Tezer stood with his hands on his hips looking all around the area. "Her prints are gone."

"No way," Reggie said with apprehension.

"What do you mean, gone?" Nik asked. "How could they be gone? Even if she split off the trail we would have seen evidence of it."

"Ah shit," Tezer turned around and trotted back the way they'd come.

The men followed him.

Reggie said, "What is he doing? We need to go forward, find another trace of her-"

Shaking his head, Garth told him, "No, somehow we missed where she left the trail."

They backtracked for half a mile before Tezer stopped again.

"Find something?" Nik asked.

"Yeah. It should have raised my suspicions but I was distracted." Silently, Tezer scolded himself. His mind was on Dove and not on Robin.

Reading his mind, grinning, Nik nodded and said, "Women will do that to you, bro. You weren't prepared for it because you've never been bitten by the love bug before. Seriously, if I was the lucky one that snagged that little beauty I would still be in bed right now-"

"Maybe you need to shut up," Tezer snarled. "There's a young woman out here and if she isn't already dead, she will be. A big cat took her."

"Fuck? No, Tez, say that isn't true." The color sieved from Garth's tanned face.

"Yeah, I saw the prints cross over the tracks earlier but I dismissed them. I thought they were made more recently, I was wrong. It was closer to the time she would have gone through here. There," he pointed at one vague print and then looked off the trail.

Gruffly ordering, "Let's go," he strode into the heavier brush.

When he got past the denser foliage he could see where the cat had gone.

"It's dragging something. Get your weapons ready, stay close." Tezer took off in a jog through the forest trailing where the cat had pressed the grass down with its heavy paws, and the weight of what it was dragging.

The further into the woods they went the less chance Tezer thought they had of finding the girl alive. He'd seen some blood here and there, fortunately, not a lot to indicate she'd bled out, or had been eaten.

But he could tell the cat still dragged her, he could see heel marks occasionally. Suddenly he stopped and bent over.

The men were afraid to ask, but Garth said somberly, "Find something, Tez?"

Tezer held up a shoe. "There's nothing else here."

Coming up alongside him, Garth asked, "Blood?"

"No," Tezer replied flatly and handed the shoe to Nik to put in his backpack. He prayed it wouldn't be necessary to have to have a family member or someone identify it as Robin's if they couldn't find any other evidence of her.

"Keep moving," he ordered, and strode out of the woods and into tall grass. At least it was easier to trace the cat.

"Wait-" he stopped, held up a hand.

They all heard it, big cats fighting.

Tezer ran towards the sound of the snarling and roaring.

When he crossed several lengths of savannah the roars and howls were close by and he could see flashes of yellow and orange. His gun cocked in his hand, Tezer moved more slowly.

The men behind him were absolutely silent; they didn't want to draw the cats' attention. At least until they had them in sight.

Tezer whispered, "Stay to the south, downwind." He crept through the almost waist high grass until he spotted the cats.

Two huge lions were going at it. Two vicious males- clawing, roaring, jumping at each other. Both would share bites and slashes and howls before leaping back and then doing it again.

Off to the side Tezer could see a bit of blue color. It had to be her. He feared the condition they'd find her in. The animals were obviously fighting over her, for their dinner.

Whether she was dead or alive, Tezer needed to recover her. "Line up. I'm going to try warning shots, but if Robin is their meal, they won't give her up easily."

The other men flanked him on both sides, shotguns drawn and ready, earplugs in.

Tezer fired off a shot.

Both animals jumped at the sharp deafening sound, then went right back to fighting.

Shit- Tezer crept closer and fired off another shot. The felines paused, looked up, but then they went back to tearing each other up.

Suddenly, Tezer took off running and shooting, bullets flew past the lions slamming into trees and blasting off shards of bark in all directions. He yelled and ran and shot, the other men stayed with him, shouting at the top of their lungs.

They got the animals' attention.

Both giant cats turned to face the running, shouting men. The loud noise of the shotguns and the big men shouting and running at them offensively did the trick.

Both lions turned and disappeared into the brush.

Tezer kept firing to ensure they cleared far away. He was glad it wasn't necessary to kill them to get to Robin's body.

His stomach clenched the closer he got to the blue color partially hidden in the tall grass.

Now he saw a hint of red, it was her all right, the carrot-colored hair was Robin's. Tezer knew his friends were feeling the same grim dread he was feeling. The girl could not possibly still be alive.

Tezer pushed aside bushes and saw Robin lying on the ground. She wasn't moving. From what he could tell she still had all her limbs.

He instructed his men, "You guys stay here, fan out in a circle around us, facing out." He kept moving towards her as his men fanned out around him keeping watch for the lions returning or other animals on attack.

When he reached the girl, Tezer crouched down.

The back of her shirt was almost in shreds. A small bit of blood leaked through the blue material.

It looked like the cat had scraped her with its teeth, but had clamped down mostly on her shirt and her hair and dragged her by them.

He reached out a hand to touch her.

"Robin, it's Chief Tezer Corseque," he spoke before touching her. If she was alive he didn't want to startle her to death.

He heard breathing and a whimper.

Tezer touched her shoulder and carefully rolled her over.

Huge grey-blue eyes were so wide with fright the whites were visible clear around the irises. Her mouth fluttered speechless, her entire body was shaking like she had feverish chills.

"Okay, honey," Tezer said softly, calmly, "you're safe now. Tell me if you're injured." He brushed his hand over her hair to help soothe her.

Her mouth just flapped open and closed, the eyes bugged out, Robin was on the very edge of being frightened to death. Her body and mind had gone into shock.

Speaking quietly, "All right," Tezer gave her a cursory once over. The only blood he saw was the little on her back, everything else looked fine. She was scraped and gouged over her legs and arms, but she had all her body parts and flesh.

"I'm going to pick you up, Robin," he told her then slid his hands under her and lifted her as he stood up. He started walking.

His men kept glancing back in his direction while scanning the area.

Garth called out solemnly, "Well?" He didn't want to ask if there was anything left of her. Then he saw Tezer get closer with Robin in his arms and his held breath oozed out of his chest. "She- she okay?"

Tezer nodded. "Yeah. Scared to death, but her body is fine. Stay in a circle around us, keep your eyes peeled, ears open and guns ready." He stalked across the grassy field.

It had taken them hours to get to Robin and get back. Tezer took her to her room and gingerly laid her down on her bed.

Garth stayed with him while Leo left to tell Braemont they had her, and Reggie went to find a female to be in the room with the men so the girl couldn't cry assault later.

Nik took off to get them all food.

Avril and Chelsee entered the room first. "Oh my God, is she okay?" Avril cried as the two women hurried to the bed.

Tezer replied, "She's fine. Just petrified and she has some scratches on her limbs and her back. I want you girls to help her get cleaned up. Braemont will have one of his troops that has medical training check her out."

He stepped back as the women went to help Robin, who was now letting loose with wails, body-wracking shaking and enormous flooding tears. Her face was as pink as bubblegum, an unfortunate clash with her red hair.

Relieved that his part was done, and thank God was successful, Tezer slipped out of the room. He just cleared the door when Braemont was there.

"Corseque, they tell me she's all right." He stopped in Tezer's path. "Good job, I can't get my money from a corpse, now can I?" His snigger held no compassion, oozed only greed.

At Tezer's cold look Braemont said, "Now she will be fucking eager to call her father to send money to my account and send a helo for her and get her the hell out of here, eh?"

"Yeah, good for you. I need to get cleaned up." Tezer started to walk but Braemont stopped him.

"You'll get extra compensation for bringing her back alive."

Tezer said nothing, just kept moving.

Braemont grasped his arm. "Corseque, I have another job for you to do."

Tezer's eyes fell to Braemont's hand on his arm then up at the man. "I'm done, Braemont. I want my pay, and then me and my men are out of here," he jerked his arm from Braemont's clutch.

Nodding with a sneering grin, Braemont said, "Yeah, and undoubtedly the blonde bitch too."

Tezer's eyes narrowed to dangerous slits and he corrected him on a growl, "My wife, Braemont. She is my wife. Don't forget it. She goes where I go."

Braemont tugged his sleeves down under the suit he wore and straightened his cuffs. "Yes, well, whatever. You can't leave yet. I need you and your men, not the fools I hired but your team, to go to the Région de Tadjourah and pick up Rodlofo Asafa and bring him here."

Tezer studied Braemont before speaking. The man looked sincere, and unyielding. "Asafa is a killer. Why would you want him here?"

A minor shrug coincided with Braemont's blasé expression. "Even killers can owe people money. You will leave tomorrow and bring him here. It won't take but a day or so, then you return and I will release you from the rest of your obligations. The extra idiots I hired to travel with you to bring those people here will be good enough to keep them corralled with my other guards until I get my money owed me."

Tezer's fingers itched to roll into fists and plow into that smug auburn haired, freaky-eyed scum's jaw.

"Braemont," shaking his head, Tezer set his tempted hands on his hips and gripped them to keep from swinging at the man.

Before he could finish his rejection, Braemont said, "You and your men will leave tomorrow for my mission, or not only will none of you get paid, but you will stay here until the bitter end when the last person coughs up my due. The longer the bitch-" he sneered his resentment, "*your wife* sticks around, the better chance of danger finding her, and you know that."

Tezer had to concede that was true, but the last thing he wanted to do was leave her here totally unprotected. "I will leave Garth and Leo here to-"

"No," Braemont shook his head, not one hair on his auburn head moved. "Right now Asafa is contained, but you know how wily he is. That's why I want you and your entire team to get him. He will get away from anyone else.

"You know that. It took my men long enough to find him and capture him, I don't want to go through that again. The men can't ferry him here because they don't have the proper visas to come to Russia. It's only for a day or two at most. So, you leave in the morning, Corseque?"

When Tezer just kept staring at him with his steely glare without saying anything, Braemont said, "Listen Corseque, it's obvious your girl has a price on her head from someone that wants her for whatever reason," he smiled at Tezer's glower.

"You have no way out of here without one of my choppers unless you go back through the jungle with her and take your chances getting her somewhere safe, with her pursuer as well as my wrath following you."

His sneering grin without mirth, he continued, "I might call in for her reward myself," and paused again while Tezer looked about to explode. "So, you bring me Asafa and you get a chopper and you are all out of here, safe and quick in a day rather than weeks or even months."

Tezer knew he had no choice. What Braemont said was true, the safest way for Dove was in a chopper and out of here as fast as possible. And, Tezer sure as hell didn't want to be hoofing it through the jungle with Damon Philippè and a huge squad of lethal soldiers after them.

Garth had researched the man and advised he was ruthless, deadly, and had the resources to come after them. Garth was still trying to locate the fucker.

Dove refused to tell Tezer where the man resided; she didn't want him going after the bastard. All she would say was that it was like a small castle and she had escaped when he was away.

She had broken a locked window, climbed out, ran for her life and didn't stop until Tezer took her.

But after casual questions here and there, Tezer got out of Dove how long she'd been on the run and the general direction. He could figure out fairly well where the general area was that Philippè lived.

He would go after the fucker after he got Dove safe.

Braemont smiled, he saw the capitulation in Tezer's hard face. "Fine. I'll have the chopper ready at dawn. You can now go find your bride."

Furious, Tezer first went and located Garth and told him to tell the others about Asafa.

He left an equally angry Garth and his other friends, and went to his room to see Dove.

Finding it empty added another match to the anger simmering in his gut.

Chapter Twenty-Eight

Tezer showered and changed. His hair still damp, he went in search again of his wife.

Hearing voices coming from the great room, he entered it slowly, wanting to take in the scene before anyone noticed him.

His stomach hardened with the angles on his face when he saw Dove across the room. She was sitting on a couch, but when Rey Siva sat down next to her she stood up and laughed at something Silva said to her.

Finding a chair on the perimeter of the room, Tezer poured himself a bourbon then sat down. The urge to go over and get her was unbearable. But he'd told her he was going to work on being less domineering with her.

Of course, what she was wearing negated everything he'd promised her. His eyes tapered to pins at the t-shirt, a pink, skintight shirt that molded to her amazing tits. They were big and full and round, encased in the tight thin material, and Tezer couldn't take his eyes off them.

Neither could anyone else. Every other man in the room was watching them bounce and jiggle. He internally growled, *Fuck me, I'm getting her and-*

"*Cheeef,*" Kitty cooed and plopped down on his lap. "I have so missed you. I heard about your bravery in rescuing red Robin. You are so- so, valiant," gushing, she threw her arms around him and pressed her gargantuan udders on his chest.

"Motherfucker," he ground out through clenched teeth. "You know I am married now," he reminded her, his eyes still on Dove.

Rey was touching her hair, her face, and she was fucking giggling. Tezer saw red. He grasped Kitty's wrists and jerked them from around his neck and pushed her off his lap as he stood up.

He moved so quickly Kitty almost landed on her butt on the floor.

Awkwardly catching her balance, "Hey! You can't-" she squawked.

Tezer stalked across the room to Dove and Rey.

"Dove," he growled from behind her.

She swung around. "Tezer! You're back!" Her smile big and bright, she said, "They told me you found Robin and that she is fine." Her smile faded at the chilled expression constricting Tezer's hard face.

Very stiffly, he said, "Please accompany me to our room." His gaze flicked down her shirt and back up icy to her face.

"Uh," he looked pissed and Dove couldn't figure out why. They talked about her not staying in their room before he left. Her brows drew down, he'd better not be angry that she was downstairs. "Tezer-"

"We will talk upstairs." He took her arm as gently as he could make himself and sent a look to Rey that they would be talking later, too. This time Tezer would tell him if he touches Dove again he will snap every one of Rey's ten fingers in half before breaking his arms.

Rather than embarrass herself by arguing with him, or balking, Dove walked compliantly with him.

Traipsing up the stairs, Dove tried to make conversation, find out what was bothering him, get him calm before she was alone with him, he looked so dreadfully fierce. She asked conversationally, "Um, uh, so, everything went okay today?"

A short grunt was his only response. He kept walking with her, they were almost to their room.

"Listen, Tezer, I don't understand, what are you upset about?" She tried to stop but he kept them moving. "I don't want to go into the room with you if you're-"

"Uh huh," he grunted, and opened the door. Pulling her in, he shut and locked the door then turned and faced her.

If she thought he was frightening before, that was nothing compared to the rage that tinged red on the tips of his ears, and beat a vein at his temple, and turned his mouth into a forbidding, brutal gash.

A slight tremble entered her voice, she asked, "Tezer, what is wrong with you?"

His eyes almost disappeared under wrathful shaded lids. "What is the matter with me?" He raked her chest with fuming disdain. "Do you recall how pissed I got that day you were flitting around in that tiny tight shirt and pants? I said you dress like a whore and I'll treat you like one. Look at yourself, you are-"

She cut him off with a haughty, "I will dress as I please." Scowling, her eyes narrowed equally as angry as his, she said, "I have told you, you do not own me! I am not property for you to command."

"Oh yeah? That's the way you see it?" He saw a brief flash of fear cross her face before he grabbed her and pushed her up against the wall.

She opened her mouth to protest and he slammed his mouth over it. Taken by surprise, she froze.

He moved his hand to behind her neck and clenched it, holding her taut while he burned her mouth with a gnarling violent kiss. Biting her cherry lips, slashing his tongue over them before stabbing inside, breaching her resistance.

Dove tore her mouth from his gasping with angry dismay, "Stop it, Tezer, stop forcing yourself on me!"

Irascible and snarling, he put his big hands just below her breasts and fought to not dig his fingers into her ribs. Struggling to cool his belligerent rage, his tough voice vicious, he said, "I will not tolerate you, my wife, being felt up by another man."

She put her hands on his bulging arms. "Don't be ridiculous, no one was feeling me up. I will not be manhandled like this, Tezer."

Seething, he moved his hard hands up to cover her breasts, so full and plush under the tight T. "I am your husband, only I have the right to touch you like this," his fingers roughly clutched her soft round flesh.

Punching furiously at his arms, Dove cried, "Stop it, you don't have any right to touch me unless I say so- let go of me!"

She pulled at his wrists but he clamped down harder squeezing her globes in his big hands. So furious with him now her face vivid red, she yelled, "You let go of me right now, go find yourself another woman to manhandle and abuse!"

Her words fired into him. Tezer swung her around to face the wall and pushed her hands up to either side of shoulders pressing her palms against the wall. Grabbing her hips he yanked her bottom torso slightly out and reached for the front of her pants.

"Te- Tezer," fear stilted her words, "what are you doing- stop, stop right now-"

He pressed his rock-hard cock into her ass and ran his hands up the front of her to clutch her breasts again. His mouth against her ear, he snarled, "I don't want another woman, Dove," he groped her, kneading her flesh roughly, then shoved the shirt up to expose her bra.

Keeping her slightly bent towards the wall, her palms flush against the wall, Tezer grabbed at the buttons on her pants and jerked them apart.

"I've told you that you are the only woman I want, Dove, ever. I'm over letting you push me away. When I get done with you, you will never push me away again."

Her face and arms hard against the wall, her shirt shoved up, breasts hanging like velveteen moons, Tezer pushed her legs to spread them apart and fiercely tore at her pants.

Dove whispered, "Don't take me in anger, Tezer."

He grasped her pants and was shoving them down her hips, then he abruptly stopped. His heart pounding against his ribcage, Tezer reined in his rage and lust.

He steadied his manic frenzy and looked at the woman so delicate and precious under the brutal siege of his mouth and hand. His rough hands kneading her breasts savagely to the point of pain, his cock shoved hard against her bottom, grinding at her as he violently stripped her.

Her small body pressed against his fevered bulk with her frantic fast breathing.

Neither of them moved while he cleared the blind fury and out of control lust from his primordial brain. Gulping deep breaths, his heart still hammered, sweat rolled down the sides of his face. He moved his hands up and around her waist, wrapped his arms around her and hugged her against his chest.

When he got a grip on his run away emotions, Tezer gently turned her around. With shaking hands, he leaned her back against the wall and set his hands on her waist.

Peering remorsefully at her half frightened, half bewildered, beautiful face, he sighed painfully. "Dove, I," he sucked in a deep breath; let the air straggle out, tenderly laid his hand on the side of her face.

"I did it again, I hurt you, overpowered you with anger and violence. I…" He just stared at her for a moment then said, "This jealousy thing is a new feeling I just can't seem to get a grip on. I want you so badly, and then I see you with another man and he's touching you, when I know things aren't solid between us. I just go…blind, flying out of control."

Her back at the wall, Dove lowered her hands and pressed them against the wall and watched the pain of guilt mar his hard face.

Calming herself, she said firmly, "Tezer, married or not, I will not be with you if you treat me like this. Dragging me out of rooms, assaulting me like a marauding squall over a tiny sailboat. I," her eyes traveled the regret and shame dogging him, "I want you, Tezer."

Her voice softened to a weightless filament, "But making love is a partnership, we do it together, not *to* each other."

His head hanging, shoulders slumped, he kept his hands on her waist as if afraid she'd turn into a mist and vanish right out of his hold.

Dejected, Tezer muttered, "I am too…crude…fierce, too hard tempered, too much of a tough man to be with a precious dainty woman like you. I continuously hurt you, the thing, the person I most care about, and I'm too much of a brute to treat you with the respect and gentleness that you deserve."

If things were different, if she hadn't been brutally assaulted by that fucker, Dove and Tezer would be enjoying a normal, healthy, lusty sexual relationship. His skills at seduction would have shaped her into a sultry kitten that would desire, revel in that rough side of him.

But Damon Philippè had replaced her natural libido with terror and pain, and Tezer needed to get a hold of his actions before he did the same to her.

The shame of his wild behavior carved deep lines around his mouth, his eyes darkened to bleak black holes. He raised them to hers.

"I just look at you, so lovely I can hardly breathe when I'm with you. And your hot body, damn baby, I want to lose myself in you, on you, over you," he snorted. "I just don't wait until the feeling is reciprocated."

Dove watched Tezer come to terms with his own vital, tough manhood. While he talked, she trickled her fingertips up and down his muscled arms.

Seeing the shame hurting him, she moved her hands up the immense biceps to smooth her palms over his powerful chest. The thing was, yes, he was overpowering and forceful and rough, but he always came to a screeching halt when she said stop.

Of course the words took a while to seep into that big, hard head of his, but he could easily throw her down and take her, but he hasn't.

Then his eyes narrowed and shifted to gleam at her. A brow cocked, he asked, "Did you just say you want me?"

Her cheeks filled with soft pink color. Lips curved up pleasingly, she nodded. "Yes. If you would just talk to me instead of freaking out and dragging me off like a Mongol warrior, we-"

Keeping his hands on her waist, Tezer lowered his head to gently kiss her. His tongue sifted over her mouth until her lips parted. This time, he carefully entered her mouth pillaging with caressing strokes and delicious sucks at her tongue.

Dove responded, caressing and twirling her tongue around his, then sucking on it like he does to her. She could feel his arms tightening, flexing; the steel limbs hardening around her as his ardor heated back up.

It was almost like he was unaware how his hips moved instinctively to hers, grinding his hard male organ against her softness.

Not viciously like before, but, her pants still half down her hips, she could feel the thick hard length of him burrowing right over her panties to fit against the crevasse of her womanhood.

When a throaty moan waxed from Dove's savoring lips, Tezer slipped his hands under her back and thighs, lifted her in his arms and carried her to the bed.

He paused there, stared down at her with a serious intent look. "Baby," he said gruffly, with more than a tinge of hopefulness, "it's your decision. If you don't want to, it's okay. I swear, I'll set you down and back right off." His dark enigmatic eyes stroked over her greens gilded with gold.

Her arms curled around his neck, her smile alluring, Dove purred, "I told you, I want you." She reached up to kiss him.

His mouth instantly settled over hers, dominating the kiss, but he realized it and held back, letting her explore and taste him without him pounding all over her. Time for that later when she learned she wanted it rough. To a point.

"Tezer," a sheen of desire brushed her creamy face. Dove's words stilted out huskily, "I…" she broke off as he laid her carefully on the bed, and looked down at her with uncertainty.

She said with a smile, "I am not a frail doll. Truthfully, your strength and vigor turn me on," her cheeks brightened as she blushed. "I don't mind, I mean, I like your aggression, your roughness with me, touching me. I just want you to not go bananas every time another man is near me, and to respect me when I say no."

He laid her on the bed and bent to grasp her shoe. With a wicked leer, he said, "Then that's a yes, right? We're going to make love, right now, right?"

Giggling, she repeated his words from the other day to him, "Yeah, it's a yes. Do you want me to put it in writing so you won't think I'll forget?"

Snatching off the other shoe, he crouched down and removed his own boots and climbed on the bed. The bed shifted and shuddered with his weight. "Thank God it doesn't creak," he grinned and loomed over her.

She looked so small and delicate, and fragile and beautiful lying back with her hair pooled around the pillows like a rippling flaxen pond, her passion laden eyes filled with innocence trustingly trained on him.

He moved to prop on one knee between her legs, the other knee braced to the side. Knowing her only experience with sex was with the bastard that had raped her and tortured her, he said softly, "I'll be as gentle as I can, baby, you need to tell me if I move too roughly or fast or hard, okay?"

Batting her lashes at him with a beguiling smile and sexy tilt of her head, she raised her arms to him and said, "I know you'll be careful with me, I trust you, Tezer. But after I, uh, we adjust, don't hold back on my account, okay?"

"Ah baby, it'll be a while before I can fully unleash my full, uh, abilities. You are too small and basically…untried. But we will enjoy working up to you taking my full strength."

With a grin he added, "From all directions." He leaned over, put his hand across her neck cupping her chin, and kissed her until her eyes were swimming and unfocused, then he leaned back with a sexy foxy grin, delighted at how quickly she grew dazed and panting from his kisses.

While she cleared the haze from her eyes, Tezer reached down and grabbed the hem of her shirt already shoved up and pulled it up her arms, off her head and threw it on the floor.

He didn't say it out loud, but he thought, *that thing gets returned to its owner tomorrow and first thing they needed to do when they got out of the mansion was go shopping for her*. Her delectable body was for his enjoyment only.

Dove smiled up at him, her hands drifted down his huge biceps that were flexing and pumping with his movements.

Her skin prickled as his gaze struck and burned over her breasts encased in the black lacy bra that was so delicate, like an embroidered spider's web. Her tiny waist curved down to the low rise pants that he'd wrenched open and down.

A growl grunted deep in his chest as he reached under her to unclasp the bra and pulled it off, it joined the shirt. The dark eyes glittered with such intense heat it was like the flames leaped out and licked over her leaving thrilling burns on her skin.

He drank her in for a moment. Plump lips, gilded eyes to drown in, lush breasts with nipples like cherry gumdrops. He leaned over setting his hands on either side of her and sucked a nipple into his mouth.

Against her breasts, he mumbled, "You taste like candy, but you smell like gingerbread with the spice of the ginger and creamy brown sugar sweetness. God, I want to taste you all over."

His tongue lathed over the nipple. He cupped her breast and turned to the other nipple, licked it then bit it hard enough she jumped, but soft enough the pain cascaded into sexual pleasure.

Dove writhed against his mouth, his hands, both cupping and kneading her breasts while he sucked one nipple then the next, then slid over to the swell of her globes to suck her soft sweet flesh until a heaving moan wrung out of her.

"*Ahh, Tezer*," groaning lustily, her hands moved to between her legs, arms stiff, slinging shots of lightning burst all around inside her body.

"Hey," he smiled, pushing her hands aside, "that's my job." He caressed her breasts, kissed her thoroughly then sat up and grasped her pants.

The buttons already popped open from his earlier jealous frenzy, he pulled them down, slowly, he didn't want to remove her panties yet.

This time he wasn't pouncing on her like a junkyard dog. Tossing the pants, and her socks, he looked at the lace that was just barely a black brush stroke of lace across her womanhood.

"So nice, baby," he ran both hands up her legs to her thighs; they quivered in his hands. He stopped at her core.

He nimbly wriggled and slid the backs of his fingertips over her sex, smiling elated at her hips bucking up to his hand.

"You are sin and fire, baby, made for love. You're wet as shit, honey," his voice quivered with her thighs. He ran a finger up then down her slit over the black lace. She pulled her legs up, lurched to his hand and whimpered.

Tezer put his palms on her thighs, pressed them back down and spread them apart. Her hips squirmed when he touched her core again, stippling his fingers over her feminine folds until she was almost weeping.

"The heat, Tezer," she cried, writhing at his fingers. "It burns, so, hot." Sucking in a coarse breath, her voice lilted on the exhale, "But so hot good."

Tezer smiled at her ramblings, she was feeling so good she wasn't coherent. *Perfect.* He pulled the wisp of panties down her slender legs and dropped them over the side of the bed and sat back on his heels to look at her.

Just like he's always fantasied her; buck naked, legs spread wide to reveal her pink petals, so tender, so fully womanly. Her breasts lush luxurious pillows tipped with cherry bud nipples. Fucking hell he would never tire of looking at her.

The toughest thing he could imagine right now was not touching her every second of the day. For sure he was going to drive her nuts. Especially when they were in public. She was such a shy little thing, she would likely be embarrassed as he lavished attention, and his hands on her. But, there was no way in hell he could be with her and not touch her.

Her lids lifted slightly, she peered at him. The seductive smile still curving her lips, Dove couldn't believe she wasn't so mortified, painfully self-conscious at being splayed out nude with Tezer, tough, dangerous mercenary, still fully clothed, just sitting there between her legs staring at her like she was a feast on a platter.

But her loins were burning, she begged, "Touch me, Tezer, please…"

Chapter Twenty-Nine

$\mathcal{A}$ crafty smile creased Tezer's hard face, *oh yeah*.

"Say the magic word, sweetheart," he teased. He smiled at her perplexed expression and grinned at her hips rolling, seeking his hands on them.

"I don't know, what magic word," she whined sweetly, sexily. "I said please." She moved her hands back down to between her legs but Tezer caught them and held them back.

"No honey, say the magic word, I will be doing the touching, the pleasuring you."

Her bottom lip nudged out in a pout. Her body rolled and slid on the soft sheet under her. He held her hands so she couldn't move them.

She whimpered, "I don't know what it is, touch me, Tezer, *please*."

He never thought he'd hear those blessed words. Letting go of her hands he slid his fingers faintly up her inner thighs almost to her core then stopped. He ordered with a slight tease, "Say, 'touch me, Husband.' "

The corners of her lips turned up as her eyes closed. Head arching back, her words oozed out silky with desire, "Ah, please touch me, Husband."

His fingers went immediately to stroke up her slit.

"Oh!" Her body jumped, shivered. Her legs went to close, but he was kneeling between them keeping them spread open.

Her head rolled to the side, Dove moaned, "Good, Tezer, Husband, you feel so good…"

"No, baby, it's you that feels so fucking- uh, wonderful. Wet, wildly wet baby, wet and wonderful." It was now him that was rambling nonsense. But he didn't care, not when her woman's silk was flowing, dampening his hand.

He stroked her, on the outside of her feminine folds, scissoring his fingers on the inside feeling her shiver of ecstasy, down around and up the tender slit. When he thumbed her tight little bud she gasped loud, her hips coiled to the side.

His fingers still stroking her, he pushed her hips back and nudged her thighs further apart and continued his sensual assault.

When she was gasping fast shallow breaths, her cheeks pink, eyes fluttering, breasts jiggling all over, he cupped a breast firmly and delved his finger slowly inside her.

She froze as he expected, but he kept going, gently, slowly. Slowly he drew it out, slicked her silk all over her tiny pink clit then stroked his finger back inside her. This time, her hips rose to meet his sensual invasion.

"That's it, baby," he soothed. Pinching a nipple at the same time he moved his finger slowly in and out of her. Her hips met his gentle thrusts.

Dove's head thrashed side-to-side, she gripped the sheet beneath her, crying out every time he circled his thumb over her wet swollen clit. She was way too tight for him to add another finger. He would make her come, get her looser then stretch her more.

Hopefully he could last that long himself. He'd never been more seduced, intoxicated by a female.

Taking his time, feeling her, letting her feel was so much sexier than a slam wham. And he was so loving watching her get excited, her little moans scintillating as she grew hotter and hotter.

He was her husband, her teacher, it made him feel even more protective of her, possessive, and that was so hot too. Curling his finger inside, stroking her hot spots, then moving his finger faster in and out, he watched the red flush her chest, goose bumps popped up her arms.

Her nipples tightened to hard pebbles, she started writhing maniacally. Lips gaping, parted to suck air deeper into her heaving lungs.

Quickened keens scraped up her throat as she whimpered, "Tezer," almost frightened of the unknown but burning to orgasm, she cried, "help me…"

"I've got you baby," he cooed, "let it go, go with it." His ramrod cock strained at his pants crazed to get at her.

He squeezed one breast then the other harder, pinched her clit and thrust his finger in her until her spine arched, her neck arched and her head fell back as she let out a wailing cry of his name, *Tezer!*" and buckled forward, folding up.

Forcing his finger deeper, he felt the tremors ratcheting through her body, contracting around his finger. Her panting gasps and cries of his name warmed his ears and made him hard as a rocketship about to blast off.

As shudders roiled through her then started to lessen, Tezer slowed his manipulations. He leaned over Dove pressing his lips on her parted ones and sucked in the rest of her release.

Dove's chest billowed with rapid concussing breaths. Her brain spiraled amok, dizzy and high, her body still vibrated coming down from the orgasm.

As Tezer moved back from her, she gulped big deep breaths and tried to orient the blazing cotton wool in her head when she felt him between her legs.

His hair brushing her belly, hands spreading her thighs, and his mouth- good Lord his mouth was on her sex!

"Tezer! Stop! What are you doing?" Pushing her palms on the mattress behind her, she tried to sit up.

He splayed his huge hand on her chest and gently forced her to lie back. Clutching her thigh, he said softly, "You're not ready yet, baby, for me. You are way too tight, you won't be able to take me in without…" he didn't want to say pain, "uh, discomfort. Just relax honey, keep trusting me. Now lie back and try to relax your legs," and he dipped his head back down and mouthed her sex.

He had to hold her hips down from squirming away while he lathed her slit and bit and sucked her clit and pushed a finger back inside her soaking channel.

When she was again bucking at his mouth, her moans sweet whimpers, he worked another finger inside her. She paused, but when he kept with slow, gentle penetrations, her hips responded arching up to him.

Still feeling tremors from her first orgasm, Tezer quickly brought her back high, to the exquisite aching hunger until she was right at the crest of the cliff crying his name, writhing all over the bed, her hands clutched the sheet in tight fists.

Tezer put his mouth over her entire sex, biting down, licking her clit until he felt her start to topple; he worked a third finger in.

"Uh," Dove groaned, "Tezer, I'm…" She groaned again, and then she crashed over, her hips went wild as he took her over the cliff and she plunged down the other side in an inferno of boiling whirlwind storms. This time she screamed his name- *"Tezer!"*

Sitting back on his heels, Tezer kept his fingers driving until her body wracked around them with quaking spasms.

While she was huffing and gasping, stilling her body's trembling aftershocks, he rolled off the bed and stripped his jeans and briefs off quickly.

He snagged a condom from his pocket and sheathed his pulsing thick phallus before climbing back on the bed and between her legs.

Her body was still writhing, undulating on the sheet growing damp with her pleasure. He grabbed her hips and sunk his shaft into her part way.

AT The size of his intrusion her body turned rigid. A scream caught in her throat, her eyes popped wide, hurt and surprised. She frantically pushed at him.

Voice like rough liquor, he soothed, "Shh, Dove." He paused to let her body acclimate to his girth and soften around his thick iron rod.

Tezer brushed her hair off her damp face and looked into her terrified golden-greens. He could see the nightmare of Damon Philippè torching her eyes.

She was blind to Tezer, she only saw the monster bearing over her that had brutalized her. She started to panic, her breaths frantic and rapid.

"Okay, honey, it's Tezer, your husband, not that beast that hurt you. Feel me, baby," he took one of her hands and laid her palm on the hard planes of his face. Almost immediately she started to calm.

Her eyes cracked open, lips trembled. "Tezer?" she whispered. Her hips bumped, she felt the thick heavy fullness of him invading her tender passage, palpitating wildly against her vulnerable inner flesh.

He felt different than that animal that had attacked her. Tezer was…bigger…harder….thicker. The chest and arms that hovered over her and held her were like superman steel, safe and protective, not sharp and painful like Damon's.

Tezer wasn't slapping her, punching or cursing her. He was waiting patiently for her to accept him, even though she felt his fierce shaft raging like an explosive metal club inside her, ready to drive, pound into her with the magnitude of a locomotive.

In the back of her mind flickered the thought of how caring and careful he was with her when he obviously wanted to take off. She was well aware that he had never had to hold back before with a woman, but he did with her because he didn't want to hurt her, and he wanted this to be good for her.

He whispered while caressing the side of her face, "Are you okay, my beautiful wife? You want to stop?" While he spoke soothingly he nestled a shade deeper inside her irresistible softness and throbbed against her velvety walls.

After a deep breath and a hard swallow, she shook her head with a tremulous smile. "I'm all right. In fact," she wriggled and her vagina palpitated, tightened around his dick with a sharp spasm.

"Whoa!" He jumped, his cock jerked, his low laugh a deep rumble, "Damn, baby, I almost lost it. Ahh," he pushed in further, just a bit and felt her tighten; squeeze his manhood before softening to allow more of his girth inside her.

His heart was racing and pumping right through his cock, she had to be able to feel his life force beating inside her.

A moan slipped out as her neck arched, "Oh, God, Tezer, you feel," the steeping moan brooked and then trailed off to a breathy wisp. Her misted eyes slipped open, and saw he had been too impatient to take off his shirt.

With a smile, she fumbled at the buttons on his shirt until she got them undone. When she tried to tug it off him, he reached behind his back grasped the shirt, wrenched it over his head and tossed it.

Admiring his chest, "So big," she sighed with simmering heat, adapting to feeling his huge hardness filling her tingling channel. "After the horror with that-freak," her skin flinched at the remembrance. "I never thought I would ever be able to be with a man."

She stroked her hands up and down, all over his broad chest, sifting her fingers through the dark hair. "But you are so caring, so strong, your muscles are insane, Tezer." Squeezing his pecs, she leaned up and sucked at a nipple until he groaned and moved out of her reach.

He huffed, "Can't take that right now, babe. Tell me how you feel." He had to clear both their minds of that fucker. It was a nightmare for her to relive, and him to rage and ache for her pain, and it was hell to think of her with another man, good or bad, especially at this moment.

With a gruff grunt, he pushed slowly until he finally reached the depth of her and he was fully engulfed in her tight sheath, she felt like hot melted wax glazing his phallus.

He paused, let her adapt, then he slowly pulled back out feeling every luscious dewy drop of her, then he shoved back in slightly harder, faster, deeper. Her groaning cry and biting gasps made him smile, yeah, she would be okay.

"I, ah…" she started to talk but Tezer was moving faster, his plunges so deep she could feel him pounding at her apex, her womb. He rocked into her with a hard rhythm, grinding against her; she felt his tight balls slapping her sensitized flesh.

She stroked her hands up to his neck then knit her fingers into his hair, and tugged his head back.

"Damn, Dove," he groaned, and couldn't help slamming into her. He felt the urgent burning eroticism of their mating and it spurred him to plunge with deeper rapid thrusts.

Now he was starting to pound into her so hard he was shoving her body up the bed, he moved a hand to wrap around her shoulder to hold her and lowered his head to conquer her sexy as hell mouth.

The hums and moans projecting from his woman and her sweet tight pussy were driving him too fast to his climax. No, he wanted this bliss to last forever.

A susurrating hum vibrated in her throat with half grunts and short groans hitching out of her with his every hard thrust. She moved her hands to dig into his shoulders.

Tezer loved it, loved her sweet tender body under and around him, the incredible sexual sounds she made when he plunged into her.

He loved the way her chubby breasts bobbled and jiggled with his thrusts, the way her nails clawed the skin off his back and shoulders, *yeah.*

Grasping one of her legs, he bent her knee and pulled it up causing him to go deeper. "Wrap your legs around my hips, baby," he muttered with a growl of edgy momentum. He was climbing, wouldn't be able to hold on much longer, he needed for her to come first.

Little hums bursting from her open lips, Dove wrapped her legs around his lean hips and cried out when he sunk hard deeper.

He stroked his hand up to clench her breast, then lowered his head to bite it until she yelped. He sucked it and she was writhing so much under him he had to release her breast to hold her from sliding away.

But he kept plunging, and sucking her fragrant flesh until red marks rose all over her fair skin. Then, roughly gripping the meat of her breast he moved to suckle a sweet nipple.

Hearing her breathing grow shallow and rapid fire with gasping mewls, he rasped, "Look at me baby," and cupped her chin to hold her head from rolling back and forth. "Look at me, Dove, my wife."

She peeped up at him in slight delirium before her lids dropped from the lusting weight that pulled on them.

With his every hard thrust, a lock of hair flopped over one of his eyes. His lips parted expelling his grunting growls, sweat beaded and trickled down the side of his face. His dark eyes gleamed pure fiery passion at her like fearsome black rapiers.

Tezer tilted slightly so his cock rubbed against her clitoris with every thrust, soon she was quaking in his hands. Her vagina clenching him, her lids were closing over her pupils enlarging so much they took over the green irises, she was on the cusp of coming.

"Look at me, Dove," he commanded.

When she forced her lids back up to look at him, he held her face and drove violently into her tender channel.

With a sharp cry of his name, Dove's spine bent, the pupils just seemed to explode as her body convulsed around him.

It was too much for Tezer.

With his own hoarse growl, he pounded faster, harder, bearing down on her until he reached his own zenith.

Shouting, "God, Dove, *fuck*-" he came hard, violent, with a thunder of release his seed spilled into the shield.

His grinding thrusts like a battering ram repeatedly bore into her until his body shattered erupting again and again in an exodus of shockwaves until there was nothing left of him and he collapsed.

His breathing so rough and frenetic he blew tendrils of her loose hair around the pillow.

Tezer's fevered brain was a blank of sizzle and synapses; it was all he could manage to move slightly so he wouldn't flatten her.

Dove could feel his heart hammering against her chest. She wrapped her arms around him, she could still feel him throbbing and jerking inside of her. Her own heart was still racing, tiny convulsions still oscillating around inside her pelvis.

After a few moments, Tezer, braced up on one elbow and looked down at her. He smoothed the strands of hair stuck to her damp face.

A beautiful sheen of perspiration like a pearlescent varnish covered her skin, she glowed.

"Ah, sweetness," his husky voice rasped, "God you are the most beautiful thing I've ever seen." His lips sought hers. When he captured them he brought her along on a breathy light as air kiss, his lips pulled gently at hers.

Lifting her trembling arms Dove pushed his hair out of his eyes. Sucking on her lower lip, he murmured, "And you are all mine."

At her frown, he said, "What?" Voice deep with warning, he told her, "Don't even think differently. You are mine. Your days of even thinking of being with another man are over."

She squirmed under him to get up but he refused to move. His penis was still semi-hard embedded inside her, and she could in no way move his bulk off her.

"Uh huh, baby," he brushed his lips over hers. "We just shared something so spectacular and intimate, you are not getting up and running off. You want to talk; you'll do it here, naked, in my arms."

He rolled slightly to the side so she could move more easily but he pinned her down with his leg.

Tezer waited, but she didn't say anything. He sat up. "Okay, I need to get rid of this, I'll be right back. Do not move."

"There you go; one hot and sweaty mind boggling night and you're bossy all over again." She tried to glare sternly at him, but the giggles got the better of her.

He bent and kissed her then rolled off the bed. "It's not going to be only one, sweetness. Don't move," he hurried into the bathroom to get rid of the condom.

When he returned he carried a warm washcloth.

Climbing back onto the bed, he said with a naughty leer, "Spread those gorgeous gams, honey, let me clean you up. We can shower later, yes," he said with a quirked lip at her query, "together. But right now, I don't have the energy for it. Spread 'em," he commanded.

Slightly embarrassed, she did as he said, then moaned at the wonderful feeling of the soft warm wet cloth dabbing at her sex.

"That's enough of that, you keep making mewing noises like that and I will be all over and in you in the shake of a lamb's tail. And I need a break first. I want to revel in, savor and cherish this fantastic moment."

Tezer tossed the cloth and lay down beside her, pulled her into his arms, and cradled her head on his chest.

Comfortably settled, "Okay," he sighed, "have at it. What is the problem with what I just said?"

Cuddling against his big hard body, Dove yawned. "Um, you said, that I am yours. What does that mean? How long, for a night? Until we get to the safe place?"

A deep groan riffed from his chest. He scowled down at her. "Come on, Dove. We have discussed this. Haven't I made it clear that we are married and I have no intention of ever getting a divorce? You think I just wanted a one-night stand with you?"

Turning to face her, he lightly grasped her jaw and lifted her head to frown at her. "Again, for the umpteenth time, I could have taken you any time I wanted if that was the case."

But she frowned right back. "Yes, but I think you wanted me willing."

She spoke again as he opened his mouth scowling. "You keep saying what you want; you have never asked me what I want." The lower lip pushed out past the upper one.

"Huh." Cupping her face with both hands, he kissed her, then said, "I can't help it. From the very start I've wanted you, body and soul. Every day, every second, it only grew stronger. I've felt that you feel at least a little of the same, I hope that you want the same thing. Do you?"

His anxious eyes flicked over hers seeking her feelings in the golden green depths.

Her brows knit then dropped. With a shrug, she said, "I don't know, Tezer. This whole experience, you have to see, has been, overwhelming. I don't know if what I feel for you, the butterflies in my stomach when I look at you are from gratefulness for taking care of me," she sucked in a breath.

"Or hero worship, or just lust." She smiled and combed her fingers through his thick hair. "Or, genuine caring for you."

The unease he felt at her words flickered across his hard face as he considered her uncertainty. "But, will you give us a try? A chance to see if what we have is real? I mean," he shrugged, "it's totally fucking real on my part. I've never felt this way before about a woman, never even close. You totally blindsided me."

The color drained slightly from his face, he still held her chin. "I love you, Dove." He paused, tasting the bizarrely foreign words. Never in a million years had he thought he'd ever feel it, much less say those words to a woman.

At first he couldn't comprehend what he was feeling it was so inexplicable, not a sensation he had ever felt before. He couldn't recognize the stabbing in his heart, the way his breath stilted whenever he looked at her.

His gaze flickered over her lovely face, he swallowed before speaking. "I fell hard the second I laid eyes on you and it only grew every day as I saw how sweet and kind, and brave you are.

"My damned heart twinges every time I even think of you. To think of losing you," the grimace crunched his face and sent a bleak dimmer in his eyes. "I can't bear it. I can't bear to lose you. Please, will you give us a try?"

He stared into her big bright orbs, and saw his own uneasy expression reflected in them.

Then Dove smiled that beautiful smile that crushed his heart like a fist. She said softly, "I can't bear to lose you either, Tezer. I've been frantic with thoughts of you taking me somewhere and leaving me, forever."

"Ah, God, baby, that's good. So good." He tipped her chin to kiss her. "So, there will be no talk of divorce or any of that shit, right?"

She snuggled back into his embrace. "For now. Until we're sure."

He wrapped his arms around her and muttered, "I told you, I'm already sure."

"Uh huh, I'm," she yawned, "so sleepy. I need a nap before I can…" he could feel her blush against him.

"Do it again?" He grinned.

"Yeah," she giggled and slung her leg over his and laid her face on his furry chest.

Tezer's response was a rumbly growl. He held her in his arms, his hand curved around to clutch a plump breast as they drifted into sated slumber.

Chapter Thirty

Tezer had been so enraptured with Dove, it wasn't until after the several times they made love through the night that he remembered he had to leave in the morning.

This time it was a moan of despair instead of desire he growled.

Dove wriggled sleepily in his strong arms, mumbled, "What?"

He moved her, and sat up. "I need to go somewhere today, until tomorrow or maybe the next day."

Stretching like a languorous satiated cat, forgetting she was stark naked, Dove rubbed her eyes. Then his words started sinking in, her eyes still languidly closed she frowned. Then they flashed open. "What? Where?"

He had already forgotten what they were talking about. Her naked body writhing on the white sheets drew all the blood to his suddenly throbbing dick.

Getting on his hands and knees, he started to climb over her with his mouth starting for a strawberry nipple when she opened her eyes and put a hand to his chest.

"God, no, Tezer. I am so sore. I won't be able to walk as it is. The last time in the shower an hour ago did me in."

He kept crawling over her; she held her arm rigid, "Seriously."

His turn to pout, he sat back on his heels and let his heated gaze roam all over her curvy body.

Dove pulled the sheet to cover herself as she struggled to sit up. She lifted a hunk of tousled hair and shoved it off her shoulder.

Her brows drew down in a worried frown, she asked, "Why are you going somewhere?"

His heavy sigh rumbling, he reached out to grab a bit of the sheet and pulled it. "Ah, some stupid shit Braemont is making us do. I have no way out of it. Believe me, even if I wasn't chomping at the bit to fuck you again, uh," his lips pursed at her frown, and she tugged the sheet out of his hand.

"I mean, make love, sorry, I was born crude, it won't go away overnight." He combed his hair back with both hands with a grunt.

"Dove, the last thing I want to do is leave you alone here. I thought we were just about done with the job and I could get you the hell out of here. But I can't until I do this thing for him."

Leaning back against the headboard, she drew her knees up and wrapped her arms around them. Her hair fluffed all around her in fat unruly curls and waves. She looked so sexy it was all Tezer could do to not pounce on her.

She asked, "What is the thing?"

"Ah," he didn't want to tell her about his dirty, dangerous, sometimes sordid work, but he didn't want any lies or secrets between them.

"There's a guy, a criminal, he wants us to bring here so he can squeeze him for money. It will take a day or so to get to him and bring him back. He's in some type of containment."

With a beleaguered sigh he moved off the bed. "I'm going to run you a hot bath with some Epsom salts, that will help with your soreness. That way you'll be all peachy and soft, and hot for me when I get back."

Before she could respond, he ambled into the bathroom and started the water flowing.

After he tumbled her again in the bath, leaning her over the side of the Roman tub he had very gently taken her from behind, later, at breakfast, a buzzing of nerves twittered around inside Tezer's gut.

His eyes on Dove chatting with that asshole, Rey, he was more and more nervous to leave her here.

It wouldn't be so bad if one or two of his team was going to be here to watch over her, not the extra hired mercenaries Braemont had hired, but Braemont was insisting they all go.

The male Braemont wanted brought, Rodlofo Asafa, was brilliant, dangerous, and slick. He could easily overpower or slip away from soldiers that didn't possess Tezer and his team's extraordinary skill set.

When breakfast was over, Tezer stood up and took Dove's hand while shooting Rey a warning. That he would bloody him up if he so much as touched her while he was gone, was crystal clear in the glare of deadly threat he shot Rey.

Tezer's team was gathered at the door when Tezer and Dove came back downstairs an hour later. His arm was wrapped so tightly around her shoulders she couldn't draw a full breath.

When they reached the guys, Tezer stopped, faced her and set both hands on her shoulders. He spoke in a low voice so the others couldn't hear, "Baby, please, please, do not leave this building. I would love for you to promise me you won't leave our locked bedroom, but I know better."

The corner of his mouth ticked up at her rueful look. "Yeah, I thought so. Okay," his voice dropped lower. "All right, I have to go. Just," he kissed her lightly, "be careful, baby, do not trust anyone."

As he said that he saw Kitty over Dove's shoulder. The buxom woman was stabbing hate into Dove's back with her hostile eyes.

When Kitty saw Tezer looking at her, the hate slipped into a seductive, 'come fuck me' look for him. He didn't even blink at her; just dipped his head to kiss Dove one more time.

Dove grabbed his jacket lapels, pulling on them to tighten their bodies together and deepened the kiss.

Then, she leaned back and said in a hushed cluck, "You be careful yourself, Tezer, husband." Her lips curved shyly. "You're the one going out there to bring back a dangerous criminal. I'll be here all safe and snug as a bug."

Her lashes fluttered at him with her sultry smile. "All cozy waiting for you. Naked. Or maybe just wearing panties, tiny sheer panties. Oh, and maybe no panties, just those stockings and garter things."

Red stormed up Tezer's face, his pants strained right away. "Damn, Dove, now I'll have that picture in my head the entire time I'm gone."

His grin lopsided, he laughed. "But then again, I would have anyway. Now," he grew serious, "you stay safe, and careful. I love you, baby." He gently brushed her lips then bore down harder on her.

His hands rode around her body to clutch behind her. Pulling her close, he ground her pelvis against his hardening, swelling, groin.

Dove's hands curled up him and twined around his neck, her firm full breasts mushed against his iron slab chest. They both groaned.

"Yeah, okay, gotta go, Chief," Leo chided with a grin. "Save it for when we get back, Romeo."

Tezer lifted his head, shook off the lustful haze that clouded his eyes and brain, kissed her one more time and turned to leave with his men.

The buzzing uneasiness had filled his stomach with trepidation and now it moved up his chest to infiltrate his head. He had a bad feeling about leaving her alone.

Even after the horrific experience she suffered, she was still terribly naive and trusting. She believed the best in everyone.

It was one of things he loved about her, how sweet and innocent she is even with her stubbornness and bluster, but it put her in danger.

"Come on, Tez," Garth said as they all strode to the chopper waiting in the back, "the sooner we get the fucker, the sooner we get back and the sooner you'll be with her."

Chapter Thirty-One

*T*ezer sat in the back of the chopper with Rodlofo Asafa cuffed and gagged between him and Garth.

Nik had a tiny jump seat behind the two front seats where Reggie sat passenger and Leo was piloting.

Tezer had gagged Asafa because he wouldn't shut up and Tezer was already on pins and needles.

Where they were they had no satellite service and he'd been unable to stay in contact with Dove, or Braemont, or even one of the other mercs that were still at the estate.

The uneasy feeling in the pit of his stomach grew bigger and bigger until he could hardly think.

"Bro, come on," Garth cajoled, "we've only been gone a couple days, nothing could have happened to her in that short of time. Relax. She's probably sitting on your bed in some transparent peignoir waiting on you."

Tezer arched a dry brow at him. Even the killer Asafa looked askance over his gag at Garth.

His mouth quirking, Tezer asked satirically, "Peignoir? You been reading Cosmo or something?"

Chuckling, Garth replied, "I've dated some models, it's all they talk about; lingerie, shoes and makeup. And food, because they don't eat but they talk nonstop about it."

Tezer had thought he'd be picturing Dove just as Garth described the entire time they were gone, but the apprehension gutting him took over and he could only think of her being in danger. Images of Dove screaming his name as a faceless menace tortured her and Tezer too far away to save her endlessly barraged him.

"Hey," he leaned forward to yell over the sound of the helicopter. "Reg, try calling again, we're out of the mountains now, we should have satellite service."

Seeing Reggie nod and reach for the radio, Tezer sat back, his knee jiggered up and down with his tension.

Nik tried calming him, "Tez, bro, come on, I'm telling you she's-"

Garth held a hand up, he saw Reggie lower his head and wipe his hand across his eyes.

When Reggie returned the radio and turned around, Tezer's gut burned, he could see it on his friend's face.

"What?" he shouted.

Reggie tried to yell back but the noise of the chopper was too loud, Tezer would have to wait until they landed.

He sat still like stone, nothing moved except a vein pounding at his temple and his big chest drawing shallow breaths.

As soon as the chopper landed in the back of the estate, Garth said, "Go, we'll take care of this piece of shit." He ignored the scowl Asafa gave him over the gag.

Tezer hopped out the back, ran around the side to Reggie.

Reggie pulled off his earphones and jumped from the chopper. The two men ran towards the mansion.

Out of range of the loud machine, the engine was off but the propeller still rotated, jogging to the building, Tezer asked, "What happened?"

That Reggie did not want to give the information was clear on his distressed face, but he said, "He took her. That guy, the one who hurt her, who she was running from."

The color drained from Tezer's tanned skin, a bleak film slipped over his eyes, he ran faster.

Inside, Tezer went for Braemont.

His auburn-haired employer was at the back door waiting for him.

Storming in, Tezer barked, "What the fuck, Braemont? Tell me."

Braemont took a step back from the enraged soldier.

"Believe me, Corseque, as much as I threatened, I would not want her in that fucker's clutches. Damon Philippè makes Genghis freakin' Khan look like a lamb. Hell man, if I'd known that sick murderous, psychopathic devil that she was hiding from would dare come here I never would have-"

Tezer grabbed Braemont's shirt, drew him up on his toes and shouted at him, "What the fuck happened? Tell me everything, *now*."

"Yeah, yeah," Braemont flushed. "Let go of me, save it for that monster."

Tezer roughly released him with a push and barked, "Speak."

"It was that bimbo, Katherine Miot, Kitty. One of the other chicks tattled on her. I don't know how she found out, it's possible she seduced my uncle to spill Dove's true name." He winced.

"Jim acts as pious as shit but he has been unfaithful to my aunt plenty of times. Anyway, after that it was easy enough to Google and find the underground reward posted for her. Kitty was insanely jealous of that bitch, uh, your wife."

At Tezer's thunderous expression, Braemont cranked his neck, making it pop and took a surreptitious step back from the enraged chief.

Coughing, Braemont shored up his bravery. "Anyway, after some, ah, torture, Kitty told me that she had contacted Philippè and told him Dove was here. She'd done that last night. This morning, his men came and fuck, I don't know how they did it, probably the bimbo let them in a back door or some shit."

His brows raised with incredulity, Tezer growled, "You've made it practically impregnable, Braemont to breech this place. How could they get by your guards?"

Eyes shifting sheepish, Braemont grimaced. "Men get lackadaisical when there's nothing going on for some time. I assume my people thought the noise in the yard was the chopper landing containing you and your team returning with Asafa. They had no reason to expect trouble."

Biting back a snarl, Tezer jerked his jaw for the man to continue.

"Yeah, so they quickly infiltrated the mansion and got Dove and were gone before my men could even rustle themselves together." He wiped sweat off his brow, took a breath.

"Ah, actually they came by motorcycle, not by chopper. It's difficult to do but not impossible. You had to park your jeeps outside the perimeter but their bikes could with a lot of careful maneuvering scrape through the dense surrounding jungle." He swiped at his brow again.

"Normally we would have heard the sounds of the engines approaching and got to them before they reached the gates but, ah, as I said, the bikes sounded as loud and rough as the helicopters."

At that moment Reynaldo came hurrying to the men. "Chief," he said to Tezer. "I saw the guy take her. It was Damon Philippè himself."

Tezer turned to the merc, commanded, "Tell me."

Rey's face paled, he was looking out the window, an enraged Tezer Corseque was too damned frightening to look directly at.

"We were all held at gunpoint. They got the drop on us. He uh, two of his men grabbed her, your girl, and carried her out and brought her to him. They dropped her in front of him on his motorcycle."

He glanced up at Tezer, gulped hard with a wince. "Damn, Chief, that girl, uh, your wife, Dove tried to fight them. She was livid. And scared, like crazy scared, but she was mad too. She was fighting for all her worth." His mouth twitched in admiration for the little blonde spitfire.

"Yeah, and- and? Fucking spit it all out, did he hurt her?" Tezer demanded, his hands rolled in tight fists.

Taking a deep breath, Rey said, "Uh, he had her sitting sideways with both her legs hanging off the side of the seat, and, his hand around her neck. He was laughing, nasty. I could hear him clearly, he was saying something like, 'Thought you could get away from me, bitch? I warned you, you-' " he broke off as Avril and Chelsee were approaching.

Pinching his lips together, Rey let out a gush of air and said, "Uh, he called her the c word, you know, cun-"

"Yeah, got it. Go on." Tezer nodded sharply.

"Uh, so, he said, 'I warned you what I would do if you ran and I caught you.' At that, damn," Rey wiped his hand across his mouth, his olive skin paled further.

"She just started shaking. She still fought him, but, damn, Chief, she was petrified. Then, uh," Rey took an imperceptible step back from Tezer.

At his hesitation, Tezer snapped, "Go on."

"Yeah, so, he uh, slapped her. Then, he grabbed her jaw and squeezed so hard tears spilled, and he forced her head back hard, forced her face up and," Rey broke off.

Then taking a swift glance at Tezer he kept going, "He kissed her, like, uh, viciously. She was punching at him but he only laughed and kissed her more violently. I could see he was really hurting her. Then, he lifted her, flipped her to face front, wrapped his arm around her and they all took off."

Tezer ground out fiercely, "Braemont, get me the fucking whore."

Surprisingly, Braemont left right away without protest.

Leo came in the door. Tezer told him, "Leo, get the best coordinates for Damon Philippè's location that you can derive. We already set a trace in place to track the phone number on the reward notice; that should help. When Garth and the others have secured Asafa, get everyone and meet me at the chopper."

A quick nod and Leo left to do as he was bid.

Braemont returned almost immediately with Kitty. He had known where she was hiding out, fearful of Tezer's wrath. He dragged her down the hall and shoved her in front of Tezer.

Through grit teeth, Tezer said, "All I want to know is if you have any idea where Damon Philippè lives."

"Oh, baby," Kitty simpered. She started on her sultriest act, but she saw the vile hate and menace in Tezer's dark infuriated eyes. He was obviously restraining himself at great effort not to put his big hands around her neck and wring it.

Her eyes flicked to Braemont then back to Tezer. Licking her suddenly dry lips, she said, "I only did it for you, for you and me, so we could-"

Tezer's biting threat barked at her, "You have one chance to answer me, anything else I break you."

Kitty blanched at the roaring fury in the powerful man. She'd never been so afraid, and turned on, in her life. But she knew he meant what he said.

She told him, "I talked with one of his men when they stormed the place looking for your…bitch."

At the murderous gleam in Tezer's eyes Kitty spoke quickly, "Uh, he said Damon's castle was near the little inhabited Règion es quartinè. At the…what'd he say, uh, border of the woods near Lake Chartreu."

She reached a hand out to Tezer.

Tezer snapped at Braemont, "I want her taken care of. Make it painful." At her frightened gasp, he turned and raced out the door.

Kitty's shoulders lifted as she braced herself. She tried a vampish smile, "Come on, Yves baby, you know I didn't mean anything by it. Let's you and me go make some beautiful music together." Then her heart stuttered at the savage, sadistic smile that lit Braemont's face.

Her hands up to ward him off, Kitty's sexual poise fled replaced by dire terror that stretched her eyes wide and made her open lips shudder with dread.

But she could not halt the monster that inhabited Braemont's sophisticated body.

Her piercing screams reverberated off the walls as he made his way to his dungeon beneath the palace with her over his shoulder.

His heart in his throat, Tezer tried not to panic.

Philippè had taken Dove only this morning and they had travelled by bike. There was a chance, a slim chance that the fucker hadn't yet- a catch in his throat, Tezer swallowed around the lump that had lodged there- hurt Dove too badly. Or killed her.

Tezer was piloting this time. Garth, Reggie and Nik were already in the copter, they were waiting on Leo.

Leo burst out the back door sprinting with his laptop in his hand. When he reached the chopper he hopped in beside Tezer.

Breathing fast, Leo said as Tezer lifted the bird in the air, "Between Kitty's description and the other info you'd gotten from Dove, I got it pinpointed. Head east."

Tezer turned the helicopter and it ducked then slashed towards the east.

He zoned like he did when he was in combat domain. Tezer clamped his brain down, eliminating any thoughts, like a kind of meditation, he emptied his mind. That enabled him to just see, listen, and act.

He couldn't think of Dove, it scared him so much what Philippè could be doing to her that it paralyzed him. So he had to go into war mode and shut everything out or he'd be no good to her.

Garth murmured grimly, "We'll get her Tez, we'll get her."

None of the men spoke again until much, much later when they saw glints of stone and iron through the treetops.

Beside Tezer, Leo craned his neck peering through the bell-shaped window of the chopper. "Yeah, I think that's it, bro."

Tezer jerked his chin.

No one else said a word.

They flew over the trees, the chopper was special op elite, it was almost soundless.

The helicopter swooped silently around the area so they could check it out, make sure it was the right place. Tezer stayed close to the trees for camouflage.

When they finally caught glimpses of the stone castle, Leo said, "Yep, bingo."

There were other helicopters scattered around the vast grounds surrounding the castle, and an array of sports cars and motorbikes in the driveway.

Nik asked, "How are we gonna do this, Tez? They're going to eventually hear the copter when we get closer, you gonna set down near the trees and we'll try to slide in along the tree-line and shadows?"

His teeth gritting, one of Tezer's hands was clenched between his legs on the cyclic pushing it forward. Then as they came out of the trees, he pushed it to the right to bank, at the same time he manipulated the collective lever on his left side, adjusting the friction control for descent.

The throttle was a governor that maintained the speed so he was relieved of that responsibility. A short grunt was his answer.

Tezer brought the bird down in a small clearing surrounded by a dense grove of evergreens he'd seen as they'd passed by.

As soon as it was down, Tezer killed the engine and the men scrambled out of the chopper and ran to the shelter of the trees.

When they gathered, Tezer told them, "Okay, we couldn't do recon, so I will totally understand if you guys want to stay here. I'll-"

"Fuck you, Tez," Garth spat.

The rest of the men glared at him.

He gave his friends a grateful smile, nodded. "All right then, let's just circle it, whoever can get in tells the others. There's satellite so we can text. Let's book."

In tandem, the men tore out of the woods and ran to circle the structure.

It was a castle, but not a huge one by normal standards, Tezer thought gratefully.

He raced around the building, slowing at windows so he could peer in. He was surprised they had not seen any guards or gates or any kind of security on the way in. Damon Philippè must be pretty secure that the place could not be found. Stupid.

As he made his way around the castle perimeter, he received texts from the other guys indicating they'd seen a few beefy men that looked like security types roaming around. Lazy bastards, no one had detected the chopper coming in.

Tezer would have shot them all for dereliction of duty. No one had seen a good way in yet.

All of the men had studied a picture from the internet of Philippè, no one had spotted him yet.

Then, Tezer received a text from Nik that said, "I'm in. Southwest corner, door is unlocked."

Like he knew the others would, Tezer raced to the location.

When he got there, the other men were already shuffling inside. Tezer slipped in the door and looked around.

They were in what looked like a den. Animal heads covered the walls. Large, heavy furniture with zebra print cushions on dark wood, and more stuffed animals hunkered on the hardwood floors.

Silently crossing the room, Reggie reached the door, opened it and peered out. He held up a thumb, coast was clear.

The men crept out the door single file and found themselves in a carpeted corridor.

Tezer made gestures for each man to go in a different direction. He chose his direction and jogged silently down the corridor until he reached open space.

He heard male voices and stayed flat against a wall.

They were coming closer, then the voices sounded muffled, as if they'd turned away.

Tezer peeked around the corner and saw three men a few yards away with their backs to him, chatting comfortably about hockey.

Sprinting soundlessly up behind the group, as he reached them, Tezer slammed his gun against the side of one man's head; he went down like a rock.

The other two didn't see their friend get struck, only saw him fall, they were too stunned to react.

One turned and saw Tezer.

Tezer bashed his fist into his jaw. The guy twirled for a second before falling to the ground unconscious.

The third man, his eyes wide with shock, grabbed at his gun holstered at his side. Before he could get his hand on it, Tezer raised his gun and aimed it at the man's head.

His voice so chilled it could make ice, he said, "Don't."

The man paused, then raised his hands in the air. He rattled off nervously, "The money is in a vault on the second floor where the jewelry and-"

"Shut. Up."

The man's mouth clamped.

"The girl, I only want the girl. Where is she?" Tezer reached and yanked the man's gun from his holster and stuffed it in his belt.

The man's eyes flit to the left then right, his lips pulled in before he started to speak.

Tezer cut him off, "You're already lying and you haven't said anything yet. I don't have any problem killing you, or maiming you, or cutting off your balls and shoving them up your ass. I ask again, where is she? You don't say and I'll take you out and grab the next guy."

"Dungeon," the man blurted, his face sheet-white.

"And that is where?"

"Uh, down that hall," he motioned with his head, his hands still in the air. "There's an iron door before you get to the kitchen on the right. That's it."

"Is it locked?" Tezer watched the man's eyes shift back and forth again. He sighed and cocked his gun.

"Uh, wait, don't shoot." He turned his head and closed his eyes. "It's- it's locked. There's a key, right over the light that's above the door." He opened his eyes and smirked. "Careless, huh?"

"Where is Philippè?"

This time he answered swiftly and without deceit. He decided Tezer was not a man to play with. The lethality of the chief just radiated out of his dark enigmatic eyes.

"He's in the dungeon with her. He likes to play with women like they're toys. Uh, I mean, he's been there a while, he's probably started her torture by now. *Uh-*" his grunt came out of his unconscious mouth as Tezer bashed his gun at his temple.

Tezer didn't wait for him to collapse; he was already on the move.

By the time he reached the iron door he could hear shouting and screams of agony behind him, his team was on the job.

At the door, he looked up at the lamp and swept his hand over it. Nothing. Fuck. He reached up and grabbed the light with both hands, wrenched it off the wall and shook it.

Several keys tinkled out and fell to the floor.

Tezer tossed the lamp, it banged and clattered on the tile floor. He crouched to get the keys.

Standing with them in his hands, he looked at the lock and then the keys and stuck one in. It turned the lock. He opened the heavy iron door and listened.

He could hear a male's voice, and then, thank God, he could just barely hear Dove.

Her voice was weak, thready, but the choked words she rasped out were strong, she was telling Philippè to basically go fuck himself, except she used more ladylike language.

That's my girl, Tezer smiled until he heard a smack and Dove cry out.

With rushed stealth, Tezer raced down the stone steps until he reached the bottom. Then he stopped, adjusted his eyes to the dim lighting and scanned the scene.

The room was large and deliberately lit for shadows to loom and slither over the hard stone floor and walls.

The horrific torture apparatus Dove had described was scattered ominously around the room along with chains attached to the walls, poles, benches, and the ceiling.

Tezer's heart clenched.

Dove was chained to what looked like an ancient torture device, the infamous rack. She was lying on her back at a slant on the device. Her delicate, torn wrists were chained up over her head and one of her ankles was chained.

Her blouse was in shreds and hanging off her, and she wasn't wearing pants, just what used to be Tezer's favorite black lace panties. He knew he'd never be turned on by them again.

Dove's blood was spattered over her heaving panicked breasts that were still partially encased in the bra, but the bra was in shreds too. Blood ran down turning the black lace red.

Tezer's gaze rose to her poor, devastated face.

Although her head was now hanging forward, he had seen that her eyes were blackened and swollen; she was covered with cuts and bruises.

His eye fell to the whip on the floor beside her. God, he prayed Philippè hadn't used it on her yet.

That she still wore her clothes, what there was of them, gave Tezer the belief that Philippè hadn't raped her yet. Or committed the savage sodomy he'd threatened to do to her with additional men if she left him. He hoped.

Philippè had drawn a knife, a butcher knife, from a sheath at his hip and was wiping the blade with a brown towel.

He said in a rough accented voice, "First, **Savá Mariè Bretèche,** I am cutting off that finger with that man's ring on it."

His mouth shook with resentful rage, "You dared give your heart to another man?" Tossing the towel, he stepped closer to the side of the rack, moved his severe face to Dove's.

Grasping her hair, he pulled her head up, forcing her to look at him. "*Da*," his thick sneer seething with detestation, "I could just remove the ring, but you, my sweet need a lesson. Every time you think to give yourself to any other man but me, you will look at that missing finger, and remember, I am the only man in your life. *Bine*, **Savá Mariè?**"

Dove murmured, the words hitched out, so soft, barely audible, "I love him," gasp, "Damon. You can…" she drew a wheezing breath, "cut off my finger, but you will have to…" she coughed, choking on the blood in her throat, "cut out my heart to make me forget him."

Ugly angry color bled through Philippè's monstrous face. He gripped her hair in his fist and shook her head, her blood showered him. "You bitch," he snarled dragging her face up to him.

A vicious calm settled back over his evil mien, enjoying her pain as she was strapped on the rack making her head fairly immobile.

"Eh," he growled darkly, his guttural accented voice lowered. "You say that now, **Savá Mariè**, you will sing a different tune before this night is over. You have noticed I left that one leg unchained, it will make it easier to spread you wide, after I flog you, you little bitch.

"Then I will take my time fucking your every orifice with my dick and then with anything else I feel will heighten my thrill of abusing your lovely body that you took from me." His voice held an edge of anger, but the grin sharp at the corners snaked up Joker style.

"Maybe I will allow you to lie on the cold stone floor for the rest of the night before we do it again tomo-" he saw Dove raise her swollen eyes and tears flooded them.

This was the first time she'd cried since he'd taken her. Even as he beat her she'd remained bravely stoic.

"Finally, my sweet, you comprehend the depths of the depraved torment I plan for you. You-" She had lifted her gaze but not to him, no, she looked beyond him and something akin to hope and relief? Shimmered through her pained eyes.

What the- he swung around just as Tezer reached the bottom step.

With a decadently sinister grin, Philippè gripped the huge knife, ran a finger down the blade and shivered, excited by the cool steel of it.

He didn't fear the man at the stairs, he had his security, they should be down and upon the interloper any second.

Tezer had his gun in his hand but he had been so overcome and shocked at Dove's harrowing appearance he had taken too long to raise it.

Philippè was too close to Dove, and now he had the wicked knife at her throat.

"*Oprire-* stop, do not come any closer whoever the fuck you are," Philippè ordered.

Tezer ignored him. Inching closer he said calmly, "Baby, are you okay?" He knew she wasn't, but he needed to stall.

"I said do not fucking move," the man in his forties barked. Damon Philippè had long black hair slicked back, it fell straight as an arrow past his collar.

To Tezer, he looked like he'd stepped out of a Dracula movie. Just as pure evil, sick and perverted as the vamp himself. He even had a Romanian-esque type accent that only creeped him out further.

Tezer gave him a quick once over.

His face wasn't white like Dracula's; it was darkly tanned with razor sharp cheekbones He had a strong Roman nose that equaled the sharp chin. Even his lips, full, yet they looked like someone had taken a scalpel to them, carving them into harsh cruelty. His physique was muscular, but nothing like Tezer's, and Tezer had a few inches on him.

Dove sobbed, wheezed with weak, broken breaths, "*Tezer*," the inhale scraped through her raw throat. "You came for me." Tears rolled through layers of blood on her bruised face.

"Always." His eyes on her, he crept closer. His hard face, an implacable mask didn't show the anguish he felt at the sight of his beloved beaten and bloody.

Philippè ordered, "*Nu*, do not move, you asshole." But his curiosity got the better of him. He asked, "Who the hell are you? Better yet, how the fuck did you find me?"

Tezer had no desire to speak with the psychopath, but he needed to get closer. "I am Tezer Corseque. **Yvetsky** Braemont hired me to bring some people in through the jungle to him."

"Ah," Philippè nodded. "Yves. That figures. He is crazy, they call him eccentric, *nu*," he shook his head, "he is fucking bonkers. So, what do you have to do with my woman here?" He lowered his knife but set his hand holding it possessively over her breast.

Fighting through the red haze of fury, Tezer said calmly, "I am taking her from you, you sick fuck, and then destroying you."

Philippè's black brows winged over dark eyes glittering hell and sadism. "*Dah,* you say, really? How do you propose to do that? Before you can raise that weapon I will have slit her throat." His arrogant smirk mocked Tezer.

"You would kill her? After all you went through and the money you paid to get her back?" Tezer shuffled another step closer.

One shoulder shrugged, he said negligently, "I would hate to take the life out of my perfect woman, but," he shrugged again with a sniff, "if it came down to her life or mine, well, as you have already probably deduced, I am a very selfish self-centered man."

Shifting the knife to his other hand, he slid the hand that was on her breast up to cup Dove's face. "Ah, but I doubt I will ever find another female as unique as this one. So damned beautiful, inside and out. I did not have her long enough before to do what I wanted to her. That inside beauty would have shriveled after a short time of, fun, with me."

He turned back to Tezer. "I was so annoyed. Right after I bought her, I had to go away for an extensive amount of time, then I was ill, took so long to recover, alas," he turned back to Dove and slipped his fingers into her mouth.

She let him without a fight. "I had so damned little time with my beauty, and I was too sick for quite a while to fuck her more than twice. I had to compensate with whippings, and," he wiggled his fingers around inside her mouth, "other delicious things."

Inch by silent inch, Tezer crept forward. His time as a soldier in the jungles of various countries amongst wild feral animals taught him how to move without appearing to do so.

His eyes flit from Philippè's to Dove's. It hurt him like a burning agony seeing her like that. Brutalized and terrorized, and humiliated.

But, wait, she didn't look humiliated, she was darting her poor, bruised, swollen eyes down. *What*?

She was darting them at Philippè's extremities. Then, Tezer saw her faintly move her foot. Realizing her intent, he imperceptibly shook his head with a frown. But she subtly nodded.

Keeping his eyes blankly on Philippè, Tezer kept Dove in his peripheral and said nonchalantly, "So, how do you know Yves Braemont?"

His black brows hopped, Philippè cocked his head to the side with a coarse smile. "Oh, a few years back we-"

Dove jerked her knee up into Philippè's balls.

He screamed and bent over.

Tezer bolted across the room- but before he could get to him, his hand clutching his wounded nuts, Philippè stabbed his knife into Dove.

A pained gasp, and her body slumped.

"No!" Tezer roared and dove on top of the man. He took him down swiftly. Rage and fear turned his fists into iron rocks pounding into Philippè's head and face, and stomach, groin and kidneys.

Tezer pummeled without mercy until Philippè was nothing but a pulpy pool of blood, muscles and bone.

Wiping his bloody knuckles on Philippè's trousers, Tezer searched the dead man's pockets for keys. Finding them, he ran to Dove.

Her head lolled forward, she would have fallen but for the chains.

"Dove!" He unlocked the chains with shaking hands, she fell into his arms.

Holding her, he knelt, grabbed up the towel and shoved it on the wound bleeding at her stomach. Calling, "Baby, Dove," he moved her hair off her face.

Her eyes were closed, skin ashen, he couldn't tell if she was breathing. He wasted no time, stood up with her and fled up the stairs.

When he was halfway down the corridor, the rest of his team caught up with him.

Tezer didn't stop or slow down, his men ran with him. They raced down the hall and out of the building to the chopper.

When they reached it, Tezer handed Dove to Garth and tossed the keys to the bird to Leo and climbed inside.

Garth handed Dove to him, they all jumped in.

Before the door was closed, Leo had the machine off the ground. It banked left and then tore through the countryside.

Tezer's arm wrapped tightly around Dove, he held the towel against her wound. Her head draped back off his arm.

Garth whispered, "Tez, is she-"

Tezer held her against his chest, his own tears mingling with the blood on her.

"He stabbed her, the fucker beat her then stabbed her-" his voice broke.

No one said a word, hardly breathed, as Leo flew the helicopter to the nearest town big enough to contain a hospital.

Epilogue

The house sat on a softly rounded green hill overlooking vast forests with a circle of blue lake shimmering down below.

The day was warm in the temperate tropical country of Iszoza. Barefoot, in a black t-shirt and black jeans, Tezer stood in the doorway that led out to the tiled deck.

A varnished wooden railing encircled the deck, so highly polished it shone as bright as the tile Dove stood on.

She rested one slender hand on the railing as she looked out over the verdant scenery. The gentle breeze lifted her blonde curls, brilliant in the dawn's rising sun.

Tezer paused, drinking her in.

For months it had been touch and go before it appeared Dove was going to survive.

He brought her to his home to recover. She not only recovered, she flourished. Fragile still, she grew more beautiful to him, and he fell more deeply in love with her every day.

Softly saying, "Sweetheart," he stepped onto the deck. His heart palpitated wildly when she turned to him with her glorious smile.

Moving to her, he handed her one of the mugs of steaming coffee he held. "Here, my wife," taking a satisfied breath, he'd never tire of saying that word.

Accepting the coffee, and the kiss he pressed softly on her lips, Dove said, "You are too good to me, Husband."

That brought a grin so broad and hard his face hurt. He moved to stand beside her at the railing. "I wish I was romantic for you, Dove, but I'm too hard of a man for flowery words."

She laughed. "You are so silly, Tezer. Every time you tell me how beautiful I am, when you get my door, pull out a chair, carry me, care for me when I'm sick, feed me, make love to me, *rescue* me, nurse me back from a knife wound and tell me you love me, Tezer my husband, you are being romantic."

Setting his big hand on her back, he sighed. "I don't know what I did to be blessed with you, but I will be forever grateful. I love you, Dove."

"I love you, Tezer," she replied. Ducking her head to the side, peering up at him with her sultry golden green eyes, she said with innocent yet coy shyness, "This is the only place in your house we haven't…christened."

"Our house," he corrected, and slid a fingertip down her smooth face. "You have pretty roses in your cheeks, finally." His gaze drifted seductively down her thin figure.

She was finally gaining back the weight she'd lost, but her amazing curves were still there.

"We are supposed to be taking it slow, baby. I try to treat you carefully, like china, but you…" he cupped her chin lifting it to kiss her again, more firmly and longer this time. "You are incorrigible, insatiable, I taught you too well, I think."

She giggled and sipped her coffee. "That you did." A soft blush colored the rest of her pale face. "But," she scolded, "you have treated me too carefully, too gently while we…make love."

The color flooded more fully across her cheeks. "I am fully recovered now, Tezer. I would like us to be more…uh," embarrassed she trailed off.

"Robust?" he helped, smiling, pleased at her blatant desire for him. His hard hand slid down her back to grasp her butt.

Squeezing the perfect round cheek over her jeans he pulled her against his thickening erection. His manhood turned to granite at the feel of her firm breasts pressing into his powerful chest.

He told her, "After you eat a good breakfast, take your vitamins and medicine, I will get the comforter and spread it here, so we can look out over the countryside while we," he kissed her, "make love all day. Okay?"

Nodding with her sweet shy smile, her hand brashly went to splay on his tight ass, snug in his black jeans. She happily agreed, "Okay."

Tezer took one quick peek at her lush cleavage showing under the draping of the soft yellow shirt, then moved his arm to her shoulders.

They leaned against the railing with their coffee, watching the sun brighten and color, and warm the land below.

He took a sip of coffee and said, "And, after here on the deck, there are a million places out there, my beloved wife," he bent and kissed her, "that we need to christen."

The End

Dear Reader, thank you for purchasing

<u>Capturing Dove</u>**!**

I know you could have picked any number of books to read, but you picked this book and for that I am extremely grateful.

I hope you enjoyed this novel, and if you did, **please leave a review where you purchased it**, *and look for other exciting titles in my name!*

About the Author

Louise Furley loves writing romance with a huge helping of suspense. She finds it exciting to study new lands and learn everything she can about the area and the natives that call it home.

Her idea of fun is researching ideas, studying enigmatic modes of science, archeology, and different ways to kill someone.

Her Significant Other finds the last to be particularly notable. He remains wary yet gives Louise his full support with her writing adventures.

Sunny Florida is home where Louise is a graduate of St. Thomas University with a master's degree in Mental Health.

Louise is the author of numerous published novels. When not researching or writing, she is dreaming of unique plots, and discovering fresh ventures she hasn't yet experienced in the world.

Ride along with her as she travels new and thrilling journeys!